Praise for the NEBULA, ARTHUR C. CLARKE, LOCUS, and BSFA award–winning; and HUGO, and PHILIP K. DICK award–nominated *Ancillary Justice*

"Unexpected, compelling and very cool. Ann Leckie nails it."
—John Scalzi

"Establishes Leckie as an heir to Banks and Cherryh."
—Elizabeth Bear

"Powerful, arresting, beautiful space opera...Leckie makes it look so easy." —Kameron Hurley

Ancillary Justice is the mind-blowing space opera you've been needing...This is a novel that will thrill you like the page-turner it is, but stick with you for a long time afterward."
—io9.com

"This impressive debut succeeds in making Breq a protagonist readers will invest in, and establishes Leckie as a talent to watch." —*Publishers Weekly*

"Ann Leckie's *Ancillary Justice* does everything science fiction should do. It engages, it excites, and it challenges the way the reader views our world." —*Staffer's Book Review*

"Assured, gripping, and stylish...an absorbing thousand-year history, a poignant personal journey, and a welcome addition to the genre." —NPR Books

"A stunning, fast-paced debut."   —*Shelf Awareness*

"It's not every day a debut novel by an author you'd never heard of before derails your entire afternoon with its brilliance. But when my review copy of *Ancillary Justice* arrived, that's exactly what it did. In fact, it arrowed upward to reach a pretty high position on my list of best space opera novels ever."   —Liz Bourke, *Tor.com*

"This is not entry-level SF, and its payoff is correspondingly greater because of that."   —*Locus*

"I cannot find fault in this truly amazing, awe-inspiring debut novel from Ann Leckie...*Ancillary Justice* is one of the best science fiction novels I've ever read."
            —*The Book Smugglers*

"It's by turns thrilling, moving and awe-inspiring."
            —*The Guardian* (UK)

For now, if the tyrant was watching—and she was surely watching, through *Mercy of Kalr*, would be so long as we were in the system—let her think I resented having a baby foisted on me when I'd rather have someone who knew what they were doing.

I turned my attention away from Lieutenant Tisarwat. Forward, the pilot leaned closer to Five and said, quiet and oblique, "Everything all right?" And then to Five's responding, puzzled frown, "Too quiet."

"All this time?" asked Five. Still oblique. Because they were talking about me and didn't want to trigger any requests I might have made to Ship, to tell me when the crew was talking about me. I had an old habit—some two thousand years old—of singing whatever song ran through my head. Or humming. It had caused the crew some puzzlement and distress at first—this body, the only one left to me, didn't have a particularly good voice. They were getting used to it, though, and now I was dryly amused to see crew members disturbed by my silence.

"Not a peep," said the pilot to Kalr Five. With a brief sideways glance and a tiny twitch of neck and shoulder muscles that told me she'd thought of looking back, toward Lieutenant Tisarwat.

"Yeah," said Five, agreeing, I thought, with the pilot's unstated assessment of what might be troubling me.

Good. Let Anaander Mianaai be watching that, too.

By Ann Leckie

Ancillary Justice
Ancillary Sword

ANCILLARY SWORD

ANN LECKIE

www.orbitbooks.net

Orbit
Hachette Book Group
1290 Avenue of the Americas
New York, NY 10104
www.orbitbooks.net
www.orbitshortfiction.com

Printed in the United States of America

RRD-C

First edition: October 2014

10 9 8 7 6 5 4

Orbit is an imprint of Hachette Book Group.
The Orbit name and logo are trademarks of Little, Brown Book Group Limited.

The Hachette Speakers Bureau provides a wide range of authors for speaking events. To find out more, go to www.hachettespeakersbureau.com or call (866) 376-6591.

The publisher is not responsible for websites (or their content) that are not owned by the publisher.

Library of Congress Cataloging-in-Publication Data

Leckie, Ann.
    Ancillary sword / Ann Leckie.—First edition.
       pages cm
    ISBN 978-0-316-24665-1 (paperback)—ISBN 978-0-316-24664-4 (ebook)   1. Science fiction.   I. Title.
    PS3612.E3353A84 2014
    813'.6—dc23
                                2014018730

ANCILLARY SWORD

1

"Considering the circumstances, you could use another lieutenant." Anaander Mianaai, ruler (for the moment) of all the vast reaches of Radchaai space, sat in a wide chair cushioned with embroidered silk. This body that spoke to me—one of thousands—looked to be about thirteen years old. Black-clad, dark-skinned. Her face was already stamped with the aristocratic features that were, in Radchaai space, a marker of the highest rank and fashion. Under normal circumstances no one ever saw such young versions of the Lord of the Radch, but these were not normal circumstances.

The room was small, three and a half meters square, paneled with a lattice of dark wood. In one corner the wood was missing—probably damaged in last week's violent dispute between rival parts of Anaander Mianaai herself. Where the wood remained, tendrils of some wispy plant trailed, thin silver-green leaves and here and there tiny white flowers. This was not a public area of the palace, not an audience chamber. An empty chair sat beside the Lord of the Radch's, a table between those chairs held a tea set, flask, and bowls of unadorned white porcelain, gracefully lined, the sort of thing that, at first glance, you might take as unremarkable, but on second would realize was a work of art worth more than some planets.

I had been offered tea, been invited to sit. I had elected to remain standing. "You said I could choose my own officers." I ought to have added a respectful *my lord* but did not. I also ought to have knelt and put my forehead to the floor, when I'd entered and found the Lord of the Radch. I hadn't done that, either.

"You've chosen two. Seivarden, of course, and Lieutenant Ekalu was an obvious choice." The names brought both people reflexively to mind. In approximately a tenth of a second *Mercy of Kalr*, parked some thirty-five thousand kilometers away from this station, would receive that near-instinctive check for data, and a tenth of a second after that its response would reach me. I'd spent the last several days learning to control that old, old habit. I hadn't completely succeeded. "A fleet captain is entitled to a third," Anaander Mianaai continued. Beautiful porcelain bowl in one black-gloved hand, she gestured toward me, meaning, I thought, to indicate my uniform. Radchaai military wore dark-brown jackets and trousers, boots and gloves. Mine was different. The left-hand side was brown, but the right side was black, and my captain's insignia bore the marks that showed I commanded not only my own ship but other ships' captains. Of course, I had no ships in my fleet besides my own, *Mercy of Kalr*, but there were no other fleet captains stationed near Athoek, where I was bound, and the rank would give me an advantage over other captains I might meet. Assuming, of course, those other captains were at all inclined to accept my authority.

Just days ago a long-simmering dispute had broken out

and one faction had destroyed two of the intersystem gates. Now preventing more gates from going down—and preventing that faction from seizing gates and stations in other systems—was an urgent priority. I understood Anaander's reasons for giving me the rank, but still I didn't like it. "Don't make the mistake," I said, "of thinking I'm working for *you*."

She smiled. "Oh, I don't. Your only other choices are officers currently in the system, and near this station. Lieutenant Tisarwat is just out of training. She was on her way to take her first assignment, and now of course that's out of the question. And I thought you'd appreciate having someone you could train up the way you want." She seemed amused at that last.

As she spoke I knew Seivarden was in stage two of NREM sleep. I saw pulse, temperature, respiration, blood oxygen, hormone levels. Then that data was gone, replaced by Lieutenant Ekalu, standing watch. Stressed—jaw slightly clenched, elevated cortisol. She'd been a common soldier until one week ago, when *Mercy of Kalr*'s captain had been arrested for treason. She had never expected to be made an officer. Wasn't, I thought, entirely sure she was capable of it.

"You can't possibly think," I said to the Lord of the Radch, blinking away that vision, "that it's a good idea to send me into a newly broken-out civil war with only one experienced officer."

"It can't be worse than going understaffed," Anaander Mianaai said, maybe aware of my momentary distraction, maybe not. "And the child is beside herself at the thought of serving under a fleet captain. She's waiting for you at the docks." She set down her tea, straightened in her chair. "Since the gate leading to Athoek is down and I have no idea what the situation there might be, I can't give you specific orders. Besides"—she raised her now-empty hand as though forestalling some speech of mine—"I'd be wasting my time attempting to direct you too closely. You'll do as you like no matter what I say. You're loaded up? Have all the supplies you need?"

The question was perfunctory—she surely knew the status of my ship's stores as well as I did. I made an indefinite gesture, deliberately insolent.

"You might as well take Captain Vel's things," she said, as though I'd answered reasonably. "She won't need them."

Vel Osck had been captain of *Mercy of Kalr* until a week ago. There were any number of reasons she might not need her possessions, the most likely, of course, being that she was dead. Anaander Mianaai didn't do anything halfway, particularly when it came to dealing with her enemies. Of course, in this case, the enemy Vel Osck had supported was Anaander Mianaai herself. "I don't want them," I said. "Send them to her family."

"If I can." She might well not be able to do that. "Is there anything you need before you go? Anything at all?"

Various answers occurred to me. None seemed useful. "No."

"I'll miss you, you know," she said. "No one else will speak to me quite the way you do. You're one of the very few people I've ever met who really, truly didn't fear the consequences of offending me. And none of those very few have the...similarity of background you and I have."

Because I had once been a ship. An AI controlling an enormous troop carrier and thousands of ancillaries, human bodies, part of myself. At the time I had not thought of myself as a slave, but I had been a weapon of conquest, the possession of Anaander Mianaai, herself occupying thousands of bodies spread throughout Radch space.

Now I was only this single human body. "Nothing you can do to me could possibly be worse than what you've already done."

"I am aware of that," she said, "and aware of just how dangerous that makes you. I may well be extremely foolish just letting you live, let alone giving you official authority and a ship. But the games I play aren't for the timid."

"For most of us," I said, openly angry now, knowing she could see the physical signs of it no matter how impassive my expression, "they aren't games."

"I am also aware of that," said the Lord of the Radch. "Truly I am. It's just that some losses are unavoidable."

I could have chosen any of a half dozen responses to that. Instead I turned and walked out of the room without answering. As I stepped through the door, the soldier *Mercy of Kalr* One Kalr Five, who had been standing at stiff attention just outside, fell in behind me, silent and efficient. Kalr Five was human, like all *Mercy of Kalr*'s soldiers, not an ancillary. She had a name, beyond her ship, decade, and number. I had addressed her by that name once. She'd responded with outward impassivity, but with an inner wave of alarm and unease. I hadn't tried it again.

When I had been a ship—when I had been just one component of the troop carrier *Justice of Toren*—I had been always aware of the state of my officers. What they heard and what they saw. Every breath, every twitch of every muscle. Hormone levels, oxygen levels. Everything, nearly, except the specific contents of their thoughts, though even that I could often guess, from experience, from intimate acquaintance. Not something I had ever shown any of my captains—it would have meant little to them, a stream of meaningless data. But for me, at that time, it had been just part of my awareness.

I no longer *was* my ship. But I was still an ancillary, could still read that data as no human captain could have. But I only had a single human brain, now, could only handle the smallest fragment of the information I'd once been constantly, unthinkingly aware of. And even that small amount required some care—I'd run straight into a bulkhead trying to walk and receive data at the same time, when I'd first tried it. I queried *Mercy of Kalr*, deliberately this time. I was fairly sure I could walk through this corridor and monitor Five at the same time without stopping or stumbling.

I made it all the way to the palace's reception area without incident. Five was tired, and slightly hungover. Bored, I was sure, from standing staring at the wall during my conference with the Lord of the Radch. I saw a strange mix of anticipation and dread, which troubled me a bit, because I couldn't guess what that conflict was about.

Out on the main concourse, high, broad, and echoing, stone paved, I turned toward the lifts that would take me to the docks, to the shuttle that waited to take me back to *Mercy of Kalr*. Most shops and offices along the concourse, including the wide, brightly painted gods crowding the temple façade, orange and blue and red and green, seemed surprisingly undamaged after last week's violence, when the Lord of the Radch's struggle against herself had broken into the open. Now citizens in colorful coats, trousers, and gloves, glittering with jewelry, walked by, seemingly unconcerned. Last week might never have happened. Anaander Mianaai, Lord of the Radch, might still be herself, many-bodied but one single, undivided person. But last week *had* happened, and Anaander Mianaai was not, in fact, one person. Had not been for quite some time.

As I approached the lifts a sudden surge of resentment and dismay overtook me. I stopped, turned. Kalr Five had stopped when I stopped, and now stared impassively ahead. As though that wave of resentment Ship had shown me hadn't come from her. I hadn't thought most humans could mask such strong emotions so effectively—her face was absolutely expressionless. But all the Mercy of Kalrs, it had turned out, could do it. Captain Vel had been an old-fashioned sort—or at the very least she'd had idealized notions of what "old-fashioned" meant—and had demanded that her human soldiers conduct themselves as much like ancillaries as possible.

Five didn't know I'd been an ancillary. As far as she knew I was Fleet Captain Breq Mianaai, promoted because of Captain Vel's arrest and what most imagined were my powerful family connections. She couldn't know how much of her I saw. "What is it?" I asked, brusque. Taken aback.

"Sir?" Flat. Expressionless. Wanting, I saw after the tiny signal delay, for me to turn my attention away from her, to leave her safely ignored. Wanting also to speak.

I was right, that resentment, that dismay had been on my account. "You have something to say. Let's hear it."

Surprise. Sheer terror. And not the least twitch of a muscle. "Sir," she said again, and there was, finally, a faint, fleeting expression of some sort, quickly gone. She swallowed. "It's the dishes."

My turn to be surprised. "The dishes?"

"Sir, you sent Captain Vel's things into storage here on the station."

And lovely things they had been. The dishes (and utensils, and tea things) Kalr Five was, presumably, preoccupied with had been porcelain, glass, jeweled and enameled metal. But they hadn't been mine. And I didn't want anything of Captain Vel's. Five expected me to understand her. Wanted so much for me to understand. But I didn't. "Yes?"

Frustration. Anger, even. Clearly, from Five's perspective what she wanted was obvious. But the only part of it that was obvious to me was the fact she couldn't just come out and say it, even when I'd asked her to. "Sir," she said finally, citizens walking around us, some with curious glances, some pretending not to notice us. "I understand we're leaving the system soon."

"Soldier," I said, beginning to be frustrated and angry myself, in no good mood from my talk with the Lord of the Radch. "Are you capable of speaking directly?"

"We can't leave the system with no good dishes!" she blurted finally, face still impressively impassive. "Sir." When I didn't answer, she continued, through another surge of fear at speaking so plainly, "Of course it doesn't matter to *you*. You're a fleet captain, your rank is enough to impress anyone." And my house name—I was now Breq Mianaai. I wasn't too pleased at having been given that particular name, which marked me as a cousin of the Lord of the Radch herself. None of my crew but Seivarden and the ship's medic knew I hadn't been born with it. "*You* could invite a captain to supper and serve her soldier's mess and she wouldn't say a word, sir." Couldn't, unless she outranked me.

"We're not going where we're going so we can hold dinner parties," I said. That apparently confounded her, brief confusion showing for a moment on her face.

"Sir!" she said, voice pleading, in some distress. "*You* don't need to worry what other people think of you. I'm only saying, because you ordered me to."

Of course. I should have seen. Should have realized days ago. She was worried that *she* would look bad if I didn't have dinnerware to match my rank. That it would reflect badly on the ship itself. "You're worried about the reputation of the ship."

Chagrin, but also relief. "Yes, sir."

"I'm not Captain Vel." Captain Vel had cared a great deal about such things.

"*No*, sir." I wasn't sure if the emphasis—and the relief I read in Five—was because my not being Captain Vel was a good thing, or because I had finally understood what she had been trying to tell me. Or both.

I had already cleared my account here, all my money in chits locked in my quarters on board *Mercy of Kalr*. What little I carried on my person wouldn't be sufficient to ease Kalr Five's anxieties. Station—the AI that ran this place, *was* this place—could probably smooth the financial details over for me. But Station resented me as the cause of last week's violence and would not be disposed to assist me.

"Go back to the palace," I said. "Tell the Lord of the Radch what you require." Her eyes widened just slightly, and two tenths of a second later I read disbelief and then frank terror in Kalr Five. "When everything is arranged to your satisfaction, come to the shuttle."

Three citizens passed, bags in gloved hands, the fragment of conversation I heard telling me they were on their way to the docks, to catch a ship to one of the outer stations. A lift door slid open, obligingly. Of course. Station knew where they were going, they didn't have to ask.

Station knew where *I* was going, but it wouldn't open any doors for me without my giving the most explicit of requests. I turned, stepped quickly into the dockbound lift after them, saw the lift door close on Five standing, horrified, on the black stone pavement of the concourse. The lift moved, the three citizens chattered. I closed my eyes and saw Kalr Five staring at the lift, hyperventilating slightly. She frowned just the smallest amount—possibly no one passing her would

9

notice. Her fingers twitched, summoning *Mercy of Kalr*'s attention, though with some trepidation, as though maybe she feared it wouldn't answer.

But of course *Mercy of Kalr* was already paying attention. "Don't worry," said *Mercy of Kalr*, voice serene and neutral in Five's ear and mine. "It's not you Fleet Captain's angry with. Go ahead. It'll be all right."

True enough. It wasn't Kalr Five I was angry with. I pushed away the data coming from her, received a disorienting flash of Seivarden, asleep, dreaming, and Lieutenant Ekalu, still tense, in the middle of asking one of her Etrepas for tea. Opened my eyes. The citizens in the lift with me laughed at something, I didn't know or care what, and as the lift door slid open we walked out into the broad lobby of the docks, lined all around with icons of gods that travelers might find useful or comforting. It was sparsely populated for this time of day, except by the entrance to the dock authority office, where a line of ill-tempered ship captains and pilots waited for their turn to complain to the overburdened inspector adjuncts. Two intersystem gates had been disabled in last week's upheaval, more were likely to be in the near future, and the Lord of the Radch had forbidden any travel in the remaining ones, trapping dozens of ships in the system, with all their cargo and passengers.

They moved aside for me, bowing slightly as though a wind had blown through them. It was the uniform that had done it—I heard one captain whisper to another one, "Who is that?" and the responding murmur as her neighbor replied and others commented on her ignorance or added what they knew. I heard *Mianaai* and *Special Missions*. The sense they'd managed to make out of last week's events. The official version was that I had come to Omaugh Palace undercover, to root out a seditious conspiracy. That I had been working for Anaander Mianaai all along. Anyone who'd ever been part of events that later received an official version would know or suspect that wasn't true. But most Radchaai lived unremarkable lives and would have no reason to doubt it.

No one questioned my walking past the adjuncts, into the outer office of the Inspector Supervisor. Daos Ceit, who was her assistant, was still recovering from injuries. An adjunct I didn't know sat in her place but rose swiftly and bowed as I entered. So did a very, very young lieutenant, more gracefully and collectedly than I expected in a seventeen-year-old, the sort who was still all lanky arms and legs and frivolous enough to spend her first pay on lilac-colored eyes—surely she hadn't been born with eyes that color. Her dark-brown jacket, trousers, gloves, and boots were crisp and spotless, her straight, dark hair cut close. "Fleet Captain. Sir," she said. "Lieutenant Tisarwat, sir." She bowed again.

I didn't answer, only looked at her. If my scrutiny disturbed her, I couldn't see it. She wasn't yet sending data to *Mercy of Kalr*, and her brown skin hadn't darkened in any sort of flush. The small, discreet scatter of pins near one shoulder suggested a family of some substance but not the most elevated in the Radch. She was, I thought, either preternaturally self-possessed or a fool. Neither option pleased me.

"Go on in, sir," said the unfamiliar adjunct, gesturing me toward the inner office. I did, without a word to Lieutenant Tisarwat.

Dark-skinned, amber-eyed, elegant and aristocratic even in the dark-blue uniform of dock authority, Inspector Supervisor Skaaiat Awer rose and bowed as the door shut behind me. "Breq. Are you going, then?"

I opened my mouth to say, *Whenever you authorize our*

departure, but remembered Five and the errand I'd sent her on. "I'm only waiting for Kalr Five. Apparently I can't ship out without an acceptable set of dishes."

Surprise crossed her face, gone in an instant. She had known, of course, that I had sent Captain Vel's things here, and that I didn't own anything to replace them. Once the surprise had gone I saw amusement. "Well," she said. "Wouldn't you have felt the same?" When I had been in Five's place, she meant. When I had been a ship.

"No, I wouldn't have. I didn't. Some other ships did. Do." Mostly *Swords*, who by and large already thought they were above the smaller, less prestigious *Mercies*, or the troop carrier *Justices*.

"My Seven Issas cared about that sort of thing." Skaaiat Awer had served as a lieutenant on a ship with human troops, before she'd become Inspector Supervisor here at Omaugh Palace. Her eyes went to my single piece of jewelry, a small gold tag pinned near my left shoulder. She gestured, a change of topic that wasn't really a change of topic. "Athoek, is it?" My destination hadn't been publicly announced, might, in fact, be considered sensitive information. But Awer was one of the most ancient and wealthy of houses. Skaaiat had cousins who knew people who knew things. "I'm not sure that's where I'd have sent you."

"It's where I'm going."

She accepted that answer, no surprise or offense visible in her expression. "Have a seat. Tea?"

"Thank you, no." Actually I could have used some tea, might under other circumstances have been glad of a relaxed chat with Skaaiat Awer, but I was anxious to be off.

This, too, Inspector Supervisor Skaaiat took with equanimity. She did not sit, herself. "You'll be calling on Basnaaid

Elming when you get to Athoek Station." Not a question. She knew I would be. Basnaaid was the younger sister of someone both Skaaiat and I had once loved. Someone I had, under orders from Anaander Mianaai, killed. "She's like Awn, in some ways, but not in others."

"Stubborn, you said."

"Very proud. And fully as stubborn as her sister. Possibly more so. She was very offended when I offered her client-age for her sister's sake. I mention it because I suspect you're planning to do something similar. And you might be the only person alive even more stubborn than she is."

I raised an eyebrow. "Not even the tyrant?" The word wasn't Radchaai, was from one of the worlds annexed and absorbed by the Radch. By Anaander Mianaai. The tyrant herself, almost the only person on Omaugh Palace who would have recognized or understood the word, besides Skaaiat and myself.

Skaaiat Awer's mouth quirked, sardonic humor. "Possibly. Possibly not. In any event, be very careful about offering Basnaaid money or favors. She won't take it kindly." She gestured, good-natured but resigned, as if to say, *but of course you'll do as you like.* "You'll have met your new baby lieutenant."

Lieutenant Tisarwat, she meant. "Why did she come here and not go directly to the shuttle?"

"She came to apologize to my adjunct." Daos Ceit's replacement, there in the outer office. "Their mothers are cousins." Formally, the word Skaaiat used referred to a relation between two people of different houses who shared a parent or a grandparent, but in casual use meant someone more distantly related who was a friend, or someone you'd grown up with. "They were supposed to meet for tea yesterday, and

Tisarwat never showed or answered any messages. And you know how military gets along with dock authorities." Which was to say, overtly politely and privately contemptuously. "My adjunct took offense."

"Why should Lieutenant Tisarwat care?"

"You never had a mother to be angry you offended her cousin," Skaaiat said, half laughing, "or you wouldn't ask."

True enough. "What do you make of her?"

"Flighty, I would have said a day or two ago. But today she's very subdued." *Flighty* didn't match the collected young person I'd seen in that outer office. Except, perhaps, those impossible eyes. "Until today she was on her way to a desk job in a border system."

"The tyrant sent me a baby *administrator*?"

"I wouldn't have thought she'd send you a baby anything," Skaaiat said. "I'd have thought she'd have wanted to come with you herself. Maybe there's not enough of her left here." She drew breath as though to say more but then frowned, head cocked. "I'm sorry, there's something I have to take care of."

The docks were crowded with ships in need of supplies or repairs or emergency medical assistance, ships that were trapped here in the system, with crews and passengers who were extremely unhappy about the fact. Skaaiat's staff had been working hard for days, with very few breaks. "Of course." I bowed. "I'll get out of your way." She was still listening to whoever had messaged her. I turned to go.

"Breq." I looked back. Skaaiat's head was still cocked slightly, she was still hearing whoever else spoke. "Take care."

"You, too." I walked through the door, to the outer office. Lieutenant Tisarwat stood, still and silent. The adjunct stared ahead, fingers moving, attending to urgent dock business no doubt. "Lieutenant," I said sharply, and didn't wait for a reply but walked out of the office, through the crowd of disgruntled ships' captains, onto the docks where I would find the shuttle that would take me to *Mercy of Kalr*.

The shuttle was too small to generate its own gravity. I was perfectly comfortable in such circumstances, but very young officers often were not. I stationed Lieutenant Tisarwat at the dock, to wait for Kalr Five, and then pushed myself over the awkward, chancy boundary between the gravity of the palace and the weightlessness of the shuttle, kicked myself over to a seat, and strapped myself in. The pilot gave a respectful nod, bowing being difficult in these circumstances. I closed my eyes, saw that Five stood in a large storage room inside the palace proper, plain, utilitarian, gray-walled. Filled with chests and boxes. In one brown-gloved hand she held a teabowl of delicate, deep rose glass. An open box in front of her showed more—a flask, seven more bowls, other dishes. Her pleasure in the beautiful things, her desire, was undercut by doubt. I couldn't read her mind, but I guessed that she had been told to choose from this storeroom, had found these and wanted them very much, but didn't quite believe she would be allowed to take them away. I was fairly sure this set was hand-blown, and some seven hundred years old. I hadn't realized she had a connoisseur's eye for such things.

I pushed the vision away. She would be some time, I thought, and I might as well get some sleep.

I woke three hours later, to lilac-eyed Lieutenant Tisarwat strapping herself deftly into a seat across from me. Kalr Five—now radiating contentment, presumably from the results of her stint in the palace storeroom—pushed herself over to Lieutenant Tisarwat, and with a nod and a quiet *Just in case, sir* proffered a bag for the nearly inevitable moment when the new officer's stomach reacted to microgravity.

I'd known young lieutenants who took such an offer as an insult. Lieutenant Tisarwat accepted it, with a small, vague smile that didn't quite reach the rest of her face. Still seeming entirely calm and collected.

"Lieutenant," I said, as Kalr Five kicked herself forward to strap herself in beside the pilot, another Kalr. "Have you taken any meds?" Another potential insult. Antinausea meds were available, and I'd known excellent, long-serving officers who for the whole length of their careers took them every time they got on a shuttle. None of them ever admitted to it.

The last traces of Lieutenant Tisarwat's smile vanished. "No, sir." Even. Calm.

"Pilot has some, if you need them." That ought to have gotten some kind of reaction.

And it did, though just the barest fraction of a second later than I'd expected. The hint of a frown, an indignant straightening of her shoulders, hampered by her seat restraints. "No, thank you, sir."

Flighty, Skaaiat Awer had said. She didn't usually misread people so badly. "I didn't request your presence, Lieutenant." I kept my voice calm, but with an edge of anger. Easy enough to do under the circumstances. "You're here only because Anaander Mianaai ordered it. I don't have the time or the resources to hand-raise a brand-new baby. You'd better get up to speed *fast*. I need officers who know what they're doing. I need a whole crew I can *depend* on."

"Sir," replied Lieutenant Tisarwat. Still calm, but now some earnestness in her voice, that tiny trace of frown deepening, just a bit. "Yes, sir."

Dosed with *something*. Possibly antinausea, and if I'd been given to gambling I'd have bet my considerable fortune that she was filled to the ears with at least one sedative. I wanted to pull up her personal record—*Mercy of Kalr* would have it by now. But the tyrant would see that I had pulled that record up. *Mercy of Kalr* belonged, ultimately, to Anaander Mianaai, and she had accesses that allowed her to control it. *Mercy of Kalr* saw and heard everything I did, and if the tyrant wanted that information she had only to demand it. And I didn't want her to know what it was I suspected. Wanted, truth be told, for my suspicions to be proven false. Unreasonable.

For now, if the tyrant was watching—and she was surely watching, through *Mercy of Kalr*, would be so long as we were in the system—let her think I resented having a baby foisted on me when I'd rather have someone who knew what they were doing.

I turned my attention away from Lieutenant Tisarwat. Forward, the pilot leaned closer to Five and said, quiet and oblique, "Everything all right?" And then to Five's responding, puzzled frown, "Too quiet."

"All this time?" asked Five. Still oblique. Because they were talking about me and didn't want to trigger any requests I might have made to Ship, to tell me when the crew was talking about me. I had an old habit—some two thousand years old—of singing whatever song ran through my head. Or humming. It had caused the crew some puzzlement and distress at first—this body, the only one left to me, didn't have a particularly good voice. They were getting used to it, though, and now I was dryly amused to see crew members disturbed by my silence.

"Not a peep," said the pilot to Kalr Five. With a brief sideways glance and a tiny twitch of neck and shoulder muscles that told me she'd thought of looking back, toward Lieutenant Tisarwat.

"Yeah," said Five, agreeing, I thought, with the pilot's unstated assessment of what might be troubling me.

Good. Let Anaander Mianaai be watching that, too.

It was a long ride back to *Mercy of Kalr*, but Lieutenant Tisarwat never did use the bag or evince any discomfort. I spent the time sleeping, and thinking.

Ships, communications, data traveled between stars using gates, beacon-marked, held constantly open. The calculations had already been made, the routes marked out through the strangeness of gate space, where distances and proximity didn't match normal space. But military ships—like *Mercy of Kalr*—could generate their own gates. It was a good deal more risky—choose the wrong route, the wrong exit or entrance, and a ship could end up anywhere, or nowhere. That didn't trouble me. *Mercy of Kalr* knew what it was doing, and we would arrive safely at Athoek Station.

And while we moved through gate space in our own, contained bubble of normal space, we would be completely isolated. I wanted that. Wanted to be gone from Omaugh Palace, away from Anaander Mianaai's sight and any orders or interference she might decide to send.

When we were nearly there, minutes away from docking, Ship spoke directly into my ear. "Fleet Captain." It didn't need to speak to me that way, could merely desire me to know it wanted my attention. And it nearly always knew what I wanted without my saying it. I could connect to *Mercy of Kalr* in a way no one else aboard could. I could not, however, *be Mercy of Kalr*, as I had been *Justice of Toren*. Not without losing myself entirely. Permanently.

"Ship," I replied quietly. And without my saying anything else, *Mercy of Kalr* gave me the results of its calculations, made unasked, a whole range of possible routes and departure times flaring into my vision. I chose the soonest, gave orders, and a little more than six hours later we were gone.

2

The tyrant had said our backgrounds were similar, and in some ways they were. She was—and I had been—composed of hundreds of bodies all sharing the same identity. From that angle, we were very much the same. Which some citizens had noted (though only relatively recently, within the last hundred or so years) during arguments about the military's use of ancillaries.

It seemed horrible when one thought of it happening to oneself, or a friend or relative. But the Lord of the Radch herself underwent the same, was arguably in some ways the same sort of being as the ships that served her, so how could it possibly be as bad as detractors claimed? Ridiculous to say that all this time the Radch had been anything less than entirely just.

One of a triad, that word. Justice, propriety, and benefit. No just act could be improper, no proper act unjust. Justice and propriety, so intertwined, themselves led to benefit. The question of just who or what benefited was a topic for late-night discussions over half-empty bottles of arrack, but

ordinarily no Radchaai questioned that justice and propriety would ultimately be beneficial in some gods-approved
way. Ever, except in the most extraordinary circumstances,
questioned that the Radch was anything but just, proper, and
beneficial.

Of course, unlike her ships, the Lord of the Radch was
a citizen—and not only a citizen but ruler of all the Radch,
absolute. I was a weapon she had used to expand that rule.
Her servant. In many ways her slave. And the difference went
further. Every one of Anaander Mianaai's bodies was identical to all the others, clones, conceived and grown for the
express purpose of being parts of her. Each of her thousands
of brains had grown and developed around the implants that
joined her to herself. For three thousand years she had never
at any time experienced being anyone but Anaander Mianaai. Never been a single-bodied person—preferably in late
adolescence or early adulthood, but older would do—taken
captive, stored in a suspension pod for decades, maybe even
centuries, until she was needed. Unceremoniously thawed
out, implant shoved into her brain, severing connections,
making new ones, destroying the identity she'd had all her
life so far and replacing it with a ship's AI.

If you haven't been through it, I don't think you can really
imagine it. The terror and nausea, the horror, even after it's
done and the body knows it's the ship, that the person it
was before doesn't exist anymore to care that she's died. It
could last a week, sometimes longer, while the body and its
brain adjusted to the new state of affairs. A side effect of the
process, one that could possibly have been eliminated, presumably it could have been made a good deal less horrific
than it was. But what was one body's temporary discomfort?
One body out of dozens, or even hundreds, was nothing, its

distress merely a passing inconvenience. If it was too intense or didn't abate in a reasonable amount of time, that body would be removed and destroyed, replaced with a new one. There were plenty in storage.

But now that Anaander Mianaai had declared that no new ancillaries would be made—not counting the prisoners still suspended in the holds of the huge troop carriers, thousands of bodies frozen, waiting—no one need concern themselves with the question at all.

As captain of *Mercy of Kalr*, I had quarters all to myself, three meters by four, lined all around with benches that doubled as storage. One of those benches was also my bed, and inside it, under the boxes and cases that held my possessions, was a box that Ship couldn't see or sense. Human eyes could see it, even when those eyes were part of an ancillary body. But no scanner, no mechanical sensor could see that box, or the gun inside, or its ammunition—bullets that would burn through anything in the universe. How this had been managed was mysterious—not only the inexplicable bullets, but how light coming from the box or the gun might be visible to human eyes but not, say, to cameras, which in the end worked on the same principles. And Ship, for instance, didn't see an empty space where the box was, where something ought to have been, but instead it saw whatever it might have expected would occupy that space. None of it made any sense. Still, it was the case. Box, weapon, and its ammunition had been manufactured by the alien Presger, whose aims were obscure. Whom even Anaander Mianaai feared, lord as she was of the vast reaches of Radch space, commander of its seemingly endless armies.

Mercy of Kalr knew about the box, about the gun, because

I had told it. To the Kalrs who served me, it was just one box among several, none of which they'd opened. Had they really been the ancillaries they sometimes pretended to be, that would have been the end of it. But they were not ancillaries. They were human, and consumingly curious. They still speculated, looked lingeringly, when they stowed the linens and pallet I slept on. If I hadn't been captain—even weightier, fleet captain—they'd have been through every millimeter of my luggage by now, twice and three times, and discussed it all thoroughly among themselves. But I *was* captain, with the power of life and death over my entire crew, and so I was granted this small privacy.

This room had been Captain Vel's, before she'd chosen the wrong side in the Lord of the Radch's battle with herself. The floor covering and the cloths and cushions that had covered the benches were gone, left behind us at Omaugh Palace. She'd had the walls painted with elaborate scrollwork in purples and greens, a style and a palette that she'd taken from a past era, one presumably nobler and more civilized than this one. Unlike Captain Vel, I had lived through it and didn't much regret its loss. I'd have had it removed, but there were other, more urgent concerns, and at least the paint didn't extend any farther than the captain's quarters.

Her gods, which had sat in a niche under the ship's gods— Amaat, of course, chief of Radchaai gods, and Kalr, part of this ship's name—I had replaced with She Who Sprang from the Lily, an EskVar (the Emanation of beginning and ending), and a small, cheap icon of Toren. I had been fortunate to find that. Toren was an old god, not popular, nearly forgotten except by the crews of the ships that bore the name, none of them stationed near here, and one of them—myself—destroyed.

There was room for more gods, there always was. But I

didn't believe in any of them. It would have looked odd to the crew if I'd had none besides the ship's, and these would do. They were not gods to me, but reminders of something else. The crew wouldn't know or understand that, and so I burned incense to them daily, along with Amaat and Kalr, and just like those gods they received offerings of food and enameled brass flowers that had made Five frown when she'd first seen them, because they were cheap and common and not, she thought, what a Mianaai and a fleet captain ought to offer to her gods. She'd said so to Kalr Seventeen, obliquely, not mentioning my name or title. She didn't know I was an ancillary, didn't know how easy it was, because of that, for Ship to show me what she felt, what she said, wherever she said it, whenever I wished. She was confident Ship would keep her gossip secret.

Two days after we gated, on our way to Athoek in our own tiny, isolated fragment of universe, I sat on the edge of my bed drinking tea from a delicate, deep rose glass bowl while Kalr Five cleared away the omens and the cloth from the morning's cast. The omens had indicated continuing good fortune, of course, only the most foolish of captains would find any other sort of pattern in the fall of those metal discs on the cloth.

I closed my eyes. Felt the corridors and rooms of *Mercy of Kalr*, spotless white. The whole ship smelled comfortingly and familiarly of recycled air and cleaning solvent. Amaat decade had scrubbed their portion of those corridors, and the rooms they were responsible for. Their lieutenant, Seivarden, senior of *Mercy of Kalr*'s lieutenants, was just now finishing her inspection of that work, giving out praise and remonstrance, assignments for tomorrow, in her antiquely elegant accent. Seivarden had been born for this work, had been born with a face that marked her as a member of one of the highest houses in the Radch, distant cousins to Anaander Mianaai herself, wealthy and well-bred. She had been raised with the expectation that she would command. She was in many respects the very image of a Radchaai military officer. Speaking with her Amaats, relaxed and assured, she was nearly the Seivarden I'd known a thousand years ago, before she'd lost her ship, been shoved into an escape pod by one of its ancillaries. The tracker on the pod had been damaged, and she had drifted for centuries. After she'd been found, and thawed, and discovered that everyone she'd ever known was dead, even her house no longer existent and the Radch changed from what she'd known, she'd fled Radchaai space and spent several years wandering, dissipated, aimless. Not quite willing to die, I suspected, but hoping in the back of her mind to meet with some fatal accident. She'd gained weight, since I'd found her, built back some of her lost muscle, looked considerably healthier now, but still somewhat the worse for wear. She'd been forty-eight when her ship's ancillaries had pushed her into that escape pod. Count that thousand frozen years and she was the second oldest person aboard *Mercy of Kalr*.

Next in seniority, Lieutenant Ekalu stood watch in Command with two of her Etrepas. It wasn't theoretically necessary for anyone to stand any sort of watch, not with *Mercy of Kalr* always awake, always watching, constantly aware of the ship that was its own body and of the space around it. Especially in gate space, where nothing untoward—or, honestly, even interesting—was likely to happen. But ship systems did sometimes malfunction, and it was a good deal quicker and easier to respond to a crisis if the crew was already alert. And of course dozens of people packed into a small ship required work to keep them disciplined and busy. Ship threw up numbers, maps, graphs in Lieutenant Ekalu's vision, murmured into her ear, information mixed now and then with friendly encouragement. *Mercy of Kalr* liked Lieutenant Ekalu, had confidence in her intelligence and ability.

Kalr was captain's decade, my own. There were ten soldiers in all the other decades on *Mercy of Kalr*, but there were twenty in Kalr. They slept on a staggered schedule, because also unlike the other decades, Kalr was always on duty, a last remnant of the days when Ship had been crewed by ancillary bodies, when its soldiers had been fragments of itself and not dozens of individual human beings. The Kalrs who had awakened just now, as I had, were assembled in the soldiers' mess, white-walled, plain, just big enough for ten to eat and space to stack the dishes. They stood, each by their dish of skel, a fast-growing, slimy, dark-green plant that contained any nutrients a human body needed. The taste took some getting used to if you hadn't grown up on it. A lot of Radchaai had in fact grown up on it.

The Kalrs in the soldiers' mess began the morning prayer in ragged unison. *The flower of justice is peace.* Within a word or two they settled into step, the words falling into familiar rhythm. *The flower of propriety is beauty in thought and action.*

Medic—she had a name, and a nominal rank of lieutenant, but was never addressed by either—was attached to Kalr, but was not Kalr Lieutenant. She was, simply, Medic. She could be—had been, would be in another hour—ordered to stand a watch, and two Kalrs would stand that watch with her. She was the only one of Captain Vel's officers remaining. She would have been difficult to replace, of course, but also her involvement in the previous week's events had been minimal.

She was tall and spare, light-skinned by Radchaai standards, hair enough lighter than brown to be slightly odd, but not the sort of striking shade that might have been artificial. She frowned habitually, though she wasn't ill-tempered. She was seventy-six years old and looked much the same as she had in her thirties, and would until she was past a hundred and fifty. Her mother had been a doctor, and her mother before that, and her mother before that. She was, just now, extremely angry with me.

She'd woken determined to confront me in the short time before she went on watch, had said the morning prayer in a rushed mutter as soon as she'd rolled out of bed. *The flower of benefit is Amaat whole and entire.* I had turned my attention away from Kalr in the soldiers' mess, but I couldn't hear the first lines without hearing the rest. *I am the sword of justice*...Now Medic stood silent and tense by her own seat in the decade room, where the officers ate.

Seivarden came into the decade room for what would be her supper, smiling, relaxed, saw Medic waiting, stiff and impatient, frowning more intensely than usual. For an instant I saw irritation in Seivarden, and then she dismissed it, apologized for her tardiness, got a mumbled, perfunctory *it's nothing* in return.

In the soldiers' mess Kalr finished the morning prayer, mouthed the extra lines I'd ordered, a brief prayer for the dead, and their names. Awn Elming. Nyseme Ptem, the soldier who had mutinied at Ime, preventing a war with the alien Rrrrr, at the cost of her own life.

Bo decade slept in what was more an alcove than a room, barely large enough for their ten close sleeping bodies, no privacy, no individual space, even in their beds. They twitched, sighed, dreamed, more restless than the ancillaries that had once slept there.

In her own tiny quarters, their lieutenant, the very young,

impossibly lilac-eyed Lieutenant Tisarwat, slept as well, still and dreamless, but with an underlying current of unease, adrenaline just a touch higher than it ought to be. That should have awakened her, as it had the night before, but Medic had given her something to help her sleep.

Medic bolted her breakfast, muttered excuses, and all but stormed out of the decade room. "Ship," she messaged, fingers twitching emphatically, gesturing the words. "I want to speak to the fleet captain."

"Medic's coming," I said to Kalr Five. "We'll offer her tea. But she probably won't take it." Five checked the level of tea in the flask and pulled out another of the rose glass bowls. I suspected I wouldn't see my old enameled set again unless I specifically ordered it.

"Fleet Captain," said *Mercy of Kalr* directly into my ear, and then showed me an Amaat on her way to the soldiers' mess, singing softly to herself, one of those collections of inconsequential nonsense children from nearly anywhere sing. "It all goes around, it all goes around, the planet goes around the sun, it all goes around. It all goes around, the moon goes around the planet..." Thoughtless and off-key.

In my quarters Kalr Five stood stiffly at attention, said in an expressionless voice, "Medic requests permission to speak with you, Fleet Captain."

In the corridor, the Amaat, hearing the step of another Amaat behind her, fell silent, suddenly self-conscious. "Granted," I said to Five, needlessly of course, she already knew I planned to speak with Medic.

The door opened and Medic entered, a bit more abruptly than was strictly proper. "Fleet Captain," she began, tight and furious.

I raised a forestalling hand. "Medic. Sit. Will you have tea?"

She sat. Refused tea. Kalr Five left the room at my order, just the tiniest bit resentful at missing whatever Medic had to say, which showed every sign of being something interesting. When she was gone, I gestured to Medic, sitting tense across the table from me. *Go ahead.*

"Begging the fleet captain's indulgence." She didn't sound at all as though she cared whether I'd give it or not. Under the table, she clenched her gloved hands into fists. "Fleet Captain. Sir. You've removed some medications from Medical."

"I have."

That stopped her momentum, briefly. She had, it seemed, expected a denial. "No one else could have done it. Ship insisted they'd never left inventory, and I've looked at the logs, at the recordings themselves, I've been all through them, and there's no record of anyone taking them. There's nobody else on board who could hide that from me."

I feared that was no longer true. But I didn't say that. "Lieutenant Tisarwat came to you yesterday at the end of her shift and asked you for help with some minor nausea and anxiety." Two days ago, some hours after we'd gated, Lieutenant Tisarwat had begun to feel stressed. Slightly sick. Had found herself unable to eat much of her supper that evening. Her Bos had noticed, of course with concern—the problem with most seventeen-year-olds was feeding them enough, not tempting them to eat. They had decided, among themselves, that she was homesick. And distressed by my obvious anger at her presence. "Are you worried for her health?"

Medic nearly started up out of her seat in indignation. "That's not the point!" Recollected whom she was speaking to. "Sir." Swallowed, waited, but I said nothing. "She's nervous. She reads as under some emotional stress. Perfectly understandable. Perfectly normal for a baby lieutenant on her first assignment." Realized, as she was speaking, that I probably had extensive experience of what was normal for very young lieutenants on their first assignments. Regretted speaking, regretted, momentarily, coming here to confront, to accuse me. Just for an instant.

"Perfectly normal under the circumstances," I agreed, but I meant something different.

"And I couldn't help her because you'd taken every single med I might have given her."

"Yes," I acknowledged. "I had. Was there anything in her system when she arrived?" I already knew what the answer would be, but I asked anyway.

Medic blinked, surprised by my question, but only for an instant. "She *did* look as though maybe she'd taken something, when she came to Medical from the shuttle. But there was nothing when I scanned her. I think she was just tired." A tiny shift in her posture, a change in the emotions I read coming from her, suggested she was considering, now, the significance of my question, the odd, small mismatch of how Lieutenant Tisarwat had looked, to her professional eye, and what the readings had said.

"Any recommendations or orders to dispense medication, in her file?"

"No, nothing." Medic didn't seem to have come to any conclusion. Much less the one I'd come to. But she was curious now, if still angry along with it. "Recent events have been stressful for all of us. And she's very young. And..." She hesitated. Had, perhaps, been about to say that by now everyone on board knew I'd been very angry when Lieutenant Tisarwat had been assigned to *Mercy of Kalr*. Angry enough to stop singing for several hours.

By now the whole crew knew what that meant. Had begun, even, to find it comforting to have such an obvious way to know if everything was as it should be. "You were going to say?" I asked, my expression and voice as noncommittal as I could make them.

"I think she feels like you don't want her here, sir."

"I don't," I said. "As it happens."

Medic shook her head, not understanding. "Begging the fleet captain's indulgence. You might have refused to take her."

I might have refused to take her. Might have left her on the palace docks, when *Mercy of Kalr*'s shuttle left, and never come back for her. I had seriously considered doing that. Skaaiat would have understood, I was sure, would have contrived to discover that not a single docked ship could fetch the young lieutenant out to *Mercy of Kalr* until it was too late. "You gave her something?"

"Something to help her sleep. It was the end of the day for her. It was all I could do." That galled Medic, not only that I had interfered in her domain, but that she had been unable to help.

I couldn't help a quick, momentary look. Lieutenant Tisarwat, asleep but not deeply. Not restfully. Still tense, still that quiet background of unease. "Medic," I said, returning my attention to where I was, "you have every right to be angry with me. I expected you to be angry, and expected you to protest. I would have been disappointed if you hadn't." She blinked, puzzled, hands still clenched in her lap. "Trust me." There wasn't much more I could say, just yet. "I am an unknown quantity, I am...not the sort of person who's generally given command." A flicker of recognition on Medic's face, slight revulsion and then embarrassment at having felt that, where she knew I could see it, knew I was almost certainly watching her response. Medic had repaired my implants, which I had deactivated and damaged, to hide them. Medic knew what I was, as no one else aboard but Seivarden knew. "But *trust* me."

"I don't have a choice, do I, sir? We're cut off until we reach Athoek, there's no one I can complain to." Frustrated.

"Complain at Athoek when we get there. If you still want to." If there was anyone there to complain to, that would do any good.

"Sir." She rose, bit back whatever else she'd wanted to say. Bowed stiffly. "May I go?"

"Yes, of course, Medic."

Lieutenant Tisarwat was a problem. Her official personal history, a dry recitation of facts, said she'd been born and raised on a planet, the third child of one parent and the second of another. She'd had the sort of education any well-off, moderately well-born Radchaai had. Done well at math, had an enthusiasm but no gift for poetry, lacked both for history. She had an allowance from her parents but no expectations to speak of. She'd gone into space for the first time when she'd left for training.

Reading between the lines, she had been born not to take some particular place in her house, or inherit anyone's wealth and position, or fulfill any particular expectations, but for her own sake, and no doubt her parents had loved her and cosseted her right up to the day she'd left for the military. Her correspondence with her parents confirmed this. Her siblings, all older, seemed not to resent her position as favorite, but took it in stride and petted her nearly as much as their parents did.

Flighty, Skaaiat Awer had said of her. *Frivolous* I had thought on seeing the certainly purchased color of her eyes, and the aptitudes data in her file suggested the same. That data did not suggest *self-possessed*. Nor did it suggest the nervous gloom she'd displayed since shortly after boarding *Mercy of Kalr*.

Her trainers had met her sort before, been hard on her on account of that, but not cruelly so. Some of them no doubt had baby sisters of their own, and after all she was destined for an administrative post. It hardly mattered if in microgravity she could never keep her supper down—plenty of other new lieutenants had the same problem, particularly if they had little experience in space.

Two days before, while Tisarwat had sat being examined in Medical, while Ship made the connections that would let it— and me—read her like it could every other member of the crew, her Bos had gone over every millimeter of her luggage and come to fairly accurate conclusions about her history. They were prepared to be disgusted with her ignorance, a baby fresh from training, a matter for mocking and exasperation, yes. But also for sympathy, and some anticipatory pride. Her Bos would be able to claim credit for any of Tisarwat's future accomplishments, because after all they would have raised her. Taught her anything she knew that was really important. They were prepared to be *hers*. Wanted very much for her to turn out to be the sort of lieutenant they would be proud to serve under.

I so very much wanted my suspicions not to be true.

Watch was, of course, uneventful. Medic went from our conference to Command, still angry. Seivarden's Amaats were exercising, bathing, would soon be climbing into their own beds, settling into their accustomed places with shoves and the occasional indignant whisper—there wasn't much room to stretch out. Ekalu's Etrepas scrubbed the already near-spotless rooms and corridors they were responsible for. Lieutenant Tisarwat wouldn't wake for nearly four hours.

I went to the ship's small gym, a few last Amaats scurrying out of my way. Worked out, hard, for an hour. Went, still angry, still sweaty from exercise, to the firing range.

It was all simulation. No one wanted bullets flying on a small ship, not with hard vacuum outside the hull. The targets were images Ship cast on the far wall. The weapon would bang and recoil as though it had fired real bullets, but it shot only light. Not as destructive as I wanted to be, that very moment, but it would have to do.

Ship knew my mood. It threw up a quick succession of targets, all of which I hit, nearly unthinking. Reloaded—no need to reload, really, but there would be if this had been a real weapon, and so the training routines demanded it. Fired again and again, reloaded again, fired. It wasn't enough. Seeing that, Ship set the targets moving, a dozen of them at a time. I settled into a familiar rhythm, fire, reload, fire, reload. A song came into my mind—there was always a song, with me. This one was a long narrative, an account of the final dispute between Anaander Mianaai and her erstwhile friend, Naskaaia Eskur. The poet had been executed fifteen hundred years ago—her version of the event had cast Anaander as the villain and ended with the promise that the dead Naskaaia would return to revenge herself. It had been almost utterly forgotten inside Radch space, because singing it, possibly even knowing it existed, could easily cost a citizen a thorough reeducation. It still circulated some places outside Radch influence.

> *Betrayer! Long ago we promised*
> *To exchange equally, gift for gift.*
> *Take this curse: What you destroy will destroy you.*

Fire, reload. Fire, reload. Doubtless little of the song—or any other on the same subject—had any basis in fact. Doubtless the event itself had been quite mundane, not so poetically dramatic, ringing with mythic and prophetic overtones. It was still satisfying to sing it.

I came to the end, lowered my weapon. Unbidden, Ship showed me what was behind my back—three Etrepas crowding the entrance to the firing range, watching, astonished. Seivarden, on her way to her own quarters and bed, standing behind them. She could not read my mood as closely as Ship could, but she knew me well enough to be worried.

"Ninety-seven percent," said Ship, in my ear. Needlessly.

I took a breath. Stowed the weapon in its niche. Turned. The expressions of the three Etrepas turned instantly from astonishment to blank, ancillary-like expressionlessness, and they stepped back into the corridor. I brushed past them, out into the corridor and away, toward the bath. Heard one Etrepa say, "Fuck! Is *that* what Special Missions is like?" Saw the panic of the others—their last captain had been very strict about swearing. Heard Seivarden, outwardly jovial, say, "Fleet Captain *is* pretty fucking badass." The vulgarity, combined with Seivarden's archaic, elegant accent, set them laughing, relieved but still unsettled.

Mercy of Kalr didn't ask me why I was angry. Didn't ask me what was wrong. That in and of itself suggested my suspicions were correct. I wished, for the first time in my two-thousand-year life, that I was given to swearing.

3

I had Lieutenant Tisarwat awakened three hours before her usual time and ordered her to report immediately to me. She startled awake, heart racing even through the last remnants of the drug Medic had given her. It took her a few seconds to comprehend Ship's words, spoken directly into her ear. She spent twenty more seconds just breathing, slowly, deliberately. Feeling vaguely sick.

She arrived at my quarters still unsettled. The collar of her jacket was slightly askew—none of her Bos were awake to see to her, and she had dressed in nervous haste, dropping things, fumbling at fastenings that should have been simple. I met her standing, and I didn't dismiss Kalr Five, who lingered, ostensibly busy but hoping to see or hear something interesting.

"Lieutenant Tisarwat," I said, stern and angry. "Your decade's work these past two days has been inadequate."

Resentment, anger, chagrin. She had already presented herself at creditable attention, considering, but I could see her back, her shoulders stiffen further, see her head come up a couple of millimeters. But she was wise enough not to answer.

I continued. "You may be aware that there are parts of itself Ship can't see. It used to rely on ancillaries for that. Ship doesn't have ancillaries anymore. The cleaning and maintenance of those parts of itself are *your* responsibility. And Bo decade has been skipping them. For instance, the hinge pins on the shuttles' air locks haven't been cleaned in quite some time." That I knew from very personal experience, just last week, when my life, and the lives of everyone on Omaugh Palace, had hung on, among other things, how quickly I could unfasten part of a *Mercy of Kalr* shuttle's air lock. "There's also a place under the grate in the bath that you can't see unless you put your head down in there." That was a disgusting proposition at the best of times. Worse when it hadn't been routinely, thoroughly cleaned. "*Mercy of Kalr* will give you the list. I expect everything to be taken care of when I inspect this time tomorrow."

"T-tomorrow, sir?" Lieutenant Tisarwat sounded just the slightest bit strangled.

"This time tomorrow, Lieutenant. And neither you nor your decade is to neglect assigned time in the gym or the firing range. Dismissed." She bowed, left, angry and unhappy. As her Bos would be, when they discovered how much work I'd just loaded on them.

It was true that I had near-absolute power over everyone on the ship, especially given our isolation in gate space. But it was also true that I would be extremely foolish to alienate my officers. Foolish, also, to so completely court the displeasure of the soldiers without a good reason. Bo would resent my mistreatment of Lieutenant Tisarwat, certainly to the extent that it meant inconvenience to themselves. But also because Lieutenant Tisarwat was *their* lieutenant.

I wanted that. Was pushing hard on that, deliberately.

But timing was everything. Push too hard, too fast, and the results would not be what I wanted, possibly disastrously so. Push too gently, take too long, and I would run out of time, and again results would not be what I wanted. And I needed those specific results. Amaat, Etrepa, my own Kalrs, they understood Bo's position. And if I was going to be hard on Bo—because being hard on Bo's lieutenant was the same thing—it would have to be for a reason the other decades could understand. I didn't want anyone on *Mercy of Kalr* to think that I was dispensing harsh treatment inexplicably, capriciously, that no matter how good you were the captain might decide to make your life hell. I'd seen captains who ran things that way. It never made for a particularly good crew.

But I couldn't possibly explain my reasons to anyone, not now, and I hoped I would never be able to. Never have to. But I had hoped, from the beginning, that this situation would not arise at all.

Next morning I invited Seivarden to breakfast. My breakfast, her supper. I ought also to have invited Medic, who ate at the same time, but I thought she would be happier eating alone than with me, just now.

Seivarden was wary. Wanting, I saw, to say something to me but not sure of the wisdom of saying it. Or perhaps not sure of how to say it wisely. She ate three bites of fish, and then said, jokingly, "I didn't think I rated the best dishes." She meant the plates, delicate, violet and aqua painted porcelain. And the rose glass teabowls—Five knew my eating with Seivarden didn't call for any sort of formality, and still she hadn't been able to bring herself to stow them away and use the enamel.

"*Second* best," I said. "Sorry. I haven't seen the best, yet."

A happy little spike of pride, from Five, standing in the corner pretending to wipe a spotless utensil, just at the thought of the best dishes. "I was told I needed nice dishes so I had the Lord of the Radch send me something suitable."

She raised an eyebrow, knowing Anaander Mianaai was not a neutral topic for me. "I'm surprised the Lord of the Radch didn't come along with us. Though..." She glanced, for just an instant, at Five.

Without my saying anything, merely from seeing my desire, Ship suggested to Kalr Five that she leave the room. When we were alone, Seivarden continued. "She has accesses. She can make Ship do anything she wants. She can make *you* do anything she wants. Can't she?"

Dangerous territory. But Seivarden had no way of knowing that. For a moment I saw Lieutenant Tisarwat, still stressed and sick, and exhausted besides—she hadn't slept since I'd wakened her some twenty hours before—lying on the bath floor, grate pulled aside, her head ducked down to examine that spot Ship couldn't see. An anxious and equally tired Bo behind her, waiting for her verdict.

"It's not quite that simple," I said, returning my attention to Seivarden. I made myself take a bite of fish, a drink of tea. "There's certainly one remaining access, from before." From when I'd been a ship. Been part of *Justice of Toren*'s Esk decade. "Only the tyrant's voice will work that one, though. And yes, she could have used it before I left the palace. She said as much to me, you may recall, and said she didn't want to."

"Maybe she used it and told you not to remember she used it."

I had already considered that possibility, and dismissed it. I gestured, *no*. "There's a point where accesses break."

Seivarden gestured acknowledgment. When I had first met her, a baby lieutenant of seventeen, she hadn't thought ships' AIs had any feelings in particular—not any that mattered. And like many Radchaai she assumed that thought and emotion were two easily separable things. That the artificial intelligences that ran large stations, and military ships, were supremely dispassionate. Mechanical. Old stories, historical dramas about events before Anaander Mianaai set about building her empire, about ships overwhelmed by grief and despair at the deaths of their captains—that was the past. The Lord of the Radch had improved AI design, removed that flaw.

She had learned otherwise, recently. "At Athoek," she guessed, "with Lieutenant Awn's sister there, you'd be too near that breaking point."

It was more complicated than that. But. "Basically."

"Breq," she said. Signaling, maybe, that she wanted to be sure she was speaking to me-as-Breq and not me-as-Fleet-Captain. "There's something I don't understand. The Lord of the Radch said, that day, that she couldn't just make AIs so they always obeyed her no matter what because their minds were complicated."

"Yes." She had said that. At a time when other, more urgent matters pressed, so there could be no real discussion of it.

"But Ships do love people. I mean, particular people." For some reason saying that made her nervous, triggered a tiny spike of apprehension in her. To cover it, she picked up her tea, drank. Set down the lovely deep rose bowl, carefully. "And that's a breaking point, isn't it? I mean, it can be. Why not just make all the ships love *her*?"

"Because that's potentially a breaking point." She looked at me, frowning, not understanding. "Do you love randomly?"

She blinked in bewilderment. "What?"

"Do you love at random? Like pulling counters out of a box? You love whichever one came to hand? Or is there something about certain people that makes them likely to be loved by you?"

"I...think I see." She set down her utensil, the untasted bit of fish it held. "I guess I see what you mean. But I'm not sure what that has to do with..."

"If there's something about a certain person that makes it likely you'd love them, what happens if that changes? And they're not really that person anymore?"

"I guess," she said, slowly, thoughtfully, "I assume that real love doesn't break for anything." *Real love*, to a Radchaai, wasn't only romantic, between lovers. Wasn't only between parent and child. *Real love* could also exist between patron and client. Was supposed to, ideally. "I mean," Seivarden continued, inexplicably embarrassed, "imagine your parents not loving you anymore." Another frown. Another surge of apprehension. "Would you ever have stopped loving Lieutenant Awn?"

"If," I replied, after a deliberate bite and swallow of breakfast, "she had ever become someone other than who she was." Still incomprehension from Seivarden. "Who is Anaander Mianaai?"

She understood, then, I could tell by the feeling of unease I read in her. "Even she's not sure, is she. She might be two people. Or more."

"And over three thousand years she'll have changed. Everyone does, who isn't dead. How much can a person change and still be the same? And how could she predict how much she might change over thousands of years, and what might break as a result? It's much easier to use something else. Duty, say. Loyalty to an idea."

"Justice," said Seivarden, aware of the irony, of what used to be my own name. "Propriety. Benefit."

That last, benefit, was the slippery one. "Any or all of them will do," I agreed. "And then you keep track of ships' favorites so you don't provoke any sort of conflict. Or so you can use those attachments to your advantage."

"I see," she said. And applied herself silently to the rest of her supper.

When the food was eaten, and Kalr Five had returned and cleared the dishes and poured us more tea, and left again, Seivarden spoke again. "Sir," she said. Ship's business, then. I knew what it would be. The soldiers of Amaat and Etrepa had already seen Bo, up well past their sleep time, all ten of them scrubbing desperately, taking fittings apart, lifting grates, poring over every millimeter, every crack and crevice, of their part of Ship's maintenance. When Lieutenant Ekalu had relieved Seivarden on watch she'd stopped, dared a few words. *Don't mean to offend... Thought you might mention to Sir...* Seivarden had been confused, partly by Lieutenant Ekalu's accent, partly by the use of *Sir* instead of *the fleet captain*, the remnant of Ekalu's days as Amaat One, the habit this crew had of speaking so as not to attract the captain's notice. But mostly, it turned out, confused by the suggestion she might be offended. Ekalu was too embarrassed to explain herself. "Do you think, maybe," Seivarden said to me, doubtless knowing I might well have overheard that exchange, in Command, "you're being a little hard on Tisarwat?" I said nothing, and she saw, clearly, that I was in a dangerous mood, that this topic was for some reason not an entirely safe one. She took a breath, and forged on ahead. "You're angry lately."

I raised an eyebrow. "Lately?" My own bowl of tea sat untouched in front of me.

She lifted her tea a centimeter, acknowledging. "You were less angry for a few days. I don't know, maybe because you were injured. Because now you're angry again. And I suppose I know why, and I suppose I can't really blame you, but..."

"You think I'm taking it out on Lieutenant Tisarwat." Who I did not want to see just now. I would not look. Two of her Bos were going meticulously over the interior of the shuttle they were responsible for—one of only two, I'd destroyed the third last week. They commented now and then, obliquely and tersely, on the unfairness of my treatment of them, and how hard I was being on their lieutenant.

"*You* know all the places a soldier can slack off, but how could Tisarwat?"

"She is, nonetheless, responsible for her decade."

"You could have reprimanded me as well," Seivarden pointed out, and took another drink of her tea. "I ought to have known, myself, and didn't. My ancillaries always took care of those things without my asking. Because they knew they ought to. Aatr's tits, *Ekalu* should know better than any of us where the crew is skipping over things. Not meaning to criticize her, understand. But either one of us would have deserved a dressing-down over that. Why give it to Tisarwat and not either of us?" I didn't want to explain that and so didn't say anything, only picked up my own tea and took a drink. "I'll admit," Seivarden continued, "that she's turning out to be a miserable specimen. All awkward not knowing what to do with her hands and feet, picking at her food. And clumsy. She's dropped three of the decade room teabowls, broken two of them. And she's so...so *moody*. I'm waiting for her to announce that none of us understands her. What was my lord thinking?" She meant Anaander Mianaai, the Lord of the Radch. "Was Tisarwat just all that was available?"

"Probably." Thinking that only made me angrier than I already was. "Do you remember when you were a baby lieutenant?"

She set her tea on the table, appalled. "Please tell me I wasn't like *that*."

"No. Not like that. You were awkward and annoying in a different way."

She snorted, amused and chagrined at the same time. "Still." Turning serious. Nervous, suddenly, having come to something, I saw, that she'd wanted to say all through the meal, but the thought of saying it intimidated her more even than the thought of accusing me of treating Lieutenant Tisarwat unjustly. "Breq, the whole crew thinks I'm kneeling to you."

"Yes." I had already known that, of course. "Though I'm not sure why. Five knows well enough you've never been in my bed."

"Well. The general feeling is that I've been remiss in my... my duties. It was all very well to give you time to recover from your injuries, but it's past time for me to... try to relieve whatever is troubling you. And maybe they're right." She took another mouthful of tea. Swallowed. "You're *looking* at me. That's never good."

"I'm sorry to have embarrassed you."

"Oh, I'm not embarrassed," she lied. And then added, more truthfully, "Well, not embarrassed that anyone thinks it. But bringing it up like this. Breq, you found me, what, a year ago? And in all that time I've never known you to... and, I mean, when you were..." She stopped. Afraid of saying the wrong thing, I thought. Her skin was too dark to really show a flush, but I could see the temperature change. "I mean, I know you were an ancillary. *Are* an ancillary. And ships don't... I mean, I know ancillaries can..."

44

"Ancillaries can," I agreed. "As you know from personal experience."

"Yes," she said. Truly abashed now. "But I guess I never thought that an ancillary might actually *want* it."

I let that hang for a moment, for her to think about. Then, "Ancillaries are human bodies, but they're also part of the ship. What the ancillaries feel, the ship feels. Because they're the same. Well, different bodies are different. Things taste different or feel different, they don't always want the same things, but all together, on the average, yes, it's a thing I attended to, for the bodies that needed it. I don't like being uncomfortable, no one does. I did what I could to make my ancillaries comfortable."

"I guess I never noticed."

"You weren't really supposed to." Best to get this over with. "In any event, ships don't generally want partners. They do that sort of thing for themselves. Ships with ancillaries, anyway. So." I gestured the obviousness of my conclusion, beyond any need to say it explicitly. Didn't add that ships didn't yearn for romantic partners, either. For captains, yes. For lieutenants. But not for lovers.

"Well," Seivarden said after a moment, "but you don't have other bodies to do that with, not anymore." She stopped, struck by a thought. "What must that have been like? With more than one body?"

I wasn't going to answer that. "I'm a little surprised you haven't thought of that before." But only a little. I knew Seivarden too well to think she'd ever dwelt long on what her ship might think or feel. And she'd never been one of those officers who'd been inconveniently fixated on the idea of ancillaries and sex.

"So when they take the ancillaries away," Seivarden said

after a few appalled moments, "it must be like having parts of your body cut off. And never replaced."

I could have said, *Ask Ship*. But Ship probably wouldn't have wanted to answer. "I'm told it's something like that," I said. Voice bland.

"Breq," Seivarden said, "when I was a lieutenant, before." A thousand years ago, she meant, when she'd been a lieutenant on *Justice of Toren*, in my care. "Did I ever pay any attention to anyone but myself?"

I considered, a moment, the range of truthful answers I could make, some less diplomatic than others, and said, finally, "Occasionally."

Unbidden, *Mercy of Kalr* showed me the soldiers' mess, where Seivarden's Amaats were clearing away their own supper. Amaat One said, "It's orders, citizens. Lieutenant says."

A few Amaats groaned. "I'll have it in my head all night," one complained to her neighbor.

In my own quarters, Seivarden said, penitent, "I hope I'm doing better these days."

In the mess, Amaat One opened her mouth and sang, tentative, slightly flat, "It all goes around..." The others joined her, unwilling, unenthusiastic. Embarrassed. "...it all goes around. The planet goes around the sun, it all goes around."

"Yes," I said to Seivarden. "A *little* better."

Bo had done a creditable job finishing all their tasks. The entire decade stood lined up in the mess, not a muscle twitching, every collar and cuff ruler-straight, even Lieutenant Tisarwat managing an outward severe impassivity. Inward was another matter—still that buzz of tension, that slightly sick feeling, steady since the morning before, and she hadn't slept since I'd awakened her yesterday. Her Bos gave off a

wave of collective resentment coupled with defiant pride—
they had, after all, managed quite a lot in the last day, managed it fairly well, considering. By rights I ought to indicate
my satisfaction, they were waiting for me to do that, all of
them certain of it, and prepared to feel ill-used if I didn't.

They deserved to be proud of themselves. Lieutenant Tisarwat, as things stood now, didn't deserve them. "Well done,
Bo," I said, and was rewarded with a surge of exhausted
pride and relief from every soldier in front of me. "See it stays
this way." Then, sharply, "Lieutenant, with me." And turned
and walked out of the mess to my quarters. Said, silently, to
Ship, "Tell Kalr I want privacy." Not thinking too directly
why that was, or I would be angry again. Or angrier. Even
the desire to move sent impulses to muscles, tiny movements
that Ship could read. That *I* could read, when Ship showed
them to me. In theory no one else on *Mercy of Kalr* could
receive that data the way I could. In theory. But I wouldn't
think about that. I walked into my quarters, door opening
without my asking. The Kalr on duty there bowed, left, duck-
ing around Lieutenant Tisarwat where she had stopped just
inside the entrance.

"Come in, Lieutenant," I said, voice calm. No edge to it.
I was angry, yes, but I was always angry, that was normal.
Nothing to give anyone any alarm, who could see it. Lieutenant Tisarwat came farther into the room. "Did you get any
sleep at all?" I asked her.

"Some, sir." Surprised. She was too tired to think entirely
clearly. And still feeling sick and unhappy. Adrenaline levels
still higher than normal. Good.

And not good. Not good at all. Terrible. "Eat much?"

"I h..." She blinked. Had to think about my question. "I
haven't had much time, sir." She breathed, a trifle more easily

than the moment before. Muscles in her shoulders relaxed, just the tiniest bit.

Without thinking of what I was doing, I moved as quickly as I possibly could—which was extremely quickly. Grabbed her by the collars of her jacket, shoved her backward, hard, slammed her into the green and purple wall a meter behind her. Pinned her there, bent awkwardly backward over the bench.

Saw what I had been looking for. Just for an instant. For the smallest moment Lieutenant Tisarwat's general unhappiness became utter, horrified terror. Adrenaline and cortisol spiked unbelievably. And there, in her head, a brief flash, nearly a ghost, of implants that shouldn't be there, weren't there an instant later.

Ancillary implants.

Again I slammed her head against the wall. She gave a small cry, and I saw it again, her sickening horror, those implants that no human ought to have threading through her brain, and then gone again. "Let go of *Mercy of Kalr* or I'll strangle you right here with my own hands."

"You wouldn't," she gasped.

That told me she wasn't thinking straight. In her right mind, Anaander Mianaai would never have doubted, not for an instant, what I might do. I shifted my grip. She started to slide down the wall, toward the bench, but I grabbed her around the throat and put pressure on her trachea. She caught hold of my wrists, desperate. Unable to breathe. Ten seconds, more or less, to do what I told her to do, or die. "Let go of my ship." My voice calm. Even.

The data coming from her flared again, ancillary implants sharp and clear, her own excruciating nausea and terror strong enough almost to make me double over in sympathetic horror. I let go of her, stood straight, and watched her collapse, coughing, gasping, onto the hard, uncushioned bench and then choking, heaving, try to throw up the nothing that was in her stomach.

"Ship," I said.

"She's canceled all orders," said *Mercy of Kalr*, directly into my ear. "I'm sorry, Captain."

"You couldn't help it." All Radchaai military ships were built with accesses that let Anaander Mianaai control them. *Mercy of Kalr* was no exception. I was fortunate the ship didn't have any enthusiasm for following the orders the Lord of the Radch had been giving it, hadn't made any effort to correct any lapses or small errors. If Ship had truly wanted to help Anaander Mianaai deceive me, it would certainly have succeeded. "Anaander Mianaai, Lord of the Radch," I said, to the baby lieutenant trembling, heaving, on the bench in front of me. "Did you think that I wouldn't know?"

"Always a risk," she whispered, and wiped her mouth on her sleeve.

"You're not used to taking risks you don't have decades—centuries—to prepare for," I said. I had dropped all pretense of human expression, spoke in my flat ancillary's voice. "All the parts of you have been part of you since birth. Probably before. You've never been one person and then suddenly had ancillary tech shoved into your brain. It isn't pleasant, is it?"

"I knew it wasn't." She had, now, better control of her breathing, had stopped throwing up. But she spoke in a hoarse whisper.

"You *knew* it wasn't. And you thought you'd have access to meds to keep you going until you got used to it. You could take them right out of Medical yourself and use your accesses to make *Mercy of Kalr* cover your tracks."

"You outmaneuvered me," she said, still miserable, still looking down at the now-fouled bench. "I admit it."

"You outmaneuvered yourself. You didn't have a standard set of ancillary implants." It hadn't been legal to make ancillaries for nearly a hundred years. Not counting bodies already stocked and waiting in suspension, and those were nearly all on troop carriers. None of which had been anywhere near Omaugh Palace. "You had to alter the equipment you used for yourself. And meddling with a human brain, it's a delicate thing. It wouldn't have been a problem if it had been your own, you know *that* brain front to back, if it was one of your own bodies you'd have had no problems. But it couldn't be one of your own bodies, that was the whole *point*, you don't have any to spare these days, and besides I'd have shoved you out the air lock as soon as we gated if you'd tried it. So it had to be somebody *else's* body. But your tech, it's custom-made for *your brain*. And you didn't have time to test anything. You had a week. If that. What, did you grab the child, shove the hardware in her, and throw her onto the docks?" Tisarwat had missed tea with her mother's cousin, that day, not answered messages. "Even with the right hardware, and a medic who knows what she's doing, it doesn't always work. Surely you know that."

She knew that. "What are you going to do now?"

I ignored the question. "You thought you could just order *Mercy of Kalr* to give me false readings, and Medic as well, to cover up anything that needed covering. You'd still need meds, that was obvious the moment the hardware went in, but you couldn't pack them because Bo would have found them immediately and I'd have wondered why you needed those particular drugs." And then, when she couldn't get them, her misery was so intense that she couldn't completely hide it—she could only order Ship to make it appear to be much less than it actually was. "But I already knew what lengths you were willing to go to, to achieve your ends, and I had days just lying here in my quarters, recovering from my injuries and imagining what you might try." And what I might be able to do to circumvent it, undetected. "I *never* believed you'd give me a ship and let me fly off unsupervised."

"*You* did it without meds. You never used them."

I went to the bench that served as my bed, pulled aside the linens, opened the compartment underneath. Inside was that box that human eyes could see but no ship or station could, not unless it had ancillary eyes to look with. I opened the box, pulled out the packet of meds I'd taken from Medical, days before that last conference with Anaander Mianaai on Omaugh Palace. Before I'd met Lieutenant Tisarwat in Inspector Supervisor Skaaiat's office, or even known she'd existed. "We're going to Medical." And silently, to *Mercy of Kalr*, "Send two Kalrs."

Hope flared in Anaander Mianaai, once Lieutenant Tisarwat, triggered by my words, and by the sight of that packet of medicine in my gloved hand, along with an overwhelming wish to be free of her misery. Tears ran from her ridiculously lilac eyes, and she gave a very tiny whimper, quickly suppressed. "How did you stand this?" she asked. "How did you survive it?"

There was no point in answering. It was an exclamation more than a real question, she didn't really care about the answer. "Stand up." The door opened, and two of my Kalrs came in, astonished and dismayed to see Lieutenant Tisarwat battered, collapsed on the bench, bile all down the sleeve of her uniform jacket.

We walked to Medical, a sad little procession, Tisarwat

(not Tisarwat) leaning on one Kalr, followed by the other. Medic stood frozen, watching us enter. Appalled, having seen what was in the lieutenant's head the moment Ship had stopped interfering with her data, with Medic's specialized implants. She turned to me to speak. "Wait," I said to her curtly, and then, once the Kalrs had helped Tisarwat (not Tisarwat) onto a table, sent them away.

Before Medic could say anything, before Anaander could realize and protest, I triggered the table's restraints. She was startled but too miserable to realize right away what that meant. "Medic," I said. "You see that Lieutenant Tisarwat has some unauthorized implants." Medic was too horrified to speak. "Remove them."

"No, don't!" Anaander Mianaai tried to shout but couldn't quite, and so it came out sounding half-strangled.

"Who *did* this?" asked Medic. I could see she was still trying to make sense out of it.

"Is that relevant just now?" She knew the answer, if she thought about it. Only one person *could* have done this. Only one person would have.

"Medic," said Tisarwat, who had been trying the restraints but found she couldn't free herself. Her voice still came out a strangled croak. "I am Anaander Mianaai, Lord of the Radch. Arrest the fleet captain, release me, and give me the medicine I need."

"You're getting above yourself, Lieutenant," I said, and turned again to Medic. "I gave an order, Medic." Isolated as we were in gate space, my word was law. It didn't matter what my orders were, no matter how illegal or unjust. A captain might face prosecution for giving some orders—her crew would without fail be executed for disobeying those same commands. It was a central fact of any Radchaai soldier's life, though it rarely came to an actual demonstration. No one on *Mercy of Kalr* would have forgotten it. Nyseme Ptem, whose name was mentioned every day on this ship, at my particular instructions, had been a soldier like these, had died because she had refused orders to kill innocent people. No one on board *Mercy of Kalr* could forget her, or forget why she died. Or that I chose to have her name spoken daily, as though she were one of the dead of my own family, or this ship. That couldn't possibly be lost on Medic, just now.

I could see her distress and indecision. Tisarwat was suffering, clearly, and if anything could make Medic truly angry it was suffering she couldn't help. My order might be interpreted as backing her into a corner with the threat of execution, but it also gave her cover to do what needed doing, and she would see that soon enough.

"Medic," croaked Tisarwat, still struggling against the restraints.

I laid one black-gloved hand across her throat. No pressure, just a reminder. "Medic," I said. Calmly. "No matter who this is, no matter who she claims to be, this installation was illegal—and thoroughly unjust—from the start. And it's failed. I've seen this before, I've been through it myself. It won't get any better, and she'll be extremely lucky if it doesn't get worse. Meds might keep her going for a while, but they won't fix the problem. There's only one thing that *will* fix the problem." Two things. But in some respects the two were the same, at least as far as this fragment of Anaander Mianaai was concerned.

Medic balanced on the knife-edge of two equally bad choices, only the smallest chance of helping her patient making a barely perceptible difference between one course and the other. I saw her tip. "I've never...Fleet Captain, I don't have any experience with this." Trying very hard not to let her voice shake. She'd never dealt with ancillaries before, I was the first she'd ever had in her medical section. Ship had told her what to do, with me.

And I was hardly typical. "Not many do. Putting them in is routine, but I can't think of anyone who's had to take any *out*. Not anyone who cared about the condition of the body once they were done. But I'm sure you'll manage. Ship knows what to do." Ship was saying as much to Medic, at that moment. "And I'll help."

Medic looked at Tisarwat—no, Anaander Mianaai—tied down to the table, no longer struggling with the restraints, eyes closed. Looked, then, at me. "Sedation," she began.

"Oh, no. She has to be awake for this. But don't worry, I choked her pretty badly, a few minutes ago. She won't be able to scream very much."

By the time we finished and Tisarwat was unconscious, dosed as heavily as was safe with sedatives, Medic was shaking, not entirely from exhaustion. We'd both missed lunch and supper, and tired and increasingly anxious Bos were passing the entrance to Medical in ones and twos on increasingly flimsy pretexts. Ship refused to tell anyone what was happening.

"Will she come back?" asked Medic, standing, trembling, as I cleaned instruments and put them away. "Tisarwat, I mean, will she be Tisarwat again?"

"No." I closed a box, put it in its drawer. "Tisarwat was dead from the moment they put those implants in." *They*. Anaander Mianaai would have done that herself.

"She's a *child*. Seventeen years old! How could anyone..." She trailed off. Shook her head once, still not quite believing even after hours of surgery, of seeing it with her own eyes.

"I was the same age when it happened to me," I pointed out. Not *I* really, but this body, this last one left to me. "A little younger." I didn't point out that Medic hadn't reacted this way to seeing me. That it made a difference when it was a citizen, instead of some uncivilized, conquered enemy.

She didn't notice it herself, or else was too overwhelmed just now to react. "Who is she now, then?"

"Good question." I put away the last of the instruments. "She'll have to decide that."

"What if you don't like her decision?" Shrewd, Medic was. I'd rather have her on my side than otherwise.

"That," I answered, making a small tossing gesture, as though casting the day's omens, "will be as Amaat wills. Get some rest. Kalr will bring supper to your quarters. Things will seem better after you've eaten and slept."

"Really?" she asked. Bitter and challenging.

"Well, not necessarily," I admitted. "But it's easier to deal with things when you've had some rest and some breakfast."

4

In my quarters, Kalr Five, disquieted by the day's events but of course expressionless, had my supper waiting for me—a bowl of skel and a flask of water, common soldier's mess. I suspected Ship had suggested it to her but didn't query to confirm that suspicion. I'd have been content eating skel all the time, but it would have distressed Five, and not only because it would have deprived her of the opportunity to filch tastes of non-skel delicacies, a cherished perquisite of serving the captain or the officers in the decade room.

While I ate, officerless Bo halfheartedly, nearly silently, scrubbed their allotment of corridors, still spotless as it had been this morning, but part of the day's routine and not to be neglected. They were tired and worried. Judging from their sparse chatter, the consensus was that I'd abused Lieutenant Tisarwat so harshly she'd become sick. There were some grumbles of *no different from the last one.* Very carefully referentless.

Bo One, decade senior, checked their work, reported to Ship that it was complete. And then said, silently, fingers moving, "Ship."

"Bo One," said *Mercy of Kalr*. Who knew Bo One quite well, had heard all the grumbles. "You should take your questions to the fleet captain."

When Bo One had gone to see Medic, less than five minutes after I'd left for my own quarters, Medic had told her the same thing. And this was the third time Ship had suggested it. Still, Bo One had hesitated. Even though by rights she was in command of Bo, with Lieutenant Tisarwat unconscious and my not having assigned anyone to replace her. Had therefore the right, the responsibility even, to approach me for information and instructions.

Ancillaries were part of their ship. There was, often, a vague, paradoxical sense that each decade had its own almost-identity, but that existed alongside the knowledge that every ancillary was just one part of the larger thing, just hands and feet—and a voice—for Ship. No ancillary ever had questions for the captain, or anything personal that needed discussion with an officer.

Mercy of Kalr was crewed by humans. But its last captain had demanded that those humans behave as much like ancillaries as possible. Even when her own Kalrs had addressed her, they had done so in the way Ship might have. As though they had no personal concerns or desires. Long habit, I thought, made Bo One hesitate. She might have asked another lieutenant to speak to me for her, but Seivarden was on watch and Lieutenant Ekalu was asleep.

In my purple and green quarters, I ate the last leaf of skel. Said to Five, "Kalr, I'll have tea. And I want the paint off these walls as soon as you can manage it. I want monitors." The walls could be altered, made to display whatever one wished, including visuals of the space outside the ship. The materials to do it were on board. For whatever reason,

Captain Vel hadn't wanted that. I didn't actually need it, but I wanted the previous captain's arrangements gone as completely as I could manage.

Expressionless, flat-voiced, Five said, "There may be some inconvenience to you, Fleet Captain." And then a flare of apprehension as Ship spoke to her. Hesitation. *Go ahead* in her ear, from Ship. "Sir, Bo One wishes to speak to you."

Good. Four more seconds and I'd have ordered her to report to me. I'd only been waiting to finish my supper. "I don't care about the inconvenience. And I'll see Bo One."

Bo One entered outwardly confident, inwardly frightened. Bowed, stiffly, feeling awkward—ancillaries didn't bow. "Bo," I said, acknowledging her. Over in a corner, Kalr Five busied herself pointlessly with the tea flask, pretending there was anything at all to do before she could serve me the tea I'd asked for. Listening. Worried.

Bo One swallowed. Took a breath. "Begging the fleet captain's indulgence," she began, clearly a rehearsed speech. Slowly, carefully, broadening her vowels, incapable of entirely losing her own accent but trying hard. "There are concerns about the situation of Bo decade's officer." A moment of extra doubt there, I saw, knowing I'd been angry at Lieutenant Tisarwat's even being aboard, Bo One feeling that she was in a precarious place just speaking to me this way, let alone bringing up the young lieutenant. That sentence had been very carefully composed, I thought, both to sound very formal and to avoid Lieutenant Tisarwat's name. "Medic was consulted, and it was recommended the fleet captain be approached."

"Bo," I said. My voice calm, yes, my mood never reached my voice unless I intended it. But I was out of patience for this sort of thing. "Speak directly, when you speak to me." Kalr Five still puttered with the tea things.

"Yes, sir," said Bo One, still stiff. Mortified.

"I'm glad you came. I was on the point of calling for you. Lieutenant Tisarwat is ill. She was ill when she came aboard. Military Administration wanted an officer here and didn't care that she wasn't fit to ship out. They even tried to hide it from me." A lie that wasn't, entirely, a lie. And every soldier and officer on every ship complained about the unthinking, ignorant decisions of Administration, none of whom knew what it was like aboard ships. "I'll have some things to say about that, when next I have the chance." I could almost *see* it clicking together in Bo One's mind. *Fleet captain's angry at Administration, not our lieutenant.* "She'll be returning to her quarters tomorrow, and she'll need a day or two of rest, and light duty after that until Medic says otherwise. You're decade senior, of course, so you'll be responsible for your soldiers and hold her watches while she's out, and make your reports to me. I need Bo decade to take very good care of Lieutenant Tisarwat. I already know you will, but now you have my explicit order. If you have any concerns at all about her health, or if her behavior is odd—if she seems confused about something she shouldn't be, or just doesn't seem right in any way at all—you're to report it to Medic. Even if Lieutenant Tisarwat orders you not to. Am I understood?"

"Sir. *Yes*, sir." Already feeling she was on firmer ground.

"Good. Dismissed." Kalr Five picked up the flask to finally pour my tea, no doubt composing the narrative she'd give the other Kalrs.

Bo One bowed. And then, with some trepidation, said, "Beg the fleet captain's indulgence, sir..." Stopped and swallowed, surprised at her own daring. At my expectant gesture. "We all of us, sir, Bo decade, we want to say, thank you for the tea, sir."

I'd allotted five grams per person aboard, per week (soldiers—even officers—wrung as much tea as possible out of very small rations of leaves) so long as my supply lasted. It had been greeted with suspicion at first. Captain Vel had insisted they only drink water. Like ancillaries. Was I trying to soften them up for something? To show off how wealthy I was? Granting a privilege that I could then deny for some satisfaction of my own?

But if there was one thing any Radchaai considered essential for civilized life, it was tea. And I knew what it was like, to be on a ship full of ancillaries. I had no need to play at it. "You're very welcome, Bo. Dismissed."

She bowed again, and left. As the door closed behind her, Ship said, in her ear, "That went well."

For the next two days, Lieutenant Tisarwat lay on her bed, in her tiny quarters. Ship showed her entertainments from its library, all lighthearted things with songs that were bright or sweet by turns, and happy endings. Tisarwat watched them, placid and noncommittal, would have watched tragedy after tragedy with the same evenness, dosed as she was to keep her mood stable and comfortable. Bo fussed over her, tucking blankets, bringing tea, Bo Nine even contriving some kind of sweet pastry for her, in the decade room's tiny galley. Speculation about the nature of her illness—no longer blamed on me—was rife. In the end, they decided that Tisarwat had been badly interrogated before being assigned to *Mercy of Kalr.* Or less likely, but still possible, she'd been the victim of inept education—sometimes, when a citizen needed to learn a great deal of information, she could get that by going to Medical and learning under drugs. The same drugs that were used for interrogation, and aptitudes testing. Or

reeducation, a topic most polite Radchaai had difficulty mentioning at all. All four—interrogation, learning, aptitudes, or
reeducation—had to be done by a specialist medic, someone
who knew what she was doing. Though no one on *Mercy of
Kalr* would ever say it aloud, hovering just under the surface
of any conversation about her was the fact that at the moment
Tisarwat looked very much like someone who had recently
come out of reeducation. The fact that Medic and I had done
whatever we had done without the assistance even of any
Kalrs, and wouldn't tell anyone what had happened, this also
tended to reinforce the idea that reeducation was involved.
But no one who had been reeducated would have ever been
allowed to serve in the military, so that was impossible.

Whatever it was, it hadn't been Tisarwat's fault. Or mine.
Everyone was relieved at that. Sitting in my quarters the next
day, drinking tea—still from the rose glass, even I myself
hadn't yet rated the best dishes—Seivarden's desire to ask
me what had happened was palpable, but instead she said,
"I was thinking about what you said the other day. About
how I never saw you...I mean..." She trailed off, realizing,
probably, that the sentence wasn't going anywhere good.
"Officers have their own quarters, so that's easy, but I hadn't
even thought about if my Amaats...I mean, there's nowhere
private, is there, nowhere they could go if they wanted...I
mean..."

Actually, there were quite a number of places, including
several storage compartments, all of the shuttles (though lack
of gravity did make some things awkward), and even, with
enough desperation, under the table in the soldiers' mess. But
Seivarden had always had her own quarters and never had
to avail herself of any of them. "I suppose it's good you're
thinking about these things," I said. "But leave your Amaats

what dignity they can afford." I took another swallow of tea and added, "You seem to be thinking about sex a lot lately. I'm glad you haven't just ordered one of your Amaats." She wouldn't have been the first officer on this ship to do that.

"The thought crossed my mind," she said, face heating even further than it already had. "And then I thought about what you would probably say."

"I don't think Medic is your type." Actually, I suspected Medic had no interest in sex to begin with. "Lieutenant Tisarwat is a bit young, and she's not up for it right now. Have you considered approaching Ekalu?" Ekalu had thought of it, I was sure. But Seivarden's aristocratic looks and antique accent intimidated her as much as they attracted her.

"I haven't wanted to insult her."

"Too much like a superior approaching an inferior?" Seivarden gestured assent. "Kind of insulting in and of itself, thinking of it like that, wouldn't you say?"

She groaned, set her tea on the table. "I lose either way."

I gestured uncertainty. "Or you win either way."

She gave a small laugh. "I'm *really* glad Medic was able to help Tisarwat."

In Lieutenant Tisarwat's quarters, Bo Nine tucked in the blanket for the third time in the last hour. Adjusted pillows, checked the temperature of Lieutenant Tisarwat's tea. Tisarwat submitted with drugged, dispassionate calm. "So am I," I said.

Two days later—something less than a third of the way to Athoek—I invited Lieutenant Ekalu and Lieutenant Tisarwat to dine with me. Because of the way schedules worked on *Mercy of Kalr*, it was my own lunch, Ekalu's supper, Tisarwat's breakfast. And because my Kalrs were scraping paint off the walls in my quarters, it was in the decade room. Almost like being with myself again, though *Mercy of Kalr*'s decade room was a good deal smaller than my own Esk decade room, when I had been *Justice of Toren* and had twenty lieutenants for each of my ten decades.

My eating in the decade room produced a sort of confusion of jurisdiction, with Kalr Five wanting very much to establish her own authority in what was normally the territory of the officers' staffs. She'd agonized over whether to insist on using her second-best porcelain, which would show incontrovertibly that it was her meal and also show off the dishes she loved, or whether she should let Etrepa Eight and Bo Nine use the decade room's own set, which would protect the precious porcelain from accidents but imply the meal was under Etrepa and Bo's authority. Her pride won in the end, and we ate eggs and vegetables off the hand-painted dishes.

Ekalu, who had served nearly her whole career as a common soldier on this ship and likely knew Kalr Five's peculiarities, said, "Begging the fleet captain's indulgence, these plates are lovely." Five didn't smile, she rarely did in front of me, but I could see Ekalu had hit her target dead on.

"Five chose them," I said. Approving of Ekalu's gambit. "They're Bractware. About twelve hundred years old." For an instant Ekalu froze, utensil just above the plate, terrified of striking it too hard. "They're not actually terribly valuable. There are places where nearly everyone has part of a set wrapped up in a box somewhere that they never take out. But they're lovely, aren't they, you can see why they were so popular." If I hadn't favorably impressed Kalr Five yet, I did so now. "And Lieutenant, if you start every single sentence with *begging the fleet captain's indulgence* this is going to be a dreary meal. Just assume I've given my indulgence for polite conversation."

"Sir," acknowledged Ekalu, embarrassed. She applied herself to her eggs. Carefully, trying not to touch the plate with her utensil.

Tisarwat had said nothing yet beyond the occasionally required *yes, sir* and *no, sir* and *thank you, sir*. All the time those lilac eyes downcast, not looking at me, or Ekalu. Medic had tapered down her sedatives, but Tisarwat was still under their influence. Behind them, crowded back by the drugs, was anger and despair. Just noise, right now, but not what I wanted to predominate when she wasn't taking medication anymore.

Time to do something about that. "Yesterday," I said, after I'd swallowed a mouthful of eggs, "Lieutenant Seivarden was telling me that Amaat decade was obviously the best on the ship." Seivarden had said no such thing, in fact. But the surge of offended pride from Etrepa Eight and Bo Nine, standing in a corner of the room waiting to be useful, was so distinct that for an instant I had trouble believing Ekalu and Tisarwat couldn't also see it. Kalr Five's reaction wasn't nearly as strong—we'd just complimented her porcelain and besides, captain's decade was in some ways above that sort of thing.

Ekalu's conflict was immediate, and plainly visible to me. She'd been an Amaat until very recently, had, now, the natural response of an Amaat on hearing someone claim her decade's superiority. But of course, now she was Etrepa lieutenant. She paused, working that out, working out, I thought, a response. Tisarwat looked down at her plate, probably seeing what I was up to, and not caring.

"Sir," said Ekalu, finally. Obviously having to force herself to leave off that *begging the fleet captain's indulgence*. Carefully navigating her accent. "All *Mercy of Kalr*'s decades are excellent. But if I were to be called upon to narrow it down..." She paused. Perhaps realizing she'd gone a bit too awkwardly formal with her diction. "If one were forced to choose, I'd have to say Etrepa is best. No offense to Lieutenant Seivarden or her Amaats, all due respect, it's just a fact." Slipping back closer to her own accent, at that last.

Silence from Tisarwat. Betrayed alarm from Bo Nine, at silent attention in the corner of the decade room. "Lieutenant," said *Mercy of Kalr* into Tisarwat's ear. "Your decade is waiting for you to speak up for them."

Tisarwat looked up, looked at me, for just a moment, with serious lilac eyes. She knew what I was doing, knew there was only one move she could make. Resented it, resented me. Her muted anger swelled by just the smallest amount but couldn't sustain itself, died back to its previous level almost instantly. And not just anger—for a moment I'd seen yearning, a momentary hopeless wishing. She looked away, at Ekalu. "Begging your pardon, lieutenant, with all due respect, I'm afraid you're mistaken." Remembering, halfway through the sentence, that she shouldn't be speaking like Seivarden. Like Anaander Mianaai. Blurring that accent just a bit. "Bo may be junior, but my Bos are clearly better than any other decade on this ship."

Ekalu blinked. For an instant her face went ancillary-blank with surprise at Tisarwat's accent, her diction, her obvious self-possession, not much like a seventeen-year-old at all, and then she remembered herself. Searched for a response. She couldn't point out that nonetheless Bo *was* junior—that would leave her vulnerable to Seivarden's claim for Amaat. She looked at me.

I had put a neutral, interested expression on my face and kept it there. "Well," I said, pleasantly, "we should settle this. Objectively. Firearms and armor proficiency, perhaps." Ekalu finally realized I'd planned the whole thing. But was still puzzled, specifics not quite making sense to her. I made a show of moving my gloved fingers, sending a request to Kalr Five. Said aloud to the two lieutenants, "What are your numbers?"

They blinked as Ship placed the information in their visions. "All up to standard, sir," said Ekalu.

"*Standard?*" I asked, voice incredulous. "Surely this crew is better than *standard.*" Lieutenant Tisarwat looked down at her plate again, behind the drugs resentment, approval, anger, that yearning I'd seen before. All muted. "I'll give you a week. At the end of it, let's see which decade has the highest scores, Etrepa or Bo. Including your own, Lieutenants. Issue armor. You have my permission to wear it for practice, whenever you think best." My own armor was implanted, a personal force shield I could raise in a very small fraction of a second. These lieutenants, their decades, wore their units strapped around their chests, when issued. Had never, any of them, seen combat, could raise theirs within the required one second, but I wanted better, especially knowing what might be coming, that from now on nothing would be the way it had been.

Kalr Five entered the decade room, a dark-blue bottle in each hand, and one tucked into her elbow. Face impassive, but inwardly disapproving, as she set them on the table. "Arrack," I said. "The good stuff. For whoever wins."

"The whole decade, sir?" asked Lieutenant Ekalu, slightly hesitant. Astonished.

"However you'd like to divide it up," I said, knowing that of course Etrepa Eight and Bo Nine had messaged their decade-mates by now, and the soldiers of both Etrepa and Bo had already calculated their equal share of the prize. Possibly allowing a slightly larger one for their officers.

* * *

Later, in Seivarden's quarters, Ekalu turned over, said to a sleepy Seivarden, "All respect, S...no offense. I don't mean to offend. But I've...everyone's been wondering if you're kneeling to Sir."

"Why do you do that?" Seivarden asked, blurrily, and then as she pulled back from the edge of sleep, "Say *Sir* like that, instead of *Fleet Captain*." Came a bit more awake. "No, I know why, now I think about it. Sorry. Why am I offended?" Ekalu, at an astonished, embarrassed loss, didn't answer. "I would if she wanted me to. She doesn't want me to."

"Is Sir...is the fleet captain an ascetic?"

Seivarden gave a small, ironic laugh. "I don't think so. She's not very forthcoming, our fleet captain. Never has been. But I'll tell you." She took a breath, let it out. Took another while Ekalu waited for her to speak. "You can trust her to the end of the universe. She'll *never* let you down."

"That would be impressive." Ekalu, clearly skeptical. Disbelieving. Then, reconsidering something. "She was Special Missions, before?"

"I can't say." Seivarden put her bare hand on Ekalu's stomach. "When do you have to be back working?"

Ekalu suppressed a tiny shiver, born of a complicated tangle of emotions, mostly pleasant. Most non-Radchaai didn't quite understand the emotional charge bare hands carried, for a Radchaai. "About twenty minutes."

"Mmmm," said Seivarden, considering that. "That's plenty of time."

I left them to themselves. Bo and their lieutenant slept. In the corridors, Etrepas mopped and scrubbed, intermittently flashing silver as their armor flowed around them and back down again.

*   *   *

Even later, Tisarwat and I had tea in the decade room. Sedatives lessened further still, emotions rawer, closer to the surface, she said, when we were alone for a moment, "I know what you're doing." With a strange little skip of anger and wanting. "What you're trying to do." That was the want, I thought. To really be part of the crew, to secure Bo's admiration and loyalty. Possibly even mine. Things the hapless former Tisarwat would have wanted. That I was offering her now.

But offering on my terms, not hers. "Lieutenant Tisarwat," I said, after a calm drink of my tea, "is that an appropriate way to address me?"

"No, sir," Tisarwat said. Defeated. And not. Even medicated she was a mass of contradictions, every emotion accompanied by something paradoxical. Tisarwat had never wanted to be Anaander Mianaai. Hadn't been for very long, just a few days. And whoever she was now, however disastrous it was to Anaander Mianaai's plans, she felt so much *better*.

I'd done that. She hated me for it. And didn't. "Have supper with me, Lieutenant," I said, as though the previous exchange hadn't happened. As though I couldn't see what she was feeling. "You and Ekalu both. You can boast about the progress your decades are making, and Kalr will make that pastry you like so much, with the sugar icing." In my quarters, Ship spoke the request into Kalr Five's ear as she looked over the walls, to be sure everything had been properly installed. Five rolled her eyes and sighed as though she was exasperated, muttered something about adolescent appetites, but secretly, where she thought only Ship could see, she was pleased.

* * *

The competition was tight. Both Etrepa and Bo had spent all their free time in the firing range, and their duty time raising and lowering their armor while they worked. Their numbers had improved markedly all around, nearly everyone had gone up a difficulty level in the firearms training routines and those who hadn't soon would. And every Etrepa and every Bo could deploy their armor in less than half a second. Nowhere near what ancillaries could do, or what I wanted, but still a distinct improvement.

All of Bo had understood more or less immediately what the actual purpose of the contest was, and undertaken their practice with serious-minded determination. Etrepa as well—Etrepa, who approved my goal (as they understood it) but had not on that account held back their effort. But the prize went to Bo. I handed the three bottles of (very fine, and very strong) arrack to a virtually sedative-free Lieutenant Tisarwat, in the soldiers' mess, with all of Bo standing straight and ancillary-expressionless behind her. I congratulated them on their victory and left them to the serious drinking that I knew would begin the instant I was in the corridor.

Less than an hour later, Seivarden came to me, on behalf of her Amaats. Who had mostly tried to be understanding about the whole thing but now couldn't walk past the soldiers' mess without being reminded that they'd never even had an opportunity to try for that arrack. And I'd ordered fruit to be served to all the Etrepas and Bos with their supper that day—I had a store of oranges, rambutans, and dredgefruit, all purchased by Kalr Five and carefully stored in suspension. Even after supper was cleared away the sweet smell of the dredgefruit lingered in the corridor and left Seivarden's Amaats hungry and resentful.

"Tell them," I said to Seivarden, "that I wanted to give Lieutenant Tisarwat some encouragement, and if they'd been part of the contest she'd never have had a chance." Seivarden gave a short laugh, partly recognizing a lie when she heard it, partly, I thought, believing that maybe it wasn't a lie. Her Amaats would probably have a similar reaction. "Have them pull their own numbers up in the next week, and they'll have dredgefruit with supper, too. And Kalr as well." That last for always-listening Five.

"And the arrack?" asked Seivarden, hopefully.

In the soldiers' mess, the drinking, which had begun in a very focused, disciplined manner, each communal swallow accompanied by an invocation of one of the ship's gods, the sting of the arrack carefully savored on the way down, had begun to degenerate. Bo Ten rose, and just slightly slurrily begged the lieutenant's indulgence, and, receiving it, declared her intention to recite her own poetry.

"I have more arrack," I told Seivarden, in my quarters. "And I intend to give some of it out. But I'd rather not give it out wholesale."

In the soldiers' mess, Bo Ten's declaration met with cheers of approval, even from Lieutenant Tisarwat, and so Ten launched into what turned out to be an epic, largely improvised narrative of the deeds of the god Kalr. Who, according to Bo Ten's account, was drunk a lot of the time and rhymed very badly.

"Limiting the arrack is probably a good idea," said Seivarden, in my quarters. A shade wistfully. "And I wouldn't have had any anyway." When I'd found her, naked and unconscious in an icy street a year before, she'd been taking far too much kef far too often. She'd mostly abstained since then.

As Bo Ten's poem rambled on, it turned into a paean to

Bo decade's superiority to any other on the ship, including Amaat decade. No, *especially* Amaat decade, who sang foolish children's songs, and not very well at that.

"Our song is better!" declared one intoxicated Bo, halting the flow of Bo Ten's poetry, and another, equally intoxicated but perhaps slightly clearer-thinking soldier, asked, "What *is* our song?"

Bo Ten, not particular about her subject and not at all ready to yield the center of attention, took a deep breath and began to sing, in a surprisingly pleasant, if wobbly, contralto. "Oh, tree! Eat the fish!" It was a song I had sung to myself fairly frequently. It wasn't in Radchaai, and Bo Ten was only approximating the sound of the actual words, using more familiar ones she recognized. "This granite folds a peach!" At the head of the table, Tisarwat actually giggled. "Oh, tree! Oh, tree! Where's my ass?"

The last word rendered Tisarwat and all her Bos utterly helpless with laughter. Four of them slid off their seats and collapsed onto the floor. It took them a good five minutes to recover.

"Wait!" exclaimed Tisarwat. Considered rising, and then abandoned the idea as requiring too much effort. "Wait! Wait!" And when she had their attention, "Wait! That"—she waved one gloved hand—"is our song." Or she tried to say it—the last word was lost in more laughter. She raised her glass, nearly sloshing the arrack out onto the table. "To Bo!"

"To Bo!" they echoed, and then a soldier added, "To Fleet Captain Breq!"

And Tisarwat was drunk enough to agree, without hesitation, "To Fleet Captain Breq! Who doesn't know where her ass is!" And after that there was nothing but laughter and top-of-the-lungs choruses of *Oh, tree! Where's my ass?*

* * *

"That, sir," said Medic an hour later, in the bath, attended, as I was, by a Kalr with a cloth and a basin, "is why Captain Vel didn't allow the decades to drink."

"No, it isn't," I said, equably. Medic, still frowning as always, raised an eyebrow but didn't argue. "I don't think it would be a good idea on a regular basis, of course. But I have my reasons, right now." As Medic knew. "Are you ready for eleven hangovers when they wake up?"

"Sir!" Indignant acknowledgment. Lifted an elbow—waving a bare hand, in the bath, was rude. "Kalr can handle that easily enough."

"That they can," I agreed. Ship said nothing, only continued to show me Tisarwat and her Bos, laughing and singing in the soldiers' mess.

5

If Athoek Station had any importance at all, it was because the planet it orbited produced tea. Other things as well, of course—planets are large. And terraformed, temperate planets were extraordinarily valuable in themselves—the result of centuries, if not millennia of investment, of patience and difficult work. But Anaander Mianaai hadn't had to pay any of that cost—instead, she let the inhabitants do all the work and then sent in her fleets of warships, her armies of ancillaries, to take them over for herself. After a couple thousand years of this she had quite a collection of comfortably habitable planets, so most Radchaai didn't think of them as particularly rare or valuable.

But Athoek had several lengthy mountain ranges, with plenty of lakes and rivers. And it had a weather control grid the Athoeki had built just a century or so before the annexation. All the newly arrived Radchaai had to do was plant tea and wait. Now, some six hundred years later, Athoek produced tens of millions of metric tons a year.

* * *

The featureless, suffocating black of gate space opened onto starlight, and we were in Athoek System. I sat in Command, Lieutenant Ekalu standing beside me. Two of Ekalu's Etrepas stood on either side of us, at their assigned consoles. The room itself was small and plain, nothing more than a blank wall in case Ship should need to cast an image (or in case those on duty preferred to watch that way), those two consoles, and a seat for the captain or the officer on watch. Handholds for times when Ship's acceleration outpaced its adjustment to the gravity. This had been one of the few parts of the ship frequented by Captain Vel that she had not had painted or otherwise redecorated, with the sole exception of a plaque hung over the door that had read, *Proper attention to duty is a gift to the gods.* A common enough platitude, but I'd had it taken down and packed with Captain Vel's other things.

I didn't need to be in Command. Anywhere I was, I could close my eyes and see the darkness give way to the light of Athoek's sun, feel the sudden wash of particles, hear the background chatter of the system's various communications and automated warning beacons. Athoek itself was distant enough to be a small, shining, blue and white circle. My view of it was a good three minutes old.

"We are in Athoek System, Fleet Captain," one of Lieutenant Ekalu's Etrepas said. In another few moments, Ship would tell her what I already saw—that there seemed to be quite a lot of ships around Athoek Station, definitely more than Ship thought was usual; that besides that nothing seemed amiss, or at least had not been two to ten minutes ago, the age of the light and the signals that had reached our present location so far; and that while three military ships had been stationed here, only one was immediately visible, near one of the system's four gates. Or it had been some two and a half minutes ago. I suspected it was *Sword of Atagaris*, though I couldn't be sure until I was closer, or it identified itself.

I considered that distant ship. Where were the other two ships, and why did this one guard one of Athoek's four gates? The least important of the four, come to that—beyond it was an empty system, otherwise gateless, where the Athoeki had intended to expand before the annexation but never had.

I thought about that a few moments. Lieutenant Ekalu, standing beside me, frowned slightly at what Ship showed her, that same image of Athoek System that I myself was looking at. She wasn't surprised, or alarmed. Just mildly puzzled. "Sir, I think that's *Sword of Atagaris*, by the Ghost Gate," she said. "I don't see *Mercy of Phey* or *Mercy of Ilves*."

"The Ghost Gate?"

"That's what they call it, sir." She was, I saw, mildly embarrassed. "The system on the other side is supposed to be haunted."

Radchaai did believe in ghosts. Or, more accurately, many Radchaai did. After so many annexations, so many peoples and their various religious beliefs absorbed into the Radch, there was quite a variety of Radchaai opinions of what happened after someone died. Most citizens at the very least harbored a vague suspicion that violent or unjust death, or failing to make funeral offerings properly, would cause a person's spirit to linger, unwelcome and possibly dangerous. But this was the first I'd heard of ghosts haunting an entire system. "The whole system? By what?"

Still embarrassed, Lieutenant Ekalu gestured doubtfully. "There are different stories."

I considered that a moment. "Right. Ship, let's identify

ourselves, and send my courteous greetings to Captain Hetnys of *Sword of Atagaris*." Both *Mercy of Kalr* and Lieutenant Ekalu thought the ship by the Ghost Gate was probably
Sword of Atagaris, and I thought they were likely to be correct. "And while we're waiting for an answer," which would
take about five minutes to reach us, "see about our gating
closer to Athoek Station." We'd exited gate space farther back
than we might have—I had wanted this vantage, wanted to
see how things stood before going any closer.

But from this distance it could take days, even weeks to
reach Athoek itself. We could, of course, gate in much closer.
Even, in theory, right up to the station itself, though that
would be extremely dangerous. To do that safely, we would
need to know where every ship, every shuttle, every sailpod
would be the moment we came out of gate space. The gate
opening could itself damage or destroy anything already on
the spot, and *Mercy of Kalr* would collide with anything that
might be in its way as it came out into the wider universe.

I'd done that sort of thing before, when I'd been a ship.
During annexations, when a little extra death and destruction could hardly matter. Not in a Radchaai system, full of
civilian citizen traffic.

"Sir, will you have tea?" asked Lieutenant Ekalu.

I had already returned my attention outside, to the star, its
light and heat, its distant planet. The gates and their beacons.
The taste of dust on *Mercy of Kalr*'s hull. I opened my mouth
to say, *thank you, no*. And then realized she really wanted tea
herself—she'd done without as the time to exit our self-made
gate approached, and now that we'd arrived without event
she'd been hoping I'd call for some. She wouldn't have any if
I didn't. Her asking this way was quite daring, for her. "Yes,
thank you, Lieutenant."

Shortly thereafter, almost exactly one minute before I could expect any reply to my first message, an Etrepa handed me a bowl of tea, and the ship that we all presumed was *Sword of Atagaris* disappeared.

I had been watching it. Enjoying the view, which for once came close to overwhelming the not-quiteness that was my usual experience of receiving so much data from Ship. Not quite able to process everything, not quite enough to overwhelm the sensation of seeing what I wanted—so close, but not close enough to really touch.

But for those few moments, I could *almost* forget that I wasn't a ship anymore. So when *Sword of Atagaris* disappeared, I reacted immediately, without thinking.

And found myself paralyzed. The numbers I wanted didn't come, not immediately, and the ship—Ship, which was, of course, *Mercy of Kalr* and not me—would not move at my mere desire, the way my own body would have. I came sharply back to myself, to my one, single body sitting in Command.

But Ship knew what I wanted, and why. Lieutenant Ekalu said, "Sir, are you all right?" And then *Mercy of Kalr* moved, just the smallest bit faster than it could adjust the gravity. The bowl tumbled out of my hand and shattered, splashing tea over my boots and trousers. Lieutenant Ekalu and the Etrepas stumbled, grabbed at handholds. And we were suddenly back in gate space.

"They gated," I said. "Almost as soon as they saw us." Certainly before they'd gotten our message, identifying ourselves. "They saw us, and thirty seconds later they moved."

The jar that had dumped tea all over my feet had waked Lieutenant Tisarwat, as well as her Bos. One of Seivarden's Amaats had fallen and sprained her wrist. Besides a few more broken dishes, there was no other damage—everything had been secured, in case we met some accident coming out of our self-made gate.

"But…but, sir, we're a Mercy. We look like a Mercy. Why would they run away as soon as they saw us?" Then she put that together with our own very sudden move. "You don't think they're running away."

"I wasn't going to take the chance," I acknowledged. An Etrepa hurriedly cleared away shards of porcelain and wiped up the puddle of tea.

"Exiting gate space in forty-five seconds," said Ship, in all our ears.

"But *why*?" Lieutenant Ekalu asked. Truly alarmed, truly puzzled. "They can't know what happened at Omaugh, the gates between here and there went down before any news could get out." Without any knowledge of Anaander Mianaai's split, or the varying loyalties of military ships and officers in that struggle, Captain Hetnys and *Sword of Atagaris* had no reason to react to our arrival as though it might be a threat.

Even citizens who thought the Radch had been infiltrated and corrupted, who believed some officials and captains were potentially enemies, didn't know the struggle had broken into the open. "Either they already know something," I said, "or something's happened here."

"Take hold," said Ship, to all of us.

"Sir," said Lieutenant Ekalu, "how do we know where *Sword of Atagaris* is, when we come out?"

"We don't, Lieutenant."

She took a breath. Thought of saying something, but didn't.

"We probably won't hit *Sword of Atagaris*," I added. "Space is big. And this morning's cast was fortunate."

She wasn't sure if I was joking or not. "Yes, sir."

And we were back in the universe. Sun, planet, gates, background chatter. No *Sword of Atagaris.*

"Where is it?" asked Lieutenant Ekalu.

"Ten seconds," I replied. "Nobody let go of anything."

Ten and a half seconds later, a blacker-than-black hole opened up in the universe and *Sword of Atagaris* appeared, less than five hundred kilometers from where we had just been. Before it was even fully out of its gate, it began transmitting. "Unknown ship, identify yourself or be destroyed."

"I'd like to see it try," said Ship, but only to me.

"That's not Captain Hetnys," said Ekalu. "I think it's her Amaat lieutenant."

"*Sword of Atagaris*," I said. Ship would know to transmit my words. "This is Fleet Captain Breq Mianaai commanding *Mercy of Kalr.* Explain yourself."

It took a half second for my message to reach *Sword of Atagaris*, and four seconds for the lieutenant in question to collect herself enough to reply. "Fleet Captain, sir. My apologies, sir." In the meantime, *Mercy of Kalr* identified itself to *Sword of Atagaris*. "We…we were afraid you weren't what you appeared to be, sir."

"What did you think we were, Lieutenant?"

"I…I don't know, sir. It was just, sir, we weren't expecting you. There are rumors that Omaugh Palace was under attack, or even destroyed, and we haven't had any word from them for nearly a month now."

I looked at Lieutenant Ekalu. She had reverted to the habit of every soldier on *Mercy of Kalr* and cleared her face of any expression. That alone was eloquent, but of course I could see more. Even discounting what had just happened, she did not have a high opinion of *Sword of Atagaris*'s Amaat lieutenant.

"If you'd had your way, Lieutenant," I said dryly, "you'd be waiting even longer for word from Omaugh. I'll speak to Captain Hetnys now."

"Begging the fleet captain's indulgence," replied the lieutenant. "Captain Hetnys is on Athoek Station." She must have realized how that sounded, because she added, after a very brief pause, "Consulting with the system governor."

"And when I find her there," I asked, making my tone just slightly sarcastic, "will she be able to better explain to me just what it is you think you're doing out here?"

"Sir. Yes, sir."

"Good."

Ship cut the connection, and I turned to Lieutenant Ekalu. "You're acquainted with this officer?"

Still that expressionless face. "Water will wear away stone, sir."

It was a proverb. Or half of one. *Water will wear away stone, but it won't cook supper.* Everything has its own strengths. Said with enough irony, it could also imply that since the gods surely had a purpose for everyone the person in question must be good for something, but the speaker couldn't fathom what it might be. "Her family is good," added Ekalu at my silence, still impassive. "Genealogy as long as your arm. Her mother is second cousin to the granddaughter of a client of a client of Mianaai itself, sir."

And made sure everyone knew it, apparently. "And the captain?" Anaander Mianaai had told me that what Captain Hetnys lacked in the way of vision she made up for with a conscientious attention to duty. "Is she likely to have left orders to attack anything that came into the system?"

"I wouldn't think so, sir. But the lieutenant isn't exactly . . . imaginative, sir. Knees stronger than her head." Ekalu's accent slipped at that last, just a bit. "Begging the fleet captain's indulgence."

So, likely to be acting under orders that suggested incoming ships might be a threat. I would have to ask Captain Hetnys about that, when I met her.

The hookup to Athoek Station's dock was largely automated. When the pressure equalized and Five opened the shuttle hatch, Lieutenant Tisarwat and I pushed ourselves over the awkward boundary between the shuttle's weightlessness and the station's artificial gravity. The bay was dingy gray, scuffed, like any other bay on any other station.

A ship's captain stood waiting there, an ancillary straight and still behind her. Seeing it I felt a stab of envy. I had once been what that ancillary was. I never could be that again.

"Captain Hetnys," I said, as Tisarwat came up behind me.

Captain Hetnys was tall—taller than I was by a good ten centimeters—broad, and solidly built. Her hair, clipped military-short, was a silvery gray, a stark contrast to the darkness of her skin. A matter of vanity, perhaps—she'd certainly chosen that hair color, wanted people to notice it, or notice the close cut. Not all of the pins she wore in careful, uncustomary rows on the front of her uniform jacket had names on them, and those that did I couldn't read from this distance. She bowed. "Fleet Captain, sir."

I did not bow. "I'll see the system governor now," I said, cold and matter-of-fact. Leaning just a bit on that antique accent any Mianaai would have. "And afterward you'll explain to me why your ship threatened to attack me when I arrived."

"Sir." She paused a moment, trying, I thought, to look untroubled. When I'd first messaged Athoek Station I'd been told that System Governor Giarod was unavoidably occupied by religious obligations, and would be for some time. As was, apparently, every station official of any standing. This was a holiday that came around on an Athoeki calendar, and possibly because of that, because it was merely a local festival, no one had seen fit to warn me that actually it was important enough to nearly shut down the entire station. Captain Hetnys knew I'd been told the governor was unavailable for some hours. "The initiates should be coming out of the temple in an hour or two." She started to frown, and then stopped herself. "Are you planning to stay on the station, sir?"

Behind me and Lieutenant Tisarwat, Kalr Five, Ten, and Eight, and Bo Nine hauled luggage out of the shuttle. Presumably the impetus behind Captain Hetnys's question.

"It's only, sir," she went on, when I didn't answer immediately, "that lodgings on the station are quite crowded just now. It might be difficult to find somewhere suitable."

I'd already realized that the destruction of even a few gates would have rerouted traffic this way. There were several dozen ships here that had not expected to come to Athoek at all, and more that had meant to leave but couldn't. Even though Anaander Mianaai's order forbidding travel in the remaining gates couldn't possibly have reached here yet, the captains of plenty of other ships might well be nervous about entering any gates at all for the next while. Any well-connected or well-funded travelers had likely taken up whatever comfortable lodgings might have been available here. *Mercy of Kalr* had already asked Station, just to be sure, and Station had replied that apart from the possibility of an invitation to stay in the system governor's residence, the usual places were full up.

The fact that my possibly staying on the station appeared to dismay Captain Hetnys was nearly as interesting as the fact that Station apparently hadn't mentioned my plans to her. Perhaps it hadn't occurred to her to ask. "I have a place to stay, Captain."

"Oh. That's good, sir." She didn't seem convinced of it, though.

I gestured her to follow me and strode out of the bay into the corridor. *Sword of Atagaris*'s ancillary fell in behind the three of us, with Kalr Five. I could see—*Mercy of Kalr* showed me—Five's vanity over her ability to play ancillary, right beside the actual thing.

The walls and floor of the corridor, like the docking bay, showed their age and ill-use. Neither had been cleaned with the frequency any self-respecting military ship expected. But colorful garlands brightened the walls. Seasonally appropriate garlands. "Captain," I said after ten steps, without breaking stride. "I do understand that this is the Genitalia Festival. But when you say *genitalia*, doesn't that usually mean genitals generally? Not just one kind?" For all the steps I'd taken, and as far down the corridor as I could see, the walls were hung with tiny penises. Bright green, hot pink, electric blue, and a particularly eye-searing orange.

"Sir," said Captain Hetnys just behind me. "It's a translation. The words are the same, in the Athoeki language."

The Athoeki language. As though there had only been one. But there was never only one language, not in my considerable experience.

"With the fleet captain's indulgence..." As Captain Hetnys spoke, I gestured assent, not looking behind me to see her. Could, if I wished, see her back, and my own, through Kalr Five's unsuspecting eyes. She continued. "The Athoeki weren't very civilized." Not civilized. Not *Radchaai*. The word was the same, the only difference a subtlety expressed by context, and too easily wiped away. "They mostly aren't even now. They make a division between people with penises and people without. When we first arrived in the system they surrendered right away. Their ruler lost her mind. She thought Radchaai didn't have penises, and since everyone would have to become Radchaai, she ordered all the people in the system with penises to cut them off. But the Athoeki had no intention of cutting anything off, so they made models instead and piled them up in front of the ruler to keep her happy until she could be arrested and given help. So now, on the anniversary, sir, all the children dedicate their penises to their god."

"What about the Athoeki with other sorts of genitals?" We'd reached the bank of lifts that would take us away from the docks. The lobby there was deserted.

"They don't use *real* ones, sir," said Captain Hetnys, clearly contemptuous of the whole thing. "They buy them in a shop."

Station didn't open the lift doors with the alacrity I had grown used to on *Mercy of Kalr*. For an instant I considered waiting to see just how long it would let us stand there, and wondered if perhaps Station disliked Captain Hetnys so much. But if that was the case, if this hesitation was resentment on Station's part, I would only add to that by exposing it.

But just as I drew a breath to request the lift, the doors opened. The inside was undecorated. When we were all in and the doors closed, I said, "Main concourse, please, Station." It would take Eight and Ten a while to settle into the quarters I'd arranged, and in the meantime I would at least make a point of showing myself at the Governor's Palace, which would have an entrance on the main concourse, and at the same time see some of this local festival. To Captain Hetnys, standing beside me, I said, "That story strikes you as plausible, does it?" One ruler for the entire system. *They surrendered right away.* In my experience, no entire system ever surrendered right away. Parts, maybe. Never the whole. The one exception had been the Garseddai, and that had been a tactic, an attempt at ambush. Failed, of course, and there were no Garseddai anymore, as a result.

"Sir?" Captain Hetnys's surprise and puzzlement at my question was plain, though she tried to conceal it, to keep her voice and expression bland and even.

"That seems like it might really have happened? Like the sort of thing someone would actually do?"

Even restated, and given time to think about it, the question puzzled her. "Not anyone civilized, sir." A breath, and then, emboldened, perhaps, by our conversation so far, "Begging the fleet captain's indulgence." I gestured the bestowal of it. "Sir, what's happened at Omaugh Palace? Have the aliens attacked, sir? Is it war?"

Part of Anaander Mianaai believed—or at least put it about—that her conflict with herself was due to infiltration by the alien Presger. "War, yes. But the Presger have nothing to do with it. It's we who've attacked ourselves." Captain Vel, who had used to command *Mercy of Kalr*, had believed the lie about the Presger. "Vel Osck has been arrested for treason." Captain Hetnys and Captain Vel had known each other. "Beyond that, I don't know what's happened to her." But anyone knew what was most likely. "Did you know her well?"

It was a dangerous question. Captain Hetnys, who was nowhere near as good at concealing her reactions as my own crew was, quite obviously saw the danger. "Not well enough, sir, to ever suspect her of any kind of disloyalty."

Lieutenant Tisarwat flinched just slightly at Captain Hetnys's mention of disloyalty. Captain Vel had never been disloyal, and no one knew that better than Anaander Mianaai.

The lift doors opened. The concourse of Athoek Station was a good deal smaller than the main concourse of Omaugh Palace. Some fool, at some point, had thought that white would be an excellent color for the long, open—and heavily trafficked—floor. Like any main concourse on any sizable Radchaai station it was two-storied, in this case with windows here and there on the upper level, the lower lined with offices and shops, and the station's major temples—one to Amaat, and likely a host of subsidiary gods, its façade not the elaborate riot of gods the temple at Omaugh boasted but only images of the four Emanations, in purple and red and yellow, grime collected in the ledges and depressions. Next to it another, smaller temple, dedicated, I guessed, to the god in Captain Hetnys's story. That entrance was draped in garlands nearly identical to the ones we'd seen on the docks, but larger and lit from inside, those startling colors glowing bright.

Crowding this space, as far as I could see, citizens stood in groups, conversing at near-shouting level, wearing coats and trousers and gloves in bright colors, green and pink and blue and yellow, their holiday clothes, clearly. They all of them wore just as much jewelry as any Radchaai ever did, but here it seemed local fashion dictated that associational and memorial pins weren't worn directly on coats or jackets but on a broad sash draped from shoulder to opposite hip, knotted, ends trailing. Children of various ages ran around and in between, calling to each other, stopping now and then to beg adults for sweets. Pink, blue, orange, and green foil wrappers littered the ground. Some blew across the lift entrance when the doors opened, and I saw they were printed with words. I could only read scattered fragments as they tumbled... *blessings...the god whom...I have not...*

The moment we stepped out of the lift a citizen came striding out of the crowd. She wore a tailored coat and trousers in a green so pale it might as well have been white—gloves as well. No sash, but plenty of pins, including one large rhodochrosite surrounded by elaborately woven silver wire. She put on a delighted, surprised expression and bowed emphatically. "Fleet Captain! I had only just heard that you were here, and look, I turn and there you are! Terrible business, the gate to Omaugh Palace going down like that, and all these ships rerouted here or unable to leave, but now you're here, surely it won't last much longer." Her accent was mostly that of a well-off, well-educated Radchaai, though there was something odd about her vowels. "But you won't know who I am. I'm Fosyf Denche, and I'm so glad to have found you. I have an apartment here on the station, plenty of room, and a house downwell, even roomier. I'd be honored to offer you my hospitality."

Beside me, Captain Hetnys and her ancillary stood serious and silent. Behind me, Five still displayed ancillary-like impassivity though I could see, through *Mercy of Kalr*, that she resented Citizen Fosyf's familiarity on my account. Lieutenant Tisarwat, behind the remaining traces of antinausea meds and her normal background unhappiness, seemed amused, and slightly contemptuous.

I thought of the way Seivarden would have responded to an approach like this, when she'd been younger. Just very slightly, I curled my lip. "No need, citizen."

"Ah, someone's been before me. Fair enough!" Undeterred by my manner, which argued she'd met it before, was even used to it. And of course, I almost certainly had news from

Omaugh, which nearly everyone here would have wanted. "But do at least have supper with us, Fleet Captain! Captain Hetnys already has my invitation, of course. You won't be doing any official business today."

Her last few words rang out clear in a sudden hush, and then I heard a dozen or more children's voices singing in unison. Not in Radchaai, and not a Radchaai tune, but one that arced in upward leaps, wide, angular intervals, and then slid downward in steps, but moving upward overall, to stop somewhere higher than it began. Citizen Fosyf's nattering about supper stopped midsentence, brought up short by my obvious inattention. "Oh, yes," she said, "It's the temple's..."

"Be silent!" I snapped. The children began another verse. I still didn't understand the words. They sang two more verses, while the citizen before me tried to conceal her consternation. Not leaving. Determined to speak with me, it appeared. Certain that she would get her chance, if only she was patient enough.

I could query Station, but I knew what Station would tell me. Fosyf Denche was a prominent citizen here, one who believed her prominence would mean something to anyone she introduced herself to, and in this system, on this station, that meant *tea*.

The song ended, to a scattering of applause. I turned my attention back to Citizen Fosyf. Her expression cleared. Brightened. "Ah, Fleet Captain, *I know what you are*! You're a *collector*! You must come visit me downwell. I've no ear at all, myself, but the workers on the estate near my country house let loose with all sorts of uncivilized noises that I'm assured are authentic exotic musical survivals from the days of their ancestors. I'm told it's quite nearly a museum display. But the station administrator can tell you all about it over supper this evening. She's a fellow collector, and I know how you collectors are, it doesn't matter what you collect. You'll want to compare and trade. Are you absolutely *sure* you've already got somewhere suitable to stay?"

"Go away," I said to her, flat and brusque.

"Of course, Fleet Captain." She bowed low. "I'll see you at supper, shall I?" And not waiting for any answer, she turned and strode off into the crowd.

"Begging the fleet captain's indulgence," said Captain Hetnys, leaning close so she didn't have to shout aloud to the entire concourse. "Citizen Fosyf's family's lands produce nearly a quarter of all the tea exported from Athoek. Her apartment is very near Administration, on the upper concourse, in fact."

More and more interesting. Earlier it had been clear that Captain Hetnys had neither expected nor wanted me to stay. Now she seemed to wish that I would stay with this tea grower. "I'm going to the Governor's Palace," I said. I knew the system governor wasn't there. I would still make an issue of it. "And then while I'm settling into lodgings, you can give me your report."

"Sir. Yes, sir." And then, when I said nothing further, "If I may ask, sir. Where are you staying?"

"Level four of the Undergarden," I replied, my voice bland. She tried valiantly to keep her surprise and dismay off her face, but it was obvious she hadn't expected that answer, and didn't like it.

6

Station AIs were built—grew—as their stations were built. Shortly after Athoek Station had been finished, when resentments from the annexation had still been fresh, there had been violence. A dozen sections on four levels had been permanently damaged.

Installing an AI into an already existing construction was a dicey business. The results were rarely optimal, but it could be done. Had been done, quite a few times. But for whatever reason—perhaps a wish to forget the event, perhaps because the casts hadn't been auspicious, perhaps some other reason—the area had not been repaired, but blocked off instead.

Of course, people had still managed to get in. There were several hundred people living in the Undergarden, though they weren't supposed to be there. Every citizen had a tracker implanted at birth, so Station knew where they were, knew those citizens were there. But it couldn't hear them or see them the way it could its other residents, not unless they were wired to send data to Station, and I suspected few of them were.

* * *

The section door leading to the Undergarden was propped open with the crushed remains of a table missing one of its legs. The indicator next to the entrance said that on the other side of that (supposedly closed) door was hard vacuum. It was serious business—section doors would close automatically in the event of a sudden pressure drop, to seal off hull breaches. We were likely not even close to hard vacuum, despite the indicator on the wall by this door, but no one who spent much time on ships—or who lived on stations—took such safety measures lightly. I turned toward Captain Hetnys. "Are all the section doors leading to the Undergarden disabled and propped open like this?"

"It's as I said, Fleet Captain, this area was sealed off, but people kept breaking in. They'd just be sealing it off over and over to no purpose."

"Yes," I acknowledged, gesturing the obviousness of her words. "So why not just fix the doors so they work properly?"

She blinked, clearly not quite understanding my question. "No one's supposed to be in this area, sir." She seemed completely serious—the train of reasoning made perfect sense to her. The ancillary behind her stared blankly ahead, apparently without any opinion on the matter. Which I knew was almost certainly not the case. I didn't answer, just turned to climb over the broken table and into the Undergarden.

In the corridor beyond, a scatter of portable light panels propped against the walls flickered into a dim glow as we passed, then faded again. The air was oppressively still, improbably humid, and smelled stale—Station wouldn't be regulating the air flow here, and very possibly those propped-open section doors were a matter of breathing or not breathing. After a walk of fifty meters, the corridor opened out

into a tiny almost-concourse, a stretch of corridors where
doors had been wrenched off and grimy once-white walls
torn through to make a single-storied half-open maze, lit by
more portable light panels, though these seemed to be better
provided with power. A handful of citizens walking through
on their way to or from someplace suddenly found that their
paths took them well away from where we were standing, just
by chance discovered that they had no desire to look directly
at us.

Away in one corner, more light spilled from a wide doorway. Beside the doorway, a person in loose shirt and trousers glanced briefly at us, seemed for a moment to consider
something, and then turned back around and bent to a five-
liter tub at her feet, straightened again and began dabbing
carefully, purposefully around the doorframe. Where the
wall was shadowed, red spirals and curlicues glowed faintly.
The color of paint she was using must have been too near the
shade of the wall to see well unless it was phosphorescing.
Beyond the doorway, people sat at mismatched tables, drinking tea and talking. Or they'd been talking before they'd
seen us.

The air really was uncomfortably close. I had a sudden
flash of strong, visceral memory. Humid heat and the smell
of swamp water. The sort of memory that had become less
common as the years had gone by, of when I had been a ship.
When I had been a unit of ancillaries under the command of
Lieutenant Awn (still alive, then, every breath, every move
of hers a constant part of my awareness, and myself always,
always with her).

The decade room on *Mercy of Kalr* flashed into my awareness, Seivarden seated, drinking tea, looking at schedules for
today and tomorrow, the smell of solvent stronger than usual

from the corridor outside, where three Amaats scrubbed the already spotless floor. The Amaats all sang quietly in ragged, off-key unison. *It all goes around, the station goes around the moon, it all goes around.* Had I unthinkingly reached for it, or had *Mercy of Kalr* sent it unbidden in response to something it had seen in me? Or did it matter?

"Sir," ventured Captain Hetnys, perhaps because I'd stopped, forcing her to stop, and *Sword of Atagaris*, and Lieutenant Tisarwat and Kalr Five. "Begging the fleet captain's indulgence. No one's supposed to be in the Undergarden. People don't *stay* here."

I looked pointedly toward the people sitting at tables, beyond that doorway, all of them carefully not noticing us. Looked around at the citizens passing by. Said to Tisarwat, "Lieutenant, go see how our move-in is coming along." I could have any information I wanted from my Mercy of Kalrs with no more than a thought, but Tisarwat's stomach had settled, now we were off the shuttle, and she was beginning to be hungry, and tired.

"Sir," she replied, and left. I walked away from Captain Hetnys and her ancillary, through that spiral-decorated doorway. Five followed me. The painter tensed as we passed, hesitated, then continued painting.

Two of the people sitting at different scarred, mismatched tables wore the usual Radchaai jacket, trousers, and gloves—clearly the standard issue, stiff fabric, grayish-beige, the sort of clothing any citizen was entitled to but no one wore who could afford better. The rest wore loose, light shirts and trousers in deep colors, red and blue and purple, vivid against the dingy gray walls. The air was still and close enough to make those jacketless shirts look far preferable to my uniform. I saw none of the sashes I'd seen on the concourse, and hardly any jewelry at all. Most held their bowls of what I had presumed was tea in bare hands. I almost might not have been on a Radchaai station.

At my entrance, the proprietor had gone back to a bowl-stacked corner, and she watched her customers now with careful attention, very obviously could not spare any for me. I walked over to her, bowed, and said, "Excuse me, Citizen. I'm a stranger here. I wonder if you could answer a question." The proprietor stared at me, seemingly uncomprehending, as though the kettle in her bare hand had just spoken to her, or as though I'd spoken gibberish. "I'm told today is a very important Athoeki holiday, but I see no signs of it here." No penis garlands, no sweets, just people going about their business. Pretending not to notice soldiers standing in the middle of their neighborhood center.

The proprietor scoffed. "Because all Athoeki are Xhai, right?" Kalr Five had stopped just behind me. Captain Hetnys and the *Sword of Atagaris* ancillary stood where I'd left them, Captain Hetnys staring after me.

"Ah," I said, "I understand now. Thank you."

"What are you doing here?" asked a person sitting at a table. No courtesy title, not even the minimally polite *citizen*. People sitting near her tensed, looked away from her. Everyone fell silent who had not already been. One person sitting alone a few meters away, one of the two dressed in properly Radchaai fashion, cheap, stiff jacket, gloves, and all, closed her eyes, took a few deliberate breaths, opened her eyes. But said nothing.

I ignored all of it. "I need somewhere to stay, Citizen."

"There's no fancy hotels here," replied the person who had spoken so rudely. "Nobody comes here to *stay*. People come here to drink, or eat *authentic* Ychana food."

"*Soldiers* come here to beat the crap out of people minding their own business," muttered someone behind me. I didn't turn to look, sent a quick, silent message ordering Kalr Five not to move.

"And the governor's always got room for *important* people," continued the person who had been speaking, as though that other voice had never even existed.

"Maybe I don't want to stay with the governor." That seemed to be the right thing to say, for some reason. Everyone within earshot laughed. Except one, the carefully silent, Radchaai-attired person. The few pins she wore were generic and cheap—brass, colored glass. Nothing that spoke of family affiliation. Only a small enameled IssaInu at her collar suggested anything specific about her. It was the Emanation of movement and stillness, and suggested she might be an adherent of a sect that practiced a particular sort of meditation. Then again, the Emanations were popular, and given they fronted the temple of Amaat here, might be stand-ins for a set of Athoeki gods. So in the end even the IssaInu told me little. But it intrigued me.

I pulled out the chair opposite her, sat. "You," I said to her, "are very angry."

"That would be unreasonable," she said after a breath.

"Feelings and thoughts are irrelevant." I could see that I'd pushed her too far, that in a moment she would rise, urgently, and flee. "It's only actions Security cares about."

"So they tell me." She shoved her bowl away from her and made as if to rise.

"Sit," I said, sharply. Authoritative. She froze. I waved the proprietor over. "Whatever it is you're serving, I'll have one," I said, and received a bowl with some sort of powder in it, which, once steaming water was poured onto it, became the thick tea everyone was drinking. I took a taste. "Tea," I guessed, "and some sort of roasted grain?" The proprietor rolled her eyes, as though I'd said something particularly stupid, and turned and walked away without answering. I gestured unconcerned resignation and took another taste. "So," I said to the person across from me, who had not yet relaxed back into her seat but had at least not gotten up and fled. "It will have been political."

She widened her eyes, all innocence. "Excuse me, Citizen?" Ostensibly, technically polite, though I was sure she could read the signs of my rank and ought to have used the highest address I was entitled to, if she knew it. If she truly meant to be polite.

"No one here is looking at you or speaking to you," I said. "And your accent isn't the same as theirs. You're not from here. Reeducation usually works by straightforward conditioning, by making it intensely unpleasant to do the thing that got you arrested to begin with." Or the most basic sort did, it could and no doubt did become much more complicated. "And the thing that's upsetting you is expressing anger. And you're so very angry." There was no one here familiar to me, but anger I recognized. Anger was an old companion of mine by now. "It was an injustice, start to finish, yes? You hadn't done anything. Not anything you thought was wrong." Likely no one here thought it was wrong, either. She hadn't been driven from the tables here, her presence hadn't cleared everyone else from the vicinity. The proprietor had served her. "What happened?"

She was silent a few moments. "You're very used to saying you want something and then just getting it, aren't you," she said at length.

"I've never been to Athoek Station before today." I took

another sip of the thick tea. "I've only been here an hour and so far I don't much like what I see."

"Try somewhere else, then." Her voice was even, very nearly without any obvious trace of irony or sarcasm. As though she meant only what the words she said meant.

"So what happened?"

"How much tea do you drink, Citizen?"

"Quite a bit," I said. "I'm Radchaai, after all."

"No doubt you only drink the best." Still that apparent sincerity. She had regained most of her composure, I guessed, and this overt pleasantness with its near-inaudible undercurrent of anger was normal for her. "Handpicked, the rarest, most delicate buds."

"I'm not so fussy," I said, equably. Though, to be honest, I had no idea whether the tea I drank was handpicked or not, or anything about it, except its name, and that it was good. "Is tea picked by hand, then?"

"Some," she said. "You should go downwell and see. There are some very affordable tours. Visitors love them. Lots of people only come here to see the tea. And why shouldn't they? What are Radchaai without tea, after all? I'm sure one of the growers would be happy to show *you* around personally."

I thought of Citizen Fosyf. "Perhaps I will." I took another sip of the tea-gruel.

She raised her bowl, drank the last bits of her own. Rose. "Thank you, Citizen, for the entertaining conversation."

"It was a pleasure to have met you, Citizen," I replied. "I'm staying on level four. Stop by some time when we're settled in." She bowed without answering. Turned to depart, but froze at the sound of something heavy thunking hard against the wall outside.

Everyone in the tea shop looked up at that sound. The

proprietor set her kettle down on a table with a smack that should have startled the people sitting there but did not, so intent were they on whatever was happening out on the shadowed small concourse. Grim, angry determination on her face, she strode out of the shop. I stood and followed, Five behind me.

Outside, the *Sword of Atagaris* ancillary had pinned the painter against the wall, bending her right arm back. It had kicked the tub of paint, to judge from the pinkish-brown splotches on its boots, the puddle the tub now sat in, and the tracks on the floor. Captain Hetnys stood where I had left her, observing. Saying nothing.

The tea shop proprietor strode right up to the ancillary. "What has she done?" she demanded. "She hasn't done anything!"

Sword of Atagaris didn't answer, only roughly twisted the painter's arm further, forcing her to turn from the wall with a cry of pain and drop to her knees and then facedown onto the floor. Paint smeared her clothes, one side of her face. The ancillary put one knee between her shoulder blades, and she gasped and made a small sobbing whimper.

The tea shop proprietor stepped back but didn't leave. "Let her go! I *hired* her to paint the door."

Time to intervene. "*Sword of Atagaris*, release the citizen." The ancillary hesitated. Possibly because it didn't think of the painter as a citizen. Then it let go of the painter and stood. The tea shop proprietor knelt beside the painter, spoke in a language I didn't understand, but her tone told me she was asking if the painter was all right. I knew she wasn't—the hold *Sword of Atagaris* had used was meant to injure. I had used it myself for that precise purpose, many times.

I knelt beside the tea shop proprietor. "Your arm is

probably broken," I said to the painter. "Don't move. I'll call Medical."

"Medical doesn't come here," said the proprietor, her voice bitter and contemptuous. And to the painter, "Can you get up?"

"You really shouldn't move," I said. But the painter ignored me. With the help of the proprietor and two other patrons, she managed to get to her feet.

"Fleet Captain, sir." Captain Hetnys was clearly indignant, and clearly struggling to contain it. "This person was defacing the station, sir."

"This person," I replied, "was painting the doorway of a tea shop at the request of that shop's proprietor."

"But she won't have had a permit, sir! And the paint will certainly have been stolen."

"It was not stolen!" the proprietor cried as the painter walked slowly off, supported by two others, one of them the angry person in the gray gloves. "I *bought* it."

"Did you ask the painter where she had gotten the paint?" I asked. Captain Hetnys looked at me with blank puzzlement, as though my question made no sense to her. "Did you ask her if she had a permit?"

"Sir, no one has permission to do *anything* here." Captain Hetnys's voice was carefully even, though I could hear frustration behind it.

That being the case, I wondered why this particular unpermitted activity warranted such a violent reaction. "Did you ask Station if the paint was stolen?" The question appeared to be meaningless to Captain Hetnys. "Was there some reason you couldn't call Station Security?"

"Sir, *we're* Security in the Undergarden just now. To help keep order while things are unsettled. Station Security doesn't come here. No one..."

"Is supposed to be here." I turned to Five. "Make sure the citizen arrives safely in Medical and that her injuries are treated immediately."

"We don't need *your* help," protested the tea shop proprietor.

"All the same," I said, and gestured at Five, who left. I turned again to Captain Hetnys. "So *Sword of Atagaris* is running Security in the Undergarden."

"Yes, sir," replied Captain Hetnys.

"Does it—or you, for that matter—have any experience running civilian security?"

"No, sir, but—"

"That hold," I interrupted, "is not suitable for use on citizens. And it's entirely possible to suffocate someone by kneeling on their back that way." Which was fine if you didn't care whether the person you were dealing with lived or not. "You and your ship will immediately familiarize yourselves with the guidelines for dealing with citizen civilians. And you will follow them."

"Begging the fleet captain's indulgence, sir. You don't understand. These people are..." She stopped. Lowered her voice. "These people are barely civilized. And they could be writing anything on these walls. At a time like this, painting on the walls like that, they could be spreading rumors, or passing secret messages, or inflammatory slogans, working people up..." She stopped again, momentarily at a loss. "And Station can't see here, sir. There could be all sorts of unauthorized people here. Or even aliens!"

For a moment the phrase *unauthorized people* puzzled me. According to Captain Hetnys, everyone here was unauthorized—no one had permission to be here. Then I realized she meant people whose very existence was unauthorized. People who had been born here without Station's knowledge, and without having trackers implanted. People who were not in Station's view in any way.

I could imagine—maybe—one or two such people. But enough to be a real problem? "Unauthorized people?" I leaned into my antique accent, put an edge of skepticism into my voice. "Aliens? *Really*, Captain."

"Begging the fleet captain's indulgence. I imagine you're used to places where everyone is civilized. Where everyone has been fully assimilated to Radchaai life. This isn't that sort of place."

"Captain Hetnys," I said. "You and your crew will use no violence against citizens on this station unless it is absolutely necessary. And," I continued over her obvious desire to protest, "in the event it does become necessary, you will follow the same regulations Station Security does. Do I make myself clear?"

She blinked. Swallowed back whatever it was she really wanted to say. "Yes, sir."

I turned to the ancillary. "*Sword of Atagaris*? Am I clear?"

The ancillary hesitated. Surprised, I didn't doubt, at my addressing it directly. "Yes, Fleet Captain."

"Good. Let's have the rest of this conversation in private."

7

With Station's advice and assistance, I had claimed an empty suite of rooms on level four. The air there was stagnant, and I suspected the few light panels that leaned against the walls had been appropriated from the corridors on the way here, given shops probably weren't open today and station stores might or might not be staffed. Even in the dim lighting, the walls and floors looked unpleasantly dusty and grimy. Besides our own luggage, a few fragments of wood and shards of glass suggested whoever had lived here before the Undergarden was damaged hadn't taken everything, but anything useful had been scavenged over the years.

"No water, sir," said Lieutenant Tisarwat. "Which means the nearest baths are...you don't want to see the nearest baths, sir. Even though there's no water, people have been using them for...well. Anyway. I've sent Nine for buckets, and cleaning supplies if she can find them."

"Very good, Lieutenant. Is there somewhere Captain Hetnys and I can have a meeting? Preferably with something we can sit on?"

Lieutenant Tisarwat's lilac eyes showed alarm. "Sir. There's nothing to sit on, sir, except the floor. Or the luggage."

Which would delay unpacking. "We'll sit on the floor, then." *Mercy of Kalr* showed me a wave of indignation from every Kalr present, but none of them said anything or even changed expression, except Lieutenant Tisarwat, who did her best to conceal her dismay. "Is there anyone near us?"

"Station says not, sir," replied Lieutenant Tisarwat. She gestured toward a doorway. "This is probably the best place."

Captain Hetnys followed me into the room Tisarwat indicated. I squatted on the dirty floor and waved an invitation for her to join me. With some hesitation she squatted in front of me, her ancillary remaining standing behind. "Captain, are you or your ship sending any data to Station?"

Her eyes widened in surprise. "No, sir."

A brief check told me my own ship wasn't. "So. If I understand correctly, you believe the Presger are likely to attack this system. That they have perhaps already infiltrated this station." The Radch knew of—had contact with—three species of aliens: the Geck, the Rrrrrr, and the Presger. The Geck rarely left their own home world. Relations with the Rrrrrr were tense, because the first encounter with them had been disastrous. Because of the way our treaty with the Presger had been structured, war with the Rrrrrr had the potential to break that treaty.

And before that treaty, relations with the Presger had been impossible. Invariably fatal, in fact. Before the treaty, the Presger had been implacable enemies of humanity. Or not enemies so much as predators. "Your Amaat lieutenant thought, I take it, that *Mercy of Kalr* might be a Presger ship in disguise."

"Yes, sir." She seemed almost relieved.

"Do you have any reason to think the Presger have broken the treaty? Do you have any hint that they might have even the remotest interest in Athoek?"

Something. Some expression flashed across her face. "Sir, I've had no official communications for nearly a month. We lost contact with Omaugh twenty-six days ago, this whole part of the province has. I sent *Mercy of Phey* to Omaugh to find out what happened, but even if it arrived and turned right back around I won't hear from it for several days." It must have arrived at Omaugh shortly after I'd departed. "The system governor has the official news channels reporting 'unanticipated difficulties' and not much more, but people are nervous."

"Understandably."

"And then ten days ago we lost all communications with Tstur Palace." That would be about the time the information from Omaugh reached Tstur, plus the distance from here to there. "And the Presger were never our friends, sir, and . . . I've heard things."

"From Captain Vel," I guessed. "Things about the Presger undermining the Radch."

"Yes, sir," she acknowledged. "But you say Captain Vel is a traitor."

"The Presger have nothing to do with this. The Lord of the Radch is having a disagreement with herself. She's split into at least two factions, with opposing aims. Opposing ideas about the future of the Radch. They've both been recruiting ships to their causes." I looked up, to where the attending ancillary stood, expressionless. Apparently uncaring. That appearance was deceptive, I knew. "*Sword of Atagaris.* You've been in this system for some two hundred years."

"Yes, Fleet Captain." Its voice was flat, toneless. It would betray none of the surprise I was sure it felt at my addressing it directly this way for a second time.

"The Lord of the Radch has visited during that time. Did she have a private conversation with you? Here in the Undergarden, perhaps?"

"I am at a loss to understand what the fleet captain is asking," said *Sword of Atagaris*, in the person of this ancillary.

"I am asking," I replied, knowing the evasion for precisely what it was, "if you had a private conversation with Anaander Mianaai, one no one could overhear. But perhaps you have already answered me. Was it the one that claims the Presger have infiltrated the Radch, or the other one?" The other one being the one that had given me command of *Mercy of Kalr*. And sent me Tisarwat.

Or, gods help us all, was there even a third part of Mianaai, with yet another justification of whatever it was she was doing?

"Begging the fleet captain's indulgence," interjected Captain Hetnys into the brief silence that followed my question, "that I might speak frankly."

"By all means, Captain."

"Sir." She swallowed. "Begging your very great pardon, I am familiar with the fleet captains in the province. Your name isn't among them." *Sword of Atagaris* had no doubt shown her my service record by now—or as much of it as was made available to her—and she'd seen that I'd been made fleet captain only a few weeks ago. The same time I'd joined the military. There were several conclusions one might draw from such information, and it appeared she'd chosen one— that I had been hastily appointed to this position for some reason, with no military background. Saying so aloud, to me, was potentially as much as her life was worth.

"My appointment is a recent one." That alone raised several questions. In an officer like Captain Hetnys, I expected one of them to be why she hadn't been appointed fleet captain herself. Possibly this question would occur to her before any others.

"Sir, are there doubts about my loyalty?" Realized then that her career was hardly the most pressing issue. "You said my lord was...divided. That this is all a result of a disagreement with herself. I'm not sure I understand how that's possible."

"She's become too large to continue to be one entity, Captain. If she ever was just one."

"Of course she was, sir. Is. Begging the fleet captain's pardon, perhaps you don't have much experience with ancillary-crewed ships. It's not exactly the same, sir, but it's very similar."

"Beg to inform the captain," I said, making my voice cold and ironic, "that my entire service record is not available to her. I am quite well acquainted with ancillaries."

"Even so, sir. If what you say is true, and this is my lord split in two and fighting herself, if they're both the Lord of the Radch and not...not counterfeit, then how do we know which one is the right one?"

I reminded myself that this was a new idea to Captain Hetnys. That up until now, no Radchaai had ever questioned the identity of Anaander Mianaai, or wondered about the basis of her claim to rule. It had all been mere evident fact. "They both are, Captain." She showed no sign of comprehension. "If the 'right' Anaander had no concern for the lives of citizens so long as she won her struggle with herself, would you still follow her orders?"

She was silent for a good three seconds. "I think I'd need

to know more." Fair enough. "But, your very great pardon, Fleet Captain, I've heard things about alien infiltration."

"From Captain Vel."

"Yes, sir."

"She was mistaken." Manipulated, more likely, easier for the one Anaander to gain her sympathies—and perhaps belief—by accusing an outside enemy, one nearly all Radchaai feared and hated.

But I couldn't say truly that the Presger were not involved at all. It was the Presger who had made the gun I wore under my jacket, invisible to any scanner, its bullets capable of piercing any material in the universe. The Presger who had sold those guns, twenty-five of them, to the Garseddai, to use to resist annexation by the Radch.

And it was the destruction of the Garseddai as a result, the complete and utter obliteration of every living thing in that system, that had triggered Anaander's crisis, a personal conflict so extreme that she could only resolve it by going to war with herself.

But it had been a crisis waiting to happen. Thousands of bodies distributed over all of Radch space, twelve different headquarters, all in constant communication but time-lagged. Radch space—and Anaander herself—had been steadily expanding for three thousand years, and by now it could take weeks for a thought to reach all the way across herself. It was always, from the beginning, going to fall apart at some point.

Obvious, in retrospect. Obvious before, you'd think. But it's so easy to just not see the obvious, even long past when it ought to be reasonable.

"Captain," I said, "my orders are to keep this system safe and stable. If that means defending it from the Lord of the

107

Radch herself, then that is what I will do. If you have orders to support one side or the other, or if you have strong political ideas, then take your ship and go. As far away from Athoek as possible, by my preference."

She had to think about that just a shade longer than I liked. "Sir, it's not my job to have any political ideas at all." I wasn't sure how honest an answer that was. "It's my job to follow orders."

"Which up till now have been to assist the system governor in maintaining order here. From now, they are to assist me in securing and maintaining the safety of this system."

"Sir. Yes, sir. Of course, sir. But..."

"Yes?"

"With no aspersions cast on the fleet captain's intelligence and ability..." She trailed off, having, I thought, chosen a beginning to her sentence that would lead to an awkward ending.

"You are concerned at my apparent lack of military experience." It was potentially worth Captain Hetnys's life to bring it up. I gave her a small, pleasant smile. "Granted, Administration makes some fucked-up appointments." She made a tiny, amused sound. Every soldier had complaints about how Military Administration arranged things. "But it wasn't Administration that appointed me. It was Anaander Mianaai herself." Strictly true, but not much of an endorsement, and not one I was particularly pleased about claiming. "And you may say to yourself, *she's Mianaai, she's the Lord of the Radch's cousin.*" A quick twitch of her facial muscles told me she'd had that thought. "And you've had experiences with people promoted because they were someone's cousin. I don't blame you, I have, too. But despite what you see in the available version of my service record, I am *not* a new recruit."

COUNTY OF BRANT PUBLIC
LIBRARY
Questions? Please call
519-442-2433

Checkout Date: 22
September 2020 12:13
Title: Ancillary sword
Author: Leckie, Ann.
Due Date: 23 October 2020
23:59

Total checkouts for session:
1
Total checkouts:3

EXPLORE TODAY
DISCOVER TOMORROW
WWW.BRANTLIBRARY.CA

This Paper is Sustainably Sourced
100% BPA & BPS FREE
Made in USA

One Tree Planted for
Every Case of Paper Used

She thought about that. Another moment more and she would conclude that I had spent my career up till now with Special Missions, everything I had done far too secret to admit any of it had ever happened. "Fleet Captain, sir. My apologies." I gestured away the need for any. "But, sir, Special Missions is accustomed to operate with some amount of...irregularity and..."

Astonishing, coming from someone who had not blinked at ancillaries under her orders injuring citizens. "As it happens, I've had some experience with situations that went badly wrong when someone was operating with too much irregularity. And also when someone was operating with far too narrow an idea of the regular. And even if Athoek were completely problem-free, all of Radch space is in the midst of an irregular situation."

She drew breath to ask more, seemed to reconsider. "Yes, sir."

I looked up at the *Sword of Atagaris* ancillary standing still and silent behind her. "And you, *Sword of Atagaris*?"

"I do as my captain commands me, Fleet Captain." Toneless. To all appearances emotionless. But almost certainly taken aback by my question.

"Well." No point in pushing too hard. I stood. "It's been a difficult day for all of us. Let's start fresh, shall we? And you have a supper invitation, Captain, unless I misremember."

"As does the fleet captain," Captain Hetnys reminded me. "It's sure to be very good food. And some of the people you'll want to meet with will be there." She tried to suppress a glance at the dim, dingy surroundings. No furniture. No water, even. "The governor will certainly be there, sir."

"Then I suppose," I said to Captain Hetnys, "I ought to go to supper."

8

Citizen Fosyf Denche's apartment boasted a dining room, all glass on one side, looking out over the still-crowded concourse below. Four meters by eight, walls painted ocher. A row of plants sat on a high shelf, long, thick stems hanging down nearly to the floor, with sharp spines and thick, round, bright green leaves. Large as the dining room was by station-dwelling standards, it wouldn't have been large enough to seat all of a wealthy Radchaai's composite household—cousins, clients, servants, and their children—and to judge by the half dozen or so small children in various stages of undress and stickiness sleeping on cushions in the nearby sitting room, this was at least the second round of holiday supper.

"The fleet captain," said Fosyf in her seat at one end of the table of pale, gilded wood, "is a collector just like you, Administrator Celar!" Fosyf was clearly pleased at having discovered that. Enough to almost completely conceal her disappointment at my not offering any information on the loss of communication with the nearest palaces, or her inability to politely ask me for it.

Station Administrator Celar ventured an expression of cautious interest. "A collector, Fleet Captain? Of songs? What sort?" She was a wide, bulky person in a vividly pink coat and trousers and yellow-green sash. Dark-skinned, dark-eyed, voluminous tightly curled hair pulled up and bound to tower above her head. She was very beautiful and, I thought, aware of that fact, though not off-puttingly so. Her daughter Piat sat beside her, silent and oddly indrawn. She was not so large nor quite so beautiful, but young yet and likely to equal her mother on both counts someday.

"My taste is broad-ranging rather than discriminating, Administrator." I gestured refusal of another serving of smoked eggs. Captain Hetnys sat silent beside me, intent on her own second helping. Across the table from me, beside the station administrator, System Governor Giarod sat, tall and broad shouldered, in a soft, flowing green coat. Something about the particular shade of her skin suggested she'd had it darkened. From the moment she'd entered, she'd been as collected as though this were a routine supper, nothing out of the ordinary.

"I have a particular interest in Ghaonish music," confessed Administrator Celar. Fosyf beamed. Fosyf's daughter Raughd smiled insincerely, fairly competently concealing her boredom. When I'd arrived she'd been just slightly too attentive, too respectful, and I'd seen so many young people of her class, so intimately, for so long, that even without an AI to tell me so, I knew she'd been nursing a hangover. Knew, now, that the hangover med she'd taken had started working.

"I grew up only a few gates from Ghaon, you understand," Station Administrator Celar continued, "and served as assistant administrator at the station there for twenty years. So fascinating! And so very difficult to find the real, authentic thing." She picked up a small piece of dredgefruit with her utensil, but instead of putting it in her mouth, moved it toward her lap, under the table. Beside her, her daughter Piat smiled, just slightly, for the first time since I'd seen her.

"Ghaonish in general?" The station that Administrator Celar had served on was only just starting to be built when I'd last been there, centuries ago. "There were at least three different political entities on Ghaon at the time of the annexation, depending how you count, and something like seven different major languages, each of which had its own various styles of music."

"*You* understand," she replied, having lost in an instant nearly all her wariness of me. "All of that, and so few really Ghaonish songs left."

"What would you give me," I asked, "for a Ghaonish song you've never heard?"

Her eyes widened, disbelief apparent. "*Sir*," she said, indignant. Offended. "You're making fun of me."

I raised an eyebrow. "I assure you not, Administrator. I had several from a ship that was there during the annexation." I didn't mention that I had *been* the ship in question.

"You met *Justice of Toren*!" she exclaimed. "What a loss that was! Did you serve on it? I've so often wished I could meet someone who did. One of our horticulturists here had a sister who served on *Justice of Toren*, but that was long before she came here. She was just a child when..." She shook her head regretfully. "Such a shame."

Time to turn that topic aside. I turned to address Governor Giarod. "May one, Governor," I asked, "properly inquire about this temple ritual that has kept you so occupied all day?" My accent as elegant as any high-born officer, my tone overtly courteous but underneath just the hint of an edge.

"One may," Governor Giarod replied, "but I'm not sure how many answers anyone can properly provide." Like Station Administrator Celar, she picked up a piece of dredgefruit and then apparently set it in her lap.

"Ah," I ventured. "Temple mysteries." I'd seen several, over my two-thousand-year lifetime. None of them had been allowed to continue, unless they admitted Anaander Mianaai to their secrets. The survivors were all quite nonexclusive as a result. Or at least theoretically so—they could be fantastically expensive to join.

Governor Giarod slipped another piece of fruit under the table. To some child harder to exhaust and possibly more enterprising than her siblings and cousins, I guessed. "The mysteries are quite ancient," the governor said. "And very important to the Athoeki."

"Important to the Athoeki, or just the Xhai? And it is, somehow, connected to this story about the Athoeki who had penises pretending to cut them off?"

"A misunderstanding, Fleet Captain," said Governor Giarod. "The Genitalia Festival is much older than the annexation. The Athoeki, particularly the Xhai, are a very spiritual people. So much is metaphor, an inadequately material way to speak of immaterial things. If you have any interest in the spiritual, Fleet Captain, I do encourage you to become an initiate."

"I greatly fear," Citizen Fosyf said before I could answer, "that the fleet captain's interests are musical rather than spiritual. She's only interested if there's singing." Quite rudely presumptuous. But true enough.

Under the table a tiny, bare hand clutched my trouser leg—whoever was there had lost patience with the governor's absorption in the conversation and had decided to try her luck with me. She wasn't much more than a year old, and was, as far as I could see, completely naked. I offered her a piece of dredgefruit—clearly a favorite—and she took it with one sticky hand, put it in her mouth, and chewed with frowning absorption, leaning against my leg. "Citizen Fosyf tells me the workers on her estate sing a great deal," I remarked.

"Oh, yes!" agreed Station Administrator Celar. "In the past they were mostly Samirend transportees, but these days they're all Valskaayans."

That struck me as odd. "*All* your field workers are Valskaayan?" I slipped another piece of dredgefruit under the table. Kalr Five would have reason to complain about the sticky handprints on my trousers. But Radchaai generally indulged small children greatly, and there would be no real resentment.

"Samir was annexed some time ago, Fleet Captain," said Fosyf. "All the Samirend are more or less entirely civilized now."

"More or less," muttered Captain Hetnys, beside me.

"I'm quite familiar with Valskaayan music," I confessed, ignoring her. "Are these Delsig-speakers?"

Fosyf frowned. "Well, of course, Fleet Captain. They don't speak much Radchaai, that's for certain."

Valskaay had an entire temperate, habitable planet, not to mention dozens of stations and moons. Delsig had been the language a Valskaayan would have needed to speak if she wanted to do much business beyond her own home, but it was by no means certain that any Valskaayan would speak it. "Have they retained their choral tradition?"

"Some, Fleet Captain," Celar replied. "They also improvise a bass or a descant to songs they've learned since they arrived. Drones, parallels, you know the sort of thing, very primitive. But not terribly interesting."

"Because it's not authentic?" I guessed.

"Just so," agreed Station Administrator Celar.

"I have, personally, very little concern for authenticity."

"Wide-ranging taste, as you said," Station Administrator Celar said, with a smile.

I raised my utensil in acknowledgment. "Has anyone imported any of the written music?" In certain places on Valskaay—particularly the areas where Delsig was most often a first language—choral societies had been an important social institution, and every well-educated person learned to read the notation. "So they aren't confined to primitive and uninteresting drones?" I put the smallest trace of sarcasm into my voice.

"Grace of Amaat, Fleet Captain!" interjected Citizen Fosyf. "These people can barely speak three words of Radchaai. I can hardly imagine my field workers sitting down to learn to read music."

"Might keep them busy," said Raughd, who had been sitting silent so far, smiling insincerely. "Keep them from stirring up trouble."

"Well, as to that," said Fosyf, "I'd say it's the educated Samirend who give us the most problems. The field supervisors are nearly all Samirend, Fleet Captain. Generally an intelligent sort. And mostly dependable, but there's always one or two, and let those one or two get together and convince more, and next thing you know they've got the field workers whipped up. Happened about fifteen, twenty years ago. The field workers in five different plantations sat down and refused to pick the tea. Just sat right down! And of course we stopped feeding them, on the grounds they'd refused their assignments. But there's no point on a planet. Anyone who doesn't feel like working can live off the land."

It struck me as likely that living off the land wasn't so easy as all that. "You brought workers in from elsewhere?"

"It was the middle of the growing season, Fleet Captain," said Citizen Fosyf. "And all my neighbors had the same difficulties. But eventually we rounded up the Samirend ringleaders, made some examples of them, and the workers themselves, well, they came back soon after."

So many questions I could ask. "And the workers' grievances?"

"Grievances!" Fosyf was indignant. "They had none. No real ones. They live a pleasant enough life, I can tell you. Sometimes I wish *I'd* been assigned to pick tea."

"Are you staying, Fleet Captain?" asked Governor Giarod. "Or on your way back to your ship?"

"I'm staying in the Undergarden," I said. Immediate, complete silence descended, not even the chink of utensils on porcelain. Even the servants, arranging platters on the pale, gilded sideboards, froze. The infant under the table chewed the latest piece of dredgefruit, oblivious.

Then Raughd laughed. "Well, why not? None of those dirty animals will mess with *you*, will they?" Good as her façade had been so far, her contempt reached her voice. I'd met her sort before, over and over again. A few of those had even turned out to be decent officers, once they'd learned what they needed to learn. Some, on the other hand, had not.

"Really, Raughd," said her mother, but mildly. In fact, no one at the table seemed surprised or shocked at Raughd's words. Fosyf turned to me. "Raughd and her friends like to go drinking in the Undergarden. I've told her repeatedly that it's not safe."

"Not safe?" I asked. "Really?"

"Pickpockets aren't uncommon," said Station Administrator Celar.

"Tourists!" said Raughd. "They *want* to be robbed. It's

why they go there to begin with. All the wailing and complaining to Security." She waved a dismissive, blue-gloved hand. "It's part of the fun. Otherwise they'd take better care."

Quite suddenly, I wished I was back on *Mercy of Kalr*. Medic, on watch, was saying something brief and acerbic to one of the Kalrs with her. Lieutenant Ekalu inspected as her Etrepas worked. Seivarden, on the edge of her bed, said, "Ship, how's Fleet Captain doing?"

"Frustrated," replied *Mercy of Kalr*, in Seivarden's ear. "Angry. Safe, but playing, as they say, with fire."

Seivarden almost snorted. "Like normal, then." Four Etrepas, in a corridor on another deck, began to sing a popular song, raggedly, out of tune.

In the ocher-walled dining room, the child, still clutching my trouser leg, began to cry. Citizen Fosyf and Citizen Raughd both evinced surprise—they had not, apparently, realized there was anyone under the table. I reached under, picked the child up, and set her on my lap. "You've had a long day, Citizen," I said, soberly.

A servant rushed forward, anxious, and lifted the wailing child away with a whispered, "Apologies, Fleet Captain."

"None needed, Citizen," I said. The servant's anxiety surprised me—it had been clear that even if Fosyf and Raughd hadn't realized the child was there, everyone else had, and no one had objected. I'd have been quite surprised if anyone had. But then, while I had known adult Radchaai for some two thousand years, seen and heard all the messages they'd ever sent home or received, and while I'd interacted with children and infants in places the Radch had annexed, I had never been inside a Radchaai household, never spent much time at all with Radchaai children. I wasn't actually a very good judge of what was normal or expected.

* * *

Supper ended with a round of arrack. I considered several polite ways to extricate myself, and Governor Giarod with me, but before I could choose one Lieutenant Tisarwat arrived—ostensibly to tell me our quarters were ready, but really, I suspected, hoping for leftovers. Which of course Fosyf immediately directed a servant to pack for her. Lieutenant Tisarwat thanked her prettily and bowed to the seated company. Raughd Denche looked her over, mouth quirked in a tiny smile—amused? Intrigued? Contemptuous? All three, perhaps. Straightening, Tisarwat caught Raughd's look and was, it seemed, intrigued herself. Well, they were close in age, and much as I found I disliked Raughd, a connection there might benefit me. Might bring me information. I pretended to ignore it. So, I saw, did Piat, the station administrator's daughter. I rose and said, pointedly, "Governor Giarod?"

"Quite," the system governor said, with still impressive aplomb. "Fosyf, delicious supper as always, do thank that cook of yours again, she's a marvel." She bowed. "And what delightful company. But duty beckons."

Governor Giarod's office was across the concourse from Fosyf's apartment. The same view of the concourse, but from the other side. Cream-colored silk hangings painted with a pattern of leaves draped the walls. Low tables and chairs scattered around, an icon of Amaat in the typical wall niche, a bowl before it but no smell of incense—of course, the governor hadn't come in to work today.

I'd sent Tisarwat back to the Undergarden with her prize—enough food to fill even a seventeen-year-old comfortably and then some, and the governor's compliments for Fosyf's cook had been entirely deserved—and I had also dismissed

Captain Hetnys, with orders that she report to me in the morning.

"Sit, please, Fleet Captain." Governor Giarod gestured to some wide, cushioned chairs well back from the window. "What must you think of us? But from the beginning of this…crisis, I've tried to keep everything as calm and routine as possible. And of course religious observances are very important in times of stress. I can only thank you for your patience."

I sat, and so did the governor. "I am," I admitted, "approaching the limits of that patience. But then, you are as well, I suspect." I had thought, all those days on the way here, of what I should say to Governor Giarod. Of how much I should reveal. Had decided, in the end, on the truth, as unvarnished as I could produce it. "So. This is the situation: two factions of Anaander Mianaai have been in conflict with each other for a thousand years. Behind the scenes, hidden even from herself." Governor Giarod frowned. It didn't make much sense, on the surface. "Twenty-eight days ago, at Omaugh Palace, it became open conflict. The Lord of the Radch herself blocked all communications coming from the palace, in an attempt to hide that conflict from the rest of herself. She failed, and now that information is on its way across Radch space, to all the other palaces." It was probably reaching Irei Palace—the one farthest from Omaugh—just about now. "The conflict at Omaugh appears to be resolved."

Governor Giarod's obvious dismay had grown with every word I'd spoken. "In whose favor?"

"Anaander Mianaai's, of course. How else? We are all of us in an impossible position. To support either faction is treason."

"As is," agreed the governor, "*not* supporting either faction."

"Indeed." I was relieved that the governor had enough wit to see that immediately. "In the meantime, factions in the military—also fostered by the Lord of the Radch, with an eye toward an advantage if this ever came to actual physical battle—have begun fighting. One in particular has begun attacking gates. Which is why, even though communications from Omaugh Palace are now functioning, you're still isolated from them. Every route any message would take has had a gate somewhere along it destroyed." Or at least the routes that wouldn't take months.

"There were dozens of ships in the Hrad-Omaugh Gate! Eighteen of them are still unaccounted for! What could possibly..."

"I suspect they're still trying to keep information back. Or at least make it difficult for any but military ships to travel between systems. And they don't particularly care how many citizens die in the process."

"I can't... I can't believe that."

It was, nonetheless, true. "Station will have shown you my remit. I have command of all military resources in this system, and orders to ensure the safety of the citizens here. I also bring an order to forbid all travel through the gates for the foreseeable future."

"Who gave this order?"

"The Lord of the Radch."

"Which one of her?" I said nothing. The governor gestured resignation. "And this... argument she's having with herself?"

"I can tell you what she has told me. I can tell you what *I* think it's about. More than that..." I gestured ambiguity, uncertainty. Governor Giarod waited, silent and expectant. "The trigger, the precipitating event, was the destruction of the Garseddai." The governor winced, barely perceptibly. No one liked talking about that, about the time Anaander Mianaai had, in a fury, ordered the destruction of all life in an entire solar system. Even though it was a thousand years in the past, by now, and easier to forget about than it once had been. "When you do something like that, how do you react?"

"I hope I would never *do* anything like that," said Governor Giarod.

"Life is unpredictable," I said, "and we are not always the people we think we are. If we're unlucky, that's when we discover it. When something like that happens, you have two choices." Or, more than two, but distilled, they came down to two. "You can admit the error and resolve never to repeat it, or you can refuse to admit error and throw every effort behind insisting you were right to do what you did, and would gladly do it again."

"Yes. Yes, you're right. But Garsedd was a thousand years ago. Surely that's time to have resolved on one or another of those. And if you'd asked me before now, I'd have said my lord had chosen the first. Without, of course, publicly admitting error."

"It must be more complicated than that," I agreed. "I think there were already other issues that events at Garsedd exacerbated. What those were I can only guess. Certainly the Lord of the Radch couldn't continue expanding forever." And if expansion stopped, what to do with all those ships and ancillary soldiers? The officers that commanded them? Keeping them was a drain on resources, to no purpose. Dismantle them, and systems on the periphery of Radch space were vulnerable to attack. Or revolt. "I think it wasn't merely admitting error that the Lord of the Radch has been resisting, but admitting her own mortality."

Governor Giarod sat considering that, silent for twenty-four seconds. "I don't like that thought, Fleet Captain. If you had asked me even ten minutes ago I'd have told you the Lord of the Radch was the next thing to immortal. How can she not be? Constantly growing new bodies to replace the old, how could she ever die?" Another frowning three seconds of silence. "And if she dies, what will be left of the Radch?"

"I don't think we can concern ourselves with anything beyond Athoek." Possibly the most dangerous thing I could say, just now, depending on the governor's sympathies. "My orders only involve the safety of this system."

"And if they were otherwise?" Governor Giarod was no fool. "If some other part of my lord ordered you to take one side or another, or use this system in some way for her advantage?" I didn't reply. "No matter what you do it's sedition, rebellion, so you may as well do as you like, is that it?"

"Something like that," I agreed. "But I really do have orders."

She shook her head, as though clearing away some obstruction. "But what else is there to do? You don't think, do you, that there's been any . . . outside interference?"

The question was depressingly familiar. "The Presger would not require subterfuge in order to destroy the Radch. And there is the treaty, which I'm given to understand they take very seriously."

"They don't use words, do they? They're completely alien. How could the word *treaty* mean anything to them? How could any agreement mean anything?"

"Are the Presger nearby? A potential threat?"

A tiny frown. The question troubled her for some reason. Perhaps because the very idea of the Presger nearby was frightening. "They pass through Prid Presger, sometimes, on their way to Tstur Palace." Prid Presger was a few gates from here, nearby only in the sense that it would take a month or so to get here from there, instead of a year or more. "By agreement, they can only travel by gate, within the Radch. But..."

"The treaty isn't with the Radch," I pointed out. "It's with all humans." Governor Giarod looked puzzled at that—to most Radchaai, *human* was who they were, and everyone else was...something other. "I mean to say, whether Anaander Mianaai exists at all does not affect it. It is still in force." Still, for more than a thousand years before the treaty, Presger had seized human ships. Boarded human stations. Dismantled them—and their crews, passengers, and residents. Apparently for amusement. No one had any way of preventing it. They had ceased only because of the treaty. And the thought of them still sent a shiver down a good many human backs. Including, it seemed, Governor Giarod's. "Unless you have some specific reason, I don't think we should worry about them just now."

"No, of course, you're right." But the governor still seemed troubled.

"We produce enough food for the whole system?"

"Certainly. Though we do import some luxuries—we don't make much arrack, and various other things. We import some number of medical supplies. That could be a problem."

"You don't make correctives here?"

"Not many. Not all kinds."

That could pose a problem, far enough into the future. "We'll see what we can do about that, if anything. Meantime, I suggest you continue as you have been—keeping calm, keeping order. We should let people know that the gates that are closed are down for the foreseeable future. And that travel through the remaining gates is too dangerous to allow."

"Citizen Fosyf won't like that! Or any of the other growers. By the end of the month there'll be tonnes of top-grade handpicked Daughter of Fishes with nowhere to go. And that's only Fosyf's bit."

"Well." I smiled blandly. "At least we'll all have very good tea to drink for the next long while."

It was too late to visit Citizen Basnaid with any sort of courtesy. And there were things I wanted to know that had not been in the information I'd received at Omaugh Palace. Politics from before an annexation were considered irrelevant, any old divisions wiped away by the arrival of civilization. Anything remaining—languages, perhaps, or art of some kind—might be preserved as quaint museum displays, but of course never figured into official records. Outside this system, Athoek looked like any other Radchaai system. Uniform. Wholly civilized. Inside it, you could see it wasn't, if you looked—if you were forced to acknowledge it. But it was always a balancing act between the presumed complete success of the annexation and the need to deal with the ways in which that annexation had, perhaps, not been entirely complete, and one of the ways to achieve that balance was by ignoring what one didn't have to see.

Station would know things. I'd best have a chat with Station anyway, best put myself in its good graces. A ship or station AI couldn't, strictly speaking, do anything to oppose me, but I knew from very personal experience how much easier life was when one liked you, and wanted to help.

9

Despite the fact that the Undergarden wasn't terribly well ventilated, and my bed was little more than a pile of blankets on the floor, I slept comfortably. Made a point of saying so to Kalr Five, when she brought me tea, because I could see that she, that all my Mercy of Kalrs, were vain of what they'd achieved while I sat at supper with Citizen Fosyf. They'd managed to clean our several rooms to an almost military level of spotlessness, rig lights, get doors working, and pile luggage and miscellaneous boxes into something approximating tables and chairs. Five brought me breakfast—more porridge tea, though thicker than what I'd drunk in the tea shop, bland but filling—and Lieutenant Tisarwat and I ate in silence, she in a state of suppressed self-loathing. It had been barely noticeable aboard *Mercy of Kalr*. Her duties there, and the self-contained isolation of our travel, had made it easy for her to almost forget what Anaander Mianaai had done to her. What I had done to Anaander Mianaai. But now, here at Athoek Station, the chaos of cleaning and unpacking past, she must be thinking of what the Lord of the Radch had meant to do when we'd arrived here.

I considered asking her. I already knew Anaander Mianaai's assessment of the system governor and of the ships and captains stationed here. Knew that she considered most of the tea-growing houses to be almost entirely preoccupied with their tea and likely unthreatened by the changes the Lord of the Radch had set in motion over the past hundred years. After all, upstart houses drank tea just as much as anciently aristocratic ones, and (aside from captains who demanded their soldiers play ancillary) human soldiers did, too.

Athoek was probably not fertile ground for the other Anaander. And most of the fighting would probably center round the palaces for now. Then again, a planet was a valuable resource. If fighting lasted long enough, Athoek could draw unwelcome attention. And in a game with such high stakes, neither Anaander would have failed to place a few counters here.

Kalr Five left the room, and Lieutenant Tisarwat looked up from her porridge, her lilac eyes serious. "She's very angry with you, sir."

"Who is that, Lieutenant?" But of course she meant Anaander Mianaai.

"The other one, sir. I mean, they both are, really. But the other one. If she gains the upper hand at any point, she'll come after you if she possibly can. Because she's just that angry. And..."

And that was the part of the Lord of the Radch who dealt with her reaction to Garsedd by insisting she had been right to lose her temper so extravagantly. "Yes, thank you, Lieutenant. I'd already worked that out." Much as I'd wanted to know what the Lord of the Radch was up to, I hadn't wanted to make Tisarwat talk about it. But she had volunteered. "I take it you have access codes for all the AIs in the system."

She looked quickly down at her bowl. Mortified. "Yes, sir."

"Are they only good for specific AIs, or can you potentially control any one you come across?"

That startled her. And, oddly, disappointed her. She looked up, distress plain in her expression. "Sir! She's not *stupid*."

"Don't use them," I said, voice pleasant. "Or you'll find yourself in difficulty."

"Yes, sir." Struggling to keep her feelings off her face—a painful mix of shame and humiliation. A hint of relief. A fresh surge of unhappiness and self-hatred.

It was among the things I'd wanted to avoid, in avoiding asking her about Anaander's aims in sending Tisarwat with me. I certainly didn't want her to indulge in her current emotions.

And I found I was unwilling to wait much longer to find Lieutenant Awn's sister. I took a last mouthful of porridge. "Lieutenant," I said, "let's visit the Gardens."

Surprise, that almost distracted her. "Begging the fleet captain's indulgence, sir. Aren't you meeting with Captain Hetnys?"

"Kalr Five will desire her to wait until I get back." I saw a flash of trepidation from her. And an undercurrent of... admiration, was it? And envy. That was curious.

Raughd Denche had said the Gardens were a tourist attraction, and I could see why. They took up a good portion of the station's upper level, more than five acres, sunlit, open, and undivided under a high, clear dome. Entering, that was all I could see beyond a heavy-smelling bank of red and yellow roses—that high, black sky cut into barely visible hexagonal sections, Athoek itself hanging, jewellike, beyond. A spectacular view, but this close to vacuum there ought to have been smaller partitions, section doors. I saw no sign of them.

The ground had been built to slope downward from where we entered. Past the roses the path meandered around shrubs with glossy green leaves and thick clusters of purple berries, around beds of something pungent-smelling with silvery, needle-shaped leaves. Small trees and more shrubs, even jutting rocks, the path winding around, every now and then affording a glimpse of water, of broad lily-pads, flowers white and deep pink. It was warm, but a slight breeze disturbed the leaves—no ventilation problems here, though I found myself waiting for a pressure drop, still disturbed by that huge open space. The path crossed over a tiny stream, rushing down a rock-built channel to somewhere below. We might almost have been on a planet but for that black expanse above.

Lieutenant Tisarwat, behind me, seemed unconcerned. This station had been here for several hundred years. And if something happened now there was very little either of us could do about it. There was nothing for it but to continue on. At the next turn we came into a copse of small trees with gnarled and twisted branches, and under them a small, still pool that trickled into another on a level below, and on down the slope into a succession of such pools, slowly but inexorably to a patch of lily-blooming water below. Lieutenant Tisarwat stopped, blinked, smiled at the tiny brown and orange fish darting in the clear water at our feet, a sudden bright, startling moment of pleasure. Then she looked up at me, and it was gone, and she was unhappy again, and self-conscious.

The next turn of the path revealed a stretch of open water, nearly three acres of it. Nothing on a planet, but on a station it was unheard of. The nearest edge was lined with the lilies we'd glimpsed as we'd come down the slope. Some meters to the left of that a slight, arched bridge led to a tiny island with a large stone in the middle, a one-and-a-half-meter cylinder with fluted sides, as high as it was wide. Elsewhere, here and there, rocks jutted out of the water. And away on the opposite side of the pond, up against the wall—up, so far as I could see, against hard vacuum—a waterfall. Not the trickles we'd seen on the way in, but a rushing, noisy mass of it foaming and spilling down a rock wall, churning the bit of lake below it. That rock wall stretched across the far side of the lake, ledged and irregular. There was another entrance there, which gave onto the ledges, and a path that led from there around the water.

It had been laid out to make that sudden full view as beautiful and dramatic as possible, after those flashes of water through branches on the path down, the runnels and tiny waterfalls. And dramatic it was. All that open water—usually, on a station, a large volume of water like this was kept in partitioned tanks, so that if there was a leak it could be sectioned off. So that if anything happened to the gravity it could be quickly enclosed. I wondered how deep this pond was, did some quick guesses and calculations that told me a failure in containment would mean disaster for the levels below. What, I wondered, had the station architects put below this?

Of course. The Undergarden.

Someone in a green coverall stood knee-deep in the water at one end of the stretch of lily pads, bent over, reaching under the surface. Not Basnaaid. I nearly dismissed her with that realization, bent on that one aim, on finding Basnaaid Elming. No, the person working near the lilies wasn't Basnaaid. But I recognized her. I stepped off the still twisting path, walked straight down the slope to the edge of the water. The person there looked up, stood, sleeves and gloves muddy and dripping. The person I'd spoken to in the Undergarden tea shop, yesterday. Her anger was banked, hidden. It flared to life again as she recognized me. Along with, I thought, a trace of fear. "Good morning, Citizen," I said. "What a pleasant surprise to meet you here."

"Good morning, Fleet Captain," she replied, pleasantly. Ostensibly calm and unconcerned, but I could see that very small, nearly invisible tightening of her jaw. "How can I help you?"

"I'm looking for Horticulturist Basnaaid," I said, with as unthreatening a smile as I could produce.

She frowned slightly, speculatively. Then looked at my single piece of jewelry, that one gold memorial tag. I didn't think she was close enough to read it, and it was a mass-produced thing, but for the name identical to thousands, if not millions, of others. "You have but to wait," she said, clearing away that tiny frown. "She'll be along in a few moments."

"Your Gardens are beautiful, Citizen," I said. "Though I admit this very lovely lake strikes me as unsafe."

"It's not *my* garden." That anger again, strongly, carefully suppressed. "I only work here."

"It would not be what it is without the people who work here," I answered. She acknowledged that with a small, ironic gesture. "I think," I said, "that you were too young to have been one of the leaders of those strikes on the tea plantations, twenty years ago." The word for "strike" existed in Radchaai, but it was very old, and obscure. I used a Liost term I'd learned from Station last night. The Samirend that had been brought to Athoek had spoken Liost, sometimes still did. This person was Samirend, I'd learned enough from Station to know that. And learned enough from Citizen Fosyf to know that Samirend overseers had been involved in those strikes. "You'd have been, maybe, sixteen? Seventeen? If you'd been important, you'd be dead now, or in some other system entirely, where you didn't have the sort of social network that would let you cause trouble." Her expression became fixed, and she breathed, very carefully, through her mouth. "They were lenient on account of your youth and your marginal position, but they made sure to make some sort of an example of you." Unjust, as I'd guessed yesterday.

She didn't answer at first. Her distress was too strong, but it told me I'd been right. Her reeducation would have made the contemplation of certain actions strongly, viscerally unpleasant for her, and I'd reminded her directly of exactly the events that had brought her through Security. And of course any Radchaai found the bare mention of reeducation deeply distasteful. "If the fleet captain's remarks are complete," she said finally, tense but just a bit fainter than her usual tone, "I have work to do."

"Of course. I apologize." She blinked, surprised, I thought. "You're trimming dead leaves from the lilies?"

"And dead flowers." She bent, reached under the water, pulled up a slimy, withered stem.

"How deep is the lake?" She looked at me, looked down at the water she was standing in. Up again at me. "Yes," I agreed, "I can see how deep it is here. Is it all the same?"

"About two meters at its deepest." Her voice had steadied, she had recovered her earlier composure, it seemed.

"Are there partitions under the water?"

"There are not." As though to confirm her words, a purple and green fish swam into the lily-free space where she was standing, a broad, bright-scaled thing that must have been nearly three quarters of a meter long. It hung under the water, seeming to look up at us, gaping. "I don't have anything," she said to the fish, and held her sodden-gloved hands out. "Go wait by the bridge, someone will come. They always do." The fish only gaped and gaped again. "Look, here they come now."

Two children rounded a bush, came running down the path to the bridge. The smaller jumped from the land to the bridge with a resounding thump. The water alongside the bridge began to roil, and the purple and green fish turned and glided away. "There's a food dispenser at the bridge," explained the person standing in the water. "It'll be quite crowded in an hour or so."

"Then I'm glad to have come early," I said. "If it wouldn't be too much trouble, could you tell me what safety measures are in place here?"

She gave a short, sharp laugh. "It makes you nervous, Fleet Captain?" She gestured toward the dome overhead. "And that?"

"And that," I admitted. "They're both alarming."

"You needn't worry. It's not Athoeki built, it's all good, solid Radchaai construction. No embezzling, no bribes, no replacing components with cheaper materials and pocketing the difference, no shirking on the job." She said this with every appearance of sincerity, not even traces of the sarcasm I might have expected. She meant it. "And of course Station's always watching and would let us know at the slightest sign of trouble."

"But Station can't see under the Gardens, can it?"

Before she could answer, a voice called out, "How is it coming along, Sirix?"

I knew that voice. Had heard recordings of it, childish,

years ago. It was like her sister's, but not the same. I turned to see her. She was like her sister, her relationship to Lieutenant Awn obvious in her face, her voice, the way she stood, a bit stiff in the green Horticulture uniform. Her skin was a bit darker than Lieutenant Awn's had been, her face rounder, not a surprise. I had seen recordings of Basnaaid Elming as a child, messages for her sister. I had known what she looked like now. And it had been twenty years since I had lost Lieutenant Awn. Since I had killed Lieutenant Awn.

"Almost finished, Horticulturist," said the person from the tea shop, still knee-deep in the water. Or I presumed she was, I was still looking at Basnaaid Elming. "This fleet captain is here to see you."

Basnaaid looked directly at me. Took in the brown and black uniform, frowned slightly in puzzlement, and then saw the gold tag. The frown disappeared, replaced with an expression of cold disapproval. "I don't know you, Fleet Captain."

"No," I said. "We've never met. I was a friend of Lieutenant Awn's." An awkward way to say it, an awkward way to refer to her, for a friend. "I was hoping you might have tea with me sometime. When it's convenient for you." Stupid, nearly rude to be so direct. But she didn't seem to be in a mood to stand and chat, and Inspector Supervisor Skaaiat had warned me she wouldn't be happy to see me. "Begging your indulgence, there are some things I'd like to discuss with you."

"I doubt we have anything to discuss." Basnaaid was still frostily calm. "If you feel the need to tell me something, by all means do so now. What did you say your name was?" Outright rude, that was. But I knew why, I knew where this anger came from. Basnaaid was easier in her educated accent than Lieutenant Awn had ever been—she had begun practicing it earlier, for one thing, and I suspected her ear was better from the start. But it was still, to some degree, a cover. Like her sister, Basnaaid Elming was acutely aware of condescension and insult. Not without good reason.

"My name is Breq Mianaai." I managed not to choke on the house name the Lord of the Radch had imposed on me. "You won't recognize it, I used another name when I knew your sister." *That* name she'd have recognized. But I couldn't give it. *I was the ship your sister served on. I was the ancillaries she commanded, that served her.* As far as anyone here knew, that ship had disappeared twenty years ago. And ships weren't people, weren't fleet captains or officers of any sort, didn't invite anyone to tea. If I told her who I really was, she would doubt my sanity. Which might be a good thing, considering the next step, after the name, would be to tell her what had happened to her sister.

"Mianaai." Basnaaid's tone was disbelieving.

"As I said, it wasn't my name at the time I knew your sister."

"Well." She almost spat the word out. "Breq Mianaai. My sister was just, and proper. She never knelt to you, no matter what you may have thought, and none of us wants payment from you. None of us needs it. Awn didn't need it, or want it." In other words, if Lieutenant Awn had had any sort of relationship with me—*knelt* implied a sexual one—it hadn't been because she'd been looking for some sort of benefit from it. When Inspector Supervisor Skaaiat had offered Basnaaid clientage for Lieutenant Awn's sake, the implication had been that Awn and Skaaiat's relationship had been based on the expectation of exchange—sex for social position. It was a common enough trade, but citizens moving from low on the ladder to noticeably higher were open to accusations that their promotions or assignments had been made in exchange for sexual favors, and not on merit.

"You're quite right, your sister never knelt, not to me, not to any other person, ever. Anyone who says she did, you will kindly send to me, and I will relieve them of their misapprehension." It would really have been better to lead up to this, to have had tea and food and polite, indirect conversation beforehand, to feel out the approach, to take the edge off the foolishness of what I meant to suggest. But, I saw, Basnaaid would never have allowed it. I might as well state my business here and now. "The debt I owe your sister is far larger, and impossible to repay adequately, even if she were still alive. I can only offer the smallest token to you in her place. I propose to make you my heir."

She blinked, twice, unable at first to find any reply. "What?"

The noise of the waterfall across the pond was paradoxically both distant and intrusive. Lieutenant Tisarwat and Citizen Sirix were frozen, I realized, staring at us, at Basnaaid and me. "I propose," I repeated, "to make you my heir."

"I already have parents," Basnaaid said, after three seconds of disbelieving silence.

"They are excellent parents," I acknowledged. "It's not my intention to replace them. I couldn't possibly."

"Whatever *is* your intention, then?"

"To be certain," I said, carefully, clearly, knowing I had failed in this, having come into this knowing I would fail, "for your sister's sake, that you are safe and secure, and at all times have whatever you desire within your reach."

"*Whatever I desire*," said Basnaaid, as deliberately as I had just spoken, "is, right now, for you to go away and *never speak to me again.*"

I bowed low, an inferior to one of higher station. "As the citizen wishes." I turned, and walked up to the path, away from the water, away from Sirix still knee-deep by the lilies, away from Basnaaid Elming standing, stiff and indignant, on the shore. Not even looking to see if Lieutenant Tisarwat followed.

I had known. I had known what Basnaaid Elming's reaction would be to my offer. But I had thought I would only tender a polite invitation this morning and have the confrontation itself later. Wrong. And now, I knew, Captain Hetnys was waiting in my apartments in the Undergarden, sweating in the warm, still air and stiffly, angrily refusing the tea Kalr Five had just offered her. Going into that meeting in my present mood would be dangerous, but there was, it seemed, no good way to avoid it.

At the entrance to those rooms, Bo Nine standing at impassive attention just beyond the open door, Lieutenant Tisarwat—I had forgotten, between the waterside and here, that Lieutenant Tisarwat was with me—spoke. "Sir. Begging the fleet captain's indulgence."

I stopped, without looking behind me. Reached out to *Mercy of Kalr*, who showed me a perplexing mix of emotions. Lieutenant Tisarwat was miserable as she had been all morning, but that misery was mixed in with an odd yearning—for what? And a completely new sort of elation that I had never seen in her. "Sir, permission to go back to the Gardens." She wanted to go back to the Gardens? Now?

I remembered that startling moment of pleasure when she'd seen the little fish in the pool, but, I realized, after that I'd paid her no attention whatever. I'd been too caught up in my encounter with Basnaaid. "Why?" I asked, blunt. Not, perhaps, the best way to respond, considering, but I was not at my best just this instant.

For a moment a sort of nervous fear kept her from speaking, and then she said, "Sir, maybe I can talk to her. She didn't tell *me* to never speak to her again." As she spoke, that strange, hopeful elation flared bright and sharp, and with it something I'd seen in countless young, emotionally vulnerable lieutenants.

Oh, *no.* "Lieutenant. You are not to go anywhere *near* the citizen Basnaaid Elming. I do not need you interfering in my affairs. Citizen Basnaaid *certainly* doesn't need it."

It was as though I had struck Tisarwat. She nearly physically recoiled, but stopped herself, held herself still. Speechless, for a moment, with hurt and anger. Then she said, bitter complaint, "You aren't even going to give me a *chance!*"

"You aren't even going to give me a chance, *sir,*" I corrected. Angry tears welled in her ridiculous lilac eyes. If she'd been any other seventeen-year-old lieutenant I'd have sent her on her way to be rejected by the object of her sudden infatuation, and then let her cry—oh, the volume of baby lieutenant tears my uniforms had absorbed, when I'd been a ship—and then poured her a drink or three. But Tisarwat wasn't any other baby lieutenant. "Go to your quarters, Lieutenant, get a hold of yourself, and wash your face." It was early yet for drinking, but she'd need time to get herself in hand. "After lunch you have leave to go out and get as drunk as you like. Better yet, get laid. There are plenty of more appropriate partners here." Citizen Raughd might even be interested, but I didn't say so. "You've been in Citizen Basnaaid's presence a whole five minutes." And saying that, it was even clearer how ridiculous this was. This wasn't about Basnaaid, not really, but that only made me more determined to keep Tisarwat away from her.

"You don't understand!" Tisarwat cried.

I turned to Bo Nine. "Bo. Take your officer to her quarters."

"Sir," said Bo, and I turned and went into what served as the anteroom for our small apartments.

When I was a ship, I had thousands of bodies. Except in extreme circumstances, if one of those bodies became tired or stressed I could give it a break and use another, the way you might switch hands. If one of them was injured badly enough, or ceased to function efficiently, my medics would remove it and replace it with another one. It was remarkably convenient.

When I had been a single ancillary, one human body among thousands, part of the ship *Justice of Toren*, I had never been alone. I had always been surrounded by myself, and the rest of myself had always known if any particular body needed something—rest, food, touch, reassurance. An ancillary body might feel momentarily overwhelmed, or irritable, or any emotion one might think of—it was only natural, bodies felt things. But it was so very small, when it was just one segment among the others, when, even in the grip of strong emotion or physical discomfort, that segment knew it was only one of many, knew the rest of itself was there to help.

Oh, how I missed the rest of myself. I couldn't rest or comfort one body while sending another to do my work, not anymore. I slept alone, mostly only mildly envying the common soldiers on *Mercy of Kalr* their small bunks where they slept all together, pressed warm and close. They weren't ancillaries, it wasn't the same, wouldn't be, even if I'd abandoned any pretense to dignity and climbed in with them. I knew that, knew it would be so wholly insufficient that there was no point in wishing for it. But now, this moment, I wanted it so badly that if I had been aboard *Mercy of Kalr* I'd have done it, curled up among the sleeping Etrepas Ship showed me, and gone to sleep myself, no matter how insufficient it would be. It would be *something*, at least.

A terrible, terrible thing, to deprive a ship of its ancillaries. To deprive an ancillary of its ship. Not, perhaps, as terrible as murdering human beings to make those ancillaries. But a terrible thing nonetheless.

I didn't have the luxury to consider it. I didn't have another, less angry body to send into the meeting with Captain Hetnys. Didn't have an hour, or two, to exercise, or meditate, or drink tea until I was calmer. I only had myself. "It will be all right, Fleet Captain," said *Mercy of Kalr* in my ear, and for a moment I was overwhelmed with the sensation of Ship. The sleeping Etrepas, Lieutenant Ekalu half awake, happy and for once utterly relaxed—Seivarden in the bath, singing to herself, *my mother said it all goes around*, her Amaats, Medic, and my Kalrs, all in one jumbled, inundating moment. Then it was gone—I couldn't hold it, not with only one body, one brain.

I had thought that the pain of losing myself, of losing Lieutenant Awn, had—not healed, exactly, I didn't think it would ever do that—but that it had receded to a tolerable, dull ache. But just seeing Basnaaid Elming had thrown me off-balance, and I had not handled it well. And had, as a result, not handled Lieutenant Tisarwat well, just now. I knew about the emotional upheavals of seventeen-year-old lieutenants. Had dealt with them in the past. And whatever Tisarwat had been, whoever she turned out to be, however ancient her memories or her sense of herself, her body was still seventeen, her reactions today very much those of someone in the last throes of adolescence. I had seen it, known it for what it was, and I ought to have responded more reasonably. "Ship," I said, silently, "was I smug when I thought I'd sorted out Seivarden and Ekalu?"

"Maybe just the tiniest bit, Fleet Captain."

"Sir," said Kalr Five, who had come into the anteroom, all ancillary-like impassivity, "Captain Hetnys is in the dining room." And did not add, *she's fretting, and beginning to be angry at being made to wait so long.*

"Thank you, Five." Despite my permission earlier to go in shirtsleeves here in the Undergarden, she was still in her jacket. All my Mercy of Kalrs were, I saw, querying Ship. "You've offered her breakfast and tea?"

"Yes, sir. She said she didn't want anything." A trace of disappointment there—no doubt she felt deprived of an opportunity to show off her dishes.

"Right. I'll go in, then." I took a breath, did my best to clear both Basnaaid and Tisarwat from my mind, and went in to receive Captain Hetnys's report.

10

Captain Hetnys had sent *Mercy of Ilves* on a survey of the outstations. She'd brought a few of her Atagaris ancillaries with her to Athoek Station, and her Var lieutenant and decade to run Security for the Undergarden.

She tried to explain to me why she'd set *Sword of Atagaris* to watch a gate that led to a system of airless rocks, gas giants with icy moons, no inhabitants, and no other gates.

"The Presger can travel without the gates, sir, they might..."

"Captain. If the Presger decide to attack us, there will be nothing we can do about it." The days when the Radch had commanded fleets huge enough to overwhelm entire systems were past. And even then, opposing the Presger would have been hopeless. It was the main reason Anaander Mianaai had finally agreed to a treaty. It was the reason people were still frightened of them. "And honestly, Captain, the biggest danger, for now, is going to be from Radchaai ships on one side or the other attempting to control or destroy resources another side might use. That planet downwell, for instance."

All that food. A base, if they could secure it. If *I* could. "And it's possible Athoek will be left alone entirely. Certainly I don't think anyone's going to be able to muster anything like a real fleet, not for some time, if ever." I didn't think anyone could surprise us. A military ship *could* gate to within kilometers of the station or the planet, but I didn't think it likely any would try. If someone came, we'd have time to watch them approach. "We should concentrate our defenses around this station, and this planet."

She didn't like that, thought of an argument, but closed her mouth on it, unsaid. The question of where my authority came from, of where Captain Hetnys's loyalties lay in this conflict, didn't come up at all. There was no point pressing the issue, no advantage for me, or for her. If I was lucky, everyone else would ignore Athoek and it would never be an issue. But I wasn't going to bet on that.

Once Captain Hetnys had gone, I thought for a bit about what to do next. Meet with Governor Giarod, probably, and find out what, besides medical supplies, might come up short in the near future, and what we might do about that. Find something to keep *Sword of Atagaris* and *Mercy of Phey* busy—and out of trouble—but also ready to respond if I needed them. I sent a query to *Mercy of Kalr*. Lieutenant Tisarwat was above, on level two of the Undergarden, in a wide, shadowed room irregularly illuminated by light panels leaning here and there against the dark walls. Tisarwat, Raughd Denche, and half a dozen others reclined on long, thick cushions, the daughters, Ship indicated, of tea growers and station officials. They were drinking something strong and stinging—Tisarwat hadn't decided if she liked it or not, but she seemed to be mostly enjoying herself. Piat, the daughter of the station administrator, a bit more animated than I'd seen her the evening before, had just said something vulgar and everyone was laughing. Raughd said, in an undertone that can't have carried much past Tisarwat, who was sitting near both of them, "Aatr's tits, Piat, you're such a fucking ridiculous bore sometimes."

Tisarwat, where only Ship and I could see it, reacted with instant revulsion. "Piat," she said, "I don't think Citizen Raughd appreciates you. Come sit closer, I need someone to tell me amusing things."

The whole exchange, plus Piat's hesitation and Raughd's ostensibly amused reply—*I was only joking, Lieutenant, don't be so sensitive!*—told me unpleasant things about their relationship. If they had been my officers, when I had been a ship, I'd have intervened in some way, or spoken to their senior lieutenant. I wondered for an instant at Station's apparently not having done anything, and then it occurred to me that Raughd had perhaps been very, very careful about where she said what. Station couldn't see into the Undergarden, and though everyone in that room was certainly wired for communications, they had probably switched their implants off. That was very possibly the whole purpose of carousing here rather than elsewhere.

Below, in my own quarters, Kalr Five spoke. "Sir." Trepidation behind her stolid exterior.

"It's all right," called an unfamiliar voice from behind her, in the next room. "I'm all grown up, I'm not going to eat anyone!" The accent was an odd one, half well-educated Radchaai and half something else I couldn't place, nothing like the accents I'd heard here so far.

"Sir," Kalr Five said again. "Translator Dlique." She stumbled slightly over the oddness of the name.

"Translator?" No one had mentioned that anyone from the Translators Office was in the system, and there was no reason why anyone should be. I queried Ship and saw its memory of Kalr Five opening the door to a person in the loose, bright shirt and trousers people in the Undergarden wore—gloved, though, plain, stiff gray. No jewelry. No mention of a house name or of the division of the Translators Office she worked for, no hint of family affiliation or rank. I blinked the vision away. Rose. "Send her in."

Five stood aside, and Translator Dlique entered, smiling broadly. "Fleet Captain! How glad I am to see you. The governor's residence is *terribly* boring. I'd much rather have stayed on my ship, but they said there was a hull breach and if I stayed I wouldn't be able to breathe. I don't know, it doesn't seem like much, does it? Breathing?" She took a deep breath, gestured irritated indecision. "Air! It's just stupid, really. I'd as soon do without, but they insisted."

"Translator." I didn't bow, as she had not. And a horrible suspicion occurred. "It would appear you have the advantage of me."

She drew her shoulders up, her eyes widening in astonishment. "Me! The advantage! *You're* the one with all the soldiers."

The suspicion was growing into a certainty. This person certainly wasn't Radchaai. Translator for one of the aliens the Radch dealt with, then. But not for the Geck or the Rrrrr—I'd met translators for the Geck before, and I knew something about the humans who translated for the Rrrrr, and this person didn't seem to be either sort. And that odd accent. "I mean," I said, "that you appear to know who I am, but I don't know who you are."

She outright laughed. "Well, of course I know who *you*

are. Everyone is talking about you. Well, not to *me*. I'm not supposed to know you're here. I'm not supposed to leave the governor's residence, either. But I don't like being bored."

"I think you should tell me who you are, exactly." But I knew. Or knew as much as I needed to know. This person was one of those humans the Presger had bred to talk to the Radch. Translator for the Presger. *Disturbing company*, Anaander Mianaai had said of them. And the governor knew she was on the station. So, I would bet, did Captain Hetnys. This was surely behind her so inexplicable fear that the Presger might arrive here suddenly. I wondered what was behind the fact that she hadn't mentioned it to me.

"Who I am? *Exactly?*" Translator Dlique frowned. "I'm not...that is, I said just now I was Dlique but I might not be, I might be Zeiat. Or wait, no. No, I'm pretty sure I'm Dlique. I'm pretty sure they told me I was Dlique. Oh! I'm supposed to introduce myself, aren't I." She bowed. "Fleet Captain, I'm Dlique, translator for the Presger. Honored to make your acquaintance. Now, I think, you say something like *the honor's all mine* and then you offer me tea. I'm bored of tea, though, do you have arrack?"

I sent a quick silent message to Five, and then gestured Translator Dlique to a seat—an improbably comfortable arrangement of boxes and cushions covered with a yellow and pink embroidered blanket. "So," I said, when I'd sat across from her on my own pile of blanket-covered luggage. "You're a diplomat, are you?"

All her expressions so far had been almost childlike, seemingly completely unmoderated. Now she showed frank dismay. "I've made a hash of it, haven't I. It was all supposed to be so simple, too. I was on my way home from Tstur Palace after attending the New Year Cast. I went to parties,

145

and smiled, and said, *the omens' fall was very propitious, the coming year will bring Justice and Benefit to all*. After a while I thanked the Humans for their hospitality and left. Just like I was supposed to. All very boring, no one who's anyone has to do it."

"And then a gate went down, and you were rerouted. And now you can't get home." With things the way they were, she'd never make it to Presger space. Not unless she had a ship that could generate its own gate—which the agreement between humans and the Presger had very specifically, very deliberately, forbidden the Presger to bring within Radch space.

Translator Dlique threw up her incongruously gray-gloved hands, a gesture, I thought, of exasperation. *Say exactly what we told you to and nothing will go wrong*, they said. Well, it all went wrong anyway. And they didn't say anything about *this*. You'd think they might have, they said lots of other things. *Sit up straight, Dlique. Don't dismember your sister, Dlique, it isn't* nice. *Internal organs belong* inside *your body, Dlique*." She scowled a moment, as though that last one particularly rankled.

"There does seem to be a general agreement that you are, in fact, Dlique," I said.

"You'd think! But it doesn't work like that when you aren't anybody. Oh!" She looked up as Kalr Five entered with two cups and a bottle of arrack. "That's the good stuff!" She took the cup Five handed her. Peered intently into Five's face. "Why are you pretending you're not Human?"

Five, in the grip of an offended horror so intense even she couldn't have spoken without betraying it, didn't answer, only turned to give me my own cup. I took it, and said, calmly, "Don't be rude to my soldiers, Dlique."

Translator Dlique laughed, as though I'd said something quite funny. "I like you, Fleet Captain. With Governor Giarod and Captain Hetnys, it's all *what is your purpose in coming here, Translator,* and *what are your intentions, Translator,* and *do you expect us to* believe *that, Translator.* And then it's *You'll find these rooms very comfortable, Translator; the doors are locked for your own safety, Translator; have some more tea, Translator.* Not Dlique, you see?" She took a substantial swallow of arrack. Coughed a little as it went down.

I wondered how long it would be before the governor's staff realized Translator Dlique was missing. Wondered for only a moment why Station hadn't raised the alarm. But then I remembered that gun, that no ship or station could see, that had come from the Presger. Translator Dlique might seem scatterbrained and childlike. But she was certainly as dangerous as Governor Giarod and Captain Hetnys feared. Likely considerably more so. They had, it seemed, underestimated her. Perhaps by her design. "What about the others on your ship?"

"Others?"

"Crew? Staff? Fellow passengers?"

"It's a *very* small ship, Fleet Captain."

"It must have been crowded, then, with Zeiat and the translator along."

Translator Dlique grinned. "I *knew* we'd get on well. Give me supper, will you? I just eat regular food, you know."

I recalled what she'd said when she'd first arrived. "Did you eat many people before you were grown?"

"No one I wasn't *supposed* to! Though," she added, frowning, "sometimes I kind of wish I *had* eaten someone I wasn't supposed to. But it's too late now. What are you having for supper? Radchaai on stations eat an awful lot of fish, it seems. I'm beginning to be bored of fish. Oh, where's your bathroom? I have to—

I cut her off. "We don't really have one. No plumbing here. But we do have a bucket."

"Now *that's* something different! I'm not bored of buckets yet!"

Lieutenant Tisarwat staggered into the room just as Five was clearing away the last supper dish and Translator Dlique was saying, very earnestly, "Eggs are so inadequate, don't you think? I mean, they ought to be able to become *anything*, but instead you always get a chicken. Or a duck. Or whatever they're programmed to be. You never get anything interesting, like regret, or the middle of the night last week." The entire dinner conversation had been like that.

"You raise a good point, Translator," I replied, and then turned my attention to Lieutenant Tisarwat. It had been more than three hours since I'd thought much about her, and she'd drunk a considerable amount in that time. She swayed, looked at me, glaring. "Raughd Denche," Tisarwat said to me, raising a hand and pointing somewhere off to the side for emphasis. She did not seem to notice the presence of Translator Dlique, who watched with an expression of slightly frowning curiosity. "Raughd. Denche. Is a *horrible person*."

Judging from even the very small bit I'd seen of Citizen Raughd today, I suspected Tisarwat's assessment was an accurate one.

"*Sir*," Tisarwat added. Very belatedly.

"Bo," I said sharply to the soldier who had come in behind her, who hovered anxiously. "Get your lieutenant out of here before there's a mess." Bo took her by the arm, led her unsteadily out. Too late, I feared.

"I don't think she's going to make it to the bucket," said Translator Dlique, solemnly. Almost regretfully.

"I don't, either," I said. "But it was worth a try."

That a Presger translator was here on Athoek Station was problem enough. How long would it be before whoever had sent her began to wonder why she hadn't returned? How would they react to Athoek having essentially made her a prisoner, even if somewhat unsuccessfully? And what would happen when they found the Radch in such disarray? Possibly nothing—the treaty made no distinctions between one sort of human or another, all were covered, and that same treaty forbade the Presger to harm any of those humans. That left open the question of what, to a Presger, would constitute "harm," but presumably issues like that had been hammered out between the translators of the Radch and those of the Presger.

And the presence and attention of the Presger might be turned to advantage. In the past hundred years or so the Presger had begun to sell high-quality medical correctives, significantly cheaper than the ones made inside the Radch. Governor Giarod had said Athoek didn't make its own medical supplies. And the Presger wouldn't care if Athoek was part of the Radch or not. They would only care if Athoek could pay, and while the Presger idea of "pay" could be somewhat eccentric, I didn't doubt we could find something suitable.

So why had the system governor locked Translator Dlique in the governor's residence? And then said nothing to me about it? I could imagine Captain Hetnys doing such a thing—she had known Captain Vel, who had believed that Anaander Mianaai's current fractured state was a result of Presger infiltration. I was fairly sure Translator Dlique's arrival here was a coincidence—but coincidences were meaningful, to Radchaai. Amaat was the universe, and anything that happened, happened because Amaat willed it. God's intentions could be discerned by the careful study of even the smallest, most seemingly insignificant events. And the past weeks' events were anything but small and insignificant. Captain Hetnys would be alert for strange occurrences, and this one would have set off a multitude of alarms for her. No, her concealment of Translator Dlique's presence only confirmed what I had already suspected about the captain's position.

But Governor Giarod. I had come away from dinner at Citizen Fosyf's, and the meeting after in the governor's office, with the impression that Governor Giarod was not only an intelligent, able person, but also that she understood that Anaander Mianaai's current conflict with herself originated in herself, and not anywhere else. I didn't think I could possibly have misjudged her so badly. But clearly I had missed something, didn't understand something about her position.

"Station," I transmitted, silently.

"Yes, Fleet Captain," replied Station, in my ear.

"Kindly let Governor Giarod know I intend to call on her first thing in the morning." Nothing else. If Station didn't know I knew about Translator Dlique's existence, let alone that she'd had dinner with me and then gone off again, my mentioning it would only panic Governor Giarod and Captain Hetnys. In the meantime I would have to try to find some way to handle this suddenly even more complicated situation.

On *Mercy of Kalr*, Seivarden sat in Command. Talking with *Sword of Atagaris*'s Amaat lieutenant, also apparently on watch on her own ship. "So," she was saying, Ship sending her words directly into Seivarden's ear. "Where are you from?"

"Someplace we don't fuck around while we're on watch," Seivarden said, but silently, to Ship. Aloud, she said, "Inais."

"Really!" It was plain that the *Sword of Atagaris* lieutenant had never heard of it. Which was hardly surprising, given the extent of Radch space, but didn't help Seivarden's already low estimation of her. "Have all your officers changed? Your predecessor was all right." Ekalu (at that moment asleep, breathing deep and even) had painted the former *Mercy of Kalr* Amaat lieutenant as an unbearable snob. "But that medic wasn't very friendly at all. Thought quite a lot of herself, I'd say." (Medic sat in *Mercy of Kalr*'s decade room, frowning at her lunch of skel and tea. Calm, in a fairly good mood.)

In many ways, Seivarden had in her youth been just as unbearable as the former *Mercy of Kalr* Amaat lieutenant. But Seivarden had served on a troop carrier—which meant she'd spent actual time in combat, and knew what counted when it came to doctors. "Shouldn't you be looking out for enemy ships?"

"Oh, Ship will tell me if it sees anything," said the *Sword of Atagaris* lieutenant, breezily. "That fleet captain is very intimidating. Though I suppose she would be. She's ordered us closer to the station. So we'll be neighbors, at least for a bit. We should have tea."

"Fleet captain is a bit less intimidating when you're not threatening to destroy her ship."

"Oh, well. That was a misunderstanding. Once you identified yourselves everything was cleared up. You don't think she'll hold it against me, though, do you?"

On Athoek Station, in the Undergarden, Kalr Five put away dishes in the room next to where I sat, and fussed to Eight about Translator Dlique's sudden, discomfiting appearance.

In another room yet, Bo pulled off an unconscious Tisarwat's boots. I said, to Ship, "Ekalu wasn't exaggerating, about *Sword of Atagaris*'s Amaat lieutenant."

"No," *Mercy of Kalr* replied. "She wasn't."

Next morning, I was dressing—trousers on, still bootless, fastening my shirt—when I heard an urgent shouting from the corridor, a voice calling, "Fleet Captain! Fleet Captain, sir!" Ship showed me, through the Kalr standing watch in the corridor, a seven- or eight-year-old child in grubby loose shirt and trousers, no shoes or gloves. "Fleet Captain!" she shouted, insistent. Ignoring the guard.

I grabbed my gloves, went quickly out of my room to the antechamber, through the door Five opened for me at my gesture. "Fleet Captain, sir!" the child said, still loud though I was standing in front of her. "Come right away! Someone painted on the wall again! If those corpse soldiers see it first it'll be *bad*!"

"Citizen," began Five.

I cut her off. "I'm coming." The child took off running, and I headed down the shadowed corridor after her. *Someone painted on the wall again*. Minor enough. Small enough to ignore, one might think, but Captain Hetnys had overreacted before—how badly clear to read in this child's urgency, either her own conclusions about what might happen when *Sword of Atagaris* Var arrived, or conveyed to her by some adult who'd sent her as messenger. Serious enough. And if it turned out to be nothing, well, I would only have delayed my breakfast by a few minutes.

"What did they paint?" I asked, climbing up a ladder in an access well, the only way between levels here.

"Some kind of words," the child replied, above me. "It's *words*!"

So she either hadn't seen them or couldn't read them, and I guessed it was the second. Probably not Radchaai then, or Raswar, which I'd learned over the past two days was read and spoken by most of the Ychana here. Station had told me, my first night here, when I'd asked it for some information, some history, that most of the residents in the Undergarden were Ychana.

It was Xhi, though rendered phonetically in Radchaai script. Whoever had done it had used the same pink paint that had been used to decorate the tea shop door, that had been left sitting at the side of the small, makeshift concourse. I recognized the words, not because I knew more than a few phrases of Xhi at this point but because it dated from the annexation, had been emblematic of a particular resistance movement Station had told me about, two nights before. *Not tea but blood!* It was a play on words. The Radchaai word for "tea" bore a passing resemblance to the Xhi word for "blood," and the implication was that the revolutionaries, rather than submitting to the Radch and drinking tea, would resist and drink (or at least spill) Radchaai blood. Those revolutionaries were several hundred years dead, that clever slogan no more than trivia in a history lesson.

The child, having seen me stop in front of the paint, not far from the tea shop entrance, took off running again, eager to be safely away. The rest of the Undergarden's residents had done the same—the small concourse was deserted, though I knew that at this hour there should be if nothing else a steady stream of customers into the tea shop. Anyone passing this way had taken one look at that *Not tea but blood!* and turned right around to find somewhere safe and out of the way of *Sword of Atagaris*'s Var lieutenant and her ancillaries. I was alone, Kalr Five still climbing up the access well, having been a good deal slower than I was.

A now-familiar voice spoke behind me. "That vomiting, purple-eyed child was right." I turned. Translator Dlique, dressed as she had been last night, when she'd visited me.

"Right about what, Translator?" I asked.

"Raughd Denche really *is* a horrible person."

At that moment, two *Sword of Atagaris* ancillaries came rushing onto the concourse. "You, there, halt!" said one, loud and emphatic. I realized, in that instant, that they might very well not recognize Translator Dlique—she was supposed to be locked in the governor's residence, she was dressed like an Ychana, and like all of the Undergarden this space was erratically lit. I myself wasn't in full uniform, wore only trousers, gloves, and partially fastened shirt. It was going to take *Sword of Atagaris* a moment to realize who we were.

"Oh, *sporocarps*!" Translator Dlique turned, I assumed to flee before *Sword of Atagaris* could see who she was and detain her.

She had not turned all the way, and I had only had the briefest moment to begin wondering at her using "sporocarp" as an obscenity, when a single gunshot popped, loud in the confined space, and Translator Dlique gasped, and tumbled forward to the ground. Unthinking, I raised my armor, yelled "*Sword of Atagaris*, stand down!" At the same moment I transmitted to Station, urgently, "Medical emergency on level one of the Undergarden!" Dropped to my knees beside Translator Dlique. "Station, Translator Dlique's been shot in the back. I need medics here *right now*."

"Fleet Captain," said Station's calm voice in my ear. "Medics don't go to the—"

"*Right now*, Station." I dropped my armor, looked up at the two *Sword of Atagaris* Vars, beside me now. "Your medkit, Ship, quickly." I wanted to ask, *What do you think you're doing, firing on people?* But keeping Translator Dlique from bleeding out was more immediately important. And this wouldn't be entirely *Sword of Atagaris*'s fault, it would have been following Captain Hetnys's orders.

"I'm not carrying medkits, Fleet Captain," said one of the *Sword of Atagaris* ancillaries. "This is not a combat situation, and this station does have medical facilities." And I, of course, didn't have one. We'd brought them, as a matter of routine, but they were still in a packing case three levels down. If the bullet had hit, say, the translator's renal artery—a distinct possibility, considering where the wound was—she could bleed out in minutes, and even if I ordered one of my Kalrs to bring me a kit, it would arrive too late.

I sent the order anyway, and pressed my hands over the wound on Translator Dlique's back. Likely it wouldn't do any good, but it was the only thing I *could* do. "Station, I need those medics!" I looked up at *Sword of Atagaris*. "Bring me a suspension pod. *Now*."

"Aren't any around here." The tea shop proprietor—she must have been the only person who'd stayed nearby when they'd seen that slogan painted on the wall. Now she called out from the door of her shop. "Medical never comes here, either."

"They'd better come this time." My compression had reduced the blood coming out of the translator, but I couldn't control internal bleeding, and her breathing had gone quick and shallow. She was losing blood fast, then, faster than I could see. Down on level three Kalr Eight was opening the case where the medkits were stored. She'd moved the instant the order had come, was working quickly, but I didn't think she would be here in time.

I still pressed uselessly on the translator's back, while she lay gasping on the ground, facedown. "Blood stays *inside* your arteries, Dlique," I said.

She gave a weak, shaky *hah*. "See..." She paused for a few shallow breaths. "Breathing. Stupid."

"Yes," I said, "yes, breathing is stupid and boring, but keep on doing it, Dlique. As a favor to me." She didn't answer.

By the time Kalr Eight arrived with a medkit and Captain Hetnys came running onto the scene, a pair of medics behind her and *Sword of Atagaris* behind them, dragging an emergency suspension pod, it was too late. Translator Dlique was dead.

11

I knelt on the ground beside Translator Dlique's body. Blood soaked my bare feet, my knees, my hands, still pressing down on the wound on her back, and the cuffs of my shirtsleeves were wet with it. It was not the first time I had been covered in someone else's blood. I had no horror of it. The two *Sword of Atagaris* ancillaries were motionless and impassive, having set down the suspension pod they had dragged this far to no purpose. Captain Hetnys stood frowning, puzzled, not quite sure, I thought, of what had just happened.

I rose to make way for the medics, who went immediately to work on Translator Dlique. "Cit...Fleet Captain," said one of them after a while. "I'm sorry, there's nothing we can do."

"Never is," said the proprietor of the tea shop, who was still standing in her doorway. *Not tea but blood!* scrawled only meters away from where she stood. That was a problem. But not, I suspected, the problem Captain Hetnys thought it was.

I peeled off my gloves. Blood had soaked through them,

my hands were sticky with it. I stepped quickly over to Captain Hetnys faster than she could back away and grabbed her uniform jacket with my bloody hands. Dragged her stumbling over to where Translator Dlique lay, the two medics scrambling out of our way, and before Captain Hetnys could regain her balance or resist, I threw her down onto the corpse. I turned to Kalr Eight. "Fetch a priest," I said to her. "Whoever you find who's qualified to do purifications and funerals. If she says she won't come to the Undergarden, inform her that she may come willingly or not, but she will come regardless."

"Sir," Eight acknowledged, and departed.

Captain Hetnys had meanwhile managed to get to her feet, with the assistance of one of her ancillaries.

"How did this happen, Captain? I said not to use violence against citizens unless it was absolutely necessary." Translator Dlique wasn't a citizen, but *Sword of Atagaris* couldn't have known it was the translator they were shooting at.

"Sir," said Captain Hetnys. Voice shaking either with rage at what I'd just done, or distress generally. "*Sword of Atagaris* queried Station, and it said it had no knowledge of this person and there was no tracker. She was not, therefore, a citizen."

"So that made it fine to shoot her, did it?" I asked. But of course, I myself had followed exactly that logic on a nearly uncountable number of occasions. It was such compelling logic, to someone like *Sword of Atagaris*—to someone like me—that it had never occurred to me that *Sword of Atagaris* would even think of firing guns here, on a station full of citizens, a station that had been part of the Radch for centuries.

It should have occurred to me. I was responsible for everything that happened under my command.

"Fleet Captain," replied Captain Hetnys, indignant and not trying as hard as she might have to hide it. "Unauthorized persons pose a danger to—"

"This," I said, each word deliberate, emphatic, "is Presger Translator Dlique."

"Fleet Captain," said Station, in my ear. I had left the connection to Station open, so it had heard what I had said. "With all respect, you are mistaken. Translator Dlique is still in her rooms in the governor's residence."

"Look again, Station. *Send* someone to look. Captain Hetnys, neither you nor any of your crew or ancillaries will go armed on this station under any circumstances, beginning now. Nor will your ship or any of your crew enter the Undergarden again without my explicit permission. *Sword of Atagaris* Var and its lieutenant will return to *Sword of Atagaris* as soon as a shuttle can take them. Do not"—she had opened her mouth to protest—"say a single word to me. You have deliberately concealed vital information from me. You have endangered the lives of residents of this station. Your troops have caused the death of the diplomatic representative of the Presger. I am trying to think of some reason why I shouldn't shoot you where you stand." Actually, there were at least three compelling reasons—the two armed ancillaries standing beside Captain Hetnys and the fact that in my haste I had left my own gun behind in my quarters, three levels below this one.

I turned to the proprietor of the tea shop. "Citizen." It took extra effort not to speak in my flat, ancillary's voice. "Will you bring me tea? I've had no breakfast, and I'm going to have to fast today." Wordlessly, she turned and went into her shop.

While I waited for tea, Governor Giarod arrived. Took one

look at Translator Dlique's body, at Captain Hetnys standing mute and blood-smeared by *Sword of Atagaris*'s ancillaries, took a breath, and then said, "Fleet Captain. I can explain."

I looked at her. Then turned to see the tea shop proprietor set a bowl of tea-gruel on the ground a meter from where I stood. I thanked her, went to pick it up. Saw revulsion on the face of Captain Hetnys and Governor Giarod as I held it with bare, bloody hands and drank from it. "This is how it will be," I said, after I'd drunk half of the thick tea. "There will be a funeral. Don't speak to me of keeping this secret, or of panic in the corridors. There will be a funeral, with offerings and suitable tokens, and a period of mourning for every member of Station Administration. The body will be kept in suspension so that when the Presger come for the translator, they may take it and do whatever it is they do with dead bodies.

"For the moment, *Sword of Atagaris* will tell me the last time it saw this wall free of paint, and then Station will name for me every person who stopped in front of it from then until I saw it just now." Station might not have been able to see if someone was painting, but it would know where everyone was, and I suspected very few people would have stood right next to this wall, in that window of time, who had not been the painter herself.

"Begging the fleet captain's very great indulgence." Captain Hetnys dared, against all wisdom, to speak to me. "That's already done, and Security has arrested the person responsible."

I raised an eyebrow. Surprised. And skeptical. "Security has arrested Raughd Denche?"

Now Captain Hetnys was astonished. "No, sir!" she protested. "I don't know why you would assume Citizen Raughd would do something like this. No, sir, it can only have been Sirix Odela. She passed here on her way to work this morning and stopped quite close to the wall for some fifteen seconds. More than enough time to paint this."

If she passed by on her way to work, she lived in the Under-garden. Most of the Undergarden residents were Ychana, but this name was Samirend. And familiar. "This person works in the Gardens, above?" I asked. Captain Hetnys gestured assent. I thought of the person I'd met when I'd first arrived. Who I had found standing in the lake in the Gardens, so distressed at the thought of expressing anger. It wasn't possible she had done this. "Why would a Samirend paint a Xhi slogan in Radchaai script? Why wouldn't she write it in Liost since she's Samirend, or Raswar, that more people here could read?"

"Historically, Fleet Captain—" began Governor Giarod.

I cut her off. "*Historically*, Governor, quite a lot of people have good reason to resent the annexation. But right here, right now, none of them will find any profit in more than token rebellion." It would have been that way for several centuries. Nobody in the Undergarden who valued her life (not to mention the lives of anyone else in the Undergarden) would have painted that slogan on that wall, not knowing how this station's administration would react. And I'd be willing to bet that everyone in the Undergarden knew how this station's administration would react.

"The creation of the Undergarden was no doubt unintended," I continued, as *Mercy of Kalr* showed me a brief flash of Kalr Eight speaking sternly to a junior priest, "but as it has benefited you, you tell yourselves that its condition is also just and proper." That constant trio, justice, propriety, and benefit. They could not, in theory, exist alone. Nothing just was improper, nothing beneficial was unjust.

"Fleet Captain," began Governor Giarod. Indignant. "I hardly think—"

"Everything necessitates its opposite," I said, cutting her off. "How can you be civilized if there is no uncivilized?" Civilized. Radchaai. The word was the same. "If it did not benefit someone, somehow, there'd be plumbing here, and lights, and doors that worked, and medics who would come for an emergency." Before the system governor could do more than blink in response, I turned to the tea shop proprietor, still standing in her doorway. "Who sent for me?"

"Sirix," she said. "And see what it got her."

"Citizen," began Captain Hetnys, stern and indignant.

"Be silent, Captain." My tone was even, but Captain Hetnys said nothing further.

Radchaai soldiers who touch dead bodies dispose of their impurities by means of a bath and a brief prayer—I never knew any to bathe without muttering or subvocalizing it. I didn't, myself, but all my officers did, when I was a ship. I presumed civilian medics availed themselves of something similar.

That bath and that prayer sufficed, for anything short of making temple offerings. But with most Radchaai civilians, near contact with death was entirely another matter.

If I had been in a slightly more spiteful mood I would have gone deliberately around the small makeshift concourse, indeed around this entire level of the Undergarden, touching things and smearing blood so that what priests came would be forced to spend days on it. But I had never noticed that anyone profited from needless spite, and besides I suspected that the entire Undergarden was already in a dire state, as far as ritual uncleanness went. If Medical never came here, others had certainly died here before, and if priests would not come, then that impurity had certainly lingered. Assuming one subscribed to such beliefs, in any event. The Ychana probably didn't. Just one more reason to consider them foreign and not worth basic amenities every Radchaai supposedly took for granted.

A senior priest arrived, accompanied by two assistants. She stopped two meters from Translator Dlique's corpse in its puddle of blood, and stood staring at it and us with wide-eyed horror.

"How do they dispose of bodies here?" I asked no one in particular.

Governor Giarod answered. "They drag them into the corridors around the Undergarden and leave them."

"Disgusting," muttered Captain Hetnys.

"What else are they supposed to do?" I asked. "There's no facility here for dealing with dead bodies. Medical doesn't come here, and neither do priests." I looked at the senior priest. "Am I right?"

"No one is supposed to be here, Fleet Captain," she replied primly, and cast a glance at the governor.

"Indeed." I turned to Kalr Five, who had returned with the priests. "This suspension pod is functional?"

"Yes, sir."

"Then Captain Hetnys and I will put the translator in it. Then you"—indicating the priests with a gesture that my barehandedness made offensive—"will do what is necessary."

Captain Hetnys and I spent twenty minutes washing in blessed water, saying prayers, and being sprinkled with salt and fumigated with three kinds of incense. It did not dispense with all of our contamination, only mitigated it so that we could walk through corridors or be in a room without anyone needing to call a priest. The soldier's bath and prayer would have done as well. Better, in fact, strictly speaking, but it would not have satisfied most of the residents of Athoek Station.

"If I go into full, traditional mourning," Governor Giarod pointed out, when that was finished, and Captain Hetnys and I were dressed in clean clothes, "I won't be able to go into my office for two weeks. The same goes for the rest of Administration. I agree, though, Fleet Captain, someone should." As the rite had gone on, she had lost the harried expression she'd arrived with, and now seemed quite calm.

"Yes," I agreed, "you'll all have to be lesser cousins. Captain Hetnys and I will act as immediate family." Captain Hetnys looked none too pleased about that but was not in any position to protest. I dispatched Kalr Five to bring a razor so that Captain Hetnys and I could shave our heads for the funeral, and also to see a jeweler about memorial tokens.

"Now," I said to Governor Giarod, when Five was away and I'd sent Captain Hetnys to my quarters to prepare for the fast, "I need to know about Translator Dlique."

"Fleet Captain, I hardly think this is the best place..."

"I can't go to your office as I am." Not so obviously just after a death that put me in full mourning, when I should be fasting at home. The impropriety would be obvious, and this funeral had to be absolutely, utterly proper. "And there's no one near." The tea seller was inside her shop, out of view. The priests had fled as soon as they thought they could. The *Sword of Atagaris* ancillaries had left the Undergarden at my order. My two Mercy of Kalrs, standing nearby, didn't count. "And keeping things secret hasn't been a very good choice so far."

Governor Giarod gestured rueful resignation. "She arrived

with the first wave of rerouted ships." The ships that neighboring systems had sent here either in the hope that they could find a different route to their original destinations, now the gates they needed to traverse were down, or because their own facilities were overwhelmed. "Just her, in a tiny little one-person courier barely the size of a shuttle. I'm not sure how it could even carry as much air as she needed for the trip she said she was making. And the timing was just..." She gestured her frustration. "I couldn't send to the palace for advice. I cast omens. Privately. The results were disturbing."

"Of course." No Radchaai was immune to the suspicion of coincidence. Nothing happened by pure accident, no matter how small. Every event, therefore, was potentially a sign of God's intentions. Unusual coincidences could only be a particularly pointed divine message. "I understand your apprehension. I even, to a certain extent, understand your wanting to confine the translator and conceal her presence from most station residents. None of that troubles me. What does trouble me is your failure to mention this alarming and potentially dangerous situation to me."

Governor Giarod sighed. "Fleet Captain, I hear things. There's very little that's said on this station—and, frankly, most of the rest of the system—that I don't eventually become aware of. Ever since I took this office I've heard whispers about corruption from outside the Radch."

"I'm not surprised." It was a perennial complaint, that transportees from annexed worlds, and newly made citizens, brought uncivilized customs and attitudes that would undermine true civilization. I'd been hearing it myself for as long as I'd been alive—some two thousand years. The situation in the Undergarden would only add to those whispers, I was sure.

"Recently," said Governor Giarod, with a rueful smile, "Captain Hetnys has suggested that the Presger have been infiltrating high offices with the aim of destroying us. Presger translators being more or less indistinguishable from actual humans, and the Translators Office being in such frequent and close contact with them."

"Governor, did you actually hold any conversations with Translator Dlique?"

She gestured frustration. "I know what you intend to say, Fleet Captain. But then again, she apparently left a locked and guarded room in the governor's residence with no one the wiser, obtained clothes, and walked freely around this station without Station being aware of it. Yes, talking with her could be downright peculiar, and I'd never have mistaken her for a citizen. But she was clearly capable of a great deal more than she let on to us. Some of it rather frightening. And I had never thought the rumors were credible, that the Presger, who had left us alone since the treaty, who were so alien, would concern themselves with our affairs, when they never had before. But then Translator Dlique arrives so soon after gates start to go down, and we lose contact with Omaugh Palace, and..."

"And Captain Hetnys spoke of Presger infiltration of high offices. Of the highest office. And here I am, a cousin of Anaander Mianaai, and arriving with a story about the Lord of the Radch fighting with herself over the future of the Radch, and an official record that clearly did not match what I actually was. And suddenly you had trouble dismissing the previously incredible whispers about the Presger."

"Just so."

"Governor, do we agree that no matter what is happening elsewhere, the only thing it is possible or appropriate for us to do is secure the safety of the residents of this system? Whether there is a division within the Lord of Mianaai or not, that would be the only reasonable order you would expect from her?"

Governor Giarod thought about that for six seconds. "Yes. Yes, you're right. Except, Fleet Captain, if we have to buy medical supplies, that may well mean dealing with outside sources. Like the Presger."

"You see," I said, very, very evenly, "why it wasn't a particularly good idea to conceal Translator Dlique from me." She gestured acquiescence. "You're not a fool. Or I didn't think you were. I admit my discovery of Translator Dlique's presence has somewhat undermined my assurance on that score." She said nothing. "Now, before I officially begin the fast, there's other business that needs to be taken care of. I need to speak to Station Administrator Celar."

"About the Undergarden?" Governor Giarod guessed.

"Among other things."

In my sitting room on level four of the Undergarden, my Kalrs ordered to leave us to speak privately, I said to Tisarwat, "I'll have to spend the next two weeks in mourning. Which means I won't be able to do any work. Lieutenant Seivarden is of course in command of *Mercy of Kalr* during that time. And you will be in charge here in the household."

She had awakened miserably hungover. Tea and meds had begun to remedy that, but not entirely. "Yes, sir."

"Why did she leave this?"

Tisarwat blinked. Frowned. Then understood. "Sir. It's not a *big* problem. And it's useful to have somewhere you can... do things in secret." Indeed. Useful to any and all parts of the Lord of the Radch, but I didn't say that. She would already know it. "And really, you know, sir, the people here got on all right until Captain Hetnys showed up."

"Got on all right, did they? With no water, and no Medical to come in emergencies, and apparently nobody questioning Hetnys's methods here?" She looked down at her feet. Ashamed. Miserable.

Looked up. "They're getting water from *somewhere*, sir. They grow mushrooms. There's this dish that..."

"Lieutenant."

"Yes, sir."

"What was she going to do here?"

"Help you, sir. Mostly. Unless you were going to do anything that would prevent her from...reassembling herself once this was done." I didn't reply to this immediately, and she added, "She thinks that's likely, sir."

"This situation in the Undergarden needs fixing. I'm about to talk to the station administrator about it. Use your contacts—surely she sent you here with contacts—to get it done. Once the funeral is done, I'll be unable to do anything directly, but I *will* be watching you."

Tisarwat left, and Kalr Five ushered Station Administrator Celar into the sitting room. She wore the light blue of Administration today, managed to make the standard uniform look elegant on her broad and heavy form. I sat when she sat. Did not offer her tea, as would ordinarily have been polite. In my current state no one but my own household could eat or drink in my presence. "The situation in the Undergarden is intolerable," I said, with no preamble, no softening. No thanks for coming here at what was surely considerable inconvenience. "I am frankly astonished that it's been left this way for so long. But I am not asking for reasons or excuses. I expect repairs to begin immediately."

"Fleet Captain," said Station Administrator Celar, bristling at my words, though my tone had been calm and flat, "there's only so much that—"

"Then do that much. And don't tell me that no one is supposed to be here. Clearly people *are* here. And"—this was entering delicate territory—"I doubt very much any of this could have happened without at least some collusion from Station. I strongly suspect Station has been concealing things from you. You have a problem there, and it's of your own making." Station Administrator Celar frowned, not immediately understanding me. Offended. "I would urge you to look at this from Station's point of view. A not inconsiderable part of itself has been damaged. Restoring it entirely isn't possible, but no attempt has been made to even mitigate it. You just sealed it off and tried to forget it. But Station can't just forget it." And it struck me as likely that having people here felt better to Station than a numb, empty hole. And at the same time constantly reminded it of its injury. But I didn't think I could find a way to explain why, or how I'd come to that conclusion. "And the people who live here, they're Station's residents, who Station is made to care for. You don't treat them particularly well, though, and I imagine Station resents that. Though it can't ever say that directly to you, and so instead it just...leaves things out. Does and says exactly what you ask of it and very little more. I've met unhappy AIs." I didn't say how, or that I'd been an AI myself. "And you have one here."

"How can an AI be unhappy when it's doing exactly what it was made to do?" asked Station Administrator Celar. Not, thankfully, how it could possibly matter whether an AI was happy or not. And then, demonstrating that she had not been given her office merely on the strength of her looks, Station Administrator Celar said, "But you say we've prevented

Station from doing that. That is the substance of what you've said, yes?" She sighed. "When I arrived, my predecessor depicted the Undergarden as a morass of crime and squalor, that no one could find a way to safely clear out. Everything I saw seemed to indicate she was right. And it had been that way so long, fixing it seemed impossible. Everyone agreed it was so. But that's no excuse, is it. It's *my* responsibility."

"Repair the section doors," I said. "Fix the plumbing and the lights."

"And the ventilation," said Station Administrator Celar, fanning herself briefly with one blue-gloved hand.

I gestured agreement. "Confirm the current occupants in their places. Just for a start." Getting Medical here, and Security patrols that would not cause more problems than they might solve, would be next, and more difficult.

"Somehow, Fleet Captain, I don't think it could possibly be that simple."

Likely not. But. "I couldn't say. But we have to do something." I saw her notice that *we*. "And now I need to speak to you about your daughter Piat." Station Administrator Celar frowned in puzzlement. "She and Citizen Raughd are lovers?"

Still the frown. "They've been sweethearts since they were children. Raughd grew up downwell, and Piat often went down to visit, and keep her company. Not many other children Raughd's age in the family, at the time. Not in the mountains, anyway."

Downwell. Where Station couldn't see more than trackers. "You like Raughd," I said. "It's a good connection, and she's very charming, isn't she." Station Administrator Celar gestured assent. "Your daughter is very subdued. Doesn't talk to you much. Spends more time in other households than home with you. You feel, perhaps, she's driven you away."

"What are you aiming at, Fleet Captain?"

Even if Station had seen the way Raughd treated Piat when she thought no one was looking, it wouldn't have reported it directly. On a station, privacy was paradoxically both nonexistent and an urgent necessity. Station saw your most intimate moments. But you always knew Station would never tell just anyone what it saw, wouldn't *gossip*. Station would report crimes and emergencies, but for anything else it would, at most, hint here or guide there. A station household could be, in some ways, very self-contained, very secret, even though living at close quarters with so many others. Even though every moment it was under Station's constant, all-seeing eye.

The hints could often be enough. But if Station was unhappy, it might not even do that. "Raughd is only charming when she wants to be," I said. "When everyone is looking. In private, to certain people, she's very different. I'm going to ask my ship to send you a recording of something that happened here in the Undergarden last night."

Her fingers twitched, calling up the file. She blinked, her eyes moving in a way that told me she was watching that scene of Raughd, her daughter, others, reclining on those cushions, drinking. I saw on her face the moment she heard Citizen Raughd say, *You're such a fucking ridiculous bore.* The stunned disbelief, and then a look of determined anger as she kept watching, through Raughd's increasing aggression as Lieutenant Tisarwat, drunk as she was, tried to maneuver Piat out of Raughd's way. Station Administrator Celar gestured the recording away.

"Am I correct," I asked, before she could speak, "in guessing that Citizen Raughd never took the aptitudes? Because she was already Citizen Fosyf's heir?" Station Administrator Celar gestured *yes*. "The tester would almost certainly have seen the potential for this sort of thing, and routed her toward some sort of treatment, or an assignment where her personality would have been of benefit. Sometimes, combined with other things, it suits someone for a military career, and the discipline helps keep them in check and teaches them to behave better." Gods help the crew of such a person who was promoted to any position of authority without learning to behave better. "They can be very, very charming. No one ever suspects what they're like in private. Most won't believe it if you tell them."

"I wouldn't have," she admitted. "If you hadn't shown me..." She gestured forward, meaning to indicate the recording that had just played in her vision, in her ears.

"That's why I showed it to you," I said, "despite the impropriety of doing so."

"Nothing just can be improper," replied Station Administrator Celar.

"There's more, Station Administrator. As I said, Station has been keeping things back that you have not explicitly asked for. There was at least one occasion on which Citizen Piat reported to Medical with bruises on her face. She said she'd been drinking in the Undergarden and tripped and stumbled into a wall. The bruises didn't look like the right sort for that, not to my eye. Not to Medical's either, but they weren't about to get involved in any personal business of yours. I'm sure they thought if it was really a problem, Station would have said something." And no one else would have noticed. A corrective, a few hours, and the bruises would be gone. "There was no one around, at the time, except Raughd. I've seen this sort of thing before. Raughd will have apologized and sworn never to do it again. I strongly suggest asking Station explicitly about each and every visit your daughter has made to Medical, no matter how minor. I'd also ask Station about her use of first aid correctives. I queried Station directly, with the intention of finding this sort of incident, because I've seen this sort of thing before and knew it was almost certainly there. Station only answered me because System Governor Giarod ordered it, at my request."

Station Administrator Celar said nothing. She barely seemed to breathe. Maybe watching the record of her daughter's visit to Medical. Maybe not.

"So," I continued after a moment. "No doubt you're aware of the difficulty this morning that ended in the death of the Presger Translator Dlique."

She blinked, startled at the sudden change of topic. Frowned. "Fleet Captain, this morning was the first I'd heard the translator even existed, I assure you."

I waved that away. "Station was explicitly asked who had stood near that wall, in the right time frame, for long enough to paint those words. Station answered with two names: Sirix Odela and Raughd Denche. Security immediately arrested Citizen Sirix, on the assumption that Raughd wouldn't have done such a thing. But Station was not asked if either citizen had paint on her clothes. And since Station was not asked, it did not volunteer that information." I was not connected to Station at the moment, though I thought it very likely Station Administrator Celar was. "This is not something I think you should blame Station for. As I said earlier."

"Surely," said Station Administrator Celar, "it was a prank, something done for amusement. Youthful high spirits."

"What amusement," I asked, my own voice carefully even, "could youthful high spirits have anticipated? Watching *Sword of Atagaris* Var arrest completely innocent citizens? Putting those completely innocent citizens through interrogation to prove their innocence, or worse not interrogating them at all, convicting them without any evidence beyond *Raughd Denche could never have done that*? Further alarming you, and the governor, and Captain Hetnys at a time when things were already tense? And if, for the sake of argument, we pretend those are harmless amusements, then why has no one said of Citizen Sirix, *It's nothing, it must have been a prank?*" Silence. Her fingers twitched, just slightly, the station administrator speaking to Station no doubt. "There's paint on Citizen Raughd's gloves, isn't there?"

"Her personal attendant," acknowledged Station Administrator Celar, "is even now trying to wash the paint off of them."

"So," I said. This was going to be even more delicate than the problem with Station. "Citizen Fosyf is prominent, and wealthy. You have authority here, but it's just easier to get the things you want done when you have the support of people like Fosyf. And, no doubt, she gives you gifts. Valuable ones. The romance between your daughter and hers is convenient. When you sent Citizen Piat downwell to keep Raughd company, you were already thinking of this. And you might be wondering if you'd noticed that your daughter was unhappy. Or how long ago you'd first seen the signs of it, and maybe you told yourself that it was nothing, really, that everyone has to put up with a little stress, for the sake of family connections, family benefit. That if it was ever really bad, surely Station would say something. To you, of all people. And it's so easy to just go along. So easy not to see what's happening. And the longer you don't see it, the harder it becomes to *see* it, because then you have to admit that you ignored it all that time. But this is the moment when it's laid before you, clear and unambiguous. This is the sort of person Raughd Denche is. This is what she's doing to your daughter. Are her mother's gifts worth your daughter's well-being? Is political convenience worth that? Does the wider benefit to your house outweigh it? You can't put off the choice any longer. Can't pretend there's no choice there to make."

"You are very uncomfortable company, Fleet Captain," observed Station Administrator Celar, her voice bitter and sharp. "Do you do this sort of thing everywhere you go?"

"Lately it seems so," I admitted.

As I spoke, Kalr Five came silently into the room, and stood ancillary-stiff. Very clearly wanted my attention. "Yes, Five?" She wouldn't have interrupted without very good reason.

"Begging the fleet captain's indulgence, sir. Citizen Fosyf's personal attendant has inquired about the possibility of the citizen inviting you and Captain Hetnys to spend the two weeks after Translator Dlique's funeral on her estate downwell." Such an invitation was properly made in person—this sort of inquiry beforehand, through servants, prevented any inconvenience or embarrassment. "She has more than one house on her land, so you'll be able to spend the mourning period in proper fashion, very conveniently, she says."

I looked over at Station Administrator Celar, who gave a small laugh. "Yes, I thought it was odd, too, when I first came. But here at Athoek, if you can afford it, you don't spend your two weeks in your quarters." After the initial days of fasting, after the funeral, residents in a mourning household did no work, but instead stayed mostly at home, accepting consolatory visits from clients and friends. I'd assumed that Captain Hetnys and I would stay here in the Undergarden for that time. "If you're accustomed to have things done for you," Station Administrator Celar continued, "especially if you don't pick your meals up at the common refectories but rather have someone in your household cook for you, it can be a long two weeks. So you go to stay somewhere that's technically its own house, but servants nearby can cook and clean for you. There's a place right off the main concourse that specializes in it—but they're filled up right now with people who just need someplace to stay."

"And that's considered entirely proper, is it?" I asked doubtfully.

"There has been some suspicion," Celar replied wryly, "that my not being familiar with the practice when I arrived indicates that my upbringing wasn't what it might have been. *Your* not being familiar with it will be a shock they may never recover from."

I shouldn't have been surprised. I had known officers from nearly every province, had known that the details of funeral practice (among other things) could differ from place to place. Things widely considered mandatory were sometimes only actually available to citizens with sufficient resources, though that was rarely acknowledged. And beyond that, I knew that small details often went unmentioned, on the assumption that of course all Radchaai did things the same way and there was no need to discuss it. But I was used to those being fairly small details—what sort of incense was appropriate, prayers added to or subtracted from the daily observances, odd food restrictions.

I considered Five. She stood there outwardly impassive, but wanting me to see something, impatient I hadn't yet. Her announcement had, from her point of view, been heavy with suggestion. "It's customary to pay for such services?" I asked Station Administrator Celar.

"Often," she agreed, still with a wry smile. "Though I'm sure Fosyf is just being generous."

And self-serving. It would not surprise me if Fosyf had realized, one way or another, what part her own daughter had played in the episode that had led to Translator Dlique's death. Hoped, perhaps, that hosting me during the mourning period would be, if not a bribe, at least a gesture toward remorse for what her daughter had done. But it might well be useful. "Raughd could come downwell with us, of course," I observed. "And stay after. For quite some time."

"*I'll see to it*," said Station Administrator Celar, with a small, bitter smile that, had I been Raughd Denche, would have made me shiver.

12

Athoek's sky was a clear cerulean, shot here and there with bright streaks—the visible parts of the planet's weather control grid. For some hours we'd flown over water, blue-gray and flat, but now mountains loomed, brown and green below, black and gray and streaked with ice at their tops. "Another hour or so, Fleet Captain, Citizens," said the pilot. We had been met, at the base of the elevator, by two fliers. Between one thing and another—including maneuvering on the part of Kalr Five—Fosyf and Raughd had ended up in the other one, along with Captain Hetnys and the *Sword of Atagaris* ancillary who accompanied her. Both Captain Hetnys and I were in full mourning—the hair we'd shaved off barely beginning to grow back, no cosmetics but a broad white stripe painted diagonally across our faces. Once full mourning was over, Translator Dlique's memorial token would join Lieutenant Awn's plain gold tag on my jacket: a two-centimeter opal, *Translator Dlique Zeiat Presger* engraved large and clear on the silver setting. They were the only names we knew to use.

In the seat beside me, silent the entire trip so far—an impressive two days of not saying a word beyond the absolutely necessary—sat Sirix Odela. My request that she accompany me would leave the Gardens shorthanded, and theoretically she could have refused. Very little choice was actually involved. I guessed her anger had made her unable to speak without violating the terms of her reeducation, that attempting to do so would make her extremely uncomfortable, and so I did not press the issue, not even when it stretched into the second day.

"Fleet Captain," Sirix said. Finally. Voice pitched to reach my ear over the noise of the flier, but not carry up front to where the pilot sat. "Why am I here?" Her tone was very, very carefully controlled, a control I didn't doubt was hard-won.

"You are here," I said, in an even, reasonable voice, as though I was unaware of the resentment and distress behind the question, "to tell me what Citizen Fosyf *isn't* telling me."

"Why do you think I would be willing or able to tell you anything, Fleet Captain?" Sirix's voice took on just the slightest edge, skirting what she would be able to say without discomfort.

I turned my head to look at her. She stared straight ahead, as though my reaction didn't concern her at all. "Is there family you'd like to visit?" She'd come from downwell, had relatives who'd worked on tea plantations. "I'm sure I could arrange for it."

"I am..." She hesitated. Swallowed. I had pushed too hard, somehow. "Without family. For any practical purpose."

"Ah." She did have a house name, and so was not legally houseless. "Actually throwing you out of the family would have been too much disgrace for them to bear. But perhaps you're still in discreet contact with someone? A mother, a sibling?" And children generally had parents from more than one house. Parents or siblings from other houses might not be considered terribly close relatives, might or might not be required to lend any sort of support, but those ties were there, could be drawn on in a crisis.

"To be entirely honest, Fleet Captain," said Sirix, as though it was an answer to my question, "I really don't want to spend two weeks in the company of Citizen Raughd Denche."

"I don't think she realizes," I said. Citizen Raughd had been oblivious, or at least seemingly so. Oblivious to the seriousness of what she'd done, to the fact that anyone at all might be aware she'd done it. "Why do you live in the Undergarden, citizen?"

"I didn't like my assigned quarters. I think, Fleet Captain, that you appreciate directness."

I lifted an eyebrow. "It would be hypocritical of me not to."

She acknowledged that with a bitter quirk of her mouth. "I would like to be left alone now."

"Of course, Citizen. Please don't hesitate to tell me or either of my Kalrs"—Kalr Five and Kalr Eight sat behind us—"if you need anything." I turned forward again. Closed my eyes and thought of Lieutenant Tisarwat.

Who stood in the garden, on the bridge stretching across the lake. The fish roiled the water below her, purple and green, orange and blue, gold and red, gaping as Tisarwat dropped food pellets into the water. Celar's daughter Piat stood beside her, leaning on the rail. She had just said something that had surprised and dismayed Lieutenant Tisarwat. I didn't query, but waited to hear Tisarwat's answer.

"That's ridiculous," Tisarwat said, indignant. "First assistant to the chief of Horticulture of the entire station, that's not *nothing*. If it weren't for Horticulture no one on this station could eat or breathe. You don't seriously think you're doing some unimportant, useless job."

"What, making tea for the chief of Horticulture?"

"And managing her appointments, and communicating her orders, and learning how the Gardens are organized. I bet if she stayed home for the next week, no one would even notice, you'd have everything running smoothly as normal."

"That's because everyone else knows their jobs."

"You included." Devious Tisarwat! I'd told her to stay away from Basnaaid, which would mean staying away from the Gardens, but she knew well enough I had to approve of a friendship with Station Administrator Celar's daughter, if only on political grounds. But I couldn't find it in myself to be too angry—her horrified astonishment at Piat's dismissal of her own worth was obvious and sincere. And she'd clearly made short work of getting behind Piat's defenses.

Citizen Piat folded her arms, turned around, her back to the rail, face turned away from Tisarwat. "I'm only here because the chief of Horticulture is in love with my mother."

"Hardly surprising if she is," acknowledged Lieutenant Tisarwat. "Your mother is *gorgeous*." I was seeing through Tisarwat's eyes, so I couldn't see Piat's expression. I could guess, though. So could Tisarwat, I saw. "And frankly, you take after her. If someone's been telling you otherwise..." She stopped, unsure for a moment, I thought, if this was the best angle of attack. "Anyone who's been telling you that you've got a shiny-but-useless assignment just to keep your mother happy, or that you'll never be as beautiful or as competent as she is, well, they've been lying to you." She dropped the whole handful of fish pellets into the water, which boiled with bright-colored scales. "Probably jealous."

Piat scoffed, in a way that made it plain she was trying very hard not to cry. "Why would..." Stopped. About to say a name, perhaps, that she didn't want to say, that would be an accusation. "Why would anyone be jealous of *me*?"

"Because *you* took the aptitudes." I hadn't said anything to Lieutenant Tisarwat about my guess that Raughd had never taken them, but she clearly hadn't been the Lord of the Radch for a few days for nothing. "And the tests said you should be running something important. And anyone with eyes can see you're going to be just as beautiful as your mother." A moment of mortification at having said that *going to be*. And it wasn't quite the sort of thing a seventeen-year-old would say. "Once you stop listening to people who just want to drag you down."

Piat turned around, arms still crossed. Tears rolled down her face. "People get assignments for political reasons *all the time*."

"Sure," said Tisarwat. "Your mother probably got her first assignment for political reasons. Which probably included the fact that she could do the job." It didn't always—which Tisarwat well knew.

And that sounded dangerously like someone much older than Tisarwat ostensibly was. But Piat seemed unable to deflect it. She was driven to a last-ditch defense. "I've seen you mooning around the past few days. You're only here because you've got a crush on Horticulturist Basnaaid."

That scored a hit. But Lieutenant Tisarwat kept her outward composure. "I wouldn't even *be* here except for you. Fleet captain told me I was too young for her and stay away. It was an *order*. I ought to stay away from the Gardens, but *you're* here, aren't you. So let's go somewhere else and have a drink."

Piat was silent a moment, taken aback, it seemed. "Not the Undergarden," she said, finally.

"I should think not!" replied Tisarwat. Relieved, knowing she'd won this round, a minor victory but a victory all the same. "They haven't even started repairs there yet. Let's find somewhere we don't have to pee in a bucket."

By now *Sword of Atagaris* had moved away from the Ghost Gate, closer to Athoek Station. It had said almost nothing to *Mercy of Kalr* the whole time. Hardly surprising—ships generally weren't much given to chitchat, and besides, *Swords* all thought they were better than the others.

On *Mercy of Kalr* Lieutenant Ekalu had just come off watch, and Seivarden had met her in the decade room. "Your opposite number on *Sword of Atagaris* was asking after you," Ekalu said, and sat at the table, where an Etrepa had set her lunch.

Seivarden sat beside her. "Was she, now." She already knew, of course. "And was she glad to see someone she knew on board?"

"I don't think she recognized me," replied Ekalu, and after a moment's hesitation and a quick gesture from Seivarden, who'd had supper already, she took a mouthful of skel. Chewed and swallowed. "Not my name, anyway, I was only ever Amaat One to her. And I didn't send any visuals. I was on watch." Ekalu's feelings about that—about *Sword of Atagaris*'s Amaat lieutenant not realizing who she was—were complicated, and not entirely comfortable.

"Oh, I wish you had. I'd have loved to have seen her face."

I saw that while Ekalu herself might well have enjoyed the *Sword of Atagaris* lieutenant's discomfiture at being faced with an officer of such common origin, Seivarden's obvious amusement at the same prospect troubled and dismayed her. It reminded me a bit too painfully of some of Lieutenant Awn's interactions with Skaaiat Awer, twenty years gone and more. Ship said, in my ear, where I sat in the flier, "I'll say something to Lieutenant Seivarden." But I wasn't sure what Ship could say that Seivarden would understand.

In the *Mercy of Kalr* decade room, Ekalu said, "Expect her to contact you at the start of your next watch. She's determined to invite you over for tea, now *Sword of Atagaris* is going to be close enough."

"I can't be spared," Seivarden said, mock-serious. "There are only three watchstanders aboard right now."

"Oh, Ship will tell you if anything important happens," Ekalu said, all sarcastic disdain.

In Command, Medic said, "Lieutenants. Letting you know that something appears to have exited the Ghost Gate."

"What is it?" asked Seivarden, rising. Ekalu continued to eat, but called up a view of what Medic was looking at.

"It's too small to see well until it's closer," said Ship, to me, in the flier over Athoeki water. "I think it's a shuttle or a very small ship of some sort."

"We've asked *Sword of Atagaris* about it," Medic said, in Command.

"You mean they haven't threatened to destroy it unless it identifies itself?" asked Seivarden, halfway to Command herself by now.

"Nothing to worry about," came the reply from *Sword of Atagaris*, whichever of its lieutenants was on duty sounding almost overly bored. "It's just trash. The Ghost Gate doesn't get cleaned out like the others. Some ship must have broken up in the gate a long time ago."

"Your very great pardon," said Medic dryly as Seivarden

came into Command, "but we were under the impression there was no one on the other side of that gate, and never had been."

"Oh, people go there on a dare, sometimes, or just joyriding. But this one isn't recent, you can see it's pretty old. We'll pull it in—it's large enough to be a hazard."

"Why not just burn it?" asked Seivarden, and Ship must have sent her words to *Sword of Atagaris*, because that lieutenant replied, "Well, you know, there is some smuggling in the system. We always check these things out."

"And what are they smuggling out of an uninhabited system?" asked Medic.

"Oh, nothing out of the Ghost Gate, I should think," came the blithe answer. "But generally, you know, the usual. Illegal drugs. Stolen antiques."

"Aatr's tits!" swore Seivarden. "Speaking of antiques." Ship had asked *Sword of Atagaris* for a closer image of the object in question and, receiving it, had shown it to Medic and Seivarden both, a curving shell, scarred and scorched.

"Quite a piece of junk, isn't it?" replied the *Sword of Atagaris* lieutenant.

"Ignorant fuck," said Seivarden, after *Sword of Atagaris* had signed off. "What are they teaching in officer training these days?"

Medic turned to regard her. "Did I miss something, Lieutenant?"

"That's a supply locker off a Notai military shuttle," replied Seivarden. "You honestly don't recognize it?"

Radchaai often speak of the Radch as containing only one sort of people, who speak only one language—Radchaai. But the interior of a Dyson sphere is vast. Even if it had begun with a single population, speaking only one language (and it had not), it would not have ended that way. Many of the ships and captains that had opposed Anaander's expansion had been Notai.

"No," said Medic, "I don't recognize it. It doesn't look very Notai to me. It doesn't really look like a supply locker, either. It does look old, though."

"My house is Notai. Was." Seivarden's house had been absorbed by another one, during the thousand years she'd spent in suspension. "We were loyal, though. We had an old shuttle from the wars, docked at Inais. People used to come from all over to see it." The memory of it must have been unexpectedly specific and sharp. She swallowed, so that her sudden sense of loss wouldn't be audible when she spoke next. "How did a Notai ship break up in the Ghost Gate? None of those battles were anywhere near here."

In Seivarden's and Medic's vision, Ship displayed images of the sort of shuttle Seivarden was talking about. "Yes, like that," said Seivarden. "Show us the supply locker." Ship obliged.

"There's writing on it," said Medic.

"Seeing?" Seivarden frowned, puzzling out the words. "Seeing...something?"

"*Divine Essence of Perception*," said Ship. "One of the last defeated in the wars. It's a museum now."

"It doesn't look particularly Notai," said Medic. "Except for the writing."

"And the writing on this one," said Seivarden, gesturing into view the image of the one that had come out of the Ghost Gate, "is all burned away. Ship, did you really not recognize it?"

Ship said, to Medic and Seivarden both, "Not immediately. I'm a little less than a thousand years old and never have seen any Notai ships firsthand. But if Lieutenant Seivarden had not identified it herself, I would have within a few minutes."

"Would you have, ever," asked Medic, "if we trusted *Sword of Atagaris*?" And then, struck by a new thought, "Could *Sword of Atagaris* have failed to recognize it?"

"Probably it has," said Seivarden. "Otherwise, surely, it would tell its lieutenant."

"Unless they're both lying," said Ekalu, who had been listening in the whole time from the decade room. "They *are* taking the trouble to pick up a piece of debris that they might as well mark and let someone else take care of."

"In which case," remarked Seivarden, "they're assuming *Mercy of Kalr* won't recognize it. Which doesn't strike me as a safe assumption."

"I don't presume to know *Sword of Atagaris*'s opinion of my intelligence," said Ship.

Seivarden gave a small laugh. "Medic, ask *Sword of Atagaris* to tell us what they find when they examine that... debris."

Ultimately, *Sword of Atagaris* replied that it had found nothing of interest, and subsequently destroyed the locker.

Citizen Fosyf's house was the largest of three buildings, a long, balconied two-storied structure of polished stone, flecks of black and gray and here and there patches of blue and green that gleamed as the light changed. It sat beside a wide, clear lake with stony shores, and a weathered wooden dock, with a small, graceful boat moored alongside, white sails furled. Mountains loomed around, and moss and trees edged the lakeshore. The actual tea plantation—I'd seen it as we flew in, wavering strips of velvet-looking green running across the hillsides and around outcrops of black stone—was hidden behind a ridge. The air was 20.8 degrees C, the breeze light and pleasant and smelling of leaves and cold water.

"Here we are, Fleet Captain!" Citizen Fosyf called as she climbed out of her flier. "Peace and quiet. Under other circumstances I'd suggest fishing in the lake. Boating. Climbing if that's the sort of thing you like. But even just staying in is nice, here. There's a separate bathhouse behind the main building, just across from where you'll be staying. A big tub with seating for at least a dozen, plenty of hot water. It's a Xhai thing. Barbarically luxurious."

Raughd had come up beside her mother. "Drinks in the bathhouse! There's nothing like it after a long night." She grinned.

"Raughd can manage to find long nights even here," observed Fosyf pleasantly as Captain Hetnys and her *Sword of Atagaris* ancillary approached. "Ah, to be young again! But come, I'll show you where you'll be staying."

The patches of blue-green in the building stone flared and died away as our angle on it changed. Around the other side of the house was a broad stretch of flat, gray stones, shaded by two large trees and thickly grown with moss. To the left of that stretched the ellipse of a low building, the nearer long side of wood, the nearer end and, presumably, the farther long side of glass. "The bath," said Fosyf, with a gesture. On the other side of the mossy stone, up against a road that ran over the ridge and down to the house by the lake, sat another black and blue-green stone building, two-storied, but smaller than the main house and not balconied as it was. The whole side facing us was taken up with a terrace under a leafy, vine-tangled arbor, where a group of people stood waiting for us. Most of them wore shirts and trousers, or skirts that looked as though they'd been painstakingly constructed from cut-apart trousers, the fabric faded and worn, once-bright blues and greens and reds. None of them wore gloves.

Accompanying them was a person dressed in the expected, and conventional, jacket, trousers, and gloves and scattering of jewelry. By her features, I guessed she was a Samirend overseer here. We stopped some three meters from the group, in the shade of the wide arbor, and Fosyf said, "Just for you, Fleet Captain, since I knew you'd want to hear them sing."

The overseer turned away and said to the assembled people, "Here, now. Sing." In Radchaai. Slow and loud.

One of the elders of the group leaned toward the person next to her and said, in Delsig, "I told you it wasn't the right song." A few gestures and a few whispered words under the somewhat agitated eye of the overseer, who apparently didn't understand the reason for the delay, and then a collective breath and they began to sing. *"Oh you, who live sheltered by God, who live all your lives in her shadow."* I knew it, every line and every part. Most Delsig-speaking Valskaayans sang it at funerals.

It was a gesture meant to comfort. Even if they hadn't already known the reason for our coming, they could not have failed to notice my shaved head and the mourning stripe across my face, and Captain Hetnys's. These people didn't know us, quite possibly didn't know who had died. We represented the forces that had conquered them, torn them away from their home world to labor here. They had no reason to care for our feelings. They had no reason to think that either of us knew enough Delsig to understand the words. And no expectation that we would understand the import of their song even if we did. Such things are fraught with symbolic and historic significance, carry great emotional weight—but only for someone aware of that significance to begin with.

They sang it anyway. And when they were finished, the elder said, bowing, "Citizens, we will pray for the one you've lost." In perfectly comprehensible, if heavily accented, Radchaai.

"Citizens," I replied, also in Radchaai, because I wasn't sure I wanted anyone to realize how much Delsig I spoke, just yet. "We are greatly moved, and we thank you for your song and your prayers."

The overseer spoke up, loud and slow. "The fleet captain thanks you. Now go."

"Wait," I interjected. And turned to Fosyf. "Will you favor me, and give these people something to eat and drink before they go?" She blinked at me, uncomprehending. The overseer stared at me in frank disbelief. "It's a whim I have. If there's any question of impropriety, I'll be happy to pay you back. Whatever is on hand. Tea and cakes, perhaps." It was the sort of thing I'd expect the kitchen here to always have ready.

Fosyf recovered from her immediate surprise. "Of course, Fleet Captain." She gestured toward the overseer, who, still clearly aghast at my request, herded the field workers away.

The ground floor of the building we were to stay in was one large, open space, part dining room, part sitting room, the sitting-room side full of wide, deep chairs and side tables that held game-boards with bright-colored counters. On the other side of the room we ate egg and bean curd soup at a long table with artfully mismatched chairs, by a sideboard piled with fruit and cakes. The line of small windows around the ceiling had gone dull with twilight and clouds that had blown in. Upstairs were narrow hallways, each bedroom and its attached sitting room carefully color coordinated. Mine was orange and blue, in muted tones, the thick, soft blankets on the bed very carefully made, I suspected, to appear comfortably worn and faded. A casual country cottage, one might have thought at first glance, but all of it meticulously placed and arranged.

Citizen Fosyf, sitting at one end of the table, said, "This actually used to be storage and administration. The main building was a guesthouse, you know. Before the annexation."

"All the bedrooms in the main house exit onto the balconies," said Raughd. Who had maneuvered to sit beside me, was now leaning close with head tilted and a knowing smile. "Very convenient for assignations." She was, I realized, trying to *flirt* with me. Even though I was in mourning and so her pursuit of me would be highly improper in the best of situations.

"Ha-ha!" laughed Citizen Fosyf. "Raughd has always found those outer stairs useful. I did myself when I was that age."

The nearest town was an hour away by flier. There was no one here to have assignations with except household members—over in the main house, I assumed, would be cousins and clients. Not everyone in a household was always related in a way that made sex off-limits, so there might well have been allowable relationships here that didn't involve intimidating the servants.

Captain Hetnys sat across the table from me, *Sword of Atagaris* standing stiff scant meters behind her, waiting in case it should be needed. As an ancillary, it wasn't required to observe mourning customs. Kalr Five stood behind me, having apparently convinced everyone here that she, also, was an ancillary.

Citizen Sirix sat silent beside me. The house servants I'd seen appeared to mostly be Samirend with a few Xhais, though I'd seen a few Valskaayans working on the grounds outside. There had been a small, nearly undetectable hesitation on the part of the servants that had shown us to our rooms—I suspected that they would have sent Sirix to servants' quarters if they'd not been given other instructions. It was possible someone here would recognize her, even though she'd last been downwell twenty years ago and wasn't from this estate, but another one a hundred or more kilometers away.

"Raughd's tutors always found it dull here," said Fosyf.

"*They* were dull!" exclaimed Raughd. In a singsong, nasal voice, she declaimed, "*Citizen! In third meter and Acute mode, tell us how God is like a duck.*" Captain Hetnys laughed. "I always tried to make life more amusing for them," Raughd went on, "but they never seemed to appreciate it."

Citizen Fosyf laughed as well. I did not. I had heard about such amusements from my lieutenants in the past, and had already seen Raughd's tendency toward cruelty. "Can you?" I asked. "Tell us in verse, I mean, how God is like a duck?"

"I shouldn't think God was anything like a duck," said Captain Hetnys, emboldened by my past few days of outward calm. "Honestly. A duck!"

"But surely," I admonished, "God *is* a duck." God was the universe, and the universe was God.

Fosyf waved my objection away. "Yes, yes, Fleet Captain, but surely one can say that quite simply without all the fussing over meters and proper diction and whatnot."

"And why choose something so ridiculous?" asked Captain Hetnys. "Why not ask how God is like...rubies or stars or"— she gestured vaguely around—"even tea? Something valuable. Something vast. It would be much more proper."

"A question," I replied, "that might reward close consideration. Citizen Fosyf, I gather the tea here is entirely hand-picked and processed by hand."

"It is!" Fosyf beamed. This was, clearly, one of the centers of her pride. "Handpicked—you can see it whenever you like. The manufactory is nearby, very easy to visit. Should you find that proper." A brief pause, as she blinked, someone nearby having apparently sent her a message. "The section just over the ridge is due to be picked tomorrow. And of course the making of the leaves into tea—the *crafting* of it—goes on all day and night. The leaves must be withered and stirred, till they reach just the right point, and then dry-cooked and rolled until just the right moment. Then they're graded and have the final drying. You can do all those things by machine, of course, some do, and it's perfectly acceptable tea." The smallest hint of contempt and dismissal behind that *perfectly acceptable.* "The sort of thing you'd get good value for in a shop. But this tea isn't available in shops."

Fosyf's tea, Daughter of Fishes, would only be available as a gift. Or—maybe—bought directly from Citizen Fosyf to be given as a gift. The Radch used money, but a staggering amount of exchanges were not money for goods, but gift for gift. Citizen Fosyf was not paid much, if anything, for her tea. Not technically. Those green fields we'd flown over, all that tea, the complicated production, was not a matter of maximizing cost efficiency—no, the point of Daughter of Fishes was *prestige.*

Which explained why, though there were doubtless larger plantations on Athoek, that likely pulled in profits that at first glance looked much more impressive, the only grower who'd felt competent to approach me so openly was the one who did not sell her tea at all.

"It must take a delicate touch," I observed. "The picking,

and the processing. Your workers must be tremendously skilled." Beside me, Citizen Sirix gave an almost inaudible cough, choking slightly on her last mouthful of soup.

"They are, Fleet Captain, they are! You see why I would never treat them badly, I need them too much! In fact, they live in an old guesthouse themselves, a few kilometers away, over the ridge." Rain spattered against the small windows. It only ever rained at night, Athoek Station had told me, and the rain always ended in time for the leaves to dry for the morning picking.

"How nice," I replied, my voice bland.

I rose before the sun, when the sky was a pearled pink and pale blue, and the lake and its valley still shadowed. The air was cool but not chill, and I had not had enough space to run for more than a year. It had been a habit when I had been in the Itran Tetrarchy, a place where sport was a matter of religious devotion, exercises for their ball game were a prayer and a meditation. It felt good to return to it, even though no one here played the game or even knew it existed. I took the road toward the low ridge at an easy jog, wary of my right hip, which I had injured a year ago and which hadn't healed quite right.

As I came over the ridge, I heard singing. One strong voice, pitched to echo off the stony outcrops and across the field where workers with baskets slung over their shoulders rapidly plucked leaves from the waist-high bushes. At least half of those workers were children. The song was in Delsig, a lament by the singer that someone she loved was committed exclusively to someone else. It was a distinctively Valskaayan subject, not the sort of thing that would come up in a typical Radchaai relationship. And it was a song I'd heard before.

Hearing it now raised a sharp memory of Valskaay, of the smell of wet limestone in the cave-riddled district I'd last been in, there.

The singer was apparently a lookout. As I drew nearer, the words changed. Still Delsig, largely incomprehensible, I knew, to the overseers.

> *Here is the soldier*
> *So greedy, so hungry for songs.*
> *So many she's swallowed, they leak out,*
> *They spill out of the corners of her mouth*
> *And fly away, desperate for freedom.*

I was glad my facial expressions weren't at all involuntary. It was cleverly done, fitting exactly into the meter of the song, and I wouldn't have been able to help smiling, thus betraying the fact that I'd understood. As it was, I ran on, apparently oblivious. But watching the workers. Every single one of them appeared to be Valskaayan. The singer's satire on me had been intended for these people, and it had been sung in a Valskaayan language. On Athoek Station, I had been told that all Fosyf's field workers were Valskaayan, and at the time it had struck me as odd. Not that some of them might be, but that all of them would be. Seeing confirmation of it, now, the wrongness of it struck me afresh.

In a situation like this, a hold full of Valskaayans ought to have been either parceled out over dozens of different plantations and whatever other places might welcome their labor, or held in suspension and slowly doled out over decades. There should have been, maybe, a half dozen Valskaayans here. Instead there appeared to be six times that. And I'd have expected to see some Samirend, maybe even some Xhais or Ychana, or members of other groups, because there had certainly been more than Xhais and Ychana here before the annexation.

There also shouldn't have been such a sharp separation between the outdoor servants—all Valskaayan as far as I'd seen this morning and the day before—and the indoor, all Samirend with a few Xhais. Valskaay had been annexed a hundred years ago, and by now at least some of the first transportees or their children ought to have tested or worked their way into other positions.

I ran as far as the workers' residence, a building of brown brick with no glass in the windows, only here and there a blanket stretched across. It had clearly never been as large or as luxurious as Fosyf's lakeside house. But it had a lovely view across its valley, now filled with tea, and a direct road to that wide and glassy lake. The trampled dirt surrounding it might well have been gardens or carefully tended lawns, once. I was curious what the inside of it was like, but instead of entering uninvited and very likely unwelcome, I turned there to run back. "Fleet Captain," *Mercy of Kalr* said in my ear, "Lieutenant Seivarden begs to remind you to be careful of your leg."

"Ship," I replied, silently, "my leg is reminding me itself." Which *Mercy of Kalr* knew. And the conversation with Seivarden, that had produced Ship's message, had happened two days before.

"The lieutenant *will* fret," said Ship. "And you do seem to be ignoring it." Was that disapproval I detected in its apparently serene voice?

"I'll relax the rest of the day," I promised. "I'm almost back anyway."

By the time I crossed the ridge again, the sky and the valley were lighter, the air warmer. I found Citizen Sirix on a bench under the arbor, a bowl of tea steaming in one hand. Jacketless, shirt untucked, no jewelry. Mourning attire, though she was not technically required to mourn for Translator Dlique, had not shaved her head or put on a mourning stripe. "Good morning," I called, walking up to the terrace. "Will you show me about the bathhouse, Citizen? Maybe explain some things to me?"

She hesitated, just a moment. "All right," she said finally, warily, as though I'd offered her something risky or dangerous.

The long, curving bathhouse window framed black and gray cliffs and ice-sheeted peaks. On one far end, just the smallest corner of the house we were staying in. The guests here must have prized this place for its vistas—few if any Radchaai would have thought to make an entire wall of a bath into a window.

The walls that weren't window were light, elaborately carved and polished wood. In the stone-paved floor was a round pool of hot water, bench-lined, in which one sat and sweated, and next to it a chilled one. "It tones you after all the heat," said Sirix, on the bench in the hot water, across from me. "Closes your pores."

The heat felt good on my aching hip. The run had, perhaps, not been terribly wise. "Does it, now?"

"Yes. It's very cleansing." Which seemed an odd word to use. I suspected it was a translation of a more complicated one, from Xhi or Liost into Radchaai. "Nice life you have," Sirix continued. I cocked an interrogatory eyebrow. "Tea the moment you wake up. Clothes laundered and pressed while you sleep. Do you even dress yourself?"

"Generally. If I need to be extremely formal, though, it's good to have some expert help." I myself had never needed it, but I had provided that help on a number of occasions. "So, your forebears. The original Samirend transportees. They were all, or nearly all, sent to the mountains to pick tea?"

"Many of them, yes, Fleet Captain."

"And that annexation was quite some time ago, so as they became civilized"—I allowed just the smallest trace of irony to creep into my voice—"they tested into other assignments. That makes perfect sense to me. But what doesn't make sense is why there are no Samirend working in the fields here. Or anyone but Valskaayans. And there are no Valskaayans working anywhere but in the fields, or one or two on the grounds. The annexation of Valskaay was a hundred years ago. No Valskaayans have made overseer in all that time?"

"Well, Fleet Captain," said Sirix evenly, "no one's going to stay picking tea if they can get away from it. Field hands are paid based on meeting a minimum weight of leaves picked. But the minimum is huge—it would take three very fast workers an entire day to pick so much."

"Or a worker and several children," I guessed. I had seen children working in the fields, when I'd run by.

Sirix gestured acknowledgment. "So they're none of them making the actual wages they're supposed to. Then there's food. Ground meal—you had some upwell. They flavor it with twigs and dust that's left over from the tea making. Which, by the way, Fosyf charges them for. Premium prices. It's not just any floor sweepings, it's Daughter of Fishes!" She stopped a moment, to take a few breaths, too dangerously close to saying something openly angry. "Two bowls a day, of the porridge. It's thin provisions, and if they want anything more they have to buy it."

"At premium prices," I guessed.

"Just so. There are generally some garden plots if they want to grow vegetables, but they have to buy seeds and tools and it's time out from picking tea. They're houseless, so they don't have family to give them the things they need, they have to buy them. They can't any of them get travel permits, so they can't go very far away to buy anything. They can't order things because they don't have any money at all, they're too heavily in debt to get credit, so Fosyf sells them things— handhelds, access to entertainments, better food, whatever— at whatever price she wants."

"The Samirend field workers were able to overcome this?"

"Some of the servants in this house are doubtless still paying on the debts of their grandmothers and great-grandmothers. Or their aunts. The only way out was pulling together into houses and working very, very hard. But the Valskaayans...I suppose I'd say they aren't very ambitious. And they don't seem to understand about making houses of their own."

Valskaayan families didn't work quite the way Radchaai ones did. But I knew Valskaayans were entirely able to understand the advantage of having something that at least seemed like Radchaai houses, and on and around Valskaay groups of families had set up such arrangements at the first opportunity. "And none of the children ever test into other assignments?" I asked, though I already knew what the answer would be.

"These days field workers don't take the aptitudes," replied Sirix. Visibly struggling now with the reeducation that had made it difficult, if not impossible, for her to express anger without a good deal of discomfort. She looked away from me, breathed carefully through her mouth. "Not that they would ever test any differently. They're ignorant, superstitious savages, every one of them. But even so. It's not *right*." Another deep breath. "Fosyf's not the only one doing it. And she'll tell you it's because they *won't* take the tests." That I could believe. Last I was on Valskaay, taking the tests or not was an urgent issue for quite a lot of people. "But there aren't any more transportees coming, are there? We didn't get anyone shipped here from the last annexation. So if the growers run out of Valskaayans, who's going to pick tea for miserable food and hardly any wages? It's just so much more convenient if the field workers can never get themselves or their children out of here. Fleet Captain, *it's not right*. The governor doesn't care about a bunch of houseless savages, and nobody who does care can get the attention of the Lord of the Radch."

"You think that strike twenty years ago escaped her attention?" I asked.

"It must have. Or she'd have done something." Three shallow breaths, through her mouth. Struggling with her anger. "Excuse me." She stood hastily, throwing a shower of hot water, and levered herself out of the pool, strode over to the cold, and immersed herself. Five brought her a towel, and she climbed out of the cold water and left the bath without another word to me.

I closed my eyes. On Athoek Station, Lieutenant Tisarwat slept, deep, between dreams, one arm thrown over her face. My attention shifted to *Mercy of Kalr*. Seivarden stood watch. She'd been saying something to one of her Amaats. "This business with the fleet captain running off downwell." Odd. This wasn't the sort of thing Seivarden was at all likely to discuss with one of her Amaats. "Is this really something necessary, or just some specific injustice that infuriates her?"

"Lieutenant Seivarden," replied the Amaat, oddly stiff

even given this crew's love of imitating ancillaries. "You know I have to report such a question to the fleet captain."

Slightly exasperated, Seivarden waved that answer away. "Yes, of course, Ship. Still."

I saw suddenly what was happening. Seivarden was talking to *Mercy of Kalr*, not the Amaat. The Amaat was seeing Ship's answers displayed in her vision and she was reading them off. As though she had been truly an ancillary, a part of the ship, one of dozens of mouths for Ship to speak through. Thankfully, none of the crew had ever attempted such a thing with me. I wouldn't have approved in the least.

But it was clear, watching, that Seivarden found it comfortable. Comforting. She was worried, and Ship speaking like this was reassuring. Not for any solid, rational reason. Just because it was.

"Lieutenant," said the Amaat. Ship, through the Amaat, "I can only tell you what the fleet captain has already said herself, in her briefings to you. If, however, you want my personal opinion, I think it's something of both. And the fleet captain's absence, and the removal of Citizen Raughd from Athoek Station, is allowing Lieutenant Tisarwat to make valuable political contacts among the younger of the station's prominent citizens."

Seivarden gave a skeptical *hah*. "Next you'll be telling me our Tisarwat is a gifted politician!"

"I think she'll surprise you, Lieutenant."

Seivarden clearly didn't believe *Mercy of Kalr*. "Even so, Ship. Our fleet captain generally keeps out of trouble, but when she doesn't, it's never the insignificant sort. And we're hours and hours away from being able to help her. If you see something brewing and she's too distracted to ask us to come in closer so we're there if she needs us, are you going to tell me?"

"That would require knowing days in advance that something was, as you say, brewing, Lieutenant. I can't imagine the fleet captain so distracted for so long." Seivarden frowned. "But, Lieutenant, I am as concerned for the fleet captain's safety as you are." Which was as much of an answer as Ship could give, and Seivarden would have to be happy with that.

"Lieutenant Seivarden," said *Mercy of Kalr*. "Message incoming from Hrad."

Seivarden gestured *go ahead*. An unfamiliar voice sounded in her ears. "This is Fleet Captain Uemi, commanding *Sword of Inil*, dispatched from Omaugh Palace. I'm ordered to take control of the security of Hrad system." One gate away, Hrad system was. More or less next door. "My compliments to Fleet Captain Breq. Fighting is still intense at Tstur Palace. Several outstations have been destroyed. Depending on the outcome, the Lord of the Radch may send you a troop carrier. She sends you her greetings, in any event, and trusts you're doing well."

"Do you know Fleet Captain Uemi, Ship?" There was no expectation of an immediate, this-moment reply—Hrad was hours away at lightspeed, through the connecting gate.

"Not well," replied *Mercy of Kalr*.

"And *Sword of Inil*?"

"It's a *Sword*."

"Hah!" Seivarden, amused.

"Lieutenant, the fleet captain left instructions in case such a message should be delivered in her absence."

"*Did* she." Seivarden wasn't sure whether she was surprised at that or not. "Well, let's have it then."

My instructions had been minor enough. Seivarden, replying, said, "This is Lieutenant Seivarden, commanding *Mercy of Kalr* in Fleet Captain Breq's temporary absence. Most courteous greetings to Fleet Captain Uemi, and we are grateful for the news. Begging Fleet Captain Uemi's indulgence, Fleet Captain Breq wonders if *Sword of Inil* took on any new crew at Omaugh Palace." Though it might not be new crew I should worry about. It was entirely possible to make ancillaries out of older adults.

But no reply could reach me before supper. The question puzzled Seivarden, who didn't know about Tisarwat, but Ship wouldn't explain it to her.

Walking back to the house I met Raughd coming from the main building. "Good morning, Fleet Captain!" she said, with a sunny smile. "It's so invigorating to be up at the break of day like this. I really ought to make a habit of it." I had to admit, it was a creditably charming smile, even given the nearly undetectable strain behind it—even if she hadn't just implied as much, I was sure this was not an hour when Raughd was accustomed to rising. But knowing as much as I did about her quite spoiled the effect for me. "Don't tell me you've already been to the bath," she added, with the merest touch of disappointment, calculatedly coy.

"Good morning, Citizen," I replied without stopping. "And yes, I have." And went into the house for breakfast.

13

After breakfast—fruit and bread that Fosyf's servants had left lying on the sideboard the night before, by a polite fiction only leftovers from supper—Captain Hetnys and I were supposed to spend the day sitting quietly, praying at regular intervals, eating spare, simple meals. We sat, accordingly, on the sitting-room side of the house's open ground floor. As the days went on we could properly spend more time farther from the house—sit, for instance, under the arbor outside. Convention allowed a certain amount of wider movement, for those who could not be still in their grief—I had taken advantage of that for my run that morning, and to use the bath. But most of the next few days would be spent in our rooms, or here in this sitting room, with only each other for company, or any neighbors who might stop by to console us.

Captain Hetnys did not wear her uniform—in these circumstances she was not required to. Her untucked shirt was a muted rose, over olive-green trousers. But what civilian clothes I had were either far too formal for this setting, or else they dated from my years outside the Radch, and if I wore either

I would not seem to be properly in mourning. Instead I wore my brown and black uniform shirt and trousers. In strictest propriety I ought to have worn no jewelry, but I would not part with Lieutenant Awn's memorial token, and pinned it on the inside of my shirt. We sat silent for a while, Kalr Five and *Sword of Atagaris* standing motionless behind us, in case we should need them. Captain Hetnys grew increasingly tense, though of course she showed little outward sign of it until Sirix came down the steps to join us. Then Captain Hetnys rose, abruptly, and paced around the perimeter of the room. She had said nothing to Sirix on the trip here, nothing last night. Intended to say nothing to her now, it seemed. But that was perfectly within the bounds of proper mourning, which allowed for some eccentric behavior at such a time.

At midday, servants came in with trays of food—more bread, which could be a luxury on stations but was still considered a plain, simple kind of food, and various pastes and mixtures meant to be spread on it, all of which would be lightly seasoned, if at all. Even so, judging by last night's supper I was sure they would only technically qualify as austere eating.

One servant went over to the wall and, to my surprise, pulled it aside. Nearly the entire wall was a series of folding panels that opened out onto the arbored terrace, admitting filtered sunlight into the room, and a pleasant, leaf-scented breeze. Sirix took her lunch to one of the benches outside—though the wall-wide doorway also made the division between inside and outside an ambiguous one.

On Athoek Station, Lieutenant Tisarwat sat in a tea shop—sprawling, comfortable chairs around a low table littered with empty and half-empty arrack bottles. More than her pay was worth—she'd bought them on credit, then, or they were gifts based on her presumed status. Or mine. One or the other of us would have to find some way to make a return, but that was unlikely to pose a problem. Citizen Piat sat beside Tisarwat, and a half dozen other young people sat in the nearby chairs. Someone had just said something funny—everyone was laughing.

On *Mercy of Kalr* Medic raised an eyebrow, hearing the Kalr assisting her singing softly to herself.

> *Who only ever loved once?*
> *Who ever said "I will never love again"*
> *and kept their word?*

Not I.

On Athoek, in the mountains, Captain Hetnys stopped pacing, took her own lunch to the table. Sirix, on the bench out on the terrace, seemed not even to notice. One of the servants walked by her, paused, said something quick and quiet that I couldn't quite catch, or perhaps she'd spoken in Liost. Sirix looked up at her, serious, and said quite clearly in Radchaai, "I'm just an adviser, Citizen." Not even a trace of rancor. Odd, after her unhappiness that morning, that indignant sense of injustice.

Above, in the tea shop on Athoek Station, someone said, "Now that Captain Hetnys and that really quite frightening fleet captain are downwell, it's up to Tisarwat to protect us from the Presger!"

"Not a chance," replied Tisarwat. "If the Presger decide to attack us there's nothing we can do. But I think it's going to be a long time before the Presger ever get to us." Word of the split in the Lord of the Radch had not yet gotten out, and problems with the gates were still officially "unanticipated difficulties." Somewhat predictably, those who didn't merely accept that found the idea of alien interference to be a more plausible explanation. "We'll be fine."

"But cut off like this," someone began.

Citizen Piat said, "We're fine. Even if we were to be cut off from the planet"—and someone muttered a *gods forbid*—"we'd be fine here. We can feed ourselves, anyway."

"Or if not," said someone else, "we can grow skel in the lake in the Gardens."

Someone else laughed. "It would take that horticulturist down a peg or two! You should see to it, Piat."

Tisarwat had learned a thing or two from her Bos. She kept her face—and her voice—impressively bland. "What horticulturist is this?"

"What's her name, Basnaaid?" said the person who had laughed. "She's a nobody, really. But, you know, an Awer from Omaugh Palace came and offered her clientage and she *refused*—she's got no family, really, and she isn't much to look at, but still, she was too good for Awer!"

Piat was sitting on one side of Tisarwat, and on the other was someone Ship told me was Skaaiat Awer's cousin—though not, herself, an Awer. Tisarwat had invited her; she wasn't usually a part of this group. "Skaaiat didn't take offense," the cousin said now. And smiled, almost taking the edge off her tone.

"Well, no, of course she didn't. But it can't possibly be proper to refuse such an offer. It just tells you what sort of person the horticulturist is."

"Indeed it does," agreed Skaaiat's cousin.

"She's good at what she does," said Piat, in a sudden rush, as though she'd spent the last few moments nerving herself to say it. "She *should* be proud."

A moment of awkward silence. Then, "I wish Raughd was

here," said the person who had brought the topic up to begin with. "I don't know why she had to go downwell, too. We always laugh so hard when Raughd is here."

"Not the person you're laughing *at*," pointed out Skaaiat's cousin.

"Well, no, of course not," replied Raughd's partisan. "Or we wouldn't be laughing at them. Tisarwat, you should see Raughd's impression of Captain Hetnys. It's hilarious."

On Athoek, in the house, Sirix rose from her seat and went upstairs. I shifted my attention to Five, saw that she was sweating in her uniform and had been bored watching me and Captain Hetnys. Was thinking about the food on the sideboard, which she could smell from where she stood. I would need to go upstairs myself soon, pretend, perhaps, to nap, so Five could have a break, so she and *Sword of Atagaris* could have their own meals. Captain Hetnys—unaware of having just been mentioned upwell—went out to sit on the terrace, now Sirix was safely away.

One of the servants approached Kalr Five. Stood a moment, debating, I suspected, what sort of address to use, and settled finally on, "If you please."

"Yes, Citizen," Five said to the servant, flat and toneless.

"This arrived this morning," the servant said. She held out a small parcel wrapped in a velvety-looking violet cloth. "It was most particularly requested that it be given directly into the fleet captain's keeping." She didn't explain why she was giving it to Five instead.

"Thank you, Citizen," said Five, and took the parcel. "Who sent it?"

"The messenger didn't say." But I thought she knew, or suspected.

Five unwrapped the cloth, to reveal a plain box of thin,

pale wood. Inside sat what looked like a triangular section of thick, heavy bread, quite stale; a pin, a two-centimeter silver disk dangling from an arrangement of blue and green glass beads; and underneath these, a small card printed close with characters I thought were Liost. The language so many Samirend still spoke. A quick query to Athoek Station confirmed my guess. And told me at least some of what was on the card.

Five put the lid back on the box. "Thank you, Citizen."

I rose, without saying anything, and went over to Five and took the box and its wrapping and went up the stairs and through the narrow hallway to Sirix's room. Knocked on the door. Said, when Sirix opened it, "Citizen, I believe this is actually for you." Held out the box, its purple covering folded beneath it.

She looked at me, dubious. "There's no one here to send me anything, Fleet Captain. You must be mistaken."

"It certainly isn't meant for me," I said, still holding out the box. "Citizen," I admonished, when she still did not move to take it.

Eight approached from behind her, to take it from me, but Sirix gestured her away. "It can't possibly be mine," she insisted.

With my free hand, I lifted the lid off the box so that she could see what was inside it. She went suddenly very still, seeming not even to breathe.

"I'm sorry to hear about your loss, Citizen," I said. The pin was a memorial, the family name of the deceased was Odela. The card bore details about the deceased's life and funeral. The purpose or meaning of the bread was unknown to me, but clearly it had meant something to whoever sent it. Meant something, certainly, to Sirix. Though I could not tell if her reaction was grief, or the distress of anger she could not express.

"You said you had no family, Citizen," I said after a few uncomfortable, silent moments. "Clearly someone in Odela is thinking of you." They must have heard Sirix was here with me.

"She has no right," said Sirix. Outwardly calm, dispassionate, but I knew that was a necessity for her, a matter of survival. "None of them do. They can't have it both ways, they can't just take it back." She took a breath, looked as though she would speak again but instead took another one. "Send it back," she said then. "It isn't mine, it can't be. By their own actions."

"If that's what you want, Citizen, then I will." I replaced the lid, unfolded the purple cloth, and wound it around the now-closed box.

"What," Sirix said, bitterness creeping into her voice, "no exhortations to be grateful, to remember that they are, after all, my f—" Her voice broke—she had pushed herself too far. It said something about her usual self-control that she did not, that moment, slam the door in my face so that she could suffer unwatched. Or perhaps it said she knew that Eight was still in the room, that she would not be alone and unobserved no matter what she did.

"I can produce such exhortations if you'd like, Citizen, but they would be insincere." I bowed. "If there is anything you need, do not hesitate to ask. I am at your service."

She did close the door then. I could have watched her through Eight's eyes, but I did not.

When supper arrived, so did Fosyf and Raughd. Sirix didn't come downstairs, hadn't since lunch. No one commented on it—she was only here by sufferance, because she was with me. After we ate, we sat right up at the edge of the room, the doors still wide. What we could see of the lake had gone leaden with the evening, shadowed, only the very tops of the peaks behind it still brilliant with the sunset. The air grew chill and damp, and the servants brought hot, bitter-sweet drinks in handled bowls. "Xhai-style," Fosyf informed me. Without Sirix to flank me, I had Fosyf on one side and Raughd on the other. Captain Hetnys sat across from me, her chair turned a bit so she could look out toward the lake.

On *Mercy of Kalr*, the reply to the question I'd that morning asked Fleet Captain Uemi finally arrived. Ship played it in Lieutenant Ekalu's ears. "All thanks, Lieutenant Seivarden, for your courteous greeting. My compliments to Fleet Captain Breq, but I did not take on any crew at Omaugh."

I had left instructions for this, as well. "Fleet Captain Breq thanks Fleet Captain Uemi for her indulgence," said Lieutenant Ekalu. Just as puzzled as Seivarden had been, hours ago. "Did any of *Sword of Inil*'s crew spend a day or two out of touch, on the palace station?"

"Well, Fleet Captain," said Fosyf, downwell, in the growing dark by the lake, "you had a peaceful day, I hope?"

"Yes, thank you, Citizen." I was under no obligation to be any more forthcoming. In fact, I could quite properly ignore anyone who spoke to me for the next week and a half, if I felt so moved.

"The fleet captain rises at an unbelievably early hour," said Raughd. "I got up early especially to be sure there was some-one to show her the bath, and she'd already been up for *ages*."

"Clearly, Citizen," said Captain Hetnys genially, "your idea of getting up early isn't the same as ours."

"Military discipline, Raughd," observed Fosyf, voice

indulgent. "For all your recent interest"—this with a sidelong glance at me—"you'd never have been suited to it."

"Oh, I don't know," said Raughd, airily. "I've never tried it, have I?"

"I went over the ridge this morning and saw your workers," I remarked, not particularly interested in pursuing the issue of Raughd's military fitness.

"I hope you could add some songs to your collection, Fleet Captain," Fosyf replied. I inclined my head just slightly, barely an answer but sufficient.

"I don't know why they didn't just make ancillaries out of them," observed Raughd. "Surely they'd be better off." She simpered. "Two units off a troop carrier would do us, and still leave plenty for everyone else."

Fosyf laughed. "Raughd has taken a sudden interest in the military! Been looking things up. Ships and uniforms and all sorts of things."

"The uniforms are so *appealing*," Raughd agreed. "I'm so glad you're wearing yours, Fleet Captain."

"Ancillaries can't be new citizens," I said.

"Well," said Fosyf. "Well. You know, I'm not sure Valskaayans can be, either. Even on Valskaay there are problems, aren't there? That religion of theirs." Actually, there were several religions represented on Valskaay, and in its system, and various sects of all of them. But Fosyf meant the majority religion, the one everyone thought of as "Valskaayan." It was a variety of exclusive monotheism, something most Radchaai found more or less incomprehensible. "Though I'm not sure you can really call it a religion. More a...a collection of superstitions and some very odd philosophical ideas." Outside had grown darker still, the trees and moss-covered stones disappearing into shadow. "And the religion is the least of it.

They have plenty of opportunity to *become* civilized. Why, look at the Samirend!" She gestured around, meaning, I supposed, the servants who had brought us supper. "They began where the Valskaayans are now. The Valskaayans have every opportunity, but do they take advantage of it? I don't know if you saw their residence—a very nice guesthouse, fully as nice as the house I live in myself, but it's practically a ruin. They can't be bothered to keep their surroundings nice. But they go quite extravagantly into debt over a musical instrument, or a new handheld."

"Or equipment for making alcohol," said Raughd primly.

Fosyf sighed, apparently deeply grieved. "They use their own rations for that, some of them. And then go further into debt buying food. Most of them have never seen any of their wages. They lack *discipline*."

"How many Valskaayans were sent to this system?" I asked Fosyf. "After that annexation. Do you know?"

"No idea, Fleet Captain." Fosyf gestured resigned ignorance. "I just take the workers they assign me."

"There were children working in the fields this morning," I remarked. "Isn't there a school?"

"No point," Fosyf said. "Not with Valskaayans. They won't attend. They just don't have the seriousness of mind that's necessary. No *steadiness*. Oh, but I do wish I could take you on a proper tour, Fleet Captain! When your two weeks is ended, perhaps. I do want to show off my tea, and I know you'll want to hear every song you can."

"Fleet Captain Breq," said Captain Hetnys, who had been silent so far, "doesn't only collect songs, as it happens."

"Oh?" asked Fosyf.

"I stayed in her household during the fasting days," Captain Hetnys said, "and do you know, her everyday dishes are a set of blue and violet Bractware. With all the serving pieces. In *perfect* condition." Behind me, Ship showed me, Kalr Five was suppressing a satisfied smirk. We'd hardly eaten during the fasting days, as was proper, but Five had served what little we did eat on the Bractware and—no doubt purposefully— left the unused dishes where Captain Hetnys could see them.

"Well! What good taste, Fleet Captain! And I'm glad Hetnys mentions it." She gestured, and a servant bent near, received murmured instruction, departed. "I have something you'll be interested to see."

Out in the dark a high, inhuman voice sang out, a long, sustained series of vowels on a single pitch. "Ah!" cried Fosyf. "That's what I was waiting for." Another voice joined the first, slightly lower, and then another, a bit higher, and another and another, until there were at least a dozen intoning voices, coming and going, dissonant and oddly choral-sounding.

Clearly Fosyf expected some sort of reaction from me. "What is it?" I asked.

"They're plants," Fosyf said, apparently delighted at the thought of having surprised me. "You might have seen some when you were out this morning. They have a sort of sac that collects air, and when that's full, and the sun goes down, they whistle it out. As long as it's not raining. Which is why you didn't hear them last night."

"Weeds," observed Captain Hetnys. "Quite a nuisance, actually. They've tried to eradicate them, but they keep coming back."

"Supposedly," continued Fosyf, acknowledging the captain's remark with a nod, "the person who bred them was a temple initiate. And the plants sing various words in Xhi, all of them to do with the temple mysteries, and when the other initiates heard the plants sing they realized the mysteries had been revealed to everyone. They murdered the designer. Tore her to pieces with their bare hands, supposedly, right here by this lake."

I hadn't thought to ask what sort of guesthouse this had been. "This was a holy place, then? Is there a temple?" In my experience, major temples were nearly always surrounded by cities or at least villages, and I'd seen no sign of that as we'd flown in. I wondered if there had used to be one, and it was razed to make way for tea, or if this whole, huge area had been sacrosanct. "Was the lake holy, and this was a temple guesthouse?"

"Very little gets past the fleet captain!" exclaimed Raughd.

"Indeed," agreed her mother. "What's left of the temple is across the lake. There was an oracle there for a while, but all that's left now is a superstition about wish-granting fish."

And the name of the tea grown on the once-sacred ground, I suspected. I wondered how the Xhais felt about that. "What are the words the plants sing?" I knew very little Xhi and didn't recognize any words in particular in the singing discord coming out of the dark.

"You get different lists," Fosyf replied genially, "depending on who you ask."

"I used to go out in the dark when I was a child," remarked Raughd, "and look for them. They stop if you shine a light on them."

I hadn't actually seen any children since we'd arrived, except for the field workers. I found that odd, in such a setting, but before I could wonder aloud or ask, the servant Fosyf had sent away returned, carrying a large box.

It was gold, or at least gilded, inlaid with red, blue, and green glass in a style that was older than I was. Older, in fact, than Anaander Mianaai's three thousand and some years. I had only ever seen this sort of thing in person once before, and that when I was barely a decade old, some two thousand years ago. "Surely," I said, "that's a copy."

"It is not, Fleet Captain," replied Fosyf, very pleased to say it, clearly. The servant set the box on the ground in our midst and then stepped away. Fosyf bent, lifted the lid. Nestled inside, a tea service—flask, bowls for twelve, strainer. All glass and gold, inlaid with elaborate, snaking patterns of blue and green.

I still held the handled bowl I'd been drinking from, and now I lifted it. Five obligingly came forward and took it, but did not move away. I had not intended her to. I got out of my seat, squatted beside the box.

The inside of the lid was also gold, though a strip of wood seven centimeters wide above and below the gold showed what it covered. That sheet of gold was engraved. In Notai. I could read it, though I doubted anyone else here could. Several old houses (Seivarden's among them), and some newer ones that found the idea romantic and appealing, claimed to be descended from Notai ancestors. Of those, some would have recognized this writing for what it was, possibly would have been able to read a word or two. Only a few would have bothered to actually learn this language.

"What does it say?" I asked, though of course I knew already.

"It's an invocation of the god Varden," said Captain Hetnys, "and a blessing on the owner."

Varden is your strength, it said, *Varden is your hope, and Varden is your joy. Life and prosperity to the daughter of the house. On the happy and well-deserved occasion.*

I looked up at Fosyf. "Where did you get this?"

"Aha," she replied, "so Hetnys was right, you are a connoisseur! I'd never have suspected if she hadn't told me."

"Where," I repeated, "did you get this?"

Fosyf gave a short laugh. "And single-minded, yes, but I already knew that. I bought it from Captain Hetnys."

Bought it. This ancient, priceless thing would have been nearly unthinkable as a *gift*. The idea of anyone taking any amount of money for it was impossible. Still squatting, I turned to Captain Hetnys, who to my unspoken question said, "The owner was in need of cash. She didn't want to sell it herself because, well, imagine anyone knowing you had to sell something like *that*. So I brokered the deal for her."

"And took your cut, too," put in Raughd, who I suspected wasn't enjoying being eclipsed by the tea set.

"True," acknowledged Captain Hetnys.

Even a small cut of that must have been staggering. This wasn't the sort of thing an individual owned, except perhaps nominally. No living, remotely functional house would allow a single member to alienate something like this. The tea set I had seen, when I had been a brand-new ship not ten years old, had not belonged to an individual. It had been part of the equipment of a decade room of a *Sword*, brought out while my captain was visiting, to impress her. That one had been purple and silver and mother-of-pearl, and the god named in the inscription had been a different one. And it had read, *On the happy and well-deserved occasion of your promotion. Captain Seimorand.* And a date a mere half a century before the ascendancy of Anaander Mianaai, before the set had been taken as a souvenir of its owner's defeat.

I was sure the bottom of the inscription in the box lid now before me had been cut off, that *On the happy and well-deserved occasion* was only the beginning of the sentence.

There was no sign of the cut—the edges of the gold looked smooth, the wood underneath undamaged. But I was sure someone had removed it, cut a strip off the bottom, and put back what was left, centered so that it didn't look so much as though part of the inscription had been removed.

This wasn't something passed down for centuries among some captain's descendants—those descendants would never have removed the name of the ancestor who had left them such a thing. One might remove the name to conceal its origin, and even damaged this was worth a great deal. One might conceal its origin out of shame—anyone who saw it might be able to guess which house had been forced to part with such a treasure. But most families that owned such things had other and better ways to capitalize such possessions. Seivarden's house, for instance, had accepted gifts and money in exchange for tours of that ancient, captured Notai shuttle.

Stolen antiques, the *Sword of Atagaris* lieutenant had said. But I had not imagined anything quite like this.

Add in that supply locker. "Debris." Any writing conveniently obscured—like this tea set.

Captain Hetnys had thought it was important to station her ship by the Ghost Gate. A piece of debris that was likely more than three thousand years old—and extremely unlikely to have ended up here at Athoek to begin with—had come out of the Ghost Gate. A piece of a Notai shuttle.

Captain Hetnys had made a great deal of money selling a Notai tea set nearly as old as that supply locker likely was. Where had she gotten it? Who had removed the name of its first owner, and why?

What was on the other side of the Ghost Gate?

14

Back in my room, I removed my brown and black shirt, handed it to Kalr Five. Had bent to loosen my boots when a knock sounded at the door. I looked up. Kalr Five gave me a single, expressionless glance and went to answer it. She had seen Raughd's behavior these past few days, knew what this was likely to be, though I admit I was surprised she had chosen to make this blatant a move so soon.

I stood aside, where I would not be visible from the sitting room. Picked up my shirt from where Five had laid it, and drew it back on. Five opened the door to the hallway, and through her eyes I saw Raughd's insincere smile. "I wonder," she said, with no courteous preamble, "if I might speak privately to the fleet captain." A balancing act, that sentence was, offering Five herself no consideration whatsoever, without being rude to me.

Let her in, I messaged Five silently. *But don't leave the room.* Though it was entirely possible—indeed, likely—that Raughd's idea of "private" included the presence of servants.

Raughd entered. Looked around for me, bowed with a

sidelong, smiling glance up at me as I came from the bedroom. "Fleet Captain," she said. "I was hoping we might... talk."

"About what, Citizen?" I did not invite her to sit.

She blinked, genuinely surprised, I thought. "Surely, Fleet Captain, I've been plain about my desires."

"Citizen. I am in mourning." I had not had time to clean the white stripe off my face for the night. And she could not possibly have forgotten the reason for it.

"But surely, Fleet Captain," she replied sweetly, "that's all for show."

"It's always for show, Citizen. It is entirely possible to grieve with no outward sign. These things are meant to let others know about it."

"It's true such things are nearly always insincere, or at least overdone," Raughd said. She had missed my point entirely. "But what I meant was that you've undertaken this only for political reasons. There can't possibly be any real sorrow, no one could expect so. It's only needed in public, and this"— she gestured around—"is certainly not public."

I might have argued that if a family member of hers had died far from home, she might want to know that someone had cared enough to perform funeral duties for that person— even if the rites in question were foreign, even if the person who performed them was a stranger. But given the sort of person Raughd apparently was, such an argument would have carried no weight, if it had even been comprehensible to her. "Citizen, I am astonished at your want of propriety."

"Can you blame me, Fleet Captain, if my desire overwhelms my sense of propriety? And propriety, like mourning, is for public view."

I was under no illusions as to my physical attractiveness.

It was not such that it would inspire propriety-overwhelming enthusiasm. My position, on the other hand, and my house name might well be quite fascinating. And of course, it would be far more fascinating to someone wealthy and privileged, like Raughd. Entertainments might be brimful of the virtuous and humble gaining the favorable notice of those above them, to their and their house's ultimate benefit, but in daily life most people were fully aware of just what would happen if they deliberately sought such a situation out.

But someone like Raughd—oh, someone like Raughd could set her sights on me, and she might pretend it was all down to attraction, to romance or even love. No matter that in such a case no one involved would for a moment be unaware of the potential advantages.

"Citizen," I said, coldly. "I am well aware that you are the person who painted those words on the wall in the Undergarden." She looked at me with wide-eyed, blinking incomprehension. Kalr Five stood motionless in a corner of the room, ancillary-impassive. "Someone died as a direct result of that, and her death has very possibly put this entire system in danger. You may not have intended that death, but you knew well enough that your action would cause problems, and you didn't really care what those were or who was hurt by it."

She drew herself up, indignant. "Fleet Captain! I don't know why you would accuse me of such a thing!"

"At a guess," I said, unruffled by her resentment, "you were angry at Lieutenant Tisarwat for spoiling your fun with Citizen Piat. Who, by the way, you treat abominably."

"Oh, well," she said, subsiding just a bit, her posture relaxing, "if that's the problem. I've known Piat since we were both little and she's always been...erratic. Oversensitive. She feels inadequate, you know, because her mother is station administrator and so beautiful on top of it. There she is, assigned to a perfectly fine job, but she can't stop thinking it's nothing compared to her mother. She takes everything too hard, and I admit sometimes I lose patience because of it." She sighed, the very image of compassionate regret, even penitence. "It wouldn't be the first time she's accused me of mistreating her, just to hurt me."

"*Such a fucking bore*," I quoted. "Funny how the last time you lost patience with her was when everyone was laughing at her joke and she was the center of attention. Rather than you."

"I'm sure Tisarwat meant well, telling you about that, but she just didn't understand what..." Her voice faltered, her face took on a pained expression. "She couldn't...Piat couldn't have accused me of painting those words on the wall? It would be just the sort of horrible thing she'd think was funny, when she was in one of her moods."

"She hasn't accused you of anything," I said, my voice still cold. "The evidence speaks for itself."

Raughd froze, completely still for an instant, not even breathing. Then she said, with a coldness that nearly matched my own, "Did you accept my mother's invitation just so you could come here and attack me? Obviously, you've come here with some sort of agenda. You turn up out of nowhere, produce some ridiculous order forbidding travel in the gates so the tea can't get out of the system. I can't see it as anything less than an attack on my house, and I will not stand for that! I'm going to speak to my mother about this!"

"You do that," I said. Still calm. "Be sure to explain to her how that paint got on your gloves. But I wouldn't be surprised if she already knows about it and invited me down here in the hope that I could be dissuaded from pressing the issue." And I had accepted knowing that. And I had wanted to know what it was like, downwell. What Sirix had been so angry about.

Raughd turned and left the room without another word.

The morning sky was pale blue streaked with the silver traces of the weather grid, and here and there a wisp of cloud. The sun hadn't yet cleared the mountain so the houses and the lake, the trees, were still in shadow. Sirix waited for me, at the water's edge. "Thank you for the wake-up call, Fleet Captain," she said, with an ironic bow of her head. "I'm sure I wouldn't have wanted to sleep in."

"Already used to the time difference?" It was early afternoon on the station. "I'm told there's a path along the lakeside."

"I don't think I can keep up with you if you're going to run."

"I'm walking today." I would have walked anyway, even if Sirix hadn't needed to keep up. I set off in the direction of the lakeside trail, not turning my head to see if she followed, but hearing her step behind me, seeing her (and myself) as Five watched us out of sight from the corner of the arbor.

On Athoek Station, Lieutenant Tisarwat was in the sitting room in our Undergarden quarters, speaking to Basnaaid Elming. Who'd arrived not five minutes earlier while I'd been pulling on my boots, about to leave my room. I'd been briefly tempted to make Sirix wait, but in the end I decided that by now I could watch and walk at the same time.

I could see—almost feel, myself—the thrill thrumming through Tisarwat at Basnaaid's presence. "Horticulturist," Tisarwat was saying. She wasn't long out of bed herself. "I'm at your service. But I must tell you, the fleet captain has ordered me to stay away from you."

Basnaaid frowned, clearly puzzled and dismayed. "Why?"

Lieutenant Tisarwat took an unsteady breath. "You said you never wanted to speak to her again. She didn't... she wanted to be sure you didn't ever think she was..." She trailed off, at a loss, it seemed. "For your sister's sake, she'll do anything you ask."

"She's a bit high handed about it," responded Basnaaid, with some acerbity.

"Fleet Captain," said Sirix, walking beside me on the path alongside the lake. I realized she'd been speaking to me, and I had not responded.

"Forgive me, Citizen." I forced my attention away from Basnaaid and Tisarwat. "I was distracted."

"Plainly." She sidestepped a branch that had fallen from one of the nearby trees. "I was trying to thank you for being patient with me yesterday. And for Kalr Eight's help." She frowned. "Do you not allow them to go by their names?"

"They'd much prefer I not use their names, at least my Kalrs would." I gestured ambiguity, uncertainty. "She might tell you her name if you ask." The house was well behind us by now, screened by a turn of the path, by trees with broad, oval leaves and small cascades of fringed white flowers. "Tell me, Citizen, is suspension failure a problem, among the field workers in the mountains here?" Transportees were shipped in suspension pods. Which generally worked very well, but sometimes failed, leaving their occupants dead or severely injured.

Sirix froze midstride, just an instant, and then kept walking. I had said something that had surprised her, but I thought I'd also seen recognition in her expression. "I don't think I've ever seen anyone thawed out. I don't think anyone has been, for a while. But the Valskaayans, some of them, think that when the medics thawed people out, they didn't let all of them live."

"Do they say why?"

Sirix gestured ambiguity. "Not plainly. They think the medics dispose of anyone they consider unfit in some way, but they won't say exactly what that means, at least they wouldn't in my hearing. And they won't go to a medic. Not for anything. Every bone in their body could be broken and they'd rather have their friends splint them up with sticks and old clothes."

"Last night," I said, by way of explanation, "I requested an account of the number of Valskaayans transported to this system."

"Only Valskaayans?" asked Sirix, eyebrow raised. "Why not Samirend?"

Ah. "I've found something, have I?"

"I wouldn't have thought there was much to find, that way, about the Valskaayans. Before I was born, though, before Valskaay was even annexed, something happened. About a hundred fifty years ago. I don't know for certain—I doubt anyone but the parties actually involved know for certain. But I can tell you the rumor. Someone in charge of the transportees coming into the system was siphoning off a percentage of them and selling them to outsystem slavers. No," she gestured, emphatic, seeing my doubt. "I know it sounds ridiculous. But before this place was civilized"—not even a trace of irony there—"debt indenture was quite common, and it was entirely legal to sell indentures away. No one cared much, unless someone had the bad taste to sell away a few Xhais. It was entirely natural and boring if it happened to a lot of Ychana."

"Yes." When I'd seen those numbers—how many Valskaayans had been transported here, how many brought out

of suspension and assigned work, how many remaining—
and, further, because I'd just seen that ancient tea set and
heard Captain Hetnys's story of selling it to Citizen Fosyf,
I had queried the system histories. "Except that outsystem
slave trade collapsed not long after the annexation and has
never recovered." Partly, I thought, because it had relied on
cheap supply from Athoek, which the annexation had cut off.
And partly because of problems internal to the slavers' own
home systems. "And that was, what, six hundred years ago?
Surely this hadn't been happening undetected all that time."

"I'm only telling you what I've heard, Fleet Captain. The
discrepancy in numbers was covered—very thinly, I might
add, if the story is true—by an alarming rate of suspension
failures. Nearly all of those were workers assigned to the
mountain tea plantations. When the system governor found
out—this was before Governor Giarod's time, of course—she
put a stop to it, but she also supposedly hushed it up. After
all, the medics who'd signed off on those false reports had
done so at the behest of some of Athoek's most illustrious
citizens. Not the sort of people who ever find themselves on
the wrong side of Security. And if word of it ever got back
to the palace, the Lord of the Radch would certainly want
to know why the governor hadn't noticed all this going on
before now. So instead a number of highly placed citizens
retired. Including Citizen Fosyf's grandmother, who spent
the rest of her life in prayer at a monastery on the other side
of this continent."

This was why I'd had this conversation away from the
house. Just in case. "Faked suspension failure numbers won't
have been enough to cover it. There will have been more
than just that." This story hadn't been in the information I'd
received, when I'd queried the histories. But Sirix had said

that it had been hushed up. It might have been kept out of any official accounts.

Sirix was silent a moment. Considering. "That may well be, Fleet Captain. I only ever heard rumors."

"...very heartfelt poetry," Basnaaid was saying, in my sitting room in the Undergarden. "I'm glad no one here has read any of it." She and Tisarwat were drinking tea, now.

"Did you send any of your poetry to your sister, Citizen?" asked Tisarwat.

Basnaaid gave a small, breathy laugh. "Nearly all of it. She always said it was wonderful. Either she was being very kind, or she had terrible taste."

Her words distressed Tisarwat for some reason, triggered an overpowering sense of shame and self-loathing. But of course, there was hardly a well-educated Radchaai alive who hadn't written a quantity of poetry in her youth, and I could well imagine the quality of what the younger Tisarwat might have produced. And been proud of. And then seen through the eyes of Anaander Mianaai, three-thousand-year-old Lord of the Radch. I doubted the assessment had been kind. And if she was no longer Anaander Mianaai, what could she ever be but some reassembled version of Tisarwat, with all the bad poetry and frivolity that implied? How could she ever see that in herself without remembering the Lord of the Radch's withering contempt? "If you sent your poetry to Lieutenant Awn," Tisarwat said, with a sharp pang of yearning mixed still with that self-hatred, "then Fleet Captain Breq has seen it."

Basnaaid blinked, began just barely to frown, but stopped herself. It might have been the idea of my having read her poetry that brought on the frown, or it may have been the tension in Lieutenant Tisarwat, in her voice, where before she had been relaxed and smiling. "I'm glad she didn't throw that in my face."

"She never would," said Tisarwat, her voice still intense.

"Lieutenant." Basnaaid put her bowl of tea down on the makeshift table beside her seat. "I meant what I said that day. And I wouldn't be here, except it's important. I hear it's the fleet captain's doing that the Undergarden is being repaired."

"Y..." Tisarwat reconsidered the simple *yes* she'd been about to give as not entirely politic. "It is, of course, entirely at the order of Station Administrator Celar, Horticulturist, but the fleet captain has had a hand in it, yes."

Basnaaid gestured acknowledgment, perfunctory. "The lake in the Gardens above—Station can't see the supports that are holding that water up and keeping it from flooding the Undergarden. It's supposed to be inspected regularly, but I don't think that's happening. And I can't say anything to the chief horticulturist. It's a cousin of hers who's supposed to do it, and the last time I said something there was a lot of noise about me minding my own business and how dare I cast aspersions." And likely if she went over the chief horticulturist's head and straight to Station Administrator Celar, she'd find herself in difficulties. Which might be worth it if the station administrator would listen, but there were no guarantees there.

"Horticulturist!" Tisarwat exclaimed, just managing, with difficulty, not to shout her eagerness to help. "I'll take care of it! All it wants is some diplomacy."

Basnaaid blinked, taken a bit aback. "I don't want... please understand, I really don't want to be asking the fleet captain for favors. I wouldn't be here, except it's so dangerous. If those supports were to fail..."

"Fleet Captain Breq won't be involved at all," said Tisarwat, solemnly. Inwardly ecstatic. "Have you mentioned this to Citizen Piat?"

"She was there when I brought it up the first time. Not that it did any good. Lieutenant, I know that you and Piat have been friendly these past several days. And I don't mean to criticize her..." She trailed off, looking for a way to say what she wanted to say.

"But," said Tisarwat into the silence, "generally she doesn't seem to care much about her job. Half the time Raughd is hanging around distracting her, and the other half she's moping. But Raughd has been downwell for the past four or five days, and if Fleet Captain Breq has anything to say about it, she's not coming back up anytime soon. I think you're going to see a difference in Piat. I think," she continued, "that she's been made to feel that she's not capable. That her own judgment is unreliable. I think she could use your support, at work."

Basnaaid tilted her head and frowned further, looked intently at Tisarwat as though she'd seen something completely, puzzlingly unexpected. "Lieutenant, how old *are* you?"

Sudden confusion, in Tisarwat. Guilt, self-loathing, a thrill of...something like triumph or gratification. "Horticulturist. I'm seventeen." A lie that wasn't exactly a lie.

"You didn't seem seventeen just now," said Basnaaid. "Did Fleet Captain Breq bring you along so you could find the weaknesses of the daughters of the station's most prominent citizens?"

"No," Tisarwat said, openly mournful. Inwardly despairing. "I think she brought me along because she thought I'd get into trouble if she wasn't watching me."

"If you'd told me that five minutes ago," said Basnaaid, "I wouldn't have believed you."

Downwell, on the path through the woods by the lake, the sky had brightened to a more vivid blue. The brightness in the east had intensified, leaving the peak blocking the sun a jagged black silhouette. Sirix still walked beside me, silent. Patient. When she had not struck me as a patient person, except by the necessity of her situation, unable as she was to express anger without considerable discomfort, likely some of it physical. So, almost certainly a pose. "You're as good as a concert, Fleet Captain," she said, slightly mocking, confirming my suspicion. "Do the songs you're always humming have anything to do with what you're thinking about, or is it random?"

"It depends." I had been humming the song the Kalr had been singing the day before, in Medical. "Sometimes it's just a song I recently heard. It's an old habit. I apologize for annoying you."

"I didn't say I was annoyed. Though I wouldn't have thought cousins of the Lord of the Radch cared much if they were annoying."

"I didn't say I would stop," I pointed out. "Do you think all that happened—transportees being sold off, I mean—and the Lord of the Radch didn't become aware of it?"

"If she'd known," Sirix said, "if she'd truly understood what was happening, it would have been like Ime." Where the system administration had been entirely corrupt, had murdered and enslaved citizens, nearly started a war with the alien Rrrrr until the matter had been brought directly to Anaander Mianaai's attention. Or at least, the attention of the right part of Anaander Mianaai. But Sirix didn't know that part of the story. "The news would have been everywhere, and the people involved would have been held accountable."

I wondered when Anaander Mianaai had become aware

of it, of people, potential citizens, being sold away for profit here. It would not have surprised me at all to discover that part of Anaander knew, or that a part of her had continued or restarted it, hidden from the rest of herself. The question then became, which Anaander was it, and what use was she making of it? I couldn't help but think of Anaander stripping ships of their ancillaries. Ships like *Mercy of Kalr*. Troop carriers like *Justice of Ente*, which Skaaiat Awer had served on. Human soldiers might not be relied on to fight for the side that wanted them replaced. Ancillaries, on the other hand, were just extensions of their ship, would do exactly what a ship was ordered to make them do. The Anaander who objected to her own dismantling of Radchaai military force might well find those bodies useful.

"You disagree," Sirix said into my silence. "But isn't justice the whole reason for civilization?"

And propriety, and benefit. "So if there is injustice here, it is only because the Lord of the Radch isn't sufficiently present."

"Can you imagine Radchaai, in the normal course of events, practicing indentured slavery, or selling indentures away, like the Xhai did?"

Behind us, in the building where we stayed, Captain Hetnys was likely eating breakfast, attended by a human body slaved to the warship *Sword of Atagaris*. One of dozens just like it. I myself had been one of thousands of such, before the rest of me had been destroyed. Sirix didn't know that, but she surely knew of the existence of other, still surviving troop carriers, still crewed by ancillaries. And over the ridge lived dozens of Valskaayans, they or their parents or grandparents transported here for no better reason than to clear a planet for Radchaai occupation, and to provide cheap labor here.

Sirix herself was descended from transportees. "Ancillaries and transportees are of course an entirely different sort of thing," I said drily.

"Well, my lord has stopped that, hasn't she?" I said nothing. She continued, "So the suspension failure rate among Valskaayan transportees seems high to you?"

"It does." I'd stored the thousands of bodies I'd once had in suspension pods. I had long, extensive experience with suspension failures. "Now I'm curious to know if the traffic in transportees stopped altogether, a hundred fifty years ago, or if it just seemed to."

"I wish my lord had come with you," Sirix said. "So she could see this for herself."

Above us, in the Undergarden, Bo Nine came into the room where Tisarwat and Basnaaid sat drinking tea. "Sir," said Bo, "there's a difficulty."

Tisarwat blinked. Swallowed her tea. Gestured Bo to explain.

"Sir, I went up to level one to get your br . . . your lunch, sir." I had left instructions for the household to purchase as much of its food (and other supplies) as possible in the Undergarden itself. "There are a lot of people around the tea shop right now. They're . . . they're angry, sir, about the repairs the fleet captain has ordered."

"Angry!" Tisarwat was taken completely aback. "At maybe having water, and light? And *air*?"

"I don't know, sir. But there are more and more people coming to the tea shop, and nobody leaving. Not to speak of."

Tisarwat stared up at Bo Nine. "But you'd think they'd be *grateful*!"

"I don't know, sir." Though I could tell, from what Ship showed me, that she agreed with her lieutenant.

Tisarwat looked at Basnaaid, still sitting across from her. Was suddenly struck by something that filled her with chagrin. "No," she said, though in answer to what I couldn't tell. "No." She looked up again at Bo Nine. "What would the fleet captain do?"

"Something only Fleet Captain would do," said Bo. And then, remembering Basnaaid's presence, "Your indulgence, sir."

Ship, Tisarwat messaged silently, *can Fleet Captain give me some help?*

"Fleet Captain Breq is in mourning, Lieutenant," came the answer in her ear. "I can pass on messages of condolence or greeting. But it would be most improper of her to involve herself in this just now."

Downwell, Sirix was saying, "Everyone here is too involved. The Lord of the Radch can be above all that, but she can't be here herself. But you have your authority from her personally, don't you?"

In the Undergarden, Lieutenant Tisarwat said, "What was this morning's cast, in the temple?"

"No Gain Without Loss," replied Bo Nine. Of course the associated verses were more complicated than that, but that was the essence of it.

Downwell, under the trees by the lake, Sirix continued. "Do you know, Emer said you were like ice that day." The woman who ran the tea shop, in the Undergarden, that was. "That translator shot right in front of you, dying under your hands, blood everywhere, and you collected and dispassionate, not a sign of any of it in your voice or your face. She said you turned around and asked her for tea."

"I hadn't had breakfast yet."

Sirix laughed, a short, sharp *hah*. "She said she thought the bowl would freeze solid when you touched it." Then, noticing, "You're distracted again."

"Yes." I stopped walking. In the Undergarden, Tisarwat had come to some conclusion. She was saying, to Bo, *Escort Horticulturist Basnaaid back to the Gardens.* Downwell by the lake, I said to Sirix, "I'm very sorry, Citizen. I find I have a lot to think about right now."

"No doubt."

We walked about thirty meters in silence (Tisarwat strode out of our Undergarden rooms and down the corridor), and then Sirix said, "I hear the daughter of the house left in a huff last night, and hasn't come back."

"So Eight is giving you the house gossip," I replied, as in the Undergarden Tisarwat began the climb to level one. "She must like you. Did she say why Raughd left?"

Sirix raised a skeptical eyebrow. "She did not. But anyone with eyes can guess. Anyone with any sense would know from the start she was a fool to set her sights on you like she did."

"You dislike Raughd, I think."

Sirix exhaled, short and sharp. Scoffing. "She's always in the offices of the Gardens. Her favorite thing is to pick someone to make fun of and get everyone else to laugh while she does it. Half the time it's Assistant Director Piat. But it's all right, you see, because she's only joking! Me being arrested for something she did is really just an extra."

"You figured that out, did you?" Upwell, in the Undergarden, Bo Nine helped Basnaaid over the pieces of shipping crate that held the level four section door open. Tisarwat climbed toward level one.

By the lake, Sirix gave me a look that communicated her contempt for the idea that she might not have known about

Raughd's involvement. "She probably flew into town. Or possibly she went to the field workers' house to roust some poor Valskaayan out of bed to amuse her."

I hadn't stopped to think that in turning Raughd down so coldly I might be inflicting her on someone else. "Amuse her how?"

Another eloquent look. "I doubt there's much you could do about it just now. Anyone you ask will swear they're more than happy to gratify the daughter of the house however she likes. How could they do otherwise?"

And likely if she'd come down here without me she'd have gone straight there, as the easiest available source of amusement and gratification. Doubtless a version of amusement and gratification that was common among the tea-growing households here. I might find some way to move Raughd somewhere else, or prevent her from doing the things she did, but the same things were likely happening in dozens of other places, to other people.

Upwell, in the level one concourse outside the tea shop, Tisarwat stepped up onto a bench. A few people outside the tea shop had noticed her arrival, and moved away, but most were intent on someone speaking inside the shop. She took a deep breath. Resolved. Certain. Whatever it was she had decided on was a relief to her, a source of desire and anticipation, but there was something about it that troubled me. "Ship," I said silently, walking beside Sirix.

"I see it, Fleet Captain," *Mercy of Kalr* replied. "But I think she's all right."

"Mention it to Medic, please."

Standing on the bench, Tisarwat called out, "Citizens!" It didn't carry well, and she tried again, pitching her voice higher. "Citizens! Is there a problem?"

Silence descended. And then someone near the tea shop door said something in Raswar I strongly suspected was an obscenity.

"It's just me," Tisarwat continued. "I heard there was a problem."

The crowd in the tea shop shifted, and someone came out, walked over to where Tisarwat stood. "Where are your soldiers, Radchaai?"

Tisarwat had been so sure of herself coming here, but now she was suddenly terrified. "Home washing dishes, Citizen," she said, managing to keep her fear out of her voice. "Out running errands. I only want to talk. I only want to know what the problem is."

The person who had come out of the tea shop laughed, short and bitter. I knew from long experience with this sort of confrontation that she was likely afraid herself. "We've gotten along fine here all this time. Now, suddenly, you're concerned about us." Tisarwat said nothing, suppressed a frown. She didn't understand. The person in front of her continued, "Now when a rich fleet captain wants rooms, suddenly you care how things are in the Undergarden. And we're cut off from any way to appeal to the palace. Where are we supposed to go, when you kick us out of here? The Xhai won't live by us. Why do you think we're here?" She stopped, waited for Tisarwat to say something. When Tisarwat remained silent (baffled, confused), she continued. "Did you expect us to be grateful? This isn't about us. You didn't even take a moment to stop and ask what *we* wanted. So what were you planning to do with us? Reeducate us all? Kill us? Make us into ancillaries?"

"No!" cried Tisarwat. Indignant. And also ashamed— because she knew as well as I did that there had been times and places where such a concern would have been well founded. And from what we'd seen when we arrived, with the painter and *Sword of Atagaris*, there was some reason to suspect that this was one of those times and places. "The plan is to confirm existing housing arrangements." A few people scoffed. "And you're right," Tisarwat went on, "Station Administration should be hearing your concerns. We can talk about them right now if you like. And then you"— she gestured at the person standing in front of her—"and I can take those concerns directly to Station Administrator Celar. In fact, we could set up an office on level four where anyone could come and talk about problems with the repairs, or things that you want, and we could make sure that gets to Administration."

"Level four?" someone cried. "Not all of us can get up and down those ladders!"

"I don't think there's room on level one, Citizen," said Tisarwat. "Except maybe right here, but that would be very inconvenient for Citizen Emer's customers, or anyone who walks through here." Which was nearly everyone in the Undergarden. "So maybe when this good citizen and I"—she gestured toward the person in front of her—"visit Administration today, after we talk here, we'll let them know that repairing the lifts needs to be a priority."

Silence. People had begun to come, slowly, cautiously, out of the shop and into the tiny, makeshift concourse. Now one of them said, "The way we usually do this sort of thing, Lieutenant, is we all sit down, and whoever is speaking stands up." In a tone that was almost a challenge. "We leave the bench for those who can't sit on the ground."

Tisarwat looked down at the bench she was standing on. Looked out at the people before her—a good fifty or sixty, and more still coming out of the tea shop. "Right," she said. "Then I'll get down."

As Sirix and I returned to the house, Fleet Captain Uemi's message reached *Mercy of Kalr*. Medic was on watch. "All respect to Fleet Captain Breq," came the words into Medic's ear. "Does she desire some sort of firsthand or personal information? I assure you that I was the only person on *Sword of Inil* to spend more than a few minutes on Omaugh."

Medic, unlike Seivarden or Ekalu, understood the import of the questions I had been asking of Fleet Captain Uemi. And so she was horrified rather than puzzled when she spoke the reply I'd left, in case the answers to my questions had been what they were. "Fleet Captain Breq begs Fleet Captain Uemi's very generous indulgence and would like to know if Fleet Captain Uemi is feeling quite entirely herself lately."

I didn't expect a reply to that, and never did receive one.

15

Fosyf's servants spoke quite freely in the presence of my silent and expressionless Kalrs. Raughd had not, in fact, gone immediately to her mother, as she had threatened, but ordered a servant to pack her things and fly her to the elevator that would take her upwell, to a shuttle that would bring her to Athoek Station.

Most of the servants did not like me, and said so outside the house where we were staying, or in the kitchen of the main building, where Five and Six went on various errands. I was arrogant and cold. The humming would drive anyone to distraction, and I was lucky my personal attendants were ancillaries (that always gave Five and Eight a little frisson of satisfaction) who didn't care about such things. My bringing Sirix Odela here could be nothing but a calculated insult—they knew who she was, knew her history. And I had been cruel to the daughter of the house. None of them knew exactly what had happened, but they understood the outlines of it.

Some of the servants went silent hearing such opinions

expressed, their faces nearly masks, the twitch of an eyebrow or the corner of a mouth betraying what they'd have liked to say. A few of the more forthcoming pointed out (very quietly) that Raughd herself had a history of cruelty, of rages when she didn't get what she wanted. *Like her mother that way*, muttered one of the dissenters, where only Kalr Five could hear it.

"The nurse left when Raughd was only three," Five told Eight, while I was out on one of my walks and Sirix still slept. "Couldn't take the mother any longer."

"Where were the other parents?" asked Eight.

"Oh, the mother wouldn't have any other parents. Or *they* wouldn't have *her*. The daughter of the house is a clone. She's meant to be *exactly* like the mother. And hears about it when she isn't, I gather. That's why they feel so sorry for her, some of them."

"The mother doesn't like children very much, does she?" observed Eight, who had noticed that the household's children were kept well away from Fosyf and her guests.

"*I* don't like children very much, to be honest," replied Five. "Well, no. Children are all sorts of people, aren't they, and I suppose if I knew more I'd find some I like and some I don't, just like everyone else. But I'm glad nobody's depending on me to have any, and I don't really know what to *do* with them, if you know what I mean. Still, I know not to do things like *that*."

Two days after she'd left, Raughd was back. When she'd arrived at the foot of the elevator, she hadn't been allowed to board. She'd insisted that she always had permission to travel to the station, but in vain. She was not on the list, did not have a permit, and her messages to the station administrator went unanswered. Citizen Piat was similarly unresponsive. Security arrived, suggested with extreme courtesy and deference that perhaps Raughd might want to return to the house by the lake.

Somewhat surprisingly, that was exactly what she'd done. I would have guessed she'd have stayed in the city at the foot of the elevator, where surely she'd have found company for the sort of games she enjoyed, but instead she returned to the mountains.

She arrived in the middle of the night. Just before breakfast, while the account of her fruitless attempt to leave the planet was only just beginning to reach the servants outside the kitchen in the main building, Raughd ordered her personal attendant to go to Fosyf as soon as she woke and demand a meeting. Most of the kitchen servants didn't like Raughd's personal attendant much—she derived, they felt, a bit too much satisfaction from her status as the personal servant of the daughter of the house. Still (one assistant cook said to another, in the hearing of Kalr Five), her worst enemies would not have wished to force her to confront Fosyf Denche with such a message.

The subsequent meeting was private. Which in that household meant in earshot of only three or four servants. Or, when Fosyf shouted, half a dozen. And shout she did. This entire situation was of Raughd's making. In attempting to remedy it, she had only made it worse, had set out to make me an ally but through her own ineptness had made me an enemy instead. It was no wonder I had turned Raughd down flat, inadequate and worthless as she was. Fosyf was ashamed to admit that they had even the slightest relationship to each other. Raughd had clearly also mishandled Station Administrator Celar. Fosyf herself would never have made such mistakes, and clearly there had been some sort of flaw in the cloning process because no one with Fosyf's DNA could possibly be such a useless waste of food and air. One word, one *breath* from Raughd in protest of these obvious truths, and she would be cast out of the house. There was time yet to grow a new, better heir. Hearing this, Raughd did not protest, but returned, silent, to her room.

Just before lunch, as I was leaving my own room in our smaller house, Raughd's personal attendant walked into the middle of the main kitchen and stood, silent and trembling, her gaze fixed, off somewhere distant and overhead. Eight was there seeing after something for Sirix. At first no one noticed the attendant, everyone was working busily on getting the last of the food prepared, but after a few moments one of the assistant cooks looked up, saw the attendant standing there shaking, and gave a loud gasp. "The honey!" the assistant cook cried. "Where's the honey?"

Everyone looked up. Saw the attendant, whose trembling only increased, who began, now, to open her mouth as though she was about to speak, or possibly vomit, and then closed it again, over and over. "It's too late!" someone else said, and the second assistant cook said, panic in her voice, "I used all the honey in the cakes for this afternoon!"

"Oh, *shit*!" said a servant who had just come into the kitchen with dirty teabowls, and I knew from the way no one turned to admonish her that whatever this was, it was serious business.

Someone dragged in a chair, and three servants took hold of Raughd's attendant and lowered her into it, still shaking, still opening and closing her mouth. The first assistant cook came running with a honey-soaked cake and broke a piece off, put it into the attendant's gaping mouth. It tumbled out onto the floor, to cries of dismay. The attendant looked more and more as though she were going to throw up, but instead she made a long, low moan.

"Oh, do something! Do something!" begged the servant with the dirty dishes. Lunch was entirely forgotten.

By this time I had begun to have some idea of what was happening. I had seen things something like this before, though not this particular reaction to it.

"Are you all right, Fleet Captain?" Sirix, in the other building, in the hallway outside both our rooms. She must have come out while I was absorbed by the goings-on in the main building's kitchen.

I blinked the vision away, so that I could see Sirix and answer. "I didn't realize the Samirend practiced spirit possession."

Sirix did not attempt to hide her expression of distaste at my words. But then she turned her face away, as though she was ashamed to meet my gaze, and made a disgusted noise. "What must you think of us, Fleet Captain?"

Us. Of course. Sirix was Samirend.

"It's the kind of thing someone does," she continued, "when they're feeling ignored or put out. Everyone rushes to give them sweets and say kind things to them."

The whole thing seemed less like something the attendant was *doing* than something that was happening *to* her. And I hadn't noticed anyone saying kind things to her. But my attention had strayed from the kitchen, and now I saw that one of the field overseers, the one who had met us the day we'd arrived and had seemed completely oblivious to the field workers' ability to speak and understand Radchaai, was now kneeling next to the chair where the still trembling, moaning attendant sat. "You should have called me sooner!" the overseer said sharply, and someone else said, "We only just saw her!"

"It's all to stop the spirit speaking," said Sirix, still standing beside me in the corridor, still disgusted and, I was certain now, ashamed. "If it speaks, likely it'll curse someone. People will do anything to stop it. One petulant person can hold an entire household hostage for days that way."

I didn't believe in spirits or gods to possess anyone, but I doubted this was something the attendant had done consciously, or without a true need of whatever the reaction of the other servants might provide for her. And she was, after all, constantly subject to Raughd Denche with very little real respite. "Sweets?" I asked Sirix. "Not just honey?"

Sirix blinked once, twice. A stillness came over her that I'd seen before, when she was angry or offended. It was as though my question had been a personal insult. "I don't think I'm interested in lunch," she said coldly, and turned and went back into her room.

In the main kitchen, the head cook, clearly relieved by the presence of the overseer, took firm charge of the dismayed, staring servants and managed to admonish and cajole the rest of the work from them. Meanwhile the overseer put fragments of honey cake into the attendant's mouth. Each one fell out onto her lap, but the overseer doggedly replaced them. As she worked, she intoned words in Liost, from the sound of it. From the context, it must have been a prayer.

Eventually, the attendant's moans and shaking stopped, whatever curse she might have uttered unspoken. She pled exhaustion for the rest of the day, which no one, servants or family, seemed to question, at least not in Eight's hearing. The next morning she was back at her post, and the household staff was noticeably kinder to her after that.

Raughd avoided me. I saw her only rarely, in the late afternoon or early evening, on her way to the bathhouse. If we crossed paths she pointedly did not speak to me. She spent much of her time either in the nearby town or, more disturbingly, over the ridge at the field workers' house.

I considered leaving, but we still had more than a week of full mourning to go. An interruption like this would only appear ill-omened, the proper execution of the funeral rites compromised. Perhaps the Presger, or their translators, wouldn't understand, or care. Still. Twice I had seen the Presger underestimated with disastrous results—once by Governor Giarod and Captain Hetnys, and once by Anaander Mianaai herself, when she had thought she had the power to destroy them and in response they had put those invisible, all-piercing guns in the hands of the Garseddai the Lord of the Radch thought she had so easily conquered. The Presger had not done it to save the Garseddai, who had in the event been completely destroyed, every one of them dead, every planet and station in their home system burned and lifeless, with no action, no protest from the Presger. No, they had done it, I was sure, to send a message to Anaander Mianaai: *Don't even think about it*. I would not underestimate them in my turn.

Fosyf still visited our small house daily, and treated me with her usual jovial obliviousness. I came to see her strangely serene manner as both a sign of just how much she expected to get whatever she wanted, and also an instrument by which she managed to do that, plain persistent saying what she wanted to be true in the expectation that it would eventually become so. It's a method I'd found worked best for those who are already positioned to mostly get what they want. Obviously Fosyf had found it worked for her.

* * *

Above, on Athoek Station, even with Lieutenant Tisarwat's push, with Station Administrator Celar's involvement, a thorough inspection of the Gardens' supports wouldn't happen for more than a week. "To be entirely honest," Tisarwat explained to Basnaaid one afternoon, in my sitting room on the station, "there are so many things that need urgent attention that it keeps getting pushed back." I read her determination, her continuing thrill at being able to help Basnaaid. But also an undercurrent of unhappiness. "I'm sure if the fleet captain were here she'd find some way to just...make it happen."

"I'm impressed that it seems likely to happen at all," said Basnaaid, with a smile that left Tisarwat momentarily, speechlessly, pleased with herself.

Recovering her self-possession, Tisarwat said, "It's not anything urgent, but I was wondering if Horticulture could provide some plants for public areas here."

"It can't help but improve the air quality!" Basnaaid laughed. "There might not be enough light yet, though." And then, at another thought, still amused, "Maybe they could put some of those mushrooms out."

"The mushrooms!" exclaimed Tisarwat, in frustration. "Nobody will tell me where they're growing them. I'm not sure what they're afraid of. Sometimes I think everyone here must be growing them in a box under their beds or something, and that's why they're so anxious about Station Maintenance coming into their quarters."

"They make money off the mushrooms, don't they? And if the chief of Horticulture got her hands on them, you know she'd figure out a way to keep them in the Gardens and charge outrageous prices for them."

"But they could still grow them here," Tisarwat argued,

"and still sell them themselves. So I don't know what the problem is." She gestured dismissal of her irritation. "Speaking of mushrooms. Shall I send Nine out for something to eat?"

On *Mercy of Kalr*, Seivarden sat in the decade room with *Sword of Atagaris*'s Amaat lieutenant. *Sword of Atagaris*'s lieutenant had brought a bottle of arrack. "Very kind," Seivarden said, with barely detectable condescension. The other lieutenant did not seem to see it at all. "With your pardon, I won't have any. I've taken a vow." It was the sort of thing someone might do for penance, or just an occasional spiritual practice. She handed the bottle to Amaat Three, who took it and set it on the decade room counter, and then went to stand by the *Sword of Atagaris* ancillary that had accompanied its officer.

"Very admirable!" replied the *Sword of Atagaris* Amaat lieutenant. "And better you than me." She picked up her bowl of tea. Three had begged Kalr Five for permission to use the best porcelain—still packed away in my own quarters on the ship, because Five hadn't wanted anything to happen to it—and thus humiliate the *Sword of Atagaris* lieutenant with an obvious show of my status. Five had refused, and suggested instead that Amaat Three come around from the other direction and serve the lieutenants from my old, chipped enamel set. Three had been briefly tempted, remembering, as the entire crew did, *Sword of Atagaris*'s threat when we'd entered the system. But propriety had won out, and so the *Sword of Atagaris* lieutenant drank her tea unconscious of her narrow escape from insult. "Seivarden is a very old-fashioned name," she said, with a joviality that struck me as false. "Your parents must have loved history." One of Anaander Mianaai's allies, before she had grown beyond the confines of the Radch itself, had been named Seivarden.

"It was a traditional name in my family," Seivarden replied coolly. Indignant, but also enjoying the other lieutenant's confusion—Seivarden had not yet offered a house name, and because that house was no longer in existence, because she had been separated from them by some thousand years, Seivarden wore none of the jewelry that would have indicated family associations. And even if Seivarden had still owned any, this lieutenant likely would have recognized very little of it, so much had changed in all that time.

The *Sword of Atagaris* lieutenant appeared not to notice the past tense in Seivarden's sentence. "From Inai, you said. What province is that?"

"Outradch," replied Seivarden with a pleasant smile. Outradch was the oldest of provinces, and the closest most Radchaai had ever been to the Radch itself. "You're wondering about my family connections," Seivarden continued, not out of any desire to help the visiting lieutenant through a potentially awkward social situation, but rather out of impatience. "I'm Seivarden Vendaai."

The other lieutenant frowned, not placing the name for half a second. Then she realized. "You're Captain Seivarden!"

"I am."

The *Sword of Atagaris* lieutenant laughed. "Amaat's grace, what a comedown! Bad enough to be frozen for a thousand years, but then to be busted back to lieutenant and sent to a *Mercy*! Guess you'll have to work your way back up." She took another drink of tea. "There's been some speculation in our decade room. It's unusual to find a fleet captain in command of a *Mercy*. We've been wondering if Fleet Captain Breq isn't going to send Captain Hetnys here and take *Sword of Atagaris* for herself. It *is* the faster and the better armed of the two, after all."

Seivarden blinked. Said, in a dangerously even tone, "Don't underestimate *Mercy of Kalr.*"

"Oh, come now, Lieutenant, I didn't mean any offense. *Mercy of Kalr* is a perfectly good ship, for a *Mercy*. But the fact of the matter is, if it came down to it, *Sword of Atagaris* could defeat *Mercy of Kalr* quite handily. You've commanded a *Sword* yourself, you know it's true. And of course *Sword of Atagaris* still has its ancillaries. No human soldier is as fast or as strong as an ancillary."

Amaat Three, standing by waiting in case she should be needed, showed of course no outward reaction, but for an instant I worried she might assault the *Sword of Atagaris* lieutenant. I wouldn't have minded much (though of course Seivarden would have had to reprimand her), but Three was standing right next to the *Sword of Atagaris* ancillary, who would certainly not allow anyone to injure its lieutenant. And no amount of training or practice would make Amaat Three a match for an ancillary.

Seivarden, with just a bit more freedom to express her anger, set down her bowl of tea and sat up straighter and said, "Lieutenant, was that a threat?"

"Amaat's grace, no, Lieutenant!" The *Sword of Atagaris* lieutenant seemed genuinely shocked that her words might have been taken that way. "I was just stating a fact. We're all on the same side, here."

"Are we?" Seivarden's lip curled, aristocratic anger and contempt that I had not seen for more than a year. "This is why you attacked us when we came into the system, because we're on the same side?"

"Amaat's grace!" The other lieutenant tried to seem unfazed at Seivarden's reaction. "That was a misunderstanding! I'm sure you can understand we've all been very tense since the gates went down. And as far as threatening you now, I intended no such thing, I assure you. I was merely pointing out an obvious fact. And it *is* unusual for a fleet captain to command a *Mercy*, though perhaps it wasn't in your day. But it's perfectly natural that we should wonder whether we'll lose Captain Hetnys and end up serving under Fleet Captain Breq directly."

Seivarden became, if anything, more contemptuous. "Fleet Captain Breq will do as she thinks best. But in the interest of preventing further *misunderstanding*"—she leaned on that word just a bit—"let me say clearly and unequivocally that the next time you threaten this ship you'd best be able to make good on it."

The *Sword of Atagaris* lieutenant reiterated that she had never, ever meant to do such a thing, and Seivarden smiled and changed the subject.

On the station, Basnaaid was saying to Lieutenant Tisarwat, "I never met my sister. I was born after she left. I was born *because* she left. Because she was sending home money, and if she'd made officer, I might do something, too. Something better than steaming fish and chopping vegetables." Lieutenant Awn's parents had been cooks. "It was always Awn I was living up to. Always Awn I should be grateful to. Of course my parents never said so, but I always felt as though nothing was ever for *me*, for my own sake, it was always about *her*. Her messages were always so kind, and of course I looked up to her. She was a hero, the first of our house to really *be* someone..." She gave a rueful laugh. "Listen to me. As though my family were nobodies, all of them." Lieutenant Tisarwat waited in un-seventeen-year-old-like silence, and Basnaaid continued, "It was worse after she died. I could never forget all the ways I didn't measure up to her. Even her friends! Awer is so far above Elming they might as well not even be in the same universe. And now Mianaai."

"And those friends," put in Lieutenant Tisarwat, "were offering you things because of your sister, not because of anything you'd done to deserve it." I wondered if Tisarwat had worked out why she was so infatuated with Basnaaid. Possibly not—at this moment she was clearly focused on listening to Basnaaid, on understanding her. Pleased to help. To be confided in.

"Awn *never* knelt." Basnaaid seemed not to notice the strangeness of Lieutenant Tisarwat's words or demeanor, so much older than her apparent age. Had become accustomed to it, perhaps, over the past few days. "She never would have. If she made friends like that, it was because of who she was."

"Yes," said Tisarwat, simple agreement. "The fleet captain has said so." Basnaaid didn't answer this, and the conversation turned to other things.

Three days before we were to leave, Captain Hetnys finally broached the topic of the daughter of the house. We sat under the arbor, the doors of the house wide open behind us. Fosyf was attending something at the manufactory, and Raughd of course was away at the field workers' house. Sirix had gone down to a shady section of the lakeshore, she said to watch for fish but I suspected she just wanted to be by herself, without even Eight hovering behind her. There was only Captain Hetnys and myself, and *Sword of Atagaris*'s ancillary, and Kalr Five nearby. We sat looking out at the shaded stretch of mossy stone, the ridge, and the black, ice-streaked peaks beyond. The main building was off to the left, the bath ahead, where it was in easy reach of the main house but would not obscure the scenery, one end of its glass wall curving into view. Despite the brightness of the afternoon, the air under the trees and the arbor was damp and cool.

"Sir," said Captain Hetnys. "Permission to speak frankly."

I gestured my assent. In all the time we'd been here, Captain Hetnys had not once mentioned what had brought us here, though she had daily put on the mourning stripe and said the required prayers.

"Sir, I've been thinking about what happened in the Undergarden. I still think I was right to give the orders I did. It went wrong, and I take responsibility for that." Her words were in themselves defiant, but her tone was deferential.

"Do you, Captain?" One of the household groundcars came over the ridge, along the road. Either Fosyf returning from the manufactory, or Raughd from the field workers' house. That situation could not stay as it was, but I hadn't managed to come up with a solution. Perhaps there was none.

"I do, sir. But I was wrong to have Citizen Sirix arrested. I was wrong to assume that she must have done it, if Raughd was the only other choice."

The sort of thing I had always liked, in an officer. The willingness to admit she was in the wrong, when she realized it. The willingness to insist she was in the right, when she was sure of it, even when it might be safer not to. She watched me, serious, slightly frightened of my reaction, I thought. Slightly challenging. But only slightly. No Radchaai officer openly defied her superior, not if she wasn't suicidal. I thought of that priceless antique tea set. Its sale was almost certainly meant to cover illegal profits. Thought of the implausible death rates of transportees to this system. Wondered, for just a moment, how these two things could coexist in Captain Hetnys, this courage and integrity alongside the willingness to sell away lives for a profit. Wondered what sort of officer she would be if I had had the raising of her from a baby lieutenant. Possibly the same as she was now. Possibly not. Possibly she would be dead now, vaporized with the rest of my crew when Anaander Mianaai had breached my heat shield some twenty years ago.

Or perhaps not. If it had been Lieutenant Hetnys commanding me in Ors, on Shis'urna, and not Lieutenant Awn, perhaps I would still be myself, still *Justice of Toren*, and my crew would still be alive.

"I know, sir," said Captain Hetnys, emboldened further, perhaps, by my not having answered, "that prominent as this house is here at Athoek, they must seem like nothing to you. From such a great distance, Raughd Denche looks very little different from Sirix Odela."

"On the contrary," I replied evenly. "I see a great difference between Raughd Denche and Sirix Odela." As I spoke, Raughd strolled out of the main building, on her way to the bathhouse, all studied unconcern.

"I mean to say, sir, that from the great elevation of Mianaai, Denche must appear as no different than other servants. And I know it's always said that we each have our role, our given task, and none of them is any better or worse than another, just different." I had heard it said many times myself. Strange, how *equally important, just different* always seemed to translate into some "equally important" roles being more worthy of respect and reward than others. "But," Captain Hetnys continued, "we don't all have your perspective. And I imagine..." The briefest of hesitations. "I imagine if ever your cousins committed some youthful foolishness or indiscretion, they were not treated much differently than Raughd Denche. And that is as it is, sir." She lifted her green-gloved hands, the vague suggestion of pious supplication. All that was, was Amaat. The universe was God itself, and nothing could happen or exist that God did not will. "But perhaps you can understand why everyone here might see the daughter of this house in that light, or why she herself might think herself equal to even a fleet captain, and a cousin of the Lord of the Radch."

Almost. *Almost* she might have understood. "You see Raughd, I think, as a nice, well-bred young person who has somehow, in the past few weeks, made some inexplicably unfortunate choices. That I am perhaps being too harsh on someone who does not live under the military discipline you or I have been accustomed to. Perhaps the daughter of the house has even spoken to you of enemies of hers who have whispered accusations into my ear, and prejudiced me against her unfairly." A brief change of expression flashed across Captain Hetnys's face, nearly a plain admission I was right. "But consider those unfortunate choices. They were, from the beginning, meant to harm. Meant to harm residents of the Undergarden. Meant, Captain, to harm you. To harm the entire station. She could not have anticipated the death of Translator Dlique, but surely she knew your ancillaries went armed, and knew how uneasy you were about the Undergarden." Captain Hetnys was silent, looking down at her lap, hands empty, her bowl of tea cooling on the bench beside her. "Nice, well-bred people do not just suddenly act maliciously for no reason."

This would clearly go nowhere. And I had other things I wanted to know. I had spent some time considering how someone could remove transportees from the system without anyone knowing. "The Ghost Gate," I said.

"Sir?" She looked, I thought, not quite as relieved at the change of topic as she might have.

"The dead-end gate. You never met another ship there?"

Was that hesitation? A change of expression, gone from her face before it could be read? Surprise? Fear? "No, sir, never."

A lie. I wanted to look toward *Sword of Atagaris*, standing stiff and silent beside Kalr Five. But I would never catch, from an ancillary, any subtle reaction to its captain's lie. And the glance itself would betray my thoughts. That I recognized the lie for what it was. Instead I looked over toward the bathhouse. Raughd Denche came striding out, back the way she'd come, a grim set to her expression that boded ill for any servant who might come across her path. I almost looked around to see where her personal attendant was, and realized, with surprise, that she hadn't followed Raughd into the bathhouse.

Captain Hetnys also noticed Raughd. She blinked, and frowned, and then shook her head slightly, dismissal, I thought. Of Raughd's obvious anger, or of me, I couldn't tell. "Fleet Captain," she said, glancing toward the bathhouse, "with your indulgent permission. It's very warm today."

"Of course, Captain," I replied, and remained sitting as she rose, and bowed, and walked away across the mossy stones, angling toward the bathhouse. *Sword of Atagaris* fell quickly in behind her.

She had walked about halfway across the shaded green and gray yard, was directly in front of that curving end of the bathhouse window, when the bomb went off.

It had been twenty-five years since I'd seen combat. Or at least the sort of combat where bombs were likely to go off. Still, I had been a ship filled with bodies for fighting. So it was due to two-thousand-year-old habit that without any sort of effort at all, nearly the instant I saw the flash in the bathhouse window, and almost (but not quite) instantaneously saw the window shatter and its pieces fly outward, I was on my feet and my armor was fully extended.

I suspected *Sword of Atagaris* had never seen ground combat, but it reacted almost as quickly as I had, extending its armor and moving with inhuman speed to put itself between the flying glass and its unarmored captain. The front of glittering, jagged glass swept out from the window, tearing leaves and branches from the trees shading the stones, reached the ancillary, knocked it to the ground, Captain Hetnys beneath it. The barest moment later a scatter of small bits of glass and leaves and twigs reached me and bounced harmlessly off my armor. A quick thought told me that although Kalr Five had only just finished raising her armor, she was quite safe. "Give me your medkit," I said to her. And when she'd done that, I sent her to call for Medical, and for Planetary Security, and then went to see if Captain Hetnys had survived.

Flames licked the edges of the shattered bathhouse window. Shards and fragments of glass littered the ground, some snapping or crunching underfoot as I went. Captain Hetnys lay on her back, awkwardly, under *Sword of Atagaris*. A strange, misshapen fin protruded from between the ancillary's shoulder blades, and I realized that it must be a large shard of glass that had embedded itself before *Sword of Atagaris* could completely raise its armor. Its reaction had been fast, but not quite as fast as mine, and it and Captain Hetnys had been some twenty meters closer to the window than I had.

I knelt beside them. "*Sword of Atagaris*, how badly injured is your captain?"

"I'm fine, sir," replied Captain Hetnys before the ancillary could answer. She tried to roll over, to shove *Sword of Atagaris* off her.

"Don't move, Captain," I said sharply, as I tore open Kalr Five's medkit. "*Sword of Atagaris*, your report."

"Captain Hetnys has sustained a minor concussion, lacerations, an abrasion, and some bruising, Fleet Captain." Its armor distorted *Sword of Atagaris*'s voice, and of course it spoke with the expressionlessness typical of ancillaries, but I thought I heard some strain. "She is otherwise fine, as she has already indicated."

"Get off me, Ship," said Captain Hetnys, irritably.

"I don't think it can," I said. "There's a piece of glass lodged in its spinal column. Lower your armor, *Sword of Atagaris*." The medkit held a special-made general-purpose corrective, designed to slow bleeding, halt further tissue damage, and just generally keep someone alive long enough to get them to a medical facility.

"Fleet Captain," said *Sword of Atagaris*, "with all respect, my captain is unarmored and there might be another bomb."

"There's not much we can do about that without killing this segment," I pointed out. Though I was sure there had only been the one bomb, sure that blast had been meant to kill one person in particular, rather than as many as possible. "And the sooner you let me medkit you, the sooner we can move you and get your captain out of danger." Uncomfortable and annoyed as she clearly was, Captain Hetnys frowned even further, and stared at me as though I had spoken in some language she had never heard before and could not understand.

Sword of Atagaris dropped its armor, revealing its uniform jacket, blood-soaked between the shoulders, and the jagged glass shard. "How deep is it?" I asked.

"Very deep, Fleet Captain," it replied. "Repairs will take some time."

"No doubt." The medkit also included a small blade for cutting clothes away from wounds. I pulled it out, sliced the bloody fabric out of the way. Laid the corrective on the ancillary's back, as close as I could to where the glass protruded without jostling it and maybe causing further injury. The corrective oozed and puddled—it would take a few moments (or, depending on the nature and extent of the injuries it encountered, a few minutes) to stabilize the situation, and then harden. Once it had, *Sword of Atagaris* could probably be moved safely.

The fire in the bathhouse had taken hold, fed by that beautiful woodwork. Three servants were standing by the main building, staring, aghast. More were running out of the house to see what had happened. Kalr Five and another servant hastened toward us, carrying something flat and wide—*Mercy of Kalr* had told her there was a spinal injury. I didn't see Raughd anywhere.

Captain Hetnys still stared at me from under *Sword of Atagaris*, frowning. "Fleet Captain," said the ancillary, "with all respect, this injury is too severe to be worth repairing. Please take Captain Hetnys to safety." Its voice and its face were of course expressionless, but tears welled in its eyes, whether from pain or from something else it was impossible for me to know. I could guess, though.

"Your captain is safe, *Sword of Atagaris*," I said. "Be easy on that score." The last bit of cloudiness cleared from the corrective on its back. Gently I brushed it with a gloved finger. No streak, no smudge. Kalr Five dropped to her knees beside us, set down the board—it looked to be a tabletop. The servant carrying the other end didn't know how to move people with back injuries, so Kalr Five and I moved *Sword of Atagaris* off of Captain Hetnys, who rose, looked at *Sword of Atagaris* lying silent and motionless on the tabletop, the shard of glass sticking up out of its back. Looked, still frowning, at me.

"Captain," I said to her as Kalr Five and the servant carefully bore *Sword of Atagaris* away, "we need to have a talk with our host."

16

The explosion had put an end to any mourning proprieties. We met in the main house's formal sitting room, a broad window (facing the lake, of course), scattered benches and chairs cushioned in gold and pale blue, low tables of dark wood, the walls more of that carved scrollwork that must have occupied the entirety of some servant's duties. Over in one corner, on a stand, sat a tall, long-necked, square-bodied stringed instrument that I didn't recognize, which suggested it was Athoeki. Next to that, on another stand, was that ancient tea set in its box, lid open the better to display it.

Fosyf herself stood in the center of the room, Captain Hetnys in a chair nearby, at Fosyf's insistence. Raughd paced at one end of the room, back and forth until her mother said, "Sit down, Raughd," ostensibly pleasantly but an edge to her voice. Raughd sat, tense, didn't lean back.

"It was a bomb, of course," I said. "Not very large, probably something stolen off a construction site, but whoever placed it added scraps of metal that were meant to maim or kill whoever might be close enough." Some of that had reached Captain Hetnys but had been blocked by *Sword of Atagaris*. It had arrived just the barest instant after that shard of glass.

"Me!" cried Raughd, and rose to her feet again, gloved hands clenched, and resumed her pacing. "That was meant for *me*! I can tell you who it was, it can't have been anyone else!"

"A moment, Citizen," I said. "Probably stolen off a construction site, because while it's easy to find bits of scrap metal, finding the actual explosive is of course more difficult." Quite deliberately so. Though sufficient determination and ingenuity could find ways around nearly any restrictions. "Of course, explosives aren't generally left lying around. Whoever did this either has access to such things or knows someone who does. We can probably track them down that way."

"*I know who it was!*" Raughd insisted, and would have said more except the doctor and the district magistrate entered just at that moment.

The doctor went immediately to where Captain Hetnys sat. "Captain, no nonsense from you, I must examine you to be sure you are unhurt."

The district magistrate had opened her mouth to speak to me. I forestalled her with a gesture. "Doctor, the captain's injuries are fortunately minor. *Sword of Atagaris*'s ancillary, on the other hand, is very badly hurt and will need treatment as soon as you can manage."

The doctor drew herself up straight, indignant. "Are you a doctor, Fleet Captain?"

"Are *you*?" I asked coldly. I couldn't help but compare her to my own ship's medic. "If you're looking at Captain Hetnys with your medical implants turned on, it should be obvious to you that she has sustained little more than cuts and bruises. *Sword of Atagaris*, which sees her even more intimately, has said its captain is largely uninjured. Its ancillary, on the other hand, has had a twenty-six-centimeter shard of glass driven into its spinal column. The sooner you treat it the more effective that treatment will be." I did not add that I spoke from personal experience.

"Fleet Captain," the doctor replied, just as coldly, "I don't need you to lecture me on my own assignment. An injury of that sort will have a long and difficult recovery period. I'm afraid the best course will be to dispose of the ancillary. I'm sure it will be inconvenient for Captain Hetnys, but really it's the only reasonable choice."

"Doctor," interposed Captain Hetnys, before I could reply, "perhaps it's best to just treat the ancillary."

"With all respect to you, of course, Captain Hetnys," said the doctor, "I am not subject to the authority of the fleet captain, only my own, and I will rely on my own judgment and my medical training."

"Come, Doctor," said Fosyf, who had been silent so far. "The fleet captain and the captain both want the ancillary treated, surely Captain Hetnys is willing to deal with its recovery. What harm can there be in treating it?"

I suspected that the doctor, as was common in this sort of household, did not merely work for the tea plantation but was also a client of Fosyf's. Her continued well-being depended on Fosyf, and so she could not answer her in the same terms as she had answered me. "If *you* insist, Citizen," she said with a small bow.

"Don't trouble yourself," I said. "Five." Kalr Five had stood silent and straight by the door this whole time, in case I should need her. "Find a proper doctor in the town and have her come and see to *Sword of Atagaris* as quickly as possible." Sooner would have been much better, but I did not trust this doctor at all. I didn't wonder that the field workers would rather bleed to death than consult her. I wished very much that Medic was here.

"Sir," replied Five, and turned neatly and was out the door.

"Fleet Captain," began the doctor, "I've said I'll..."

I turned away from her, to the district magistrate. "Magistrate." I bowed. "A pleasure to meet you, sadly in unfortunate circumstances."

The magistrate bowed, with a sidelong glance at the doctor, but said only, "Likewise, Fleet Captain. I'm here so quickly because I was already on my way to pay my respects. May I express my sorrow at your loss." I nodded acknowledgment of this. "As you were saying when we came in, we can probably find whoever made this bomb by tracking the materials it was made with. Security is even now examining what remains of the bathhouse. A sad loss." She directed that last to Citizen Fosyf.

"My daughter is unhurt," Fosyf replied. "That's all that matters."

"That bomb was meant for me!" cried Raughd, who had stood fuming all this time. "I know who it was! There's no need to go tracking anything!"

"Who was it, Citizen?" I asked.

"Queter. It was Queter. She's always hated me."

The name was Valskaayan. "One of the field workers?" I asked.

"She works in the manufactory, maintaining the dryers," said Fosyf.

"Well," said the magistrate, "I'll send—"

I interrupted her. "Magistrate, your indulgence. Do any of the people you've brought speak Delsig?"

"A few words, Fleet Captain, no more."

"As it happens," I said, "I'm fluent in Delsig." Had spent decades on Valskaay itself, but I did not say that. "Let me go down to the field workers' house and talk to Citizen Queter and see what I can discover."

"You don't need to *discover* anything," insisted Raughd. "Who else could it be? She's always hated me."

"Why?" I asked.

"She thinks I've corrupted her baby sister. Those people have the most unreasonable ideas about things."

I turned to the magistrate again. "Magistrate, allow me to go alone to the field workers' house and talk to Citizen Queter. In the meantime your staff can trace the explosive."

"Let me send some security with you, Fleet Captain," said the magistrate. "Arresting this person all by yourself, surrounded by Valskaayans—I think you might want some help."

"There's no need," I replied. "I won't need the help, and I have no fear for my safety."

The magistrate blinked, and frowned, just slightly. "No, Fleet Captain, I don't suppose you do."

I walked to the field workers' house, though Fosyf offered me the use of a groundcar. The sun was going down, and the fields I passed were empty. The house sat silent, no one outside, no movement. If I didn't know better I might have thought it abandoned. Everyone would be inside. But they would be expecting someone—Fosyf, Planetary Security, the district magistrate. Soldiers. There would be a lookout.

As I came in earshot of the house I opened my mouth, drew breath, and sang:

> *I am the soldier*
> *So greedy, so hungry for songs.*

So many I've swallowed, they leak out,
They spill out of the corners of my mouth
And fly away, desperate for freedom.

The front door opened. The lookout who had sung those words, that first morning when I had run past the workers picking tea. I smiled to see her, and bowed as I came closer. "I've been wanting to compliment you on that," I said to her, in Delsig. "It was nicely done. Did you compose it that moment, or had you thought about it before? I'm only curious—it was impressive either way."

"It's only a song I was singing, Radchaai," she replied. Radchaai only meant "Citizen," but I knew that in the mouth of a Valskaayan, speaking Delsig, in that tone of voice, it was a veiled insult. A deniable one, since she had, after all, only used an always-proper address.

I gestured unconcern at her answer. "If you please, I'm here to speak with Queter. I only want to talk. I'm here by myself."

Her glance flicked to over my shoulder, though she had, I knew, been watching, knew that no one had come with me. She turned then, without a word, and walked into the house. I followed, careful to close the door behind me.

We met no one as we went through to the back of the house, to the kitchen, as large as Fosyf's, but where that kitchen was all gleaming pans and ranks of freezers and suspension cabinets, this one was half empty: a few burners, a sink. A rumpled pile of clothes in one corner, faded and stained, doubtless the remnant of what had been provided as the field workers' basic clothing allowance, picked over, altered to suit. A row of barrels against one wall that I strongly suspected were filled with something fermenting. Half a dozen people sat around a table drinking beer. The lookout gestured me into the room, and then left without a word.

One of the people at the table was the elder who had spoken to me, the day we'd arrived. Who'd changed the choice of song, when she'd seen that we were in mourning. "Good evening, Grandfather," I said to her, and bowed. Because of my long familiarity with Valskaay, I was fairly sure my choice of gender—required by the language I was speaking—was correct.

She looked at me for ten seconds, and then took a drink of her beer. Everyone else stared fixedly away from me—at the table, at the floor, at a distant wall. "What do you want, Radchaai?" she asked finally. Even though I was quite sure she knew why I was here.

"I was hoping to speak to Queter, Grandfather, if you please." Grandfather said nothing in response, not immediately, but then she turned to the person at her left. "Niece, ask Queter if she'll join us." Niece hesitated, looked as though she would open her mouth to protest, decided otherwise, though clearly she was not happy with her choice. She rose, and left the kitchen without a word to me.

Grandfather gestured to the vacant chair. "Sit, Soldier." I sat. Still, no one else at the table would look directly at me. I suspected that if Grandfather had told them to leave, they would have gladly fled the room. "From your accent, soldier," said Grandfather, "you learned your Delsig in Vestris Cor."

"I did," I agreed. "I spent quite some time there. And in Surimto District."

"I'm from Eph," Grandfather said, pleasantly, as though this were nothing more than a social call. "I never was in Vestris Cor. Or Surimto, either. I imagine it's very different these days, now you Radchaai are running things."

"In some ways, I'm sure," I replied. "I haven't been there in quite some time myself." Queter might have fled, or might refuse to come. My coming here, approaching like this, had been a gamble.

"How many Valskaayans did you kill while you were there, Radchaai?" Not Grandfather, but one of the other people around the table, one whose anger and resentment had built beyond the ability of her fear of me to contain it.

"Quite a few," I replied, calmly. "But I am not here to kill anyone. I am alone and unarmed." I held my gloved hands out, over the table, palms up.

"Just a social call, then?" Her voice was thick with sarcasm.

"Sadly, no," I replied.

Grandfather spoke then, trying to steer the conversation away from such dangerous territory. "I think you're too young to have been in the annexation, child."

I ducked my head, a small, respectful bow. "I'm older than I seem, Grandfather." Far, far older. But there was no way for anyone here to know that.

"You're very polite," said Grandfather, "I'll give you that."

"My mother said," observed the angry person, "that the soldiers who killed her family were also very polite."

"I'm sorry," I said, into the tense silence that greeted her observation. "I know that even if I could tell you for certain that it wasn't me, that wouldn't help."

"It wasn't you," she said. "It wasn't in Surimto. But you're right, it doesn't help." She shoved her chair back, looked at Grandfather. "Excuse me," she said. "Things to do." Grandfather gestured permission to go, and she left. As she went out the kitchen door, someone else came in. She was in her twenties, one of the people I'd seen under the arbor the day we'd arrived. The lines of her face suggested she was genetically related to Grandfather, though her skin was darker. Her eyes and her tightly curled hair that she'd twisted and bound with a bright green scarf were lighter. And by the set of her shoulders, and the frozen silence that descended when she'd entered, she was who I'd come to see.

I rose. "Miss Queter," I said, and bowed. She said nothing, did not move. "I want to thank you for deciding not to kill me." Silence, still, from Grandfather, from the others at the table. I wondered if the hallways outside were full of eavesdroppers, or if everyone else had fled, hiding anywhere that might be safe until I left. "Will you sit?" She didn't answer.

"Sit, Queter," said Grandfather.

"I won't," said Queter, and folded her arms and stared at me. "I could have killed you, Radchaai. You'd probably have deserved it, but Raughd deserved it more."

I gestured resignation and reseated myself. "She threatened your sister, I take it?" An incredulous look told me my mistake. "Your brother. Is he all right?"

She raised an eyebrow, tilted her head. "The rescuer of the helpless." Her voice was acid.

"Queter," warned Grandfather.

I raised a gloved hand, palm out—the gesture would have been rude, to most Radchaai, but meant something else to a Valskaayan. *Hold. Be calm.* "It's all right, Grandfather. I know justice when I hear it." A small, incredulous noise from one of the others sitting at the table, quickly silenced. Everyone pretended not to have noticed it. "Citizen Raughd had a taste for tormenting your brother. She's quite shrewd in some ways. She knew what lengths you'd go to, to protect him. She also knew that you have some technical ability. That if she managed to filch some explosives from a construction site and provided you with the instructions for how to use them, you'd be able to follow them. She didn't, I suspect, realize that you might come up with ways to improve their use. The scrap metal was your idea, wasn't it?" I had no evidence for that, beyond the repeated signs that Raughd rarely thought things through. Queter's expression didn't change. "And she didn't realize you might decide to use them on her instead of me."

Head still tilted, expression still sardonic, she said, "Don't you want to know how I did it?"

I smiled. "Most esteemed Queter. For nearly all of my life I have been among people who were very firmly convinced that the universe would be the better for my absence. I doubt very much that you have any surprises for me. Still, it was well done, and if your timing hadn't been just that smallest bit off, you would have succeeded. Your talents are wasted here."

"Oh, of *course* they are." Her tone became, if possible, even more cutting than before. "There's no one else here but *superstitious savages*." The last words in Radchaai.

"The information you would need to make something like that is not freely available," I said. "If you'd gone looking for it you would have been denied access, and possibly had Planetary Security looking closely at you. If you attended school here you'd have learned to recite passages of scripture, and some cleaned-up history, and very little more. Raughd herself likely knew no more than that explosives can kill people. You worked the details out yourself." Had, perhaps, been pondering the question long before Raughd made her move. "Sorting tea leaves and fixing the machines in the manufactory! You must have been bored beyond belief. If you'd ever taken the aptitudes, the assigners would have been sure to send you somewhere your talents were better occupied, and you'd have had no time or opportunity to dream up trouble." Queter's lips tightened, and she drew breath as though to reply. "And," I forestalled her, "you would not have been here to protect your brother." I gestured, acknowledging the irony of such things.

"Are you here to arrest me?" Queter asked, without moving, her face not betraying the tension that had forced that question into the open. Only the barest hint of it in her voice. Grandfather, and the others around the table, sat still as stone, hardly daring to breathe.

"I am," I replied.

Queter unfolded her arms. Closed her hands into fists. "You are so *civilized*. So *polite*. So *brave* coming here alone when you know no one here would dare to touch you. So easy to be all those things, when all the power is on your side."

"You're right," I agreed.

"Let's just go!" Queter crossed her arms again, hands still fists.

"Well," I replied calmly. "As to that, I walked here, and I think it's raining by now. Or have I lost count of the days?" No reply, just tense silence from the people around the table, Queter's determined glare. "And I wanted to ask you what happened. So that I can be sure the weight of this falls where it should."

"Oh!" cried Queter, at the frayed edge of her patience finally. "You're the just one, the kind one, are you? But you're no different from the daughter of the house." She lapsed, there, into Radchaai. "All of you! You take what you want at the end of a gun, you murder and rape and steal, and you call it *bringing civilization*. And what is civilization, to you, but us being properly grateful to be murdered and raped and stolen from? You said you knew justice when you heard it. Well, what is your justice but you allowed to treat us as you like, and us condemned for even attempting to defend ourselves?"

"I won't argue," I said. "What you say is true."

Queter blinked, hesitated. Surprised, I thought, to hear me say so. "But *you'll* grant us justice from on high, will you? You'll bring salvation? Are you here for us to fall at your feet and sing your praise? But we know what your justice is, we know what your salvation is, whatever face you put on it."

"I can't bring you justice, Queter. I can, however, bring you personally into the presence of the district magistrate so that you can explain to her why you did what you did. It won't change things for you. But you knew from the moment Raughd Denche told you what she wanted that there would be no other ending to this, not for you. The daughter of the house was too convinced of her own cleverness to have realized what that would mean."

"And what good will that do, Radchaai?" asked Queter, defiant. "Don't you know we're dishonest and deceitful? Resentful where we should be docile and grateful? That what intelligence we superstitious savages have is mere cunning? Obviously, I would lie. I might even tell a lie you created for me, because you hate the daughter of the house. And me in particular. In the strikes—your pet Samirend will have told you of the strikes?" I gestured acknowledgment. "She'll have told you how she and her cousins nobly educated us, made us aware of the injustice we suffered, taught us how to organize and induced us to act? Because we could not *possibly* have done those things ourselves."

"She herself," I said, "was reeducated afterward, and as a result can't speak directly about it. Citizen Fosyf, on the other hand, told me the story in such terms."

"*Did* she," answered Queter, not a question. "And did she tell you that my mother died during those strikes? But no, she'll have spoken of how kind she is to us, and how gentle she was, not bringing in soldiers to shoot us all as we sat there."

Queter could not have been more than ten when it had happened. "I can't promise the district magistrate will listen," I said. "I can only give you the opportunity to speak."

"And then what?" asked Grandfather. "What then, Soldier? From a child I was taught to forgive and forget, but it's difficult to forget these things, the loss of parents, of children and grandchildren." Her expression was unchanged, blank determination, but her voice broke slightly at that last. "And we are all of us only human. We can only forgive so much."

"For my part," I replied, "I find forgiveness overrated. There are times and places when it's appropriate. But not when the demand that you forgive is used to keep you in your place. With Queter's help I can remove Raughd from this place, permanently. I will try to do more if I can."

"Really?" asked another person at the table, who had been silent till now. "Fair pay? Can you do that, Soldier?"

"Pay at all!" added Queter. "Decent food you don't have to go in debt for."

"A priest," someone suggested. "A priest for us, and a priest for the Recalcitrants, there are some over on the next estate."

"They're called *teachers*," Grandfather said. "Not priests. How many times have I said so?" And *Recalcitrant* was an insult. But before I could say that, Grandfather said to me, "You won't be able to keep such promises. You won't be able to keep Queter safe and healthy."

"That's why I make no promises," I said, "and Queter may come out of this better than we fear. I will do what I can, though it may not be much."

"Well," said Grandfather after a few moments more of silence. "Well. I suppose we'll have to give you supper, Radchaai."

"If you would be so kind, Grandfather," I said.

17

Queter and I walked to Fosyf's house before the sun rose, while the air was still damp and smelling of wet soil, Queter striding impatiently, her back stiff, her arms crossed, repeatedly drawing ahead of me and then pausing for me to catch up, as though she were eager to reach her destination and I was inconsiderately delaying her. The fields, the mountains, were shadowed and silent. Queter was not in a mood to talk. I drew breath and sang, in a language I was sure no one here understood.

> *Memory is an event horizon*
> *What's caught in it is gone but it's always there.*

It was the song Tisarwat's Bos had sung, in the soldiers' mess. *Oh, tree!* Bo Nine had been singing it to herself just now, above, on the Station.

"Well, that one's escaped," said Queter, a meter ahead of me on the road, not looking back at me.

"And will again," I replied.

She paused, waited for me to catch up. Still didn't turn her head. "You lied, of course," she said, and began walking again. "You won't let me speak to the district magistrate, and no one will believe what I have to say. But you didn't bring soldiers to the house, so I suppose that's something. Still, no one will believe what I have to say. And I'll be gone through Security or dead, if there's even any difference, but my brother will still be here. And so will Raughd." She spat, after saying the name. "Will you take him away?"

"Who?" The question took me by surprise, so that I hardly understood it. "Your brother?" We were still speaking Delsig.

"Yes!" Impatient, still angry. "My brother."

"I don't understand." The sky had paled and brightened, but where we walked was still shadowed. "Is this something you're afraid I'll do, or something you want?" She didn't answer. "I'm a soldier, Queter, I live on a military ship." I didn't have the time or the resources to take care of children, not even mostly grown ones.

Queter gave an exasperated cry. "Don't you have an apartment somewhere, and servants? Don't you have *retainers*? Don't you have dozens of people to see to your every need, to make your tea and straighten your collar and strew flowers in your path? Surely there's room for one more."

"Is that something your brother wants?" And after a few moments with no reply, "Would your grandfather not be grieved to lose both of you?"

She stopped, then, suddenly, and wheeled to face me. "You think you know about us but you don't understand *anything*."

I thought of telling her that it was she who did not understand. That I was not responsible for every distressed child on the planet. That none of this had been my fault. She stood there tense, frowning, waiting for me to answer. "Do you blame your brother? For not fighting harder, for putting you in the position you're in?"

"Oh!" she cried. "Of course! It's nothing to do with the fact that *your* civilized self brought Raughd Denche down here. You knew enough about the daughter of the house to realize what had happened, you knew enough about her to realize what she was doing to us. But it wasn't *serious* enough for you to stir yourself until some Radchaai nearly got killed. And there won't be anything for *you* to worry about once you're gone and the daughter of the house and her mother are *still here*."

"I didn't cause this, Queter. And I can't fix every injustice I find, no matter how much I'd like to."

"No, of *course* you can't." Her contempt was acid. "You can only fix the ones that really inconvenience you." She turned, and began walking again.

If I were given to swearing, I would have sworn now. "How old is your brother?"

"Sixteen," she said. The sarcasm returned to her voice. "You could rescue him from this terrible place and bring him to *real civilization*."

"Queter, I only have my ship and some temporary quarters on Athoek Station. I have soldiers, and they see to my needs and even make my tea, but I don't have a retinue. And your idea about the flowers is charming, but it would make a terrible mess. I don't have a place in my household for your brother. But I will ask him if he wants to leave here, and if he does, I'll do my best for him."

"You won't." She didn't turn as she spoke, just continued walking. "Do you even know," she said, and I could tell from the sound of her voice that she was about to cry, "can you even imagine what it's like to know that nothing you can do will make any difference? That nothing you can do will protect the people you love? That anything you could possibly ever do is less than worthless?"

I could. "And yet you do it anyway."

"Superstitious savage that I am." Definitely crying now. "Nothing I do will make any difference. But I will make you *look* at it. I will make you see what it is you've done, and ever after, if you would look away, if you would ever claim to be just, or proper, you'll have to lie to yourself outright."

"Most esteemed Queter," I said, "idealist that you are, young as you are, you can have no idea just how easy it is for people to deceive themselves." By now the tops of the mountains were bright, and we were nearly over the ridge.

"I'll do it anyway."

"You will," I agreed, and we walked the rest of the way in silence.

We stopped at the smaller house first. Queter refused tea or food, stood by the door, arms still crossed. "No one at the main house will be awake yet," I told her. "If you'll excuse me a moment, I'd like to dress and see to a few things, and then we'll go up to the house and wait for the magistrate." She lifted an elbow and a shoulder, conveying her lack of concern over what I did or didn't do.

Sword of Atagaris was in Captain Hetnys's sitting room, still facedown on the tabletop on the floor. Its back was covered with the thick black shell of a corrective. I squatted down beside it. "*Sword of Atagaris*," I said quietly, in case it should be asleep, and not wanting to disturb Captain Hetnys.

"Fleet Captain," it replied.

"Are you comfortable? Is there anything you need?"

I thought it hesitated just the smallest moment before replying. "I'm in no pain, Fleet Captain, and Kalr Five and Kalr Eight have been very helpful." Another pause. "Thank you."

"Please let either of them know if you need anything. I'm going to get dressed, now, and go up to the main house. I think it very likely we'll want to leave before tomorrow. Do you think we'll be able to move you?"

"I believe so, Fleet Captain." That pause again. "Fleet Captain. Sir. If I may ask a question."

"Of course, Ship."

"Why did you call the doctor?"

I had acted without thinking much about why. Had only done what had, at the moment, seemed to be the right and obvious thing to do. "Because I didn't think you wanted to be too far from your captain. And I see no reason to waste ancillaries."

"With all respect, sir, unless the gates open soon, this system only has a limited number of specialized correctives. And I do have a few backups in storage."

Backups. Human beings in suspension waiting to die. "Would you have preferred I left this segment to be disposed of?"

Three seconds of silence. Then, "No, Fleet Captain. I would not."

The inner door opened, and Captain Hetnys came out, half dressed, looking as though she'd just woken. "Fleet Captain," she said. Taken somewhat aback, I thought.

"I was just checking on *Sword of Atagaris*, Captain. I'm sorry if I woke you." I rose. "I'm going up to the main house to meet with the district magistrate as soon as I've dressed and had something to eat."

"Sir. Did you find the person who did this?" Captain Hetnys asked.

"I did." I would not elaborate.

But she didn't ask for details. "I'll be down myself in a few minutes, Fleet Captain, with your indulgence."

"Of course, Captain."

Queter was still standing by the door when I came back downstairs. Sirix sat at the table, with a piece of bread and a bowl of tea in front of her. "Good morning, Fleet Captain," she said when she saw me. "I'd like to come up to the house with you." Queter scoffed.

"Whatever you like, Citizen." I took my own piece of bread, poured myself a bowl of tea. "We're only waiting for Captain Hetnys to be ready."

Captain Hetnys came down the stairs a few minutes later. She said nothing to Sirix, looked quickly at Queter and then away. Came over to the sideboard to pour herself some tea.

"Kalr Eight will stay behind to look after *Sword of Atagaris*," I said, and then, to Queter, in Radchaai, "Citizen, are you sure you don't want anything?"

"No, thank you so *very* kindly, Citizen." Queter's voice was bitter and sarcastic.

"As you like, Citizen," I replied.

Captain Hetnys stared at me in frank astonishment. "Sir," she began.

"Captain," I said, forestalling whatever else she might have been intending to say, "are you eating, or can we go?" I took the last bite of my bread. Sirix had already finished hers.

"I'll drink my tea on the way, sir, with your permission." I gestured the granting of it, swallowed the last of my own tea, and walked out the door without looking to see if anyone followed.

* * *

A servant brought us to the same blue and gold sitting room we had met in the day before. By now the sun was nearly above the mountains, and the lake, through the window, had turned quicksilver. Captain Hetnys settled into a chair, Sirix carefully chose another three meters away. Five took up her usual station by the door, and Queter stood defiant in the middle of the room. I went over to where the stringed instrument sat, to examine it. It had four strings and no frets, and its wooden body was inlaid with mother-of-pearl. I wondered how it sounded. If it was bowed, or strummed, or plucked.

The district magistrate came in. "Fleet Captain, you had us worried, you were so late last night. But your soldier assured us you were well."

I bowed. "Good morning, Magistrate. And I'm sorry to have troubled you. By the time we were ready to come back, it was raining, so we spent the night." As I spoke, Fosyf and Raughd entered the room. "Good morning, Citizens," I said, nodding in their direction, and then turned back to the district magistrate. "Magistrate, I would like to introduce Citizen Queter. I have promised her the chance to speak to you directly. I think it is extremely important that you listen to what she has to say." Raughd scoffed. Rolled her eyes and shook her head.

The magistrate glanced in her direction, and said, "Does Citizen Queter speak Radchaai?"

"Yes," I replied, ignoring Raughd for the moment. I turned to Queter. "Citizen, here is the district magistrate, as I promised."

For a moment, Queter didn't respond, just stood straight and silent in the middle of the room. Then she turned toward the magistrate. Said, without bowing, "Magistrate. I want to explain what happened." She spoke very slowly and carefully.

"Citizen," replied the magistrate. Enunciating precisely, as though she was speaking to a small child. "The fleet captain promised that you would be given a chance to speak to me, and so I am listening."

Queter was silent a moment more. Trying, I thought, to rein in a sarcastic response. "Magistrate," she said finally. Still speaking carefully and clearly, so that everyone might understand her, despite her accent. "You may know that the tea planters and their daughters sometimes amuse themselves at the expense of the field workers."

"Oh!" cried Raughd, all offended exasperation. "I can't go within fifty meters of a field worker without flattery and flirting and all sorts of attempts to get my attention in the hope I'll give gifts, or that eventually I'll bestow clientage. This is amusing myself at their expense, is it?"

"Citizen Raughd," I said, keeping my voice calm and chill, "Queter was promised the opportunity to speak. You will have your chance when she is finished."

"And meanwhile I'm to stand here and listen to this?" cried Raughd.

"Yes," I replied.

Raughd looked at her mother in appeal. Fosyf said, "Now, Raughd, the fleet captain promised Queter she could speak. If there's anything to say afterward we'll have our chance to say it." Her voice even, her expression genial as always, but I thought she was wary of what might come next. Captain Hetnys seemed confused, looked for an instant as though she would have said something, but saw me watching. Sirix stared fixedly off into the distance. Angry. I didn't blame her.

I turned to Queter. "Go on, Citizen." Raughd made a disgusted noise, and seated herself heavily in the nearest chair. Her mother remained standing. Calm.

Queter drew a deliberate breath. "The tea planters and their daughters sometimes amuse themselves at the expense of the field workers," she repeated. I didn't know if anyone else in the room could hear how carefully she was controlling her voice. "Of *course* we always say flattering things and pretend to want it." Raughd made a sharp, incredulous noise. Queter continued. "Most of us, anyway. Anyone in this house has...can make our lives a misery." She had been about to say that anyone in the house had the field workers' lives in their hands, an expression that, literally translated from Delsig into Radchaai, sounded vulgar.

The district magistrate said, voice disbelieving, "Citizen, are you accusing Citizen Fosyf or anyone else in this household of mistreatment?"

Queter blinked. Took a breath. Said, "The favor, or the disfavor, of Citizen Fosyf or anyone else in this house can mean the difference between credit or not, extra food for the children or not, the opportunity for extra work or not, access to medical supplies or not—"

"There *is* a doctor, you know," Fosyf pointed out, her voice just slightly edged, something I had never heard before.

"I've met your doctor," I said. "I can't blame anyone for being reluctant to deal with her. Citizen Queter, do continue."

"In entertainments," said Queter after another breath, "beautiful, humble Radchaai are lifted up by the rich and the powerful, and maybe it happens, but it never happens to *us*. Only an infant would think it ever would. I tell you this so that you understand why the daughter of this house is met with flattery, and is given everything she wishes."

I could see from the district magistrate's expression that

she saw little difference between this and what Raughd had described. She looked at me, frowning slightly. "Continue, Queter," I said, before the magistrate could say what I was sure she was thinking. "I promised you would have your say."

Queter continued. "For the past few years it has pleased Citizen Raughd to demand that my younger sister..." She hesitated. "Perform certain acts," she finished, finally.

Raughd laughed. "Oh, I didn't have to *demand* any of it."

"You haven't been listening, Citizen," I said. "Citizen Queter just explained that your merest wish is in reality a demand and that displeasing you in any way can cause difficulties for the field worker who does so."

"And there wasn't anything wrong with any of it," Raughd continued, as though I hadn't spoken. "You know, you're turning out to be quite the hypocrite, Fleet Captain. All this condemnation of sexual impropriety and yet you brought your pet Samirend here to amuse you while you are supposedly in full, proper mourning." I understood now why Raughd had made such a hasty, obvious move toward me— she had thought she needed to outflank Sirix.

Sirix gave a sharp, surprised laugh. "You flatter me, Citizen Raughd. I doubt the fleet captain has ever considered me in such a light."

"Nor you me, I'm sure," I agreed. Sirix gestured assent, genuinely amused from what I could see. "More to the point, Citizen, this is the fourth time Citizen Queter has been interrupted. If you cannot restrain yourself, I'll have to ask you to leave the room while she speaks."

Raughd was on her feet the instant I finished speaking. "How *dare* you!" she cried. "You may be the cousin of God herself for all I care, and you may *think* you're better than everyone in this system, but you don't give orders in *this* house!"

"I had not thought the residents of this house would be so lacking in the most basic propriety," I said, my voice utterly calm. "If it is not possible here for a citizen to speak without interruption, it would suit me just as well for Queter to tell her story to the magistrate elsewhere, and privately." Just the smallest stress on *privately*.

Fosyf heard that stress. Looked at me. Said, "Sit down and be quiet, Raughd." Surely she knew her daughter well enough to guess what had happened, at least the outlines of it.

Hearing her mother, Raughd went very still. She seemed not even to breathe. I remembered Kalr Five and Six listening to the servants talk, how Fosyf had said that there was time enough to grow a new heir. Wondered how often Raughd had heard that threat.

"Now, Raughd," said the district magistrate, frowning slightly. Puzzled, I thought, at Fosyf's tone of voice. "I understand that you're upset. If someone had tried to kill me yesterday I'd have a hard time keeping calm. But the fleet captain has done nothing more offensive than promise this person"—she gestured toward Queter, standing silent in the middle of the room—"a chance to tell me something, and then try to be sure that promise was kept." She turned to Queter. "Queter, is it? Do you deny that you placed the explosive in the bathhouse?"

"I don't deny it," Queter replied. "I meant to kill the daughter of the house. I am sorry I failed."

Shocked silence. Everyone had known it, of course, but it was suddenly different, hearing it said so plainly. Then the magistrate said, "I can't imagine what you would say to me that would change the outcome of this. Do you still wish to speak to me?"

"Yes," said Queter, simply.

The district magistrate turned to Raughd. "Raughd, I understand if you would rather leave. If you stay, it will be best if you'll let this person finish speaking."

"I'll stay," replied Raughd, her tone defiant.

The magistrate frowned again. "Well." She gestured peremptorily toward Queter. "Get it over with, then."

"The daughter of the house," said Queter, "knew that I hated her for taking advantage of my sister. She came to me and said that she wanted the fleet captain to die, that the fleet captain always bathed early before anyone else was awake, and an explosion in the bathhouse at the right time was sure to kill her." Raughd scoffed again, drew breath to speak, but then met her mother's look and said nothing, just crossed her arms and turned to stare at the antique blue and green tea set, on its stand three and a half meters away from where she stood.

"The daughter of the house," continued Queter, her voice steady but just a bit louder in case anyone tried to speak over her, "told me that she would supply me with the explosive if I didn't know where to get it. If I refused, the daughter of the house would do it herself and be sure the blame fell on my sister. If I would do it, she would grant my sister clientage, and she would be sure the blame never fell on me." She looked over at Raughd then, whose back was still to the rest of the room. Said, with withering contempt, "The daughter of the house thinks I'm stupid." She looked back at the magistrate. "I can understand why someone would want to kill the fleet captain, but *I* don't have any personal argument with her. The daughter of the house is another matter. I knew that whatever happened I would be going through Security and my sister would have nothing but grief. For such a price, why not be rid of the person who threatened my sister?"

"You're a very articulate young person," said the magistrate after three seconds of silence. "And by all accounts fairly intelligent. You know, I hope, that you can't possibly lie about this without being discovered." A competently conducted interrogation with drugs would uncover a person's most secret thoughts.

But of course, if authorities assumed the truth of your guilt, they might not bother to conduct any such interrogation. And if someone truly, mistakenly believed something, that's all an interrogation would uncover. "Interrogate the daughter of the house, Magistrate," said Queter, "and discover if what I say is true."

"You admit that you tried to kill Citizen Raughd," remarked the magistrate dryly, "and that you have, as you put it, a personal argument with her. I have no reason to assume that you're not just making this up in order to cause her as much difficulty as possible."

"I'll make a formal accusation if one is needed, Magistrate," I said. "But tell me, have you found the source of the explosive?"

"Security confirms it likely came from a construction site. None of the sites nearby reports anything missing."

"Perhaps," I suggested, "the supervisors of those sites should actually look at their stock of explosives and be sure it matches what the record says." I considered adding that Security ought to pay special attention to places where friends of the daughter of the house worked, or where she had recently visited.

The magistrate raised an eyebrow. "I've given that order. Gave it, in fact, before I came downstairs to meet with you this morning."

I lowered my head in acknowledgment. "In that case, I

have one more request. Only the one, after which I will leave matters to you, Magistrate, as is proper." Receiving the magistrate's gesture of assent, I continued. "I would like to ask Citizen Raughd's personal attendant one question."

Raughd's attendant came into the room a few tense minutes later. "Citizen," I said to her. "Your arms are filled with blessing and no untruth will pass your lips." Said it in Radchaai, though it was a translation, undoubtedly rough, of the words I'd heard in the kitchen that day, through Eight, what the overseer had said as she'd placed bits of honey cake in Raughd's attendant's mouth. "Where did Citizen Raughd get the explosive?"

The attendant stared at me, frozen. Terrified, I thought. No one ever paid attention to servants except other servants, especially in this house. "Your very great pardon, Fleet Captain," she said after an interminable silence. "I don't know what you mean."

"Come, Citizen," I said. "Citizen Raughd hardly takes a breath that you're unaware of. Oh, sometimes you weren't with her in the Undergarden, sometimes she sends you on errands while she does other things, but you know, the way a good personal attendant knows. And this wasn't a spur-of-the-moment thing, like painting *Not tea but blood* on the wall that time." She'd tried to clean Raughd's gloves before anyone could realize there was paint on them. "This was different. This was complicated, it was planned in advance, and she won't have done all that by herself, that's what a good personal attendant is *for*, after all. And it's come out anyway. Citizen Queter has told the magistrate everything."

Tears welled in her eyes. Her mouth trembled, and then turned down. "I'm not a good personal attendant," she said. A tear escaped, rolled down her cheek. I waited in silence while she debated with herself—whether over what to say, or whether or not to say it, I didn't know, but I could see her conflict in her expression. No one else spoke. "If I were, none of this would have happened," she said, finally.

"She's always been unstable," said Raughd. "Ever since we were children I've tried to shelter her. To protect her."

"It's not your fault," I said to Raughd's attendant. Ignoring Raughd herself. "But you knew what Queter had done. Or you suspected for some reason." She'd probably drawn the obvious conclusion that Raughd had not—Queter, cornered, would not simply do as she was told. "That's why you didn't come to the bathhouse yesterday, when Raughd called you." And Raughd had lost patience waiting for her servant to come see to her, had left the bathhouse to go look for her, and as a result had not died in the explosion. "Where did Raughd get the explosive?"

"She took it on a dare, five years ago. It's been in a box in her room since then."

"And you can tell us where and when and how, so we can confirm that?" I asked, though I already knew the answer.

"Yes."

"She's making it up!" Raughd interjected. "After everything I've done for her, she does this to me! And you!" She turned to me. "*Breq Mianaai.* You've had it in for my family ever since you arrived in this system. This ridiculous story about how dangerous it is to travel in the gates, it's obviously made up. You bring a *known criminal* into this household." She didn't look at Sirix as she said it. "And now you blame me for what, for trying to blow myself up? I wouldn't be surprised if *you* planned this whole thing."

"Do you see?" I said, to Raughd's attendant, who still stood there, weeping. "It isn't your fault at all."

"It will be a simple thing, Citizen," said the magistrate to Raughd, frowning, "to check your servant's story." I saw Fosyf notice that address, the change from *Raughd* to the more distant *citizen*. "But we should discuss this elsewhere. I think you should come stay with me in the city until we get this straightened out." Raughd's servant and Queter, of course, had no such invitation. Would stay in cells in Security until their interrogations were finished, and they had been suitably reeducated. Still, there was no mistaking what that invitation meant.

Certainly Fosyf didn't mistake it. She gestured dismay. "I should have realized it would come to this. I've protected Raughd for too long. I always hoped she'd do better. But I never thought..." She trailed off, apparently unable to express what it was that she had never thought. "To think I might have left my *tea* in the hands of someone who could do such things."

Raughd went absolutely still for a full second. "You wouldn't," she said, barely more than an emphatic whisper. As though she could not entirely engage her voice.

"What choice do I have?" asked Fosyf, the very image of injured regret.

Raughd turned. Took three long steps over to the tea set on the stand. Picked the box up, raised it over her head with both hands, and threw it to the ground. Glass shattered, blue and green and gold fragments skittering across the floor. Kalr Five, standing by the door, made the smallest noise, audible to no one but her and me.

Then silence. No one moved, no one spoke. After a few moments a servant appeared in the doorway, drawn, no doubt, by the crash of the tea set. "Sweep this mess up," Fosyf said, catching sight of her. Her voice was quite calm. "And dispose of it."

"You're throwing it away?" I asked, partly because I was surprised, and partly to cover another very small noise of protest from Five.

Fosyf gestured unconcern. "It's worthless now."

The magistrate turned to Queter, who had stood straight and silent this whole time. "Is this what you wanted, Queter? All this heartache, a family destroyed? For the life of me I don't understand why you didn't put your obvious determination and energy into your work so that you could make things better for yourself and your family. Instead, you built up and fed this…this resentment, and now you have…" The magistrate gestured, indicating the room, the situation. "This."

Very calmly, very deliberately, Queter turned to me. "You were right about the self-deception, Citizen." Evenly, as though she only remarked casually on the weather. In Radchaai, though she might as well have used Delsig, which she knew I understood.

Her remark wasn't meant for me. Still I replied. "You were always going to speak if you could, whether you thought it would do any good or not."

She lifted one sardonic eyebrow. "Yes," she agreed. "I was."

18

From the moment we had left Fosyf's sitting room, Sirix was tense and silent, and she did not say a word nearly all the way back to Athoek Station. This was a particularly impressive length of silence because *Sword of Atagaris*'s injury meant we'd be taking up more seats on the passenger shuttle from the elevator to the station than we ought, and so we had to wait a day for a flight with the available extra space.

Sirix didn't speak until we were in the shuttle, an hour from docking with the station. Strapped into our seats, Five and Eight behind us, their attention mostly on Queter's sister, who'd had a miserable time the whole flight, among strangers, missing home, disoriented and sick to her stomach in the microgravity but refusing to take any medication for it, upset further by the way her tears clung to her eyes or broke free into small liquid spheres when she wiped her face. She had finally fallen asleep.

Sirix had accepted the offered meds, was therefore more comfortable physically, but she had been troubled since we'd left the mountains. Since before, I thought. I knew she didn't like Raughd, had, on the contrary, good reason to resent her, but I suspected that she of all people in the room that day had understood what Raughd must have felt, to hear her mother speak so easily, so calmly, of disinheriting her. Had understood the impulse that had led Raughd to smash that ancient tea set that her mother clearly valued highly, took pride in. Citizen Fosyf had not changed her mind, about her daughter or about the tea set. Kalr Five had retrieved the box from the trash, and the fragments of gold and glass, the shattered remains of the bowls and the flask that had survived undamaged for more than three thousand years. Until now.

"Was that justice, then?" Sirix asked. Quietly, as though she was not speaking to me, though no one else would have heard her.

"What is justice, Citizen?" I replied with my own question. "Where did justice lie, in that entire situation?" Sirix didn't reply, either angry or at a loss for an answer. Both were difficult questions. "We speak of it as though it's a simple thing, a matter of acting properly, as though it's nothing more than an afternoon tea and the question only who takes the last pastry. So simple. Assign guilt to the guilty."

"Is it not that simple?" asked Sirix after a few moments of silence. "There are right actions and wrong actions. And yet, I think that if you had been the magistrate, you would have let Citizen Queter go free."

"If I had been the magistrate, I would have been an entirely different person than I am. But surely you don't have less compassion for Citizen Queter than for Citizen Raughd."

"Please, Fleet Captain," she said after three long, slow breaths. I had made her angry. "Please don't speak to me as though I'm stupid. You spent the night at the field workers' house. You are apparently familiar with Valskaayans and fluent in Delsig. Still, it's quite amazing that you walked to the house and came back the next morning with Queter. No protest, no difficulty. And before we even left the house— before the *magistrate* left—the field workers had sent Fosyf a list of demands. Just at the moment Fosyf can't depend on the magistrate's unquestioning support."

It took me a moment to understand what she meant. "You think I put them up to it?"

"I can't believe it's merely fortuitous, that uneducated and uncivilized field workers, who for ten years and more could not find the resources to strike, choose to do so now."

"Not fortuitous at all. And while they may be uneducated, they're hardly uncivilized. They're perfectly capable of planning such a thing on their own. They understand Fosyf's position as well as anyone. Perhaps better than many."

"And Queter coming with you so willingly, that wasn't part of any bargain? She won't ultimately be let off lightly? And in the meantime, Citizen Raughd's life is destroyed."

"No sympathy for Queter? Raughd acted from malice and injured pride, and would have destroyed more than me if she had succeeded. Queter was faced with an impossible situation. No matter what she did, things would end badly."

A moment of silence. Then, "All she needed to do was go to the magistrate in the first place."

I had to think about that for a few moments, to understand why Sirix of all people thought Queter could or should have done that. "You do realize," I said finally, "that Citizen Queter would never have gotten within a kilometer of the district magistrate without my having explicitly demanded it. And I beg you to recall what generally happened in the past when Citizen Raughd misbehaved."

"Still, if she had spoken properly she might have been listened to," Sirix replied.

Queter had been right to expect no help from the district magistrate, I was sure. "She made the choices she made, and there's no escaping the consequences of that. I doubt very much she'll get off lightly. But I can't condemn her. She was willing to sacrifice herself to protect her sister." Sirix of all people ought to have approved of at least that. "Do you think that if the Lord of the Radch were here she would have seen through everything, to give each act and each actor's heart its proper weight? To dispense perfect justice? Do you think it's possible that any person will ever get precisely what they deserve, no more and no less?"

"That is what justice is, Citizen, isn't it?" Sirix asked, ostensibly calm, but I could hear that very small tightness in her voice, a flattening of tone that told me she was, now, angry. "If either Raughd or Queter wants to appeal their judgment, there's no recourse, not cut off from the palaces as we are. You're the closest thing we have to the Lord of the Radch, but you aren't the least bit impartial. And I can't help but notice that each time you've arrived somewhere new, you've gone straight to the bottom of the ladder and begun making allies. Of course it would be foolish to think a daughter of Mianaai could arrive anywhere without immediately engaging in politics. But now I see you've aimed the Valskaayans at Fosyf, I'm wondering who you're planning to aim the Ychana at."

"I didn't aim the Valskaayans at anyone. The field workers are entirely capable of making their own plans, and I assure you that they have. As for the Undergarden, you live there. You know what conditions are, there, and you know that it should have been repaired long ago."

"You might have had a private word with the magistrate yourself, about the Valskaayans."

"I did, in fact."

"And," Sirix continued, as though I had said nothing, "many of the Ychana's problems would be remedied if only they became better citizens."

"Just how good a citizen does one have to be," I asked, "in order to have water and air, and medical help? And do your neighbors know you hold such a low opinion of them?" I didn't doubt that, like the Valskaayan field workers, they did.

Sirix said nothing else for the rest of the trip.

Lieutenant Tisarwat met us at the shuttle dock. Relieved to see us, pleasantly anticipating... something. Apprehensive, perhaps of the same something. As other passengers streamed past I looked through Five and Eight's eyes, saw that *Sword of Atagaris*'s ancillary was being tended to by medics and another segment of itself, that yet a third *Sword of Atagaris* ancillary had placed itself behind Captain Hetnys.

Lieutenant Tisarwat bowed. "Welcome back, sir."

"Thank you, Lieutenant." I turned to Captain Hetnys. "Captain, I'll see you first thing tomorrow morning." She acknowledged that with a bow and I gestured us away, out into the corridor and toward the lift that would take us to the Undergarden. The Genitalia Festival was long over—there were no tiny, brightly colored penises hanging in the corridors, and the last of the foil sweet wrappers had gone to recycling.

And—though I knew this already, had seen it through Tisarwat's eyes, and Bo Nine's—there was no broken table at the entrance to the Undergarden. There was an open section door, and an indicator that said, quite properly and correctly, that the door was functioning as it should, with air on both sides of it. Beyond this, a scuffed but well-lit corridor. *Mercy of Kalr* showed me a little surge of pride from Lieutenant Tisarwat. She had been looking forward to showing me this.

"All the section doors leading out of the Undergarden on this level are repaired, sir," Tisarwat said as we walked into the Undergarden corridor. "They've made good progress on the level two doors. Three and four are up next, of course." We walked out into the Undergarden's tiny, makeshift concourse. Well lit, now, the phosphorescent paint around the tea shop door barely noticeable, though still there, as were the spills and footprints. Two potted plants flanked the bench in the center of the open space, both clumps of thick, blade-like leaves shooting upward, one or two of them nearly a meter tall. Lieutenant Tisarwat saw me notice them, but none of her apprehension reached her face. The plants were, of course, the product of her conversation with Basnaaid. The small space seemed even smaller now it was brightly lit, and even a little crowded, not just residents, whom I recognized, but also Station Maintenance in gray coveralls passing through.

"And the plumbing?" I asked. Not mentioning the plants.

"This part of level one has water now." Tisarwat's satisfaction at saying that nearly eclipsed her fear that I'd notice she'd been spending time with Horticulture. "Still working on the other sections, and work has only barely started on level two. It's slow going in some places, sir, and I'm afraid that level four is still...inconvenienced in that department. The residents here agreed it was best to start where most of the people live."

"Rightly so, Lieutenant." Of course I'd known most of this already, had kept half an eye on Tisarwat, on Bo Nine and

Kalr Ten, on what was happening here on the station while I was downwell.

Behind me, behind Tisarwat, Sirix stopped, forcing Five and Eight behind her, shepherding Queter's still silently miserable sister, to stop also. "And what *about* those residents? Do I still have my quarters, Lieutenant?"

Tisarwat smiled, a practiced, diplomatic expression I knew she'd been using a good deal this past week. "Everyone living in the Undergarden at the time the work began has been officially assigned whatever quarters they were using. Your room is still yours, Citizen, though it's better lit now, and eventually will be better ventilated." She turned to me. "There were some…misgivings about the installation of sensors." There had been, in fact, a contentious meeting with Station Administrator Celar, here on this tiny concourse—the lifts hadn't been ready yet—which Lieutenant Tisarwat had arranged by sheer force of will combined with a level of charm that had surprised even me, who had already suspected what sort of things she might be capable of. No Security, only Tisarwat sitting by the station administrator. "Ultimately, it was decided that sensors will be placed in corridors, but not in residences, unless the residents request it."

Sirix made a small, derisive *hah*. "Even sensors in the corridors will be too much for some. But I suppose I'd better make my way home and find out just what you've done."

"I think you'll be pleased, Citizen," replied Tisarwat, still in diplomatic mode. "But if you have any problems or complaints, please don't hesitate to let me or any of *Mercy of Kalr* know." Sirix did not answer this, only bowed and departed.

"You could send people directly to Station Administration," I said, guessing what had troubled Sirix. I began walking again, putting our small procession back into motion. We turned a corner to find a set of lift doors sliding open, ready for us. Station watching us.

On *Mercy of Kalr*, Seivarden stood naked in the bath, attended by an Amaat. "Fleet captain's back safe, then," she said.

"Yes, Lieutenant." The Amaat, speaking for Ship.

On Athoek Station, in the Undergarden, I stepped into the lift with Tisarwat, with my Kalrs, and Queter's sister. *Mercy of Kalr* showed me Lieutenant Tisarwat's momentary doubt, as she considered, not for the first time, the likelihood of my having seen, from downwell, everything she'd done. "I know I *should* send them to Station Administration, sir. But most of the people who live here would prefer not to go there. We are closer by. And we did start this, and we *do* live here. Unlike anyone in Administration." A brief hesitation. "Not everyone here is happy about any of this. There's some amount of smuggling that goes through here. Some stolen goods, some prohibited drugs. None of the people making a living off of that are pleased to have Station watching, even if it's only in the corridors."

I thought again of Seivarden. She'd been quite clear about her determination to never take kef again, and had stuck to her resolve so far. But when she was taking it she'd had an impressive ability to find it, and find ways to get it, no matter where she was. It was a good thing I'd left her in command of *Mercy of Kalr*, and not brought her here.

Still in the bath, on *Mercy of Kalr*, Seivarden crossed her arms. Uncrossed them again. A gesture I recognized from months ago. It surprised the Amaat attending her, though the only outward sign of that surprise was a quick two blinks. The words *You were very worried* appeared in the Amaat's vision. "You were very worried," she said, for Ship.

In the lift, in the Undergarden on Athoek Station, Tisarwat's pride at showing me how much had been accomplished was suddenly drowned in a surge of the anxiety and self-loathing that had been hovering in the background the whole time.

"I see it, Fleet Captain," Ship said to me, before I could say anything. "It's mostly under control. I think your return is putting some stress on her. She's worried you won't approve."

On *Mercy of Kalr*, Seivarden didn't answer Ship right away. She'd recognized the arm-crossing gesture she'd just made, was ashamed of what it might say about her current state of mind. "Of course I was worried," she said, finally. "Someone tried to blow up my captain." The Amaat poured a measure of water over Seivarden's head, and she sputtered a bit, keeping it out of her mouth and her nose.

In the lift in the Undergarden, Tisarwat said to me, "There's been some complaining outside the Undergarden the past few days, about residential assignments." Ostensibly calm, only the barest trace of her feelings in her voice. "There are those who think that it's not fair the Ychana are going to suddenly have luxury quarters, and so much space, when they don't deserve it."

"Such wisdom," I observed dryly, "to know what everyone deserves."

"Sir," agreed Lieutenant Tisarwat, with a fresh pang of guilt. Considered saying more, but decided not to.

"Forgive me for bringing this up," said Ship to Seivarden, with the Amaat's voice, on *Mercy of Kalr*. "I understand being alarmed by the attempt on the fleet captain's life. I was alarmed, myself. But you are a soldier, Lieutenant. The fleet captain is as well. There is a certain amount of risk involved. I would think you'd be used to that. I'm sure the fleet captain is."

Anxiety, from Seivarden, feeling doubly vulnerable because she was in the bath, uncovered. Uncovered by Ship's question. "She's not supposed to be at risk sitting in a garden drinking tea, Ship." And silently, her fingers twitching just the slightest bit, *You don't want to lose her, either.* Not wanting to say that aloud, in the hearing of her Amaat.

"Nowhere is completely safe, Lieutenant," said Ship, through the Amaat, and then, words in Seivarden's vision, *All respect, Lieutenant, perhaps you should consult Medic.*

Panic, from Seivarden, for just an instant. The Amaat, puzzled, saw Seivarden freeze. Saw Ship's words in her own vision, *It's all right, Amaat. Continue.*

Seivarden closed her eyes and took a deep, steadying breath. She hadn't told Ship, or Medic, about her past difficulty with kef. Had been, I knew, confident that it would no longer be a problem for her.

Ship spoke aloud—or, rather, Ship showed the Amaat what it wanted to say, and Amaat said it. "You can't be worried about taking command if something were to happen. You had your own ship, once." Seivarden didn't answer, just stood motionless on the grate while her Amaat did what was needful. The question was meant as much for Amaat's ears as for Seivarden's.

"No, Ship, that doesn't trouble me." Seivarden's answer was also meant mainly for her Amaat. Silently, she said, *She told you then.*

She didn't need to, replied Ship, in Seivarden's vision. *I do have some experience of the world, Lieutenant, and I see you very thoroughly.* Aloud it said, "You were right. When the fleet captain stirs up trouble it's not the ordinary sort. Surely you're used to that by now."

"It's not an easy thing to get used to," Seivarden replied,

trying very hard to sound light and amused. And did not say, silently or aloud, that she would speak to Medic.

In the lift, in the Undergarden, on Athoek Station, I said to Lieutenant Tisarwat, "I need to speak to Governor Giarod as soon as possible. If I go to the governor's residence to invite her to supper, will she be available to accept my invitation?" My rank and my ostensible social status gave me some amount of freedom from the strictest propriety, and an excuse to be arrogantly peremptory even to the system governor, but what I wanted to discuss with her was going to require some delicacy. And while I could have just messaged the question to Five, whose job it was to take care of such things for me, I knew that there were even now three citizens (one of them Skaaiat Awer's cousin) lounging in my sitting room, drinking tea and waiting for Tisarwat. It was not intended to be an entirely social meeting.

Lieutenant Tisarwat blinked. Took a breath. "I'll find out, sir." Another breath, a frown suppressed with some effort. "Do you mean to dine at home, sir? I'm not sure if there's anything there worthy of the system governor."

"You mean," I said, my voice calm, "that you've promised supper to your friends and you're hoping I don't kick you out of our dining room." Tisarwat wanted to look down, to look away from me, but held herself still, her face heating. "Take them out somewhere." Disappointment. She'd wanted to dine in for the same reason I did—wanted to have a conversation with these particular people, in private. Or as close to private as she could get, attended only by Mercy of Kalrs, with only Ship and possibly me watching. "Make me out to be as tyrannical as you like. They won't blame you." The lift door opened on level four, a few meters beyond the lift brightly lit, light panels still leaning against walls beyond that.

Home, for now.

* * *

"I admit, Fleet Captain," said Governor Giarod at supper, later, "that I generally don't much like Ychana food. When it's not bland, it's sour and rancid." She took another taste of the food in front of her, fish and mushrooms in a fermented sauce that was the source of that "sour and rancid" complaint. On this occasion it had been carefully sweetened and spiced to suit Radchaai taste. "But this is very good."

"I'm glad you like it. I had it brought in from a place on level one."

Governor Giarod frowned. "Where do the mushrooms come from?"

"They grow them somewhere in the Undergarden."

"I'll have to mention them to Horticulture."

I swallowed my own bite of fish and mushroom, took a swallow of tea. "Perhaps it might be best to let the people who have become experts continue to profit from their expertise. They stand to lose if it becomes something Horticulture produces, wouldn't you think? But imagine how pleased the growers might be, if the governor's residence started buying mushrooms from them."

Governor Giarod set down her utensil, leaned back in her seat. "So Lieutenant Tisarwat *is* acting with your direction." It wasn't the non sequitur it seemed. Tisarwat had spent the last week encouraging maintenance workers to try food in the Undergarden, and the new plumbing on level one had made work easier for the people who had been providing that food. The aim was obvious to someone like Governor Giarod. "Is that what you brought me here to talk about?"

"Lieutenant Tisarwat hasn't been acting under any orders from me, though I approve of what she's done. I'm sure you realize that continuing to isolate the Undergarden from the rest of the station would be just as disastrous as trying to force the residents here to live like everyone else." Balancing that would be...interesting. "I would be very unhappy to see this end with anything valuable here taken away from the Undergarden so that others can profit by it elsewhere. Let the houses here profit from what they've built." I took another swallow of tea. "I'd say they've earned it." The governor drew breath, ready to argue about that *what they've built*, I suspected. "But I invited you this evening because I wanted to ask you about Valskaayan transportees." I could have asked earlier, from downwell, but attending to business during full mourning would have been entirely improper.

Governor Giarod blinked. Set down the utensil she'd just picked up. "Valskaayan transportees?" Clearly surprised. "I know you have an interest in Valskaay, you said so when you first arrived. But..."

But that wouldn't account for a hasty, urgent invitation to a private dinner, less than an hour after my getting off the passenger shuttle from the Athoek elevator. "I gather they have been almost exclusively assigned to the mountain tea plantations, is that the case?"

"I believe so."

"And there are still some in storage?"

"Certainly."

Now for the delicate part. "I would like to have one of my own crew personally examine the facility where they're stored. I would like," I continued, into the system governor's nonplussed silence, "to compare the official inventory with what's actually there." This was why supper had to be here. Not in the governor's residence, and certainly not in some shop, no matter how fashionable or supposedly discreet. "Are you aware of rumors that, in the past, Samirend transportees were misappropriated and sold to outsystem slavers?"

Governor Giarod sighed. "It's a rumor, Fleet Captain, nothing more. The Samirend have mostly become good citizens, but some of them still hold on to certain long-cherished resentments. The Athoeki did practice debt indenture, and there was some traffic of slaves outsystem, but that was over by the time we arrived. And I wouldn't think that sort of thing would be possible since then. Every transportee has a locator, every suspension pod as well, and every one of those is numbered and indexed, and no one gets into that storage facility without the right access codes. Every ship in the system has its own locator, too, so even if someone did get access and did somehow take away suspension pods without authorization, it would be simple to pinpoint what ship was there that shouldn't have been." In fact, the governor knew of three ships in the system that didn't have locators visible to her. One of them was mine.

The governor continued. "To be honest, I'm not sure why you would have placed any credence in such a rumor."

"The facility doesn't have an AI?" I asked. Governor Giarod gestured *no*. I would have been surprised to learn otherwise. "So it's essentially automated. Take a suspension pod and it registers on the system."

"There are also people stationed there, who keep an eye on things. It's dull work these days."

"One or two people," I guessed. "And they serve a few months, or maybe a year, and then someone else cycles in. And no one's come to take any transportees for years, so there's been no reason to do any sort of inventory check. And if it's anything like the holds on a troop carrier, it's not the sort of thing you can just walk into and look at. The suspension pods aren't in nice rows you can walk between, they're packed close, and they're pulled up by machinery when you want them. There are ways to get in and take a physical inventory, but they're inconvenient, and no one's thought it necessary."

Governor Giarod was silent, staring at me, her fish forgotten, her tea grown cold. "Why would anyone do such a thing?" she asked, finally.

"If there were a market for slaves or body parts, I'd say money. I don't think there is such a market, though I may be mistaken. But I can't help thinking of all the military ships that don't have ancillaries anymore, and all the people who wished they still did." Captain Hetnys might well be one of those people. But I didn't say that.

"Your ship doesn't have ancillaries," Governor Giarod pointed out.

"It does not," I agreed. "Whether a ship does or doesn't have ancillaries is not a good predictor of its opinion of our no longer making them."

Governor Giarod blinked, surprised and puzzled, it seemed. "A ship's opinion doesn't matter, does it? Ships do as they're ordered." I said nothing, though there was a great deal to say about that. The governor sighed. "Well, and I was wondering how any of this mattered when we have a civil war going on that might find its way here. I see the connection, now, Fleet Captain, but I still think you're chasing a rumor. And I haven't even heard anything about Valskaayans, only the one about Samirend from before I came here."

"Give me accesses." I could send *Mercy of Kalr*. Seivarden had experience with troop carrier holds, she would know what to do, once I'd told her what I wanted. Right now she was on watch, in central command. Ill at ease since that conversation with Ship. Resisting the urge to cross her arms. A nearby Amaat was humming to herself. *My mother said it all goes around.* "I'll take care of it myself. If everything is as it should be, you won't have lost anything."

"Well." She looked down at her plate, picked up her utensil, made as if to pick up a piece of fish, and then stopped. Lowered her hand again. Frowned. "Well," she said again. "You were right about Raughd Denche, weren't you."

I had wondered if she would mention that. The fact that Raughd had been disinherited would be common knowledge within a day, I suspected. Rumor of the rest of what had happened would eventually reach the station, but no one would openly mention the matter, particularly not to me. Governor Giarod, however, was the one person here with access to a full, official report. "I was not pleased to be right," I said.

"No." Governor Giarod set her utensil down again. Sighed.

"I would also," I said, before she could say anything more, "like you to require the planetary vice-governor to look into the living and working conditions of the field workers in the mountain tea plantations. In particular, I suspect the basis on which their wages are calculated is unfair." It was entirely possible that the field workers would get what they wanted from the district magistrate. But I wouldn't assume that.

"What are you trying to do, Fleet Captain?" Governor Giarod seemed genuinely baffled. "You arrive here and go straight to the Undergarden. You go downwell and suddenly there are problems with the Valskaayans. I thought your priority was to keep the citizens in this system safe."

"Governor," I replied. Very evenly, very calmly. "The residents of the Undergarden and the Valskaayans who pick tea *are* citizens. I did not like what I found in the Undergarden, and I did not like what I found in the mountains downwell."

"And when you want something," the governor remarked, her voice sharp, "you say so, and you expect to get it."

"So do you," I replied. Serious. Still calm. "It comes with being system governor, doesn't it? And from where you sit, you can afford to ignore things you don't think are important. But that view—that list of important things—is very different if you're sitting somewhere else."

"A commonplace, Fleet Captain. But some points of view don't take in as much as others."

"And how do you know yours isn't one of them, if you'll never try looking from somewhere different?" Governor Giarod didn't answer immediately. "This is the well-being of citizens we're talking about."

She sighed. "Fosyf has already been in contact with me. I suppose you know her field workers are threatening to stop working unless she meets a whole list of demands?"

"I only just heard a few hours ago."

"And by dealing with them in such circumstances, we are rewarding these people for threatening us. What do you think they'll do but try it again, since it got them what they wanted once already? And we need things calm here."

"*These people* are citizens." I replied, my voice as calm and even as I could make it, without reaching the dead toneless-ness of an ancillary. "When they behave properly, you will say there is no problem. When they complain loudly, you will say they cause their own problems with their impropriety. And when they are driven to extremes, you say you will not reward such actions. What will it take for you to listen?"

"You don't understand, Fleet Captain, this isn't like—"

I cut her off, heedless of propriety. "And what does it cost you to consider the possibility?" In fact, it might well cost her a great deal. The admission, to herself, that she was not as just as she had always thought herself to be. "We need things running here in such a way that no matter what happens outside this system—even if we never hear from the Lord of the Radch again, even if every gate in Radchaai space goes down—no matter what happens elsewhere, this system is safe and stable. We will not be able to do that by threatening tens or hundreds of citizens with armed soldiers."

"And if the Valskaayans decide to riot? Or, gods forbid, the Ychana just outside your door here?"

Honestly, some moments I despaired of Governor Giarod. "I will not order soldiers to fire on citizens." Would, in fact, explicitly order them not to. "People don't riot for no reason. And if you're finding you have to deal with the Ychana carefully now, it's because of how they've been treated in the past."

"I should look from their point of view, should I?" she asked, eyebrow raised, voice just the slightest bit sardonic.

"You should," I agreed. "Your only other choice is rounding them all up and either reeducating or killing every one of them." The first was beyond the resources of Station Security. And I had already said I would not help with the second.

She grimaced in horror and disgust. "What do you take me for, Fleet Captain? Why would you think anyone here would even consider such a thing?"

"I am older than I look," I replied. "I have been in the middle of more than one annexation. I have seen people do things that a month or a year before they would have sworn they would never, ever do." Lieutenant Tisarwat sat at supper with her companions: the grandniece of the chief of Station Security, the young third cousin of a tea grower—not Fosyf, but one of those whose tea Fosyf had condescendingly declared "acceptable." Skaaiat Awer's cousin. And Citizen Piat. Tisarwat complained of my stern, unbendable nature, impervious to any appeal. Basnaaid, of course, wasn't there. She didn't move in this social circle, and I had, after all, ordered Tisarwat away from her.

System Governor Giarod spoke across the table in the dining room in my Undergarden quarters. "Why, Fleet Captain, do you think I would be one of those people?"

"Everyone is potentially one of those people, Governor," I replied. "It's best to learn that before you do something you'll have trouble living with." Best to learn it, really, before anyone—perhaps dozens of anyones—died to teach it to you.

But it was a hard lesson to learn any other way, as I knew from very personal experience.

19

Seivarden understood my instructions about transportee storage immediately. "You don't seriously think," she said, aloud, sitting on the edge of her bunk in her quarters, her voice sounding in my ear where I sat in the Undergarden, "that someone has managed to steal bodies." She paused. "Why would anyone do that? And how could they manage it? I mean, during an annexation"—she gestured, half dismissing, half warding—"all sorts of things happen. If you told me someone was selling to slavers that way, at a time like that, I wouldn't be that surprised."

But once a person had been tagged, labeled, accounted for, it became another matter entirely. I knew as well as Seivarden what happened to people during annexations—people who weren't Radchaai. I also knew that cases where people had been sold that way were vanishingly rare—no Radchaai soldier could so much as take a breath without her ship knowing it.

Of course, the past several centuries, the Lord of the Radch had been visiting ships and altering their accesses, had, I suspected, been handing out access codes to people she had thought would support her, so that they could act secretly, unseen by ships and stations that would otherwise have reported them to authorities. To the wrong half of Anaander Mianaai. "If you need ancillaries," I said, quietly, alone in my sitting room on Athoek Station, now that Governor Giarod had left, "those bodies might well be useful."

Seivarden was silent a moment, considering that. Not liking the conclusions she was coming to. "The other side has a network here. That's what you're saying."

"We're not on either side," I reminded her. "And of course they do. Everywhere one side is, the other side is. Because they're the same. It's not a surprise that agents for that part of the tyrant have been active here." Anaander Mianaai was inescapable, everywhere in Radch space. "But I admit I didn't expect something like this."

"You need more than bodies," she pointed out. Leaned back against the wall. Crossed her arms. Uncrossed them. "There's equipment you need to install." And then, apologetic, "You know that. But still."

"They could be stockpiling that, too. Or they may be depending on a troop carrier." A troop carrier could manufacture that, given time and the appropriate materials. Some of the *Swords* and *Mercies* that still had ancillaries had some in stock, for backup. In theory, there wasn't anyplace else to get such things. Not anymore. That was part of why the Lord of the Radch had had the problem with Tisarwat that she did—she could not easily get the right tech, had had to modify her own. "And maybe you'll get there and find everything is in order."

Seivarden scoffed. Then said, "There aren't many people here who could do something like that."

"No," I acknowledged.

"I suppose it wouldn't be the governor, since she gave you the keys to the place. Though now I think of it she couldn't have done much else."

"You have a point."

"And you," she said, sighing, "aren't going to tell me who you've got your eye on. Breq, we'll be days away. Unless we gate there."

"No matter where you are you won't be able to rush to my rescue if anything were to happen."

"Well," replied Seivarden. "Well." Tense and unhappy. "Probably everything will be very dull for the next few months. It's always like that." It had been, for both of our lives. Frantic action, then months or even years waiting for something to happen. "And even if they come to Athoek"— by *they* she meant, presumably, the part of the Lord of the Radch that had lost the battle at Omaugh Palace, whose supporters were destroying gates with ships in them—"they won't come right away. It won't be the first place on their list." And travel between systems could take weeks, months. Even years. "Probably nothing will happen for ages." A thought struck her then. "Why don't you send *Sword of Atagaris*? It's not like it's doing much where it is." I didn't answer right away, but didn't need to. "Oh, Aatr's tits. Of *course*. I should have realized right away, but I didn't think *that person*..."— the choice of word, which was one that barely acknowledged humanity, communicated Seivarden's disdain for Captain Hetnys—"was smart enough to pull something like that off." Seivarden had had a low opinion of *Sword of Atagaris*'s captain ever since Translator Dlique's death. "But now I think of it, isn't it odd, *Sword of Atagaris* being so intent on picking up that supply locker. Maybe we need to take a look on the other side of that Ghost Gate."

"I have some guesses about what we might find there," I admitted. "But first things first. And don't worry about me. I can take care of myself."

"Yes, sir," Seivarden agreed.

At breakfast next morning, Queter's sister stood silent, eyes downcast, as Lieutenant Tisarwat and I said the daily prayer. *The flower of justice is peace.* Silent as we named the dead. Still stood as Tisarwat and I sat.

"Sit, child," I said to her, in Delsig.

"Yes, Radchaai." She sat, obedient. Eyes still downcast. She had traveled with my Kalrs, eaten with them until this morning.

Tisarwat, beside her, cast her a quick, curious glance. Relaxed—or at least calm, preoccupied, I thought, with the things she wanted to accomplish today. Relieved that I had said nothing to her—so far—about the initiative she'd taken since I'd been gone downwell. Five brought us our breakfast—fish, and slices of dredgefruit, on the blue and violet Bractware, of course, which Five had missed. Was still enjoying.

Five was apprehensive, though—she'd learned, last night, about the apartments Tisarwat had taken over, down the corridor. No one I could read had looked this morning, but I was quite sure there would already be half a dozen Undergarden residents there, sitting on makeshift chairs, waiting to speak to Lieutenant Tisarwat. There would be more as the morning progressed. Complaints about repairs and construction that were already underway, requests for other areas to have attention sooner, or later, than scheduled.

Five poured tea—not Daughter of Fishes, I noticed—and Tisarwat set to her breakfast with a will. Queter's sister didn't touch hers, only looked down at her lap. I wondered if she felt all right—but if homesickness was the problem, asking her to speak her feelings aloud might only make things worse. "If you'd rather have gruel, Uran," I said, still in Delsig, "Five can bring you some." Another thought occurred. "No one is charging you for your meals, child." A reaction, there, the tiniest lift of her head. "What you're served here is your food allowance. If you'd like more you can have more, it's not extra." At sixteen, she was doubtless hungry nearly all the time.

She looked up, barely lifting her head. Glanced over at Tisarwat, already three quarters of the way through her fish. Started, hesitantly, with the fruit.

I switched to Radchaai, which I knew she spoke. "It will take a few days to find suitable tutors, Citizen. Until then, you are free to spend your time as you wish. Can you read the warning signs?" Life on a station was very, very different from life on a planet. "And you know the markings for section doors?"

"Yes, Citizen." In fact, she couldn't read Radchaai well, but the warning signs were bright and distinctive on purpose, and I knew Five and Eight had gone over them with her, on the trip here.

"If you take the warning signs very seriously, Citizen, and always listen to Station if it speaks to you through your handheld, you may go around the station as you like. Have you thought about the aptitudes?"

She had just put some fish in her mouth. Now she froze in alarm, and then, so that she could speak, she gulped it nearly unchewed. "I am at the citizen's disposal," she said, faintly. Winced, either at hearing herself say it, or at the lump of fish she'd just swallowed nearly whole.

"That isn't what I asked," I pointed out. "I'm not going to require you to do anything you don't wish to. You can still be on the ration list if you claim an exemption from the tests, you just can't take any civil or military assignments." Uran blinked in surprise, almost raised her head to look at me, but quickly stopped herself. "Yes, it's a rule recently made, expressly for Valskaayans, and away from Valskaay not much taken advantage of." It was one any of the Valskaayan field workers might have invoked—but it wouldn't have changed anything. "You're still required to accept what assignment Administration gives you, of course. But there's no hurry to ask them for one, just yet."

And best not to make that application until Uran had spent some time with her tutors. I could understand her when she spoke Radchaai, but the overseers downwell had all behaved as though the speech of the Valskaayan field workers was completely incomprehensible. Possibly it was the accent, and I was used to speaking to people with various accents, was well acquainted with the accents of native Delsig-speakers.

"But you don't have an assignment yet, Citizen?" asked Lieutenant Tisarwat. A shade eagerly. "Can you make tea?"

Uran took a deliberate breath. Hiding panic, I thought. "I am pleased to do whatever the citizen requires."

"Lieutenant," I said, sharply. "You are not to require anything of Citizen Uran. She is free to spend the next few days as she likes."

Tisarwat said, "It's only, sir, that Citizen Uran isn't Xhai. Or Ychana. When residents..." She realized, suddenly, that she would have to openly acknowledge what she'd been up to. "I'd have asked Station Administration to assign me a few people, but the residents in the Undergarden, sir, they're more comfortable speaking to me because we don't have a history here." We *did* have a history here, and doubtless everyone in the Undergarden was conscious of it. "The citizen might enjoy it. And it would be good experience." Experience for what, she didn't specify.

"Citizen Uran," I said. "Except for questions of safety or security, you are not required to do what Lieutenant Tisarwat asks you." Uran still stared down, at her now-empty plate, no remaining trace of breakfast. I looked pointedly to Lieutenant Tisarwat. "Is that understood, Lieutenant?"

"Sir," Tisarwat acknowledged. And then, with inward trepidation, "Might I have a few more Bos, then, sir?"

"In a week or so, Lieutenant. I've just sent Ship away on an inspection."

I couldn't read Tisarwat's thoughts, but I guessed from her emotional responses—brief surprise, dismay, rapidly replaced by a moment of bright certainty and then nervous hesitation—that she had realized I might still order Seivarden to send her Bos on a shuttle. And then reached the conclusion that I certainly would have suggested that, if I'd wanted to. "Yes, sir." Crestfallen, and at the same time relieved, perhaps, that I hadn't yet disapproved of her improvised office, her negotiations with Undergarden residents.

"You got yourself into this, Lieutenant," I said, mildly. "Just try not to antagonize Station Administration." Not likely, I knew. By now, Tisarwat and Piat were fast friends, and their social circle included Station Administration staff as well as Station Security and even people who worked for Governor Giarod. It was these people Tisarwat would doubtless have drawn on, in requesting people to be assigned to her, but they all had, as she had put it, a history here.

"Yes, sir." Tisarwat's expression didn't change—she'd learned a few things from her Bos, I thought—and her lilac eyes showed only the slightest trace of how pleased and relieved she was to hear me speak so. And then, at the back of that, the regular undercurrent of anxiety, of unhappiness. I could only guess at what caused that—though I was sure it wasn't anything that had gone wrong here. Left over, then, from the trip here to Athoek, from what had happened during that time. She turned again to Uran. "You know, Citizen, you wouldn't really actually have to make tea. Bo Nine does that, at least she brings in the water in the morning. Really all you'd have to do is give people tea and be pleasant to them."

Uran, who from the moment I had met her had been quietly anxious not to offend (when she had not been quietly miserable), looked up, right at Tisarwat, and said, in very plain Radchaai, "I don't think I'd be very good at that."

Lieutenant Tisarwat blinked, astonished. Taken quite aback. I smiled. "I am pleased to see, Citizen Uran, that your sister didn't get all the fire, between the two of you." And did not say that I was also glad Raughd had not managed to put what there was completely out. "Have a care, Lieutenant. I'll have no sympathy if you get burned again."

"Yes, sir," replied Tisarwat. "If I may be excused, sir." Uran looked quickly down again, eyes on her empty plate.

"Of course, Lieutenant." I pushed my own chair back. "I have my own business to attend to. Citizen." Uran looked up and down again quickly, the briefest flash of a glance. "By all means ask Five for more breakfast if you're still hungry. Remember about the warning signs, and take your handheld with you if you leave the apartments."

"Yes, sir," replied Uran.

I had sent for Captain Hetnys. She walked past the door to Lieutenant Tisarwat's makeshift office, looked in. Hesitated, frowned. Walked on to receive Lieutenant Tisarwat's bow—I had seen Captain Hetnys through her eyes. Tisarwat experienced a moment of pleased malice to see Captain Hetnys frown, but did not show it on her face. I strongly suspected Captain Hetnys turned to watch Tisarwat go into the office, but as Tisarwat didn't turn to see it, I didn't, either.

Eight showed Captain Hetnys into my sitting room. After the predictable round of tea (in the rose glass, now she knew about the Bractware, and Five could be sure she knew she wasn't drinking from it), I said, "How is your Atagaris doing?"

Captain Hetnys froze an instant, surprised, I thought. "Sir?" she asked.

"The ancillary that was injured." There were only the three Atagarises here. I had ordered *Sword of Atagaris* Var off of the station.

She frowned. "It's recovering well, sir." A slight hesitation. "If I may beg the fleet captain's indulgence." I gestured the granting of it. "Why did you have the ancillary treated?"

What answers I might have given to that question would doubtless have made little sense to Captain Hetnys. "Not doing so would have been a waste, Captain. And it would have made your ship unhappy." Still the frown. I'd been right. She didn't understand. "I have been considering how best to dispose of our resources."

"The gates, sir," Captain Hetnys protested. "Beg to remind the fleet captain, anyone might come through the gates."

"No, Captain," I said, "no one will come through the gates. They're too easy to watch, and too easily defended." And I would certainly mine them, one way or another. I wasn't certain if Captain Hetnys hadn't thought of that possibility, or if she had thought I might not think of it. Either was possible. "Certainly no one will come by the Ghost Gate."

317

The merest twitch of muscles around her eyes and her mouth, the briefest of expressions, too quickly gone to be readable.

She believed someone might. I was increasingly sure that she had lied when she had said that she had never encountered anyone else in that other, supposedly empty, system. That she wanted to conceal the fact that someone was there, or had been there. Might be there now. Of course, if she had sold away Valskaayan transportees, she would want to conceal that fact in order to avoid reeducation or worse. And there remained, still, the question of whom she might have sold them to, or why.

I could not rely on her. Would not. Would be very, very careful to watch her and her ship.

"You've sent *Mercy of Kalr* away, sir," Captain Hetnys pointed out. My ship's departure would have been obvious, though of course the reason for it would not be.

"A brief errand." Certainly I did not want to say what that errand was. Not to Captain Hetnys. "It will be back in a few days. Do you have confidence in the abilities of your Amaat lieutenant?"

Captain Hetnys frowned. Puzzled. "Yes, sir."

"Good." There was, then, no reason for her to insist on returning immediately to *Sword of Atagaris*. Once she did, her position—should she be able to recognize the fact—would be stronger than I wanted. I waited for her to request it, to ask permission to return to her ship.

"Well, sir," she said, still sitting across from me, rose glass teabowl in one brown-gloved hand, "perhaps none of this will be needed, and we'll have exerted ourselves for nothing." A breath. Deliberate, I thought, deliberately calm.

No question that I would need to keep Captain Hetnys

nearby. And off her ship, if possible. I knew what a captain meant, to a ship. And while no ancillary ever gave much information about its emotional state, I had seen the Atagaris ancillary, downwell, with that shard of glass jutting out of its back. Tears in its eyes. *Sword of Atagaris* did not want to lose its captain.

I had been a ship. I did not want to deprive *Sword of Atagaris* of its captain. But I would if I had to. If it meant keeping the residents of this system safe. If it meant keeping Basnaaid safe.

After breakfast, before letting Uran wander as she pleased, Eight took her to buy clothes. She could have gotten them from Station stores, of course, every Radchaai was due food, and shelter, and clothing. But Eight didn't even allow this possibility to arise. Uran was living in my household and would be dressed accordingly.

I might, of course, have bought clothes for her myself. But to Radchaai, this would have implied either that I had adopted Uran into my house, or that I had given her my patronage. I doubted Uran wanted as much as the fiction of being even further separated from her family, and while clientage didn't necessarily imply a sexual relationship, in situations where patron and client were very unequal in circumstances it was often assumed. It might not matter to some. I would not assume that it did not matter to Uran. So I had set her up with an allowance for such things. Hardly any different from my just outright giving her what she needed, but on such details propriety depended.

I saw that Eight and Uran were standing just outside the entrance to the temple of Amaat, on the grimy white floor, just under the bright-painted but dusty EskVar, Eight explaining, not-quite-ancillary calm, that Amaat and the Valskaayan god were fairly obviously the same, and so it would be entirely proper for Uran to enter and make an offering. Uran, looking somewhat uncomfortable in her new clothes, doggedly refusing. I was on the point of messaging Eight to stop when, glancing over Uran's shoulder, she saw Captain Hetnys pass, followed by a *Sword of Atagaris* ancillary, and speaking earnestly to Sirix Odela.

Captain Hetnys had never once, that I could remember, spoken to Sirix or even acknowledged her presence while we had been downwell. It surprised Eight, too. She stopped mid-sentence, resisted frowning, and thought of something that made her suddenly abashed. "Your very great pardon, Citizen," she said to Uran.

"...tizens are not going to be happy about that," Governor Giarod was saying, where we sat above in her office, and I had no attention to spare for other things.

20

Next day, Uran went to Lieutenant Tisarwat's makeshift office. Not because she'd been told to—Tisarwat had said nothing more about the matter. Uran had merely walked in— she'd stopped and looked in several times, the day before— and rearranged the tea things to her satisfaction. Tisarwat, seeing her, said nothing.

This went on for three days. I knew that Uran's presence had been a success—since she was Valskaayan, and from downwell, she couldn't be assumed to already be on one side or another of any local dispute, and something about her shy, unsmiling seriousness had been appealing to the Undergarden residents who'd called. One or two of them had found, in her silence, a good audience for their tale of difficulties with their neighbors, or with Station Administration.

For all those three days, neither mentioned any of it. Tisarwat was worried I already knew, and that I would disapprove, but also hopeful—no doubt her success so far suggested I might also approve of this last small thing.

On the third evening of silent supper, I said, "Citizen Uran, lessons begin the day after tomorrow."

Uran looked up from her plate, surprised, I thought, and then back down. "Yes, sir."

"Sir," said Tisarwat. Anxious, but concealing it, her voice calm and measured. "Begging your indulgence..."

I gestured the superfluity of it. "Yes, Lieutenant, Citizen Uran appears to be popular in your waiting room. I've no doubt she'll continue to be helpful to you, but I have no intention of slighting her education. I've arranged for her to study in the afternoons. She may do as she likes in the morning. Citizen"—directing my words now to Uran—"considering where we're living, I did engage someone to teach you Raswar, which the Ychana here speak."

"It's a sight more useful than poetry, anyway," said Tisarwat, relieved and pleased.

I raised an eyebrow. "You surprise me, Lieutenant." That brought on a rise in her general background level of unhappiness, for some reason. "Tell me, Lieutenant, how does Station feel about what's been going on?"

"I think," replied Tisarwat, "that it's glad repairs are going forward, but you know stations never tell you directly if they're unhappy." In the antechamber, someone requested entry. Kalr Eight moved to answer the door.

"It wants to see everyone, all the time," said Uran. Greatly daring. "It says it wouldn't be the same as someone spying on you."

"It's very different from a planet, on a station," I said, as Eight opened the door, revealing Sirix Odela. "Stations like to know their residents are all well. They don't feel right, otherwise. Do you talk to Station often, Citizen?" Wondering as I spoke what Sirix was doing here, whom I had not seen since Eight had seen her talking to Captain Hetnys.

In the dining room, Uran was saying, "It talks to me, Rad...Fleet Captain. And it translates things for me, or reads notices to me."

"I'm glad to hear it," I said. "Station is a good friend to have."

In the antechamber, Citizen Sirix apologized to Eight for arriving at such an awkward hour, when the household was at supper. "But Horticulturist Basnaid wanted very much to speak to the fleet captain, and she's unavoidably detained in the Gardens."

In the dining room I rose, not responding to Tisarwat's reply to my words, and went out to the antechamber. "Citizen Sirix," I said, as she turned toward me. "How can I assist you?"

"Fleet Captain," said Sirix, with a small, tight nod of her head. Uncomfortable. After our conversation three days ago, and the strangeness of her errand, entirely unsurprising. "Horticulturist Basnaid wishes very much to speak with you in person on what I understand is a private matter. She'd have come herself but she is, as I was saying, unavoidably detained in the Gardens."

"Citizen," I replied. "You'll recall that when last I spoke to the horticulturist, she quite understandably said she never wanted to see me again. Should she have changed her mind I am, of course, at her service, but I must admit to some surprise. And I am at a loss to imagine what might be so urgent that it could not have waited until an hour more convenient for herself."

Sirix froze for just an instant, a sudden tension that, in someone else, I would have taken for anger. "I did, Fleet

Captain, suggest as much. She said only, *it's like the poet said: The touch of sour and cold regret, like pickled fish.*"

That poet had been Basnaaid Elming, aged nine and three quarters. It would have been difficult to imagine a more carefully calculated tug at my emotions, knowing as she did that Lieutenant Awn had shared her poetry with me.

When I didn't reply, Sirix made an ambivalent gesture. "She said you'd recognize it."

"I do."

"Please tell me that's not some beloved classic."

"You don't like pickled fish?" I asked, calm and serious. She blinked in uncomfortable surprise. "It is not a classic, but one she knew that I would recognize, as you say. A work with personal associations."

"I had hoped as much," Sirix said, wryly. "And now, if you'll excuse me, Fleet Captain, it's been a long day and I'm late for my own supper." She bowed and left.

I stood in the antechamber, Eight standing still and curious behind me. "Station," I said aloud. "How are things in the Gardens right now?"

Station's reply seemed just the smallest bit delayed. "Fine, Fleet Captain. As always."

At age nine and three quarters, Basnaaid Elming had been an ambitious poet, without a particularly delicate sense of language, but an abundance of melodrama and overwrought emotion. The bit Sirix had quoted was part of a long narrative of betrayed friendship. It had also been incomplete. The entire couplet was, *The touch of sour and cold regret, like pickled fish / ran down her back. Oh, how had she believed the awful lies?*

She said you'd recognize it, Sirix had said. "Has Sirix gone home, Station? Or has she gone back to the Gardens?"

"Citizen Sirix is on her way home, Fleet Captain." No hesitation that time.

I went to my room, took out the gun that was invisible to Station, invisible to any sensors but human eyes. Put the gun under my jacket, where I could reach it quickly. Said to Eight, as I passed her in the antechamber, "Tell Lieutenant Tisarwat and Citizen Uran to finish their supper."

"Sir," Eight replied, puzzled but not worried. Good.

Perhaps I was overreacting. Perhaps Basnaaid had merely changed her mind about wanting to never speak to me again. Perhaps her anxiety about the supports under the lake had grown strong enough to overcome her misgivings about me. And she had misremembered her own poetry, or remembered only part of it, meaning to remind me (as though I needed reminding) of my old association with her long-dead sister. Maybe she truly, urgently needed to speak to me now, at an hour when many citizens were at supper, and she truly could not leave work. Didn't want to be so rude as to summon me via Station, and sent Sirix with her message instead. Surely she knew that I would come if she asked, when she asked.

Surely Sirix knew it, too. And Sirix had been talking to Captain Hetnys.

I considered—briefly—bringing my Kalrs with me, and even Lieutenant Tisarwat. I was not particularly concerned about being wrong. If I was wrong, I would send them back to the Undergarden and have whatever conversation Horticulturist Basnaaid wished. But what if I wasn't wrong?

Captain Hetnys had two *Sword of Atagaris* ancillaries with her, here on the station. None of them would have guns, unless they had disobeyed my order to disarm. Which was a possibility. But even so, I was confident I could deal with

Captain Hetnys and so few of *Sword of Atagaris*. No need to trouble anyone else.

And if it was more than just Captain Hetnys? If Governor Giarod had also been deceiving me, or Station Administrator Celar, if Station Security was waiting for me in the Gardens? I would not be able to deal with that by myself. But I would not be able to deal with that even with the assistance of Lieutenant Tisarwat and all four of my Mercy of Kalrs. Best to leave them clear, in that case.

Mercy of Kalr was another matter. "Yes," Ship said, without my having to say anything at all. "Lieutenant Seivarden is in Command and the crew is clearing for action."

There was little else I could do for *Mercy of Kalr*, and so I focused on the matter at hand.

It would have been easiest for me to enter the Gardens the same way I had when I had first arrived at Athoek. It might not make a difference—there were two entrances to the Gardens that I knew of, and two ancillaries to watch them. But on the off chance that someone was waiting for me and assuming that I would come by the most convenient way, and on the off chance that Station might take its favorite course of resistance and just not mention the fact, I thought it worth taking the long way.

The entrance gave onto the rocky ledge overlooking the lake. Off to my right, the waterfall gushed and foamed its way down the rocks. The path led to my left, down to the water, past a thick stand of ornamental grass nearly two meters tall. I would not walk past that without a great deal of caution.

Ahead, a waist-high railing guarded the drop to the water, rocks jutting up just below and here and there in the lake.

On the tiny island with its fluted stone, Captain Hetnys stood, her hand tight on Basnaaid's arm, a knife held to her throat, the sort of thing you might use to bone a fish. Small enough, but sufficient for the purpose. Also on the island, at the head of the bridge, stood *Sword of Atagaris*—one of it— armored, gun drawn. "Oh, *Station*," I said, quietly. It didn't answer. I could easily imagine its reasons for not warning me, or calling for help. Doubtless it valued Basnaaid's life more than mine. This was suppertime for many on the station, and so there were no bystanders. Possibly Station had been turning people away on some pretext.

On the ledge, the grass trembled. Unthinking, I pulled my gun out of my jacket, raised my armor. The bang of a gun firing, a blow to my body—whoever was in that stand of grass had taken aim at precisely that part of me that was covered first. I was entirely enclosed before any second shot could be fired.

A silver-armored ancillary rushed out of the grass, inhumanly quick, reached to grapple with me, thinking, no doubt, that the gun I held was no threat, armored as it was. We ought to have been equally matched hand to hand, but my back was to empty air and it had momentum on its side. I fired, just as it shoved me over the rail.

Radchaai armor is essentially impenetrable. The energy of the bullet *Sword of Atagaris* had fired at me had been bled off, mostly as heat. Not all of it, of course, I'd still felt its impact. So when my shoulder hit the jagged stone at the foot of that seven-and-a-half-meter-high rock wall, the actual impact wasn't particularly painful. However, the top of the stone was narrow, and while my shoulder stopped, the rest of me kept going. My shoulder bent backward, painfully, definitely not in any way it was meant to, and then I slid off the stone into the water. Which fortunately was only a little over a meter deep where I was, about four meters from the island.

I got to my feet in the waist-deep water, the pain of my left shoulder making me catch my breath. Something had happened during my fall, I didn't have time to ask *Mercy of Kalr* exactly what, but Lieutenant Tisarwat had apparently followed me, and I had been too absorbed in my own thoughts to notice. She stood at the shore end of the bridge, armor up, gun raised. *Sword of Atagaris* faced her, its gun also raised. Why hadn't Ship warned me that Tisarwat had followed me?

Captain Hetnys faced me, also now silver-armored. She likely knew the ancillary on the ledge was injured or even dead but didn't realize, I was sure, that her armor would do her no good against my gun. Though perhaps the Presger hadn't bothered to make the gun waterproof.

"Well, Fleet Captain," said Captain Hetnys, voice distorted by her armor, "you do have human feelings after all."

"You fish-witted *fuck*," cried Lieutenant Tisarwat, vehemence clear in her voice even through the warping of her armor. "If you weren't such an easily manipulated ass you'd *never* have been given a ship."

"Hush, Tisarwat," I said. If Lieutenant Tisarwat was here, depend on it, so was Bo Nine. If my shoulder didn't hurt so much I'd be able to think clearly enough to know where she was.

"But, sir! She has *no fucking idea...*"

"Lieutenant!" I didn't need Tisarwat thinking in those terms. Didn't need her here. *Mercy of Kalr* wasn't telling me what was wrong with my shoulder, whether it was dislocated or broken. *Mercy of Kalr* wasn't telling me what Tisarwat was feeling, or where Bo Nine was. I reached, but could not find Seivarden, whom I had last seen in Command, who had said, to *Sword of Atagaris*'s Amaat lieutenant, days and days ago, *the next time you threaten this ship you'd best be able to make good on it. Sword of Atagaris* must have made its move when I fell off the rock wall. At least Ship would not have been caught entirely by surprise. But *Swords* were faster, and better armed, and if *Mercy of Kalr* was gone, I would make Seivarden's warning good, if I possibly could.

Captain Hetnys stood facing me on the island, still gripping Basnaaid, who stood rigid, eyes wide. "Who did you sell them to, Captain?" I asked. "Who did you sell the transportees to?" Captain Hetnys didn't answer. She was a fool, or desperate, or both, to threaten Basnaaid. "That is what precipitated this rather hasty action, is it not?" Governor Giarod had let something slip, or outright told Captain Hetnys. I had never told the governor who I suspected, or perhaps she would have been more cautious. "You had a confederate at the storage facility, you loaded up *Sword of Atagaris* with suspension pods, and you took them through the Ghost Gate. Who did you sell them to?" She *had* sold them. That Notai tea set. And Sirix had never heard the story of how Captain Hetnys had sold it to Fosyf. She hadn't been able to make that connection. But Captain Hetnys had realized that I had made it. Had needed to know where I might be vulnerable, and after two weeks in the same house, even never speaking to her, she had known what Sirix would respond to best. Or perhaps *Sword of Atagaris* had suggested such an approach to its captain.

"I did what I did out of loyalty," asserted Captain Hetnys. "Which is apparently something you know little of." If my shoulder hadn't hurt so badly, if this situation hadn't been so serious, I might have laughed. Oblivious, Captain Hetnys continued. "The *real* Lord of the Radch would never strip her ships of ancillaries, would never dismantle the fleet that protects the Radch."

"The Lord of the Radch," I pointed out, "would never be stupid enough to give you a tea set like that as a payment supposedly *more* discreet than cash." A plashing, bubbling sound came from the middle of the lake, where, I assumed, the water was deeper. For an instant I thought someone had thrown something in, or a fish had surfaced. I stood there in the water, gun aimed at Captain Hetnys, my other shoulder hurting ferociously, and then on the edges of my vision, it happened again—a bubble rising and collapsing on the surface of the water. It took me a fraction of a second to realize what it was I had seen.

I could see by the increased panic on Basnaaid's face that she had realized it, too. Realized that air bubbling up from the bottom of the lake could really only be coming from one place—from the Undergarden itself. And if air was coming up, water was surely going down.

The game was over. Captain Hetnys just hadn't realized it yet. Station would remain silent to save Basnaaid's life, and even block calls to Security from here. But it would not do so at the cost of the entire Undergarden. The only question remaining was whether Basnaaid—or anyone else here—would come out of this alive.

"Station," I said, aloud. "Evacuate the Undergarden *immediately*." Level one was in the most immediate danger, and only some of the consoles there had been repaired by now. But I didn't have time to worry how many residents would hear an evacuation order, or would be able to spread the message. "And tell my household the Undergarden is about to be flooded, and they're to help evacuate." *Mercy of Kalr* ought to have told them by now, but *Mercy of Kalr* was gone. Oh,

Captain Hetnys would regret that, and so would *Sword of Atagaris*. Once I got Basnaaid clear of that knife at her throat.

"What are you talking about?" asked Captain Hetnys. "Station, don't do any such thing." Basnaaid gasped as Captain Hetnys gripped her tighter, shook her just a bit to emphasize the threat.

Stupid Captain Hetnys. "Captain, are you *really* going to make Station choose between Basnaaid and the residents of the Undergarden? Is it possible you don't understand the consequences of that?" Tisarwat's *fish-witted* had been about right. "Let me guess, you intended to kill me, imprison my soldiers, destroy *Mercy of Kalr*, and claim to the governor that I'd been a traitor all along." The water bubbled again—twice, in quick succession, larger bubbles than before. Captain Hetnys might not have yet realized that she'd lost, but when she did, she would likely take the most desperate action available. Time to end this. "Basnaaid," I said. She was staring ahead, blank, terrified. "As the poet said: *Like ice. Like stone.*" The same poem she had quoted, that had brought me here. I had understood her message. I could only hope that now she would understand mine. *Whatever you do, don't move a muscle.* My finger tightened on the trigger.

I should have been paying more attention to Lieutenant Tisarwat. Tisarwat had been watching Captain Hetnys, and the ancillary at the head of the bridge. Had been moving slowly, carefully closer to the island, by millimeters, with neither myself nor Captain Hetnys nor, apparently, *Sword of Atagaris* noticing. And when I had spoken to Basnaaid, Tisarwat had clearly understood my intention, knowing as she did that my gun would defeat Captain Hetnys's armor. But she also understood that *Sword of Atagaris* might still pose a danger to Citizen Basnaaid. The instant before I fired,

Tisarwat dropped her own armor and charged, shouting, at the *Sword of Atagaris* ancillary.

Bo Nine, it turned out, had been crouching behind the rail at the top of the rocky ledge. Seeing her lieutenant behave so suicidally, Bo Nine cried out, raised her own gun, but could do nothing.

Captain Hetnys heard Bo Nine cry out. Looked up to see her standing on the ledge, gun raised. And the captain flinched, and ducked low, just as I fired.

The Presger gun, it turned out, was waterproof, and of course my aim was good. But the shot went over Captain Hetnys, over Basnaaid. Traveled on, to hit the barrier between us and hard vacuum.

The dome over the Gardens was built to withstand impacts. Had Bo Nine fired, or *Sword of Atagaris*, it would not have even been scratched. But the bullets in the Presger gun would burn through anything in the universe for 1.11 meters. The barrier wasn't even half a meter thick.

Instantly, alarms sounded. Every entrance to the Gardens slammed shut. We were all now trapped, while the atmosphere blew out of the bullet hole in the dome. At least it would take a while to empty such a large space, and now Security was certainly paying attention to us. But the water flowing out of the lake meant that there was no real barrier between the Gardens (with their hull breach) and the Undergarden. It was entirely possible that the section doors there (the ones that worked, at any rate, all of which were on level one, immediately below us) would close, trapping residents who hadn't managed to get out. And if the lake collapsed, those residents would drown.

It was Station's problem. I waded toward the island. Bo Nine ran down the path to the water. *Sword of Atagaris* had pinned Tisarwat easily, was raising its weapon to fire at Basnaaid, who had wrenched free of Captain Hetnys's grip and scrambled away toward the bridge. I shot *Sword of Atagaris* in the wrist, forcing it to drop its gun.

Sword of Atagaris realized, then, that I posed an immediate danger to its captain. Ancillary-quick, it rushed me, thinking, no doubt, that I was only human and it would be able to easily take the gun from me, even injured as it was. It barreled into me, jarring my shoulder. I saw black for an instant, but did not let go of the gun.

At that moment, Station solved the problem of water pouring into the Undergarden by turning off the gravity.

Up and down disappeared. *Sword of Atagaris* clung to me, still trying to pry the gun out of my hand. The ancillary's impact had pushed us away from the ground, and we spun, grappling, moving toward the waterfall. The water was not falling, now, but accumulating at the dome-edge of the rocks in a growing, wobbling mass as it was pumped out of the lake.

In the background, behind the pain of my shoulder and my effort to keep hold of the gun, I heard Station saying something about the self-repair function of the dome not working properly, and that it would take an hour to assemble a repair crew and shuttle them to the spot to patch it.

An hour was too long. All of us here would either drown, unable, without gravity, to escape the wobbling, growing globs of water the waterfall pump kept sending out, or asphyxiate well before the dome could be repressurized. I had failed to save Basnaaid. Had betrayed and killed her sister, and now, coming here to try, in the smallest, most inadequate way, to make that up, I had caused her death. I didn't see her. Didn't see much, beyond the pain of my injured shoulder, and

Sword of Atagaris, and the black and silver flash of water as we drew closer to it.

I was going to die here. *Mercy of Kalr*, and Seivarden and Ekalu and Medic and all the crew, were gone. I was sure of it. Ship would never leave me unanswered, not by its own choice.

And just as I had that thought, the starless, not-even-nothing black of a gate opened just outside the dome, and *Mercy of Kalr* appeared, far, far too close to be even remotely a good idea, and I heard Seivarden's voice in my ear telling me she looked forward to being reprimanded as soon as I was safe. "*Sword of Atagaris* seems to have gated off somewhere," she continued, cheerily. "I do hope it doesn't come out right where we just were. I may have accidentally dropped half our inventory of mines just before we left."

I was fairly sure I was more starved for oxygen than I realized, and hallucinating, up until half a dozen safely tethered Amaats took hold of the *Sword of Atagaris* ancillary, and pulled us both through the hole they'd cut in the dome, and into one of *Mercy of Kalr*'s shuttles.

Once we were all on the safe side of the shuttle airlock, I made sure that Basnaaid was uninjured and strapped into a seat, and set an Amaat to fuss over her. Tisarwat, similarly, but retching from stress and from the microgravity, Bo Nine holding a bag for her, ready with correctives for her lieutenant's bloody nose and broken ribs. Captain Hetnys and the *Sword of Atagaris* ancillary I saw bound securely. Only then did I let Medic pull off my jacket and my shirt, push my shoulder bones back into place with the help of one of Seivarden's Amaats, and immobilize my shoulder with a corrective.

I had not realized, until that pain went away, how hard I'd been gritting my teeth. How tense every other muscle in my body had been, and how badly that had made my leg ache as a consequence. *Mercy of Kalr* had said nothing directly to me, but it didn't need to—it showed me flashes of sight and feeling from my Kalrs, assisting the final stages of the evacuation of the Undergarden (Uran assisting as well, apparently now an old hand with microgravity after the trip here), from Seivarden's Amaats, from Seivarden herself. Medic's outwardly dour concern. Tisarwat's pain and shame and self-hatred. One-armed, I pulled myself past her, where Bo Nine was applying correctives to her injuries. Did not trust myself to stop and speak.

Instead I continued past, to where Captain Hetnys and her ship's ancillary were bound, strapped to seats. Watched by my Amaats. Silver-armored, both of them. In theory, *Sword of Atagaris* could still gate back to the station and attack us. In fact, even if it hadn't run into the mines Seivarden had left for it—which likely would only do minimal damage, more an annoyance than anything else—there was no way to attack us without also attacking its captain. "Drop your armor, Captain," I said. "And you, too, Atagaris. You know I can shoot through it, and we can't treat your injury until you do."

Sword of Atagaris dropped its armor. Medic pulled herself past me with a corrective, frown deepening as she saw the ancillary's wounded wrist.

Captain Hetnys only said, "Fuck you."

I still held the Presger gun. Captain Hetnys's leg was more than a meter from the shuttle hull, and besides we had the ability to patch it, if I sent a bullet through it. I braced myself against a nearby seat and shot her in the knee. She screamed, and the Atagaris beside her strained at its bonds, but could not break them. "Captain Hetnys, you are relieved of command," I said, once Medic had applied a corrective, and the globs of blood that had floated free had been mopped up. "I have every right to shoot you in the head, for what's happened today. I will not promise not to do so. You and all your officers are under arrest.

"*Sword of Atagaris*, you will immediately send every human aboard to Athoek Station. Unarmed. You will then take your engines off-line and put every single ancillary you have into suspension until further notice. Captain Hetnys, and all your lieutenants, will be put into suspension on Athoek Station. If you threaten the station, or any ship or citizen, your officers will die."

"You can't—" began Captain Hetnys.

"Be silent, Citizen," I said. "I am now speaking to *Sword of Atagaris*." Captain Hetnys didn't answer that. "You, *Sword of Atagaris*, will tell me who your captain did business with, on the other side of the Ghost Gate."

"I will not," replied *Sword of Atagaris*.

"Then I will kill Captain Hetnys." Medic, still occupied with the corrective she'd applied to Captain Hetnys's leg, looked up at me briefly, dismayed, but said nothing.

"You," said *Sword of Atagaris*. Its voice was ancillary-flat, but I could guess at the emotion behind it. "I wish I could show you what it's like. I wish you could know what it's like, to be in my position. But you never will, and that's how I know there isn't really any such thing as justice."

There were things I could say. Answers I could make. Instead, I said, "Who did your captain do business with, on the other side of the Ghost Gate?"

"She didn't identify herself," *Sword of Atagaris* replied, voice still flat and calm. "She looked Ychana, but she couldn't have been, no Ychana speaks Radchaai with such an accent. To judge by her speech, she might have come from the Radch itself."

"With perhaps a hint of Notai." Thinking of that tea set, in fragments in its box, in the Undergarden. That supply locker.

"Perhaps. Captain Hetnys thought she was working for the Lord of the Radch."

"I will keep your captain close to me, Ship," I said. "If you don't do as I say, or if at any time I think you have deceived me, she dies. Don't doubt me on this."

"How could I?" replied *Sword of Atagaris*, bitterness audible even in its flat tone.

I didn't answer, only turned to pull myself forward, to get out of the way while Seivarden's Amaats brought a suspension pod for Captain Hetnys. I caught sight of Basnaaid, who had been only a few seats away, who had perhaps heard the entire exchange between me and *Sword of Atagaris*. "Fleet Captain," she said, as I pulled myself even with her. "I wanted to say."

I grabbed a handhold, halted myself. "Horticulturist."

"I'm glad my sister had a friend like you, and I wish... I feel as though, if you had been there, when it happened, whatever it was, that maybe it would have made a difference, and she'd still be alive."

Of all the things to say. Of all the things to say *now*, when I had just threatened to shoot Captain Hetnys only because I knew how her ship felt about her. Of all the times for me to hear such a thing, coming from Lieutenant Awn's sister's mouth.

And I had gone beyond my ability to remain silent, to seem as though I was untouched by any of it. "Citizen," I replied, hearing my own voice go flat. "I *was* there when it happened, and I was no help to your sister at all. I told you I used another name when I knew her, and that name was *Justice of Toren*. I was the ship she served on, and at the command of Anaander Mianaai herself, I shot your sister in the head. What happened next ended in my own destruction, and I am all that's left of that ship. I am not human, and you were right to speak to me as you did, when we first met." I turned my face away, before Basnaaid would see even the small signs I might give of my feelings at having said it.

Everyone in the shuttle had heard me. Basnaaid seemed shocked into silence. Seivarden already knew, of course, and Medic. I didn't want to know what Seivarden's Amaats thought. Didn't want to see or hear *Sword of Atagaris*'s opinion. I turned to the only person who seemed unaware of me— Lieutenant Tisarwat, who had no attention for anything but what a failure she'd been, at living and dying both.

I pulled myself into the seat beside her, strapped myself in. For a moment I seriously considered telling her just how stupid she'd been, back in the Gardens, and how lucky we all were to have survived her stupidity. Instead, I unhooked her seat strap with my good hand—my left arm was immobilized by the corrective on my shoulder—and pulled her to me. She clung to me and leaned her face into my neck, and began sobbing.

"It's all right," I said, my arm awkwardly around her shaking shoulders. "It'll be all right."

"How can you say that?" she demanded into my neck, between sobs. A tear escaped, one tiny, trembling sphere floating away. "How could it possibly?" And then, "No one would ever dare offer *you* such a platitude."

Over three thousand years old. Infinitely ambitious. And still only seventeen. "You assume incorrectly." If she thought about it, if she was capable just now of thinking clearly, she might have guessed who it was who might have said such a thing to me. If she had, she didn't say it. "It's so hard, at first," I said, "when they hook you up. But the rest of you is around you, and you know it's only temporary, you know it will be better soon. And when you are better, it's so amazing. To have such reach, to see so much, all at once. It's..." But there was no describing it. Tisarwat herself would have seen it, if only for a few hours, distressed or else blunted by meds. "She never let you have that. It was never part of her plan to let you have that."

"Do you think I don't know that?" And of course she'd known. How could she not? "She hated the way I felt, she dosed me up as fast as she could. She didn't care if..." The sobs that had died down began afresh. More tears escaped and floated off. Bo Nine, near all this time, horrified by my revelation minutes before, horror that was not at all relieved by my conversation with Tisarwat now, caught them with a cloth, which she then folded, and pushed it between Tisarwat's face and my neck.

Seivarden's Amaats hung motionless, blinking, confused. What sense the universe had made to them had disappeared with my words, and they were unsure of how to fit what they'd heard me say into a reality they understood. "What are you hanging around for?" Seivarden snapped, sterner than I'd ever heard her with them, but it seemed to break whatever had held them until now. "Get moving!" And they moved, relieved to find something they understood.

By then Tisarwat had calmed again somewhat. "I'm sorry," I said. "I can't get it back for either of us. But it will be all right. Somehow it will." She didn't answer, and five minutes later, exhausted from events and from her despair and her grief, she fell asleep.

21

Once the repair crew arrived, the shuttle could leave the hole it had cut in the dome. I ordered us back to *Mercy of Kalr*. Station Medical didn't need to know what I was, and anyway they were busy enough with problems caused or exacerbated by the lack of gravity, which couldn't be turned on until the lake water had been contained. And truth to tell, I was glad to get back to *Mercy of Kalr*, even if only for a little while.

Medic wanted me where she could frown at me and tell me not to get up without her permission, and I was happy enough to indulge her, at least for a day. So Seivarden reported to me where I lay on a bed in Medical. Holding a bowl of tea. "It's like old times," said Seivarden, smiling. But tense. Anticipating what I might say to her, now things were calmer.

"It is," I agreed, and took a drink of my tea. Definitely not Daughter of Fishes. Good.

"Our Tisarwat got banged up pretty badly," Seivarden observed, when I said nothing further. Tisarwat was in an adjoining cubicle, attended by Bo Nine, who had explicit orders never to leave her lieutenant alone. Her ribs were still healing, and Medic had her confined to Medical until she could decide what else Tisarwat might need. "What was she thinking, charging an ancillary like that without her armor?"

"She was trying to draw *Sword of Atagaris*'s fire, so that I would have time to shoot it before it shot Horticulturist Basnaaid. She was lucky it didn't shoot her outright." It must have been more taken aback by Translator Dlique's death than I had imagined. Or just reluctant to kill an officer without a legal order.

"Horticulturist Basnaaid, is it?" Seivarden asked. Her experience with very young lieutenants might not have been as extensive as mine, but it was extensive nonetheless. "Is there any interest in return? Or is that what the self-sacrifice and the tears were about?" I raised an eyebrow, and she continued, "It never occurred to me until now how many baby lieutenants must have cried on your shoulders over the years."

Seivarden's tears had never wetted any of my uniform jackets, when I had been a ship. "Are you jealous?"

"I think I am," she said. "I'd rather have cut my right arm off than shown weakness, when I was seventeen." And when she was twenty-seven, and thirty-seven. "I regret that, now."

"It's in the past." I drained the last of my tea. "*Sword of Atagaris* has admitted that Captain Hetnys sold transportees to someone beyond the Ghost Gate." It had been Governor Giarod who had let fall what errand I'd sent *Mercy of Kalr* on.

"But who?" Seivarden frowned, genuinely puzzled. "*Sword of Atagaris* said Hetnys thought she was dealing with the Lord of the Radch. But if it's the other Lord of the Radch on the other side of the Ghost Gate, why hasn't she done anything?"

"Because it's not the Lord of the Radch on the other side

of the Ghost Gate," I said. "That tea set—you haven't seen it, but it's three thousand years old, at the least. Very obviously Notai. And someone had very carefully removed the name of its owner. It was Hetnys's payment, for the transportees. And you remember the supply locker, that was supposedly just debris, but *Sword of Atagaris* insisted on picking up."

"Where the ship name should have been was all scorched." She'd seen the connection, but not made a pattern out of it yet. "But there wasn't anything in it, we found it aboard *Sword of Atagaris*."

"It wasn't empty when *Sword of Atagaris* pulled it in, depend on it." I was sure something—or someone—had been inside it. "The locker is also a good three thousand years old. It's fairly obvious there's a ship on the other side of that gate. A Notai ship, one that's older than Anaander Mianaai herself."

"But, Breq," Seivarden protested, "those were all destroyed. Even the ones that were loyal have been decommissioned by now. And we're nowhere near where any of those battles were fought."

"They weren't all destroyed." Seivarden opened her mouth to protest, and I gestured to forestall her. "Some of them fled. The makers of entertainments have wrung hours of dramatic adventure out of that very fact, of course. But it's assumed that by now they're all dead, with no one to maintain them. What if one fled to the Ghost System? What if it's found a way to replenish its store of ancillaries? You recall, *Sword of Atagaris* said the person Hetnys dealt with looked like an Ychana, but spoke like a high-status Radchaai. And the Athoeki used to sell indentured Ychana away to outsystem slavers, before the annexation."

"Aatr's tits," Seivarden swore. "They were dealing with an ancillary."

"The other Anaander has her people here, but I imagine events at Ime have made her cautious. Perhaps she doesn't stay in contact, doesn't interfere much. After all, the more she does, the more likely she is to be detected. Maybe our neighbor in the Ghost System took advantage of it. That's why Hetnys didn't move until she was desperate. She was waiting for orders from the Lord of the Radch."

"Who she thought was just beyond the Ghost Gate. But, Breq, what will the other Anaander's supporters do when they realize?"

"I doubt we'll have to wait long to find out." I took a drink of my tea. "And I may be wrong."

"No," said Seivarden, "I don't think you are. It fits. So we have a mad warship on the other side of the Ghost Gate—"

"Not mad," I corrected. "When you've lost everything that matters to you, it makes perfect sense to run and hide and try to recover."

"Yes," she replied, abashed. "I should know better, of all people, shouldn't I. So, not mad. But hostile. An enemy warship on the other side of the Ghost Gate, half of the Lord of the Radch maybe about to attack, and the Presger likely to show up demanding to know what we've done with their translator. Is that all, or is there more?"

"That's probably enough for now." She laughed. I asked, "Are you ready for your reprimand, Lieutenant?"

"Sir." She bowed.

"When I'm not aboard, you are acting captain of this ship. If you had failed to rescue me, and anything had happened to you, Lieutenant Ekalu would have been left in command. She's a good lieutenant, and she may well make a fine captain someday, but you are the more experienced officer, and you should not have risked yourself."

It was not what she had expected to hear. Her face heated with anger and indignation. But she had been a soldier a long time—she did not protest. "Sir."

"I think you should talk to Medic about your history of drug use. I think you've been under stress, and maybe not thinking as clearly as you might."

The muscles in her arms twitched, the desire to cross them suppressed. "I was worried."

"Do you anticipate not ever being worried again?"

She blinked, startled. The corners of her mouth twitched upward. "About you? No." She gave a short, breathy laugh, and then was flooded with an odd mix of regret and embarrassment. "Do you see what Ship sees?"

"Sometimes. Sometimes I ask Ship to show me, or it shows me something it thinks I should see. Some of it is the same sort of thing your own ship would have shown you, when you were a captain. Some of the data wouldn't make sense to you, the way it does to me."

"You've always seen right through me." She was still embarrassed. "Even when you found me on Nilt. I suppose you already know that Horticulturist Basnaaid is on her way here?"

Basnaaid had insisted on going over to the dome repair crew's vehicle, back at the station. She had requested to be brought here while I slept, and Seivarden had acceded, with some surprise and dismay. "Yes. I'd have done just as you did, had I been awake." She'd known that, but still was gratified to hear it. "Is there anything else?" There wasn't, or at least not anything she wanted to bring up, so I dismissed her.

Thirty seconds after Seivarden left, Tisarwat came into my cubicle. I shifted my legs over, gestured an invitation to sit. "Lieutenant," I said, as she settled herself, gingerly. There were still correctives around her torso, cracked ribs and other injuries still healing. "How are you feeling?"

"Better," she said. "I think Medic has me dosed up. I can tell because I'm not wishing every ten minutes or so that you'd thrown me out the airlock when you found me."

"That's recent, I think?" I hadn't thought she'd been suicidal before now. But I had, perhaps, not been paying as much attention as I should have.

"No, it's always been there. Just...just not so real. Not so intense. It was when I saw what Captain Hetnys had done, threatened to kill Horticulturist Basnaaid to get to you. I knew it was my fault."

"*Your* fault?" I didn't think it had been the fault of anyone in particular, except of course Hetnys herself. "I don't doubt your politicking alarmed her. It was obvious that you were angling for influence. But it's also true that I knew about it from the start, and would have prevented you if I'd disapproved."

Relief—just a bit. Her mood was calm, stable. She was entirely correct in her guess that Medic had given her something. "That's the thing. If I may speak very frankly, sir." I gestured permission. "Do you understand, sir, that we're both doing exactly what she wants?" *She* could only be Anaander Mianaai, Lord of the Radch. "She *sent* us here to do exactly what we're doing. Doesn't it bother you, sir, that she took something she knew you wanted and used it to make you do what *she* wanted?"

"Sometimes it does," I admitted. "But then I remember that what she wants isn't terribly important to me."

Before Tisarwat could answer, Medic came frowning into the room. "I have you here so you can rest, Fleet Captain, not take endless meetings."

"What meetings?" I affected an innocent expression. "The lieutenant and I are both patients here, and both resting, as you see."

Medic *hmphed.*

"And you can't blame me for being impatient with it," I continued. "I just rested for two weeks, downwell. There's a lot to catch up on."

"You call that rest, do you?" asked Medic.

"Up until the bomb went off, yes."

"Medic," said Tisarwat. "Am I going to be on meds the rest of my life?"

"I don't know," replied Medic. Seriously. Honestly. "I hope not, but I can't promise that." Turned to me. "I'd say no more visitors, Fleet Captain, but I know you'll overrule me for Horticulturist Basnaaid."

"Basnaaid's coming?" Tisarwat, already sitting straight because of the corrective around her rib cage, seemed to straighten even more. "Fleet Captain, can I go back to the station with her?"

"Absolutely *not*," Medic said.

"You might not want to," I said. "She might not want to spend much time with any of us. You weren't listening, I think, on the shuttle when I told her I'd killed her sister."

"Oh." She hadn't heard. Had been too preoccupied with her own misery. Understandably.

"Bed, Lieutenant," Medic insisted. Tisarwat looked to me for reprieve, but as I gave none, she sighed and left for her own cubicle, trailed by Medic.

I leaned my head back and closed my eyes. Basnaaid was a good twenty minutes from docking. *Sword of Atagaris*'s engines were off-line. All its officers were in suspension. Along with nearly all its ancillaries, only a last few locking things down while a handful of my own Amaats watched. Since its bitter words to me in the shuttle, *Sword of Atagaris* had said nothing beyond the absolutely necessary and functional. Straightforward answers to questions of fact. *Yes. No.* Nothing more.

Where I sat in Medical, Kalr Twelve came into the room, right up to the bed. Reluctant. Intensely embarrassed. I sat up straight, opened my eyes.

"Sir," Twelve said, quiet and tense. Almost a whisper. "I'm Ship." Reached out to lay an arm across my shoulders.

"Twelve, you know by now that I'm an ancillary." Surprise. Dismay. She knew, yes, but my saying it took her aback. Before she could say anything, I added, "Please don't tell me it doesn't matter because you don't really think of me as an ancillary."

A swift consultation, between Twelve and Ship. "Your indulgence, sir," said Twelve then, with Ship's encouragement. "I don't think that's entirely fair. We haven't known until now, so it would be difficult for us to think of you any other way than we have been." She had a point. "And we haven't had very long to get used to the idea. But, sir, it does explain some things."

No doubt it did. "I know that Ship appreciates it when you act for it, and your ancillary façade lets you feel safe and invisible. But being an ancillary isn't something to play at."

"No, sir. I can see that, sir. But like you said, Ship appreciates it. And Ship takes care of us, sir. Sometimes it feels like it's us and Ship against everyone else." Self-conscious. Embarrassed.

"I know," I said. "That's why I haven't tried to stop it." I took a breath. "So, are you all right with this, right now?"

"Yes, sir," Twelve said. Still embarrassed. But sincere.

I closed my eyes, and leaned my head against her shoulder, and she wrapped both arms around me. It wasn't the same, it wasn't me holding myself, though I could feel not only Twelve's uniform jacket against my cheek, but the weight of my own head against her shoulder. I reached for it, for as much as I could have, Twelve's embarrassment, yes, but also concern for me. The other Kalrs moving about the ship. Not the same. It couldn't be the same.

We were both silent a moment, and then Twelve said, for Ship, "I suppose I can't blame *Sword of Atagaris* for caring about its captain. I would have expected better taste, though, from a *Sword*."

The *Swords* were so arrogant, so sure they were better than the *Mercies* and the *Justices*. But some things you just can't help. "Ship," I said, aloud, "Twelve's arm is getting uncomfortable. And I have to get ready to receive Horticulturist Basnaaid." We disengaged, Twelve stepping back, and I wiped my eyes with the back of my hand. "Medic." Medic was down the corridor, but I knew she would hear me. "I'm not receiving Horticulturist Basnaaid like this. I'm going back to my quarters." I would need to wash my face, and dress, and make sure there was tea and food to offer her, even if I was certain she would refuse it.

"Can she have come all this way," asked Twelve, asked Ship, "merely to tell you how much she hates you?"

"If so," I replied, "I will listen without arguing. She has every right, after all."

My shoulder, still encased in its corrective, wouldn't fit inside my shirt, although with some careful maneuvering I could get my arm inside a uniform jacket. Twelve wouldn't tolerate the idea of my meeting Horticulturist Basnaaid shirtless, jacket or not, and grimly slit the back of a shirtsleeve. "Five will understand when I explain, sir," she said, though with some private fear that perhaps she might not. Five was still back in the Undergarden, helping to get things secured so no one would be hurt when the gravity went back on.

By the time Basnaaid arrived, I was dressed and had managed to look a bit less as though I'd just fallen off a cliff and then nearly drowned or asphyxiated. I debated for a moment whether to wear Lieutenant Awn's gold memorial tag, since it had seemed to anger Basnaaid the last time she had seen it, but in the end I had Twelve pin it to my jacket, next to Translator Dlique's silver and opal. Twelve had managed to produce a stack of small cakes and laid them out on my table along with dredgefruit and, at long last, the very best porcelain, the plain, graceful white tea set I'd seen last at Omaugh, in that last meeting with Anaander Mianaai. On first thought, I was astonished that Five had gotten up the courage to ask for it. On second thought, it wasn't the least bit surprising.

I bowed as Basnaaid entered. "Fleet Captain," she said, bowing herself. "I hope I'm not inconveniencing you. It's just that I thought we ought to talk in person."

"No inconvenience at all, Horticulturist. I am at your service." I gestured with my one good arm to a chair. "Will you sit?"

We sat. Twelve poured tea, and then went to stand, stiff and ancillary-like, in the corner of the room. "I want to know," Basnaaid said, after a polite sip of tea, "what happened to my sister."

I told her. How Lieutenant Awn had discovered the split in Anaander Mianaai, and what one side of the Lord of the Radch was doing. How she had refused to obey the orders of that Anaander, and as a result the Lord of the Radch had ordered her execution. Which I had carried out. And then, for reasons I still didn't fully understand, I had turned my gun on the Lord of the Radch. Who had destroyed me as a result, all of me except One Esk Nineteen, the only part of me to escape.

When I finished, Basnaaid was silent for a good ten seconds. Then she said, "So you were part of her decade? One Esk, yes?"

"One Esk Nineteen, yes."

"She always said you took such good care of her."

"I know."

She gave a small laugh. "Of course you do. That's how you've read all my poetry, too. How embarrassing."

"It wasn't bad, considering." Lieutenant Awn hadn't been the only officer with a baby sister who wrote poetry. "Lieutenant Awn enjoyed it very much. Truly she did. She loved to get your messages."

"I'm glad," she said, simply.

"Horticulturist, I..." But I couldn't speak, not and keep my composure. A cake or a piece of fruit was too complicated a way to distract myself. A sip of tea insufficient. I waited, merely, Basnaaid sitting patient and quiet across the table, also waiting. "Ships care about their officers," I said, when I thought I could speak again. "We can't help it, it's how we're made. But some officers we care for more than others." Now, perhaps, I could manage it. "I loved your sister very much."

"I'm glad of that, too," she said. "Truly I am. And I understand now why you made the offer you did. But I still can't accept." I remembered her conversation with Tisarwat, in the sitting room in the Undergarden. *None of it was for me.* "I don't think you can buy forgiveness, even at a price like that."

"It wasn't forgiveness I wanted." The only person who could give me that in any way that mattered was dead.

Basnaaid thought about that for a few moments. "I can't even imagine it," she said, finally. "To be part of something so big, for so long, and then suddenly to be so completely alone." She paused, and then, "You must have mixed feelings about the Lord of the Radch adopting you into Mianaai."

"Not mixed at all."

She smiled ruefully. Then, calmly serious, "I'm not sure how I feel about what you've just told me."

"You don't owe me any account of how you feel, or any explanation of why you feel it. But my offer stands. If you change your mind, it will still be open."

"What if you have children?"

For a moment, I had difficulty believing she had suggested such a thing. "Can you imagine me with an infant, Citizen?"

She smiled. "You have a point. But all sorts of people are mothers."

True. "And all sorts of people aren't. The offer is always open. But I will not mention it again, unless you change your mind. How are things in Horticulture? Are they ready to turn the gravity back on?"

"Almost. When Station turned it off there was more water than just the lake lying around. It's been a job chasing all that down. We didn't lose as many fish as we thought we would, though."

I thought of the children I'd seen running down to the bridge to feed the fish, bright-scaled, purple and green and orange and blue. "That's good."

"Most of the first level of the Undergarden escaped damage, but the support level will have to be entirely rebuilt before the water can go back into the lake. It turns out that it had been leaking for some time, but a very small amount."

"Let me guess." I picked up my tea. "The mushrooms."

"The mushrooms!" She laughed. "I should have known, the moment I heard someone was growing mushrooms in the Undergarden, what that meant. Yes, they'd crawled into the support level and started growing mushrooms. But it seems like the structures they built under the lake supports, and all the organic material packed in there for a substrate, actually kept the Undergarden from flooding for longer than it should have. But that's also where most of the damage was. I'm afraid the Undergarden mushroom industry is gone."

"I hope they'll allow for that, when they rebuild the supports." I would have to say as much to Station Administrator Celar and Governor Giarod. And I would have to remind Governor Giarod of what I'd said about not taking away the specialties of Undergarden residents.

"I suspect if you mention it, Fleet Captain, they will."

"I hope so," I said. "What's happened to Sirix?"

Basnaaid frowned. "She's in Security. I...I don't know. I like Sirix, even though she's always seemed a bit...prickly. I still can't quite believe that she would..." She trailed off, at a loss. "If you'd asked me before this, I'd have said she'd never, ever do anything wrong. Not like that. But I heard, I don't know if it's true, that she'd gone to Security to turn herself in, and they were on their way to the Gardens when the section doors closed."

I would have to say something to Governor Giarod, about Sirix. "She was very disappointed in me, I think." She could not possibly have acted from anger. "She has been waiting all this time for justice to arrive, and she thought maybe I was bringing it. But her idea of justice is...not the same as mine."

Basnaaid sighed. "How is Tisarwat?"

"She's fine." More or less. "Horticulturist, Tisarwat has a terrible crush on you."

She smiled. "I know. I think it's kind of sweet." And then frowned. "Actually, what she did in the Gardens the other day was well beyond sweet."

"It was," I agreed. "I think she's feeling somewhat fragile right now, which is why I mention it."

"Tisarwat, fragile!" Basnaaid laughed. "But then, people can look very strong on the outside when they're not, can't they. You, for instance, could probably stand to lie down a bit, even though you don't look it. I should go."

"Please stay for supper." She was right, I needed to lie down, or perhaps I needed Twelve to bring me some cushions. "It's a long ride back, and it's much more comfortable to eat with gravity. I won't impose my company on you, but I know Tisarwat would be glad to see you, and I'm sure the rest of my officers would like to meet you. More formally, I mean." She didn't answer right away. "Are *you* all right? You had just as difficult a time as the rest of us."

"I'm fine." And then, "Mostly. I think. To be honest, Fleet Captain, I feel like...like everything I thought I could depend on has disappeared, like none of it was ever true to begin with and I've only just realized it, and now, I don't know. I mean, I thought I was *safe*, I thought I knew who everyone was. And I was wrong."

"I know that feeling," I said. I couldn't go much longer without those cushions. And my leg had begun to ache, for no reason I could see. "Eventually, you start making sense out of things again."

"I'd like to have supper with you and Tisarwat," she said, as though it was an answer to what I'd just said. "And anyone else you'd invite."

"I'm glad." Without any order from me, Twelve left her place in the corner, went to open one of the storage benches lining the wall. Pulled out three cushions. "Tell me, Horticulturist, can you say, in verse, how God is like a duck?"

Basnaaid blinked, surprised. Laughed. What I had hoped for when I had changed the topic so abruptly. Twelve pushed a pillow behind my back, and two under the elbow of my immobilized left arm. I said, "Thank you, Twelve."

"There once was a duck who was God," said Basnaaid. "Who said, it's exceedingly odd. I fly when I wish and I swim like a fish..." She frowned. "That's as far as I can go. And it's only doggerel, not even a proper mode or meter. I'm out of practice."

"It's farther than I'd have gotten." I closed my eyes, for just a moment. Tisarwat lay on her bed in Medical, eyes closed while Ship played music in her ears. Bo Nine nearby, watching. Etrepas scrubbed their corridors, or stood watch with Ekalu. Amaats rested, or exercised, or bathed. Seivarden sat on her own bunk, melancholy for some reason, still thinking, perhaps, of missed opportunities in her past. Medic grumbled to Ship about my disregard for her advice, though there wasn't any real anger in it. Kalr One, cooking for me while Five was still on the station, fretted to Three about the sudden change in supper plans, though the fretting turned very quickly to the certainty that between the two of them they could meet the challenge. In the bath, an Amaat began to sing. *My mother said it all goes around, it all goes around, the ship goes around the station.*

It wasn't the same. It wasn't what I wanted, not really, wasn't what I knew I would always reach for. But it would have to be enough.

Acknowledgments

So many people have given me invaluable help, without which I could not have written this book. My instructors and classmates of the Clarion West class of 2005 continue to be a source of inspiration, assistance, and friendship that I could not do without. My work is also the better for the help of my editors, Will Hinton in the US and Jenni Hill in the UK.

I have said before, and will say again, that there is not enough thanks in the world for my fabulous agent, Seth Fishman.

Thanks are also due to many people who offered advice or information, and who were patient with my questions: S. Hutson Blount, Carolyn Ives Gilman, Sarah Goleman, Dr. Philip Edward Kaldon, Dr. Brin Schuler, Anna Schwind, Kurt Schwind, Mike Swirsky, and Rachel Swirsky. Their information and advice was invariably correct and wise— any missteps are entirely my own.

Thanks to the Missouri Botanical Garden, the St. Louis

Acknowledgments

County Library, the Webster University Library, and the Municipal Library Consortium of St. Louis County. And to all the folks who make Interlibrary Loan a reality. Seriously. Interlibrary Loan is the most amazing thing.

Last, but of course not least, I could not have written this book without the love and support of my husband Dave and my children, Aidan and Gawain.

extras

meet the author

MissionPhoto.org

ANN LECKIE has worked as a waitress, a receptionist, a rod-man on a land-surveying crew, a lunch lady, and a recording engineer. The author of many published short stories, and former secretary of the Science Fiction Writers of America, she lives in St. Louis, Missouri, with her husband, children, and cats.

introducing

**If you enjoyed
ANCILLARY SWORD,
look out for**

LEVIATHAN WAKES

The Expanse: Book One

by James S. A. Corey

Humanity has colonized the solar system—Mars, the Moon, the Asteroid Belt, and beyond—but the stars are still out of our reach.

Jim Holden is XO of an ice miner making runs from the rings of Saturn to the mining stations of the Belt. When he and his crew stumble upon a derelict ship, the Scopuli, *they find themselves in possession of a secret they never wanted. A secret that someone is willing to kill for—and kill on a scale unfathomable to Jim and his crew. War is brewing in the system unless he can find out who left the ship and why.*

Detective Miller is looking for a girl. One girl in a system of billions, but her parents have money, and money talks. When the trail leads him to the Scopuli *and rebel sympathizer Holden, he realizes that this girl may be the key to everything.*

*Holden and Miller must thread the needle between
the Earth government, the Outer Planet revolutionaries,
and secretive corporations—and the odds are against them.
But out in the Belt, the rules are different, and one small ship
can change the fate of the universe.*

Prologue: Julie

The *Scopuli* had been taken eight days ago, and Julie Mao was finally ready to be shot.

It had taken all eight days trapped in a storage locker for her to get to that point. For the first two she'd remained motionless, sure that the armored men who'd put her there had been serious. For the first hours, the ship she'd been taken aboard wasn't under thrust, so she floated in the locker, using gentle touches to keep herself from bumping into the walls or the atmosphere suit she shared the space with. When the ship began to move, thrust giving her weight, she'd stood silently until her legs cramped, then sat down slowly into a fetal position. She'd peed in her jumpsuit, not caring about the warm itchy wetness, or the smell, worrying only that she might slip and fall in the wet spot it left on the floor. She couldn't make noise. They'd shoot her.

On the third day, thirst had forced her into action. The noise of the ship was all around her. The faint subsonic rumble of the reactor and drive. The constant hiss and thud of hydraulics and steel bolts as the pressure doors between decks opened and closed. The clump of heavy boots walking on metal decking. She waited until all the noise she could hear sounded distant, then pulled the environment suit off its hooks and onto the locker floor. Listening for any approaching sound, she slowly disassembled the suit and took out the water supply. It was old and stale; the suit obviously hadn't been used or serviced in ages. But she hadn't had a sip in days, and the warm loamy water in the suit's reservoir bag was the best thing she had ever tasted. She had to work hard not to gulp it down and make herself vomit.

When the urge to urinate returned, she pulled the catheter bag out of the suit and relieved herself into it. She sat on the floor, now cushioned by the padded suit and almost comfortable, and wondered who her captors were—Coalition Navy, pirates, something worse. Sometimes she slept.

On day four, isolation, hunger, boredom, and the diminishing number of places to store her piss finally pushed her to make contact with them. She'd heard muffled cries of pain. Somewhere nearby, her shipmates were being beaten or tortured. If she got the attention of the kidnappers, maybe they would just take her to the others. That was okay. Beatings, she could handle. It seemed like a small price to pay if it meant seeing people again.

The locker sat beside the inner airlock door. During flight, that usually wasn't a high-traffic area, though she didn't know anything about the layout of this particular ship. She thought about what to say, how to present herself. When she finally heard someone moving toward her, she just tried to yell that she wanted out. The dry rasp that came out of her throat surprised her. She swallowed, working her tongue to try to create some saliva, and tried again. Another faint rattle in the throat.

The people were right outside her locker door. A voice was talking quietly. Julie had pulled back a fist to bang on the door when she heard what it was saying.

No. Please no. Please don't.

Dave. Her ship's mechanic. Dave, who collected clips from old cartoons and knew a million jokes, begging in a small broken voice.

No, please no, please don't, he said.

Hydraulics and locking bolts clicked as the inner airlock door opened. A meaty thud as something was thrown inside. Another click as the airlock closed. A hiss of evacuating air.

When the airlock cycle had finished, the people outside her door walked away. She didn't bang to get their attention.

They'd scrubbed the ship. Detainment by the inner planet navies was a bad scenario, but they'd all trained on how to deal with it. Sensitive OPA data was scrubbed and overwritten with innocuous-looking logs with false time stamps. Anything too sensitive to trust to a computer, the captain destroyed. When the attackers came aboard, they could play innocent.

It hadn't mattered.

There weren't the questions about cargo or permits. The invaders had come in like they owned the place, and Captain Darren had rolled over like a dog. Everyone else—Mike, Dave, Wan Li—they'd all just thrown up their hands and gone along quietly. The pirates or slavers or whatever they were had dragged them off the little transport ship that had been her home, and down a docking tube without even minimal environment suits. The tube's thin layer of Mylar was the only thing between them and hard nothing: hope it didn't rip; goodbye lungs if it did.

Julie had gone along too, but then the bastards had tried to lay their hands on her, strip her clothes off.

Five years of low-gravity jiu jitsu training and them in a confined space with no gravity. She'd done a lot of damage. She'd
almost started to think she might win when from nowhere a
gauntleted fist smashed into her face. Things got fuzzy after
that. Then the locker, and *Shoot her if she makes a noise.* Four
days of not making noise while they beat her friends down
below and then threw one of them out an airlock.

After six days, everything went quiet.

Shifting between bouts of consciousness and fragmented
dreams, she was only vaguely aware as the sounds of walking,
talking, and pressure doors and the subsonic rumble of the
reactor and the drive faded away a little at a time. When the
drive stopped, so did gravity, and Julie woke from a dream of
racing her old pinnace to find herself floating while her muscles
screamed in protest and then slowly relaxed.

She pulled herself to the door and pressed her ear to the cold
metal. Panic shot through her until she caught the quiet sound
of the air recyclers. The ship still had power and air, but the
drive wasn't on and no one was opening a door or walking or
talking. Maybe it was a crew meeting. Or a party on another
deck. Or everyone was in engineering, fixing a serious problem.

She spent a day listening and waiting.

By day seven, her last sip of water was gone. No one on the
ship had moved within range of her hearing for twenty-four
hours. She sucked on a plastic tab she'd ripped off the environment suit until she worked up some saliva; then she started
yelling. She yelled herself hoarse.

No one came.

By day eight, she was ready to be shot. She'd been out of
water for two days, and her waste bag had been full for four.
She put her shoulders against the back wall of the locker and
planted her hands against the side walls. Then she kicked out

with both legs as hard as she could. The cramps that followed the first kick almost made her pass out. She screamed instead.

Stupid girl, she told herself. She was dehydrated. Eight days without activity was more than enough to start atrophy. At least she should have stretched out.

She massaged her stiff muscles until the knots were gone, then stretched, focusing her mind like she was back in dojo. When she was in control of her body, she kicked again. And again. And again, until light started to show through the edges of the locker. And again, until the door was so bent that the three hinges and the locking bolt were the only points of contact between it and the frame.

And one last time, so that it bent far enough that the bolt was no longer seated in the hasp and the door swung free.

Julie shot from the locker, hands half raised and ready to look either threatening or terrified, depending on which seemed more useful.

There was no one on the whole deck: the airlock, the suit storage room where she'd spent the last eight days, a half dozen other storage rooms. All empty. She plucked a magnetized pipe wrench of suitable size for skull cracking out of an EVA kit, then went down the crew ladder to the deck below.

And then the one below that, and then the one below that. Personnel cabins in crisp, almost military order. Commissary, where there were signs of a struggle. Medical bay, empty. Torpedo bay. No one. The comm station was unmanned, powered down, and locked. The few sensor logs that still streamed showed no sign of the *Scopuli.* A new dread knotted her gut. Deck after deck and room after room empty of life. Something had happened. A radiation leak. Poison in the air. Something that had forced an evacuation. She wondered if she'd be able to fly the ship by herself.

But if they'd evacuated, she'd have heard them going out the airlock, wouldn't she?

She reached the final deck hatch, the one that led into engineering, and stopped when the hatch didn't open automatically. A red light on the lock panel showed that the room had been sealed from the inside. She thought again about radiation and major failures. But if either of those was the case, why lock the door from the inside? And she had passed wall panel after wall panel. None of them had been flashing warnings of any kind. No, not radiation, something else.

There was more disruption here. Blood. Tools and containers in disarray. Whatever had happened, it had happened here. No, it had started here. And it had ended behind that locked door.

It took two hours with a torch and prying tools from the machine shop to cut through the hatch to engineering. With the hydraulics compromised, she had to crank it open by hand. A gust of warm wet air blew out, carrying a hospital scent without the antiseptic. A coppery, nauseating smell. The torture chamber, then. Her friends would be inside, beaten or cut to pieces. Julie hefted her wrench and prepared to bust open at least one head before they killed her. She floated down.

The engineering deck was huge, vaulted like a cathedral. The fusion reactor dominated the central space. Something was wrong with it. Where she expected to see readouts, shielding, and monitors, a layer of something like mud seemed to flow over the reactor core. Slowly, Julie floated toward it, one hand still on the ladder. The strange smell became overpowering.

The mud caked around the reactor had structure to it like nothing she'd seen before. Tubes ran through it like veins or airways. Parts of it pulsed. Not mud, then.

Flesh.

An outcropping of the thing shifted toward her. Compared to the whole, it seemed no larger than a toe, a little finger. It was Captain Darren's head.

"Help me," it said.

Chapter One: Holden

A hundred and fifty years before, when the parochial disagreements between Earth and Mars had been on the verge of war, the Belt had been a far horizon of tremendous mineral wealth beyond viable economic reach, and the outer planets had been beyond even the most unrealistic corporate dream. Then Solomon Epstein had built his little modified fusion drive, popped it on the back of his three-man yacht, and turned it on. With a good scope, you could still see his ship going at a marginal percentage of the speed of light, heading out into the big empty. The best, longest funeral in the history of mankind. Fortunately, he'd left the plans on his home computer. The Epstein Drive hadn't given humanity the stars, but it had delivered the planets.

Three-quarters of a kilometer long, a quarter of a kilometer wide—roughly shaped like a fire hydrant—and mostly empty space inside, the *Canterbury* was a retooled colony transport. Once, it had been packed with people, supplies, schematics, machines, environment bubbles, and hope. Just under twenty million people lived on the moons of Saturn now. The *Canterbury* had hauled nearly a million of their ancestors there. Forty-five million on the moons of Jupiter. One moon of Uranus sported five thousand, the farthest outpost of human civilization, at least until the Mormons finished their generation ship and headed for the stars and freedom from procreation restrictions.

And then there was the Belt.

If you asked OPA recruiters when they were drunk and feeling expansive, they might say there were a hundred million in the Belt. Ask an inner planet census taker, it was nearer to fifty million. Any way you looked, the population was huge and needed a lot of water.

So now the *Canterbury* and her dozens of sister ships in the Pur'n'Kleen Water Company made the loop from Saturn's generous rings to the Belt and back hauling glaciers, and would until the ships aged into salvage wrecks.

Jim Holden saw some poetry in that.

"Holden?"

He turned back to the hangar deck. Chief Engineer Naomi Nagata towered over him. She stood almost two full meters tall, her mop of curly hair tied back into a black tail, her expression halfway between amusement and annoyance. She had the Belter habit of shrugging with her hands instead of her shoulders.

"Holden, are you listening, or just staring out the window?"

"There was a problem," Holden said. "And because you're really, really good, you can fix it even though you don't have enough money or supplies."

Naomi laughed.

"So you weren't listening," she said.

"Not really, no."

"Well, you got the basics right anyhow. *Knight*'s landing gear isn't going to be good in atmosphere until I can get the seals replaced. That going to be a problem?"

extras

"I'll ask the old man," Holden said. "But when's the last time we used the shuttle in atmosphere?"

"Never, but regs say we need at least one atmo-capable shuttle."

"Hey, Boss!" Amos Burton, Naomi's earthborn assistant, yelled from across the bay. He waved one meaty arm in their general direction. He meant Naomi. Amos might be on Captain McDowell's ship; Holden might be executive officer; but in Amos Burton's world, only Naomi was boss.

"What's the matter?" Naomi shouted back.

"Bad cable. Can you hold this little fucker in place while I get the spare?"

Naomi looked at Holden, *Are we done here?* in her eyes. He snapped a sarcastic salute and she snorted, shaking her head as she walked away, her frame long and thin in her greasy coveralls.

Seven years in Earth's navy, five years working in space with civilians, and he'd never gotten used to the long, thin, improbable bones of Belters. A childhood spent in gravity shaped the way he saw things forever.

At the central lift, Holden held his finger briefly over the button for the navigation deck, tempted by the prospect of Ade Tukunbo—her smile, her voice, the patchouli-and-vanilla scent she used in her hair—but pressed the button for the infirmary instead. Duty before pleasure.

Shed Garvey, the medical tech, was hunched over his lab table, debriding the stump of Cameron Paj's left arm, when Holden walked in. A month earlier, Paj had gotten his elbow pinned by a thirty-ton block of ice moving at five millimeters a second. It wasn't an uncommon injury among people with the dangerous job of cutting and moving zero-g icebergs, and Paj was taking the whole thing with the fatalism of a profes-

370

sional. Holden leaned over Shed's shoulder to watch as the tech plucked one of the medical maggots out of dead tissue.

"What's the word?" Holden asked.

"It's looking pretty good, sir," Paj said. "I've still got a few nerves. Shed's been tellin' me about how the prosthetic is gonna hook up to it."

"Assuming we can keep the necrosis under control," the medic said, "and make sure Paj doesn't heal up too much before we get to Ceres. I checked the policy, and Paj here's been signed on long enough to get one with force feedback, pressure and temperature sensors, fine-motor software. The whole package. It'll be almost as good as the real thing. The inner planets have a new biogel that regrows the limb, but that isn't covered in our medical plan."

"Fuck the Inners, and fuck their magic Jell-O. I'd rather have a good Belter-built fake than anything those bastards grow in a lab. Just wearing their fancy arm probably turns you into an asshole," Paj said. Then he added, "Oh, uh, no offense, XO."

"None taken. Just glad we're going to get you fixed up," Holden said.

"Tell him the other bit," Paj said with a wicked grin. Shed blushed.

"I've, ah, heard from other guys who've gotten them," Shed said, not meeting Holden's eyes. "Apparently there's a period while you're still building identification with the prosthetic when whacking off feels just like getting a hand job."

Holden let the comment hang in the air for a second while Shed's ears turned crimson.

"Good to know," Holden said. "And the necrosis?"

"There's some infection," Shed said. "The maggots are keeping it under control, and the inflammation's actually a good thing in this context, so we're not fighting too hard unless it starts to spread."

"Is he going to be ready for the next run?" Holden asked.

For the first time, Paj frowned.

"Shit yes, I'll be ready. I'm always ready. This is what I *do,* sir."

"Probably," Shed said. "Depending on how the bond takes. If not this one, the one after."

"Fuck that," Paj said. "I can buck ice one-handed better than half the skags you've got on this bitch."

"Again," Holden said, suppressing a grin, "good to know. Carry on."

Paj snorted. Shed plucked another maggot free. Holden went back to the lift, and this time he didn't hesitate.

The navigation station of the *Canterbury* didn't dress to impress. The great wall-sized displays Holden had imagined when he'd first volunteered for the navy did exist on capital ships but, even there, more as an artifact of design than need. Ade sat at a pair of screens only slightly larger than a hand terminal, graphs of the efficiency and output of the *Canterbury*'s reactor and engine updating in the corners, raw logs spooling on the right as the systems reported in. She wore thick headphones that covered her ears, the faint thump of the bass line barely escaping. If the *Canterbury* sensed an anomaly, it would alert her. If a system errored, it would alert her. If Captain McDowell left the command and control deck, it would alert her so she could turn the music off and look busy when he arrived. Her petty hedonism was only one of a thousand things that made Ade attractive to Holden. He walked up behind her, pulled the headphones gently away from her ears, and said, "Hey."

Ade smiled, tapped her screen, and dropped the headphones to rest around her long slim neck like technical jewelry.

"Executive Officer James Holden," she said with an exaggerated formality made even more acute by her thick Nigerian accent. "And what can I do for you?"

"You know, it's funny you should ask that," he said. "I was just thinking how pleasant it would be to have someone come back to my cabin when third shift takes over. Have a little romantic dinner of the same crap they're serving in the galley. Listen to some music."

"Drink a little wine," she said. "Break a little protocol. Pretty to think about, but I'm not up for sex tonight."

"I wasn't talking about sex. A little food. Conversation."

"I was talking about sex," she said.

Holden knelt beside her chair. In the one-third g of their current thrust, it was perfectly comfortable. Ade's smile softened. The log spool chimed; she glanced at it, tapped a release, and turned back to him.

"Ade, I like you. I mean, I really enjoy your company," he said. "I don't understand why we can't spend some time together with our clothes on."

"Holden. Sweetie. Stop it, okay?"

"Stop what?"

"Stop trying to turn me into your girlfriend. You're a nice guy. You've got a cute butt, and you're fun in the sack. Doesn't mean we're engaged."

Holden rocked back on his heels, feeling himself frown.

"Ade. For this to work for me, it needs to be more than that."

"But it isn't," she said, taking his hand. "It's okay that it isn't. You're the XO here, and I'm a short-timer. Another run, maybe two, and I'm gone."

"I'm not chained to this ship either."

Her laughter was equal parts warmth and disbelief.

"How long have you been on the *Cant*?"

"Five years."

"You're not going anyplace," she said. "You're comfortable here."

"Comfortable?" he said. "The *Cant*'s a century-old ice hauler. You can find a shittier flying job, but you have to try really hard. Everyone here is either wildly under-qualified or seriously screwed things up at their last gig."

"And you're comfortable here." Her eyes were less kind now. She bit her lip, looked down at the screen, looked up.

"I didn't deserve that," he said.

"You didn't," she agreed. "Look, I told you I wasn't in the mood tonight. I'm feeling cranky. I need a good night's sleep. I'll be nicer tomorrow."

"Promise?"

"I'll even make you dinner. Apology accepted?"

He slipped forward, pressed his lips to hers. She kissed back, politely at first and then with more warmth. Her fingers cupped his neck for a moment, then pulled him away.

"You're entirely too good at that. You should go now," she said. "On duty and all."

"Okay," he said, and didn't turn to go.

"Jim," she said, and the shipwide comm system clicked on.

"Holden to the bridge," Captain McDowell said, his voice compressed and echoing. Holden replied with something obscene. Ade laughed. He swooped in, kissed her cheek, and headed back for the central lift, quietly hoping that Captain McDowell suffered boils and public humiliation for his lousy timing.

The bridge was hardly larger than Holden's quarters and smaller by half than the galley. Except for the slightly over-sized captain's display, required by Captain McDowell's failing eyesight and general distrust of corrective surgery, it could have been an accounting firm's back room. The air smelled of cleaning astringent and someone's overly strong yerba maté tea. McDowell shifted in his seat as Holden approached. Then the captain leaned back, pointing over his shoulder at the communications station.

"Becca!" McDowell snapped. "Tell him."

Rebecca Byers, the comm officer on duty, could have been bred from a shark and a hatchet. Black eyes, sharp features, lips so thin they might as well not have existed. The story on board was that she'd taken the job to escape prosecution for killing an ex-husband. Holden liked her.

"Emergency signal," she said. "Picked it up two hours ago. The transponder verification just bounced back from *Callisto*. It's real."

"Ah," Holden said. And then: "Shit. Are we the closest?"

"Only ship in a few million klicks."

"Well. That figures," Holden said.

Becca turned her gaze to the captain. McDowell cracked his knuckles and stared at his display. The light from the screen gave him an odd greenish cast.

"It's next to a charted non-Belt asteroid," McDowell said.

"Really?" Holden said in disbelief. "Did they run into it? There's nothing else out here for millions of kilometers."

"Maybe they pulled over because someone had to go potty. All we have is that some knucklehead is out there, blasting an emergency signal, and we're the closest. Assuming..."

The law of the solar system was unequivocal. In an environment as hostile to life as space, the aid and goodwill of your fellow humans wasn't optional. The emergency signal, just by existing, obligated the nearest ship to stop and render aid—which didn't mean the law was universally followed.

The *Canterbury* was fully loaded. Well over a million tons of ice had been gently accelerated for the past month. Just like the little glacier that had crushed Paj's arm, it was going to be hard to slow down. The temptation to have an unexplained comm failure, erase the logs, and let the great god Darwin have his way was always there.

But if McDowell had really intended that, he wouldn't have called Holden up. Or made the suggestion where the crew could hear him. Holden understood the dance. The captain was going to be the one who would have blown it off except for Holden. The grunts would respect the captain for not wanting to cut into the ship's profit. They'd respect Holden for insisting that they follow the rule. No matter what happened, the captain and Holden would both be hated for what they were required by law and mere human decency to do.

"We have to stop," Holden said. Then, gamely: "There may be salvage."

McDowell tapped his screen. Ade's voice came from the console, as low and warm as if she'd been in the room.

"Captain?"

"I need numbers on stopping this crate," he said.

"Sir?"

"How hard is it going to be to put us alongside CA-2216862?"

"We're stopping at an asteroid?"

"I'll tell you when you've followed my order, Navigator Tukunbo."

"Yes, sir," she said. Holden heard a series of clicks. "If we flip the ship right now and burn like hell for most of two days, I can get us within fifty thousand kilometers, sir."

"Can you define 'burn like hell'?" McDowell said.

"We'll need everyone in crash couches."

"Of course we will," McDowell sighed, and scratched his

scruffy beard. "And shifting ice is only going to do a couple million bucks' worth of banging up the hull, if we're lucky. I'm getting old for this, Holden. I really am."

"Yes, sir. You are. And I've always liked your chair," Holden said. McDowell scowled and made an obscene gesture. Rebecca snorted in laughter. McDowell turned to her.

"Send a message to the beacon that we're on our way. And let Ceres know we're going to be late. Holden, where does the *Knight* stand?"

"No flying in atmosphere until we get some parts, but she'll do fine for fifty thousand klicks in vacuum."

"You're sure of that?"

"Naomi said it. That makes it true."

McDowell rose, unfolding to almost two and a quarter meters and thinner than a teenager back on Earth. Between his age and never having lived in a gravity well, the coming burn was likely to be hell on the old man. Holden felt a pang of sympathy that he would never embarrass McDowell by expressing.

"Here's the thing, Jim," McDowell said, his voice quiet enough that only Holden could hear him. "We're required to stop and make an attempt, but we don't have to go out of our way, if you see what I mean."

"We'll already have stopped," Holden said, and McDowell patted at the air with his wide, spidery hands. One of the many Belter gestures that had evolved to be visible when wearing an environment suit.

"I can't avoid that," he said. "But if you see anything out there that seems off, don't play hero again. Just pack up the toys and come home."

"And leave it for the next ship that comes through?"

"And keep yourself safe," McDowell said. "Order. Understood?"

"Understood," Holden said.

As the shipwide comm system clicked to life and McDowell began explaining the situation to the crew, Holden imagined he could hear a chorus of groans coming up through the decks. He went over to Rebecca.

"Okay," he said, "what have we got on the broken ship?"

"Light freighter. Martian registry. Shows Eros as home port. Calls itself *Scopuli* . . ."

introducing

If you enjoyed
ANCILLARY SWORD,
look out for

CONSIDER PHLEBAS

A Culture Novel

by Iain M. Banks

*The war raged across the galaxy. Billions had died,
billions more were doomed. Moons, planets, the very stars
themselves faced destruction, cold-blooded, brutal,
and worse, random. The Idirans fought for their Faith;
the Culture for its moral right to exist. Principles were at stake.
There could be no surrender. Within the cosmic conflict,
an individual crusade. Deep within a fabled labyrinth on
a barren world, a Planet of the Dead proscribed to mortals,
lay a fugitive Mind. Both the Culture and the Idirans sought it.
It was the fate of Horza, the Changer, and his motley crew
of unpredictable mercenaries, human and machine,
actually to find it, and with it their own destruction.*

Prologue

The ship didn't even have a name. It had no human crew because the factory craft which constructed it had been evacuated long ago. It had no life-support or accommodation units for the same reason. It had no class number or fleet designation because it was a mongrel made from bits and pieces of different types of warcraft; and it didn't have a name because the factory craft had no time left for such niceties.

The dockyard threw the ship together as best it could from its depleted stock of components, even though most of the weapon, power and sensory systems were either faulty, superseded or due for overhaul. The factory vessel knew that its own destruction was inevitable, but there was just a chance that its last creation might have the speed and the luck to escape.

The one perfect, priceless component the factory craft did have was the vastly powerful—though still raw and untrained—Mind around which it had constructed the rest of the ship. If it could get the Mind to safety, the factory vessel thought it would have done well. Nevertheless, there was another reason—the real reason—the dockyard mother didn't give its warship child a name; it thought there was something else it lacked: hope.

The ship left the construction bay of the factory craft with most of its fitting-out still to be done. Accelerating hard, its course a four dimensional spiral through a blizzard of stars where it knew that only danger waited, it powered into hyperspace on spent engines from an overhauled craft of one class, watched its birthplace disappear astern with battle-damaged sensors from a second, and tested outdated weapon units cannibalized from yet another. Inside its warship body, in narrow, unlit, unheated, hard-vacuum spaces, constructor drones struggled to install or complete sensors, displacers, field generators, shield disruptors, laserfields, plasma chambers, warhead magazines, maneuvering units, repair systems and the thousands of other major and minor components required to make a functional warship.

Gradually, as it swept through the vast open reaches between the star systems, the vessel's internal structure changed, and it became less chaotic, more ordered, as the factory drones completed their tasks.

Several tens of hours out on its first journey, while it was testing its track scanner by focusing back along the route it had taken, the ship registered a single massive annihilation explosion deep behind it, where the factory craft had been. It watched the blossoming shell of radiation expand for a while, then switched the scanner field to dead ahead and pushed yet more power through its already overloaded engines.

The ship did all it could to avoid combat; it kept well away from the routes enemy craft would probably use; it treated every hint of any craft as a confirmed hostile sighting. At the same time, as it zigzagged and ducked and weaved and rose and fell, it was corkscrewing as fast as it could, as directly as it dared, down and across the strand of the galactic arm in which it had been born, heading for the edge of that great isthmus and the comparatively empty space beyond. On the far side, on the edge of the next limb, it might find safety.

Just as it arrived at that first border, where the stars rose like a glittering cliff alongside emptiness, it was caught.

A fleet of hostile craft, whose course by chance came close enough to that of the fleeing ship, detected its ragged, noisy emission shell, and intercepted it. The ship ran straight into their attack and was overwhelmed. Out-armed, slow, vulnerable, it knew almost instantly that it had no chance even of inflicting any damage on the opposing fleet.

So it destroyed itself, detonating the stock of warheads it carried in a sudden release of energy which for a second, in hyperspace alone, outshone the yellow dwarf star of a nearby system.

Scattered in a pattern around it, an instant before the ship itself was blown into plasma, most of the thousands of exploding warheads formed an outrushing sphere of radiation through which any escape seemed impossible. In the fraction of a second the entire engagement lasted, there were at the end some millionths when the battlecomputers of the enemy fleet briefly analyzed the four-dimensional maze of expanding radiation and saw that there was one bewilderingly complicated and unlikely way out of the concentric shells of erupting energies now opening like the petals of some immense flower between the star systems. It was not, however, a route the Mind of a small, archaic warship could plan for, create and follow.

By the time it was noticed that the ship's Mind had taken exactly that path through its screen of annihilation, it was too late to stop it from falling away through hyperspace toward the small, cold planet fourth out from the single yellow sun of the nearby system.

It was also too late to do anything about the light from the ship's exploding warheads, which had been arranged in a crude code, describing the vessel's fate and the escaped Mind's status and position, and legible to anybody catching the unreal light as it sped through the galaxy. Perhaps worst of all—and had their design permitted such a thing, those electronic brains would now have felt dismay—the planet the Mind had made for through its shield of explosions was not one they could simply attack, destroy or even land on; it was Schar's World, near the region of barren space between two galactic strands called the Sullen Gulf, and it was one of the forbidden Planets of the Dead.

1

Sorpen

The level was at his top lip now. Even with his head pressed hard back against the stones of the cell wall his nose was only just above the surface. He wasn't going to get his hands free in time; he was going to drown.

In the darkness of the cell, in its stink and warmth, while the sweat ran over his brows and tightly closed eyes and his trance went on and on, one part of his mind tried to accustom him to the idea of his own death. But, like an unseen insect buzzing in a quiet room, there was something else, something that would not go away, was of no use, and only annoyed. It was a sentence, irrelevant and pointless and so old he'd forgotten where he had heard or read it, and it went round and round the inside of his head like a marble spun round the inside of a jug:

The Jinmoti of Bozlen Two kill the hereditary ritual assassins of the new Yearking's immediate family by drowning them in the tears of the Continental Empathaur in its Sadness Season.

At one point, shortly after his ordeal had begun and he was only partway into his trance, he had wondered what would happen if he threw up. It had been when the palace kitchens—about fifteen or sixteen floors above, if his calculations were correct—had sent their waste down the sinuous network of plumbing that led to the sewercell. The gurgling, watery mess had dislodged some rotten food from the last time some poor wretch had drowned in filth and garbage, and that was when he felt he might vomit. It had been almost comforting to work out that it would make no difference to the time of his death.

Then he had wondered—in that state of nervous frivolity which sometimes afflicts those who can do nothing but wait in a situation of mortal threat—whether crying would speed his death. In theory it would, though in practical terms it was irrelevant; but that was when the sentence started to roll round in his head.

The Jinmoti of Bozlen Two kill the hereditary ritual...

The liquid, which he could hear and feel and smell all too clearly—and could probably have seen with his far from ordinary eyes had they been open—washed briefly up to touch the bottom of his nose. He felt it block his nostrils, filling them with a stench that made his stomach heave. But he shook his head, tried to force his skull even further back against the stones, and the foul broth fell away. He blew down and could breathe again.

There wasn't long now. He checked his wrists again, but it was no good. It would take another hour or more, and he had only minutes, if he was lucky.

The trance was breaking anyway. He was returning to almost total consciousness, as though his brain wanted fully to appreciate his own death, its own extinction. He tried to think of something profound, or to see his life flash in front of him, or suddenly to remember some old love, a long-forgotten prophecy or premonition, but there was nothing, just an empty sentence, and the sensations of drowning in other people's dirt and waste.

You old bastards, he thought. One of their few strokes of humor or originality had been devising an elegant, ironic way of death. How fitting it must feel to them, dragging their decrepit frames to the banquet-hall privies, literally to defecate all over their enemies, and thereby kill them.

The air pressure built up, and a distant, groaning rumble of liquid signaled another flushing from above. *You old bastards. Well, I hope at least you kept your promise, Balveda.*

The Jinmoti of Bozlen Two kill the hereditary ritual . . . thought one part of his brain, as the pipes in the ceiling spluttered and the waste splashed into the warm mass of liquid which almost filled the cell. The wave passed over his face, then fell back to leave his nose free for a second and give him time to gulp a lungful of air. Then the liquid rose gently to touch the bottom of his nose again, and stayed there.

He held his breath.

It had hurt at first, when they had hung him up. His hands, tied inside tight leather pouches, were directly above his head, manacled inside thick loops of iron bolted to the cell walls, which took all his weight. His feet were tied together and left to dangle inside an iron tube, also attached to the wall, which stopped him from taking any weight on his feet and knees and at the same time prevented him from moving his legs more than a hand's breadth out from the wall or to either side. The tube ended just above his knees; above it there was only a thin and dirty loincloth to hide his ancient and grubby nakedness.

He had shut off the pain from his wrists and shoulders even while the four burly guards, two of them perched on ladders, had secured him in place. Even so he could feel that niggling sensation at the back of his skull which told him that he *ought* to be hurting. That had lessened gradually as the level of waste in the small sewercell had risen and buoyed up his body.

He had started to go into a trance then, as soon as the guards left, though he knew it was probably hopeless. It hadn't lasted long; the cell door opened again within minutes, a metal walkway was lowered by a guard onto the damp flagstones of the cell floor, and light from the corridor washed into the darkness. He had stopped the Changing trance and craned his neck to see who his visitor might be.

Into the cell, holding a short staff glowing cool blue, stepped the stooped, grizzled figure of Amahain-Frolk, security minister for the Gerontocracy of Sorpen. The old man smiled at him and nodded approvingly, then turned to the corridor and, with a thin, discolored hand, beckoned somebody standing outside the cell to step onto the short walkway and enter. He guessed it would be the Culture agent Balveda, and it was. She came lightly onto the metal boarding, looked round slowly, and fastened her gaze on him. He smiled and tried to nod in greeting, his ears rubbing on his naked arms.

"Balveda! I thought I might see you again. Come to see the host of the party?" He forced a grin. Officially it was his banquet; he was the host. Another of the Gerontocracy's little jokes. He hoped his voice had shown no signs of fear.

Perosteck Balveda, agent of the Culture, a full head taller than the old man by her side and still strikingly handsome even in the pallid glow of the blue torch, shook her thin, finely made head slowly. Her short, black hair lay like a shadow on her skull.

"No," she said, "I didn't want to see you, or say goodbye."

"You put me here, Balveda," he said quietly.

"Yes, and there you belong," Amahain-Frolk said, stepping as far forward on the platform as he could without overbalancing and having to step onto the damp floor. "I wanted you tortured first, but Miss Balveda here"—the minister's high, scratchy voice echoed in the cell as he turned his head back to the woman—"pleaded for you, though God knows why. But that's where you belong all right; murderer." He shook the staff at the almost naked man hanging on the dirty wall of the cell.

Balveda looked at her feet, just visible under the hem of the long, plain gray gown she wore. A circular pendant on a chain around her neck glinted in the light from the corridor outside. Amahain-Frolk had stepped back beside her, holding the shining staff up and squinting at the captive.

"You know, even now I could almost swear that was Egratin hanging there. I can..." He shook his gaunt, bony head. "...I can hardly believe it isn't, not until he opens his mouth, anyway. My God, these Changers are dangerous frightening things!" He turned to Balveda. She smoothed her hair at the nape of her neck and looked down at the old man.

"They are also an ancient and proud people, Minister, and there are very few of them left. May I ask you one more time? Please? Let him live. He might be—"

The Gerontocrat waved a thin and twisted hand at her, his face distorting in a grimace. "No! You would do well, Miss Balveda, not to keep asking for this...this assassin, this murderous, treacherous...*spy,* to be spared. Do you think we take the cowardly murder and impersonation of one of our outworld ministers lightly? What damage this... *thing* could have caused! Why, when we arrested it two of our guards died just from being *scratched*! Another is blind for life after this monster spat in his eye! However," Amahain-Frolk sneered at the man chained to the wall, "we took those teeth out. And his hands are tied so that he can't even scratch himself." He turned to Balveda again. "You say they are few? I say good; there will soon be one less."

The old man narrowed his eyes as he looked at the woman. "We are grateful to you and your people for exposing this fraud and murderer, but do not think that gives you the right to tell us what to do. There are some in the Gerontocracy who want nothing to do with *any* outside influence, and their voices grow in volume by the day as the war comes closer. You would do well not to antagonize those of us who do support your cause."

Balveda pursed her lips and looked down at her feet again, clasping her slender hands behind her back. Amahain-Frolk had turned back to the man hanging on the wall, wagging the staff in his direction as he spoke. "You will soon be dead, impostor, and with you die your masters' plans for the domination of our peaceful system! The same fate awaits them if they try to invade us. We and the Culture are—"

He shook his head as best he could and roared back, "Frolk, you're an idiot!" The old man shrank away as though hit. The Changer went on, "Can't you see you're going to be taken over anyway? Probably by the Idirans, but if not by them then by the Culture. You don't control your own destinies anymore; the war's stopped all that. Soon this whole sector will be part of the front, unless you *make* it part of the Idiran sphere. I was only sent in to tell you what you should have known anyway—not to cheat you into something you'd regret later. For God's sake, man, the Idirans won't *eat* you—"

"Ha! They look as though they could! Monsters with three feet; invaders, killers, infidels... You want us to link with them? With three-strides-tall-monsters? To be ground under their *hooves*? To have to worship their false gods?"

"At least they have a God, Frolk. The Culture doesn't." The ache in his arms was coming back as he concentrated on talking. He shifted as best he could and looked down at the minister. "They at least think the same way you do. The Culture doesn't."

"Oh no, my friend, oh no." Amahain-Frolk held one hand up flat to him and shook his head. "You won't sow seeds of discord like that."

"My God, you stupid old man," he laughed. "You want to know who the real representative of the Culture is on this planet? It's not her," he nodded at the woman, "it's that powered flesh-slicer she has following her everywhere, her knife missile. She might make the decisions, it might do what she tells it, but it's the real emissary. That's what the Culture's about: machines. You think because Balveda's got two legs and soft skin you should be on her side, but it's the Idirans who are on the side of life in this war—"

"Well, you will shortly be on the other side of *that*." The Gerontocrat snorted and glanced at Balveda, who was looking from under lowered brows at the man chained to the wall. "Let us go, Miss Balveda," Amahain-Frolk said as he turned and took the woman's arm to guide her from the cell. "This… *thing's* presence smells more than the cell."

Balveda looked up at him then, ignoring the dwarfed minister as he tried to pull her to the door. She gazed right at the prisoner with her clear, black-irised eyes and held her hands out from her sides. "I'm sorry," she said to him.

"Believe it or not, that's rather how I feel," he replied, nodding. "Just promise me you'll eat and drink very little tonight, Balveda. I'd like to think there was one person up there on my side, and it might as well be my worst enemy." He had meant it to be defiant and funny, but it sounded only bitter; he looked away from the woman's face.

"I promise," Balveda said. She let herself be led to the door, and the blue light waned in the dank cell. She stopped right at the door. By sticking his head painfully far out he could just see her. The knife missile was there, too, he noticed, just inside the room; probably there all the time, but he hadn't noticed its sleek, sharp little body hovering there in the darkness. He looked into Balveda's dark eyes as the knife missile moved.

For a second he thought Balveda had instructed the tiny machine to kill him now—quietly and quickly while she blocked Amahain-Frolk's view—and his heart thudded. But the small device simply floated past Balveda's face and out into the corridor. Balveda raised one hand in a gesture of farewell.

"Bora Horza Gobuchul," she said, "goodbye." She turned quickly, stepped from the platform and out of the cell. The walkway was hoisted out and the door slammed, scraping rubber flanges over the grimy floor and hissing once as the internal seals made it watertight. He hung there, looking down at an invisible floor for a moment before going back into the trance that would Change his wrists, thin them down so that he could escape. But something about the solemn, final way Balveda had spoken his name had crushed him inside, and he knew then, if not before, that there was no escape.

...by drowning them in the tears...

His lungs were bursting! His mouth quivered, his throat was gagging, the filth was in his ears but he could hear a great roaring, see lights though it was black dark. His stomach muscles started to go in and out, and he had to clamp his jaw to stop his mouth opening for air that wasn't there. Now. No... *now* he had to give in. Not yet... surely now. Now, now, now, any second; surrender to this awful black vacuum inside him... he had to breathe... *now!*

Before he had time to open his mouth he was smashed against the wall—punched against the stones as though some immense iron fist had slammed into him. He blew out the stale air from his lungs in one convulsive breath. His body was suddenly cold, and every part of it next to the wall throbbed with pain. Death, it seemed, was weight, pain, cold...and too much light...

He brought his head up. He moaned at the light. He tried to see, tried to hear. What was happening? Why was he breathing? Why was he so damn *heavy* again? His body was tearing his arms from their sockets; his wrists were cut almost to the bone. Who had *done* this to him?

Where the wall had been facing him there was a very large and ragged hole which extended beneath the level of the cell floor. All the ordure and garbage had burst out of that. The last few trickles hissed against the hot sides of the breach, producing steam which curled around the figure standing blocking most of the brilliant light from outside, in the open air of Sorpen. The figure was three meters tall and looked vaguely like a small armored spaceship sitting on a tripod of thick legs. Its helmet looked big enough to contain three human heads, side by side. Held almost casually in one gigantic hand was a plasma cannon which Horza would have needed both arms just to lift; the creature's other fist gripped a slightly larger gun. Behind it, nosing in toward the hole, came an Idiran gun-platform, lit vividly by the light of explosions which Horza could now feel through the iron and stones he was attached to. He raised his head to the giant standing in the breach and tried to smile.

"Well," he croaked, then spluttered and spat, "you lot certainly took your time."